DACUS,
A Tale of Power

DACUS,
A Tale of Power

Jim Malone

For Doretta, my wife since 1952,
the mother of my two fine
children, Beverly and
Jim B.,
my business partner,
my Ms. Smith,
a confidant
and love
always

ACKNOWLEDGEMENT TO:

Stephanie Cogshell
Consultant

Graduate
University of Arkansas at Pine Bluff
Bachelor of Arts Degree
English/Liberal Arts

*   *   *

Graduate
Webster University
Saint Louis, Missouri
Master of Arts Degree
Marketing

CHAPTER 1

A late afternoon thunderstorm drenched A. D. coming in from the lab. His agile, five foot ten, balanced physique took steps up onto the covered veranda two at a time. Peeling out of the wet shirt, he ran it across toned, broad shoulders that defied a clue as to age. Draping it over the railing, he slipped his boots off before going inside to strip completely.

Something had been eluding him all day. The shower's hot, pelting spray wasn't bringing it to the surface. Turning it off, he pulled a towel from the bar, rubbed himself nearly dry and tucked it in around a firm-bellied, 'no ass a'all' waist. Passing a brush through thick, dark hair, A. D. met pale greenish eyes in the mirror. *If these feelings are referred to as an emotional binge, I'll have scotch on the rocks,* entered his mind. Unconsciously, he stroked the thin lined, black moustache while dressing, not quite able to dismiss the encroachment into his thoughts.

A.D. Mays had been denied an indulgence in fantasy early on in life. It gave him the focused concentration to mastermind an inconceivable plan for a little diversion and a lot of wealth. However, it blocked power for imagining all possible events that were destined to be played out. How could he predict a need to use 'Dācus', a second identity he'd set up on a whim twenty-five years ago? Or, foresee profiting from a business relationship with a savvy, beautiful woman who would stir desire once again in his groin, rub Mafia elbows, reap the wrath of the metals cartel, and encounter a drawdown with the Cuban and U.S. Governments?

The clouds and rain moved on. From his mountain retreat in north Arkansas, A. D. stared through a picture window into the valley below. *It's ready*, he seriously counseled himself. *But are you truly ready to parade such a novel concept? Fact is, pursuing an intricate plot for huge gains invites problems, whatever the means used. When these are presented, expect and be prepared to meet unpredictable consequences. Involve others, as surely you must, risks will multiply. And no telling what else!*

His resolve to sort out the variables was unrelenting. Intensity of the concentration pulsated in his temples. Strong fingers traced a set jaw through groomed sideburns to apply pressure . . . *You'd better give genuine thought to how you'll handle it if things go sour. Every attempt you've made to lead a normal life has ended up with bastard results! Like those posed by a mother's one-night stand somewhere in Texas and a name tag of A. D. Mays, attached by foster parents. No doubt about it, your personality, even your existence thus far, is warped from having an identity problem! Life's been as complex as you've been accused of being . . .*

Shadows stretched, and A. D. mentally fortified his cause. *I am not happy where I am, as I am*, he reflected. *What good is the power I've uncovered if it can't be converted to wealth? The millennium is not far away. Technology is exploding more rapidly than national, and even international, entities can absorb. There's definitely a whisper of unrest. Odds are, my ploy stands a fair chance of coming in conflict with whatever's out there. Yet the times seem ripe to pull this thing off. As the old saying goes, nothing ventured, nothing gained.*

Rabbit's summons that dinner was served, had interrupted. Challenged by last thoughts, A. D. persisted, "Sit down with me tonight, Rabbit. As my comrade, you're entitled to know my plans for the engineering feat we've put together. Power is money, and vice versa. The power is assured and it minimizes most risk factors. Trouble is, using it to make money must include others. With that in mind, let me fill you in on a few old acquaintances that are skilled at the type of deception it'll take. If their boredom doesn't turn 'em on, then the prospect of big money should entice them to join us.

"These guys and the gal have key attributes perfect to help execute the plot. Their word is as good as gold, being graduates from the old school of hard knocks. Ed's the thinking, careful, rational one of the bunch. He gives balance, where Harry is a born pessimist, taking issue with anything and everything. W. T. Farris did a stint on the crap tables as a stickman. That past lets him roll with ease on any playing field, and he'd be the main man on our first venture. You'd find Art, an expert safecracker, to be quiet and observing. I'm thinking he'll be essential to banking operations down in the Caribbean. Sam's the youngest, and perhaps the most versatile player. His enormous size and strength always gave an edge if we were forced into a confrontation," he added.

"Then there's Tom and Vivian, better known as the Colonel and his Lady. They're hoots! Old ones at that! Their expertise in processing gold dates way back."

"Sounds ta me like your past had more color to it than I've got. Probably a whole lot less confinement than mine had too," Rabbit commented. "I'm on my way down to see Lulu for a while," he related, excusing himself.

A. D. nodded, absorbed in thoughts. The now took precedence over the uncertainties. He punched in numbers and put the cell phone to his ear. The call was going through. "Is that you, Ed? This is A. D. Mays, a past runnin' buddy from yesteryears."

Art Crissel, passing as forty-five or so, rather than fifty-nine, strode down the long corridor from his Chicago flight to the lobby of Little Rock National Airport. Reaching foot of the down escalator, he saw a familiar face.

Looking up, W. T. Farris shouted, "Art! How long has it been? Let's head for baggage checkout together and talk."

Scanning the lobby, mostly intent upon the purpose for being there, Art remarked, "Guess A. D. called us all in for a business meeting. Said he'd meet us, but I don't see him. Then again, I might not recognize the guy. It must have been a couple of decades ago that he went straight. Wonder what he's done with his degree in electrical engineering?"

W. T. spotted him first and used restraint to keep from yelling out. Instead, he quickly zigzagged over to grasp A. D.'s elbow. "God, you look good, man! What's up?"

"The ultimate of all scams!" A. D. greeted, putting an arm around Art while shaking W. T.'s hand. "You'll learn about it at the motel. Everyone is here. Sam, Ed, and Harry flew in from Jersey earlier today. We even have the esteemed presence of the Colonel and his Lady. He must be seventy-something but doesn't look it. Quirky as ever too. Vivian tells me he still requires her to tie him up and whip his little fat ass with a lash so that he can get his kicks. She's pretty versatile herself. It's common knowledge she's sexually AC/DC and a dominatrix. I gather time has cooled her down quite a bit. Let's get your bags and move on to our accommodations," A. D. urged.

The motel was new, state of the art, and located in a quiet commercial addition on Chenal Parkway. A. D. directed Art and W. T. toward the desk to get checked in, prompting, "As soon as you can, after luggage is in your rooms, meet the rest of us in reserved suite 222."

When A. D. departed, Art leaned across to W. T., remarking, "He hasn't changed a bit, has he? Still sober minded as ever."

Designed as a hospitality room, the suite was outfitted with wet bar, ice maker, and coffee machine. A. D. walked in to find everyone talking and drinking . . . Coffee, that is. Upon W. T. and Art's entry, he turned, mounting a small dais, with podium and slide screen to his back, so he could address them. "You have no idea how hard it has been to locate each of you after these many years. Getting everyone together at the same time became practically impossible. Perhaps one could say what we're doing here is of manifest destiny! We'll see," he remarked stoically.

"There are major decisions to be reached in a short period of time. Many factors beg to be examined. Also, your time is likely more valuable than mine. In order to move on I propose friendships be renewed later." The ayes had nods of agreement.

"Here are the bare bones of a vast, highly lucrative plan I've brought you in to consider. It involves altering the world's slender gold supply and means exactly what it implies. We stand to profit! The inventory of gold roughly twenty years ago was only about fifty thousand tons. It hasn't varied much since then," he explained. "Obvious too is the fact that the price of gold is being stabilized and controlled by manipulators. You ask me how these operators control the price of gold? My answer is, by regulating supply, which brings us to case in point."

A. D. hesitated. "This part is heavy. It's loaded with details," he warned. "To understand where I'm coming from, don't get lost or lose me in the process of trying to relay it to you. There is a potential for millions and millions of dollars to slide down into our pockets by tapping a supply of gold the present-day operators have ignored. If a problem arises, it'll lie in just how covertly the gold supply can be altered, castrating the strict control of the gold cartel. As for supply, there is only one place on earth where volumes of gold reserves exist. That place happens to be the ocean. The reason no gold is being extracted from seawater today is economic. Compared to its value, the cost of setting up and employing an electrical field between a cathode and an anode of gold for its extraction is, thus far, prohibitive."

Covering all bases, he added, "Simply put, friends, the holder of expertise to bring this gold into production becomes an instant gold market manipulator. So, what's the bottom line, you ask? It is that I have recovered a method for drawing out free electricity from the earth, which I am prepared to prove. Moreover, the applied physics of it supports gleaning gold particles from the ocean to the tune of a ton per week! Initially tho, there's the matter of securing operating expenses to get started. A 'nut', larger than any you've tried for in the past, must be raised and squirreled. Ultimately, the job will necessitate a sizeable, equipped, sea-going vessel to give you an idea of the tremendous monetary needs required."

When A. D. paused, expecting a reaction, there was not a sound. His colleagues had practically ceased breathing. They instinctively knew he had not gone to so much expense and coordinated planning to present the impossible. The potential was awesome.

Before an eye blinked, A. D. set forth again, "There is a kicker. Developing the capital to finance could be touchy, unless two other schemes can be executed. Pulling them off should be equally challenging, since they would involve unrelated and absolutely different subjects. The bulk of the money from these two schemes would be laundered, for obvious purposes. Inasmuch, every participant will be required to possess a current valid passport. In addition to your known abilities at the confidence game, you each have succeeded in avoiding a police record. Considering all those years you've spent in the rackets, it's quite phenomenal and impressive. Now, it's important to know that the entire operation is predicted to take a maximum of three years. However, within a year and a half, I predict we'll be well heeled and fabulously wealthy upon its completion."

A. D. cleared his throat and impulsively shuffled his papers. He had shocked himself by his own misdirection, but went on. "First things first. Further disclosure of details regarding the two scams chosen to raise the nut is on hold until we're banded into an organization. Anyone not interested and wanting to withdraw is asked to decide by ten tomorrow morning. It'll allow time to make plane reservations to get you back home. The rest are invited to go on up to my place for a full layout and demonstration. Incidentally, dinner this evening has been prearranged. In private dining at Vincenzo's, terms and agreements for an association can be formulated. Afterward, a question and answer session pertaining to the main scam would be in order. To provide a base and key reference material, my field notes have been compiled and copies made for each of you."

Yielding to the now, he tendered, "I'm certain highest priority of the day is to catch up on lost years, so let's indulge. One other thing though. We'll leave from here at six thirty to claim our dinner reservations." Within ten minutes, A. D. Mays bowed out on pretense of completing some work, excused himself, and left.

The group got up, mingling and everyone talking at once. In no time they'd divided into knots of two or three, holding discussions on the biggest item to come their way in a while. Harry Annemann and, huge as an elk,

Sam Thorenson gravitated toward the older Ed Bemis. "Well, Ed," Harry pried, "what's your educated opinion?"

Ed ignored him to study the field notes before replying, "The scam is classic. The gold market is already being managed, as A. D. related. True, it's being orchestrated through the international metals market, both in spot prices and in futures. Any individual, who has a supply of gold costing practically nothing, can afford to geometrically multiply the effect of his presence in the marketplace. It's done through the use of margin puts or calls. However, coming into the market, blatantly selling large amounts of gold will result in being stopped, one way or another. If A. D. has actually uncovered a way to cheaply remove gold from the ocean, then with what we know about human nature and greed, the market is open to being systematically raided." Sam showed his approval.

"To grasp A. D.'s reference to manipulating the supply of gold, I'll draw from an example for comparison. Do you recall the enormously wealthy Percival family who attempted to corner the silver market with privileged access to money?" Ed prompted. "They went into the futures market, selling off large quantities of silver futures, to drive the price down. As prices fell and they continued to sell, their holdings rose. Understand, fellows, no margin calls had been made on them. It seemed foolproof. However, the powers that be were hurting financially. If left unchecked, the Percivals were on line to dominate the world market, control its price, and shut them out. Astute consortium resources were pooled to buy up silver futures in greater quantities than the Percival's had in future sales. This countermove propelled the price of silver back up, causing margin calls on the Percivals, and proved their undoing. Point in case is that they didn't have actual silver to cover margin calls." Ed was sorting it out for them and selling himself.

"Conversely, let's analyze A. D.'s scheme. There'd be actual gold to sell. It'd be available to sell in small amounts on the spot market to pay expenses and to cover anticipated sales in the futures market. In turn, vast amounts of gold could be sold under another firm's title by use of futures contracts, which are considered as paper transactions in the metals market. When the time comes to cash in, that gold will be secured in certified depositories. Delivery can readily be made on all futures contracts. Any adverse reaction by the metals cartel will come after the fact. From A. D.'s field notes, my prediction is roughly a half billion dollars worth can be sold in one year. One other thing," Ed surveyed. "Larger sums of money should be converted into the seven leading currencies. It'd be a wise move to consider, since we'd be dealing with fiat money."

"Hold it, Ed," Harry interrupted. "Explain 'fiat', as you put it."

"It means, Harry," exemplified Ed, "no currency in the world is backed up by anything. Money is not worth any more than its perceived value. That's why nations continuously buy each other's currency. It helps to keep the relationship between them stable. Consequently, money kept in a number of currencies is stabilized by world influence. It wouldn't be based on whether or not the price of gold goes to hell."

Harry wrinkled up his brow, frowning. "Ah, I'm getting the picture. Something smells quite familiar. Let's see! There's this big pot of gold at the end of the rainbow. All you've gotta do is put up so much, and your dreams come true. It becomes a cinch, I suppose, 'cause we're going to steal it from those who already have made a potful!"

Ed indulged Harry to finish before nailing him. "If you had been invited to contribute money to get in on this scam, I'd agree. All you've been approached to do is put up your ass. As a provident man, Harry, you need to consider whether it's worth putting on the line. May I remind you that A. D. could maybe profit if money were put up and lost. For the life of me tho, I can't conceive of any way he can benefit from you losing your ass. Fact is, he'd probably lose his too."

The heated dialogue gained the attention of everyone else. They gathered around to another interest being ignited.

Harry was incensed. He'd been tastefully one-upped. It was difficult to swallow. Disposed to finding fault in the proposal's outline, his mouth had overloaded his ass. Collecting wits, Harry rationalized, "Ed, what you've said makes sense. I can accept it and am damn glad to have it spelled out. My problem is, A. D. has dangled a golden carrot out in front of us, failing to mention two other 'somethings' until last. Then, he shortened the string with a condition . . ."

Fueling his own mania, Harry blustered, "Talk about a 'bait and switch'. What does he take us for? Who would be here if the unwritten rule of living up to a commitment hadn't been followed? Sure, one caper calls for another, 'cause you gotta have the green to live on and be ready for that next one. But being asked to commit, not knowing the first damn thing about two other plans, won't hunt! A. D.'s hiding out behind this 'association' bit for a reason. We gotta decide among ourselves, right now, whether to join his little society before knowing the score or go ahead and form our own union. Ed, I think even you'd agree it'd be smart business."

The ranting remarks of Harry held substance. A muffled murmur by the others developed into a brief, intense discussion of the matter. Perceiving an accord, Vivian spoke out. "Ladies first. Tom and I approve. We vote for this body of persons to form an elite association, here and now!"

Art quickly affirmed. "W. T. and I are in agreement. You, guys, need to get with it on a position and start writin' some bylaws!"

"Hell, let's make it unanimous," bellowed Sam Thorenson, giving Ed a handshake and slapping Harry on the back. Three abreast, they headed for the door and the motel's bar.

In his suite above, A. D. smiled, flipping off the covert tap. He was immensely pleased with the turn of events.

CHAPTER 2

At ten minutes until seven, A. D. and his van of recruits turned onto West Markham Street seeking a parking place. One was found vacated inside a block west of destination, before the street turned into a rundown district. In Vincenzo's foyer, reservations were claimed on time. The private room was ready. A tuxedo-clad maitre d' ushered them in to be seated at a lengthy table set for eight. A single place, set on the opposite side from all others, came as a surprise.

Vincenzo's featured hand-tossed pizza baked in stone-lined ovens, Neapolitan food, wonderfully succulent steaks, and a selective wine list . . . A. D. recognized the collective average age of this crew, including himself, was almost past doing justice to thick choice cuts of beef. He had chosen Vincenzo's not only for fine cuisine but as importantly for its reputation to provide truly private dining.

Being served a magnificent meal, having toasted the occasion several times, and after a lot of yesteryear reminiscing, A. D. rose. "I am open to questions regarding field notes relating to the main order of business." He pointed to Harry who seemed poised for input.

Harry stood, issuing a statement instead. "This afternoon the rest of us formed our own league. We may or may not go along with you. It'll be based upon what you're willing to put out. So far, all that's been offered is two pieces of stink bait for a taste of caviar."

Scanning the table to make eye contact, A. D. nodded. "You've made me very happy. And yes I did have concerns! For even one to decline posed problems with the amount of information that's been made available. I'd already decided it must be either you all go with me or everyone splits. If it couldn't be resolved, I too had to go another way. By your having banded together today, I am more comfortable to divulge how three coordinated schemes can bring millions in for each of us," he applauded.

"Success of the overall scheme depends upon talents you represent as a group in expediting the first two scams." Without rising, A. D. swept the room again for reaction and undivided attention. "The first plan I foresee," he continued, "involves the casino trade, lying alongside the Mississippi River. An uncontrolled and rapid growth of low resort places has jeopardized their entire industry. In the absence of adequate supervision, weaker segments are trying to survive by operating 'juice joints'. You are aware of the significance! Our mark is one such casino called the Lavender Peacock. The electric wires going into its offshore structure are enormous. They are supporting at least one dice table, positively wired for high rollers. The classic situation for a con, wouldn't you say? In hard times, an organization used loaded dice to steal from its customers. Today, they're more sophisticated with dice dubbed 'missers and passers', which respond to a magnetic field in the table . . . One push of a button under that table by the stickman is all it takes to regulate the playing field." W. T.'s thumbs-up didn't break his stride.

"Operators of these types of gaming tables are bound by adhering to a rigid routine in order to win. In itself, it's a plus for our purposes. Put it with knowledge and ability to electrically interrupt their sequence of operation and they become prime subjects to be psychologically set up for a payoff. Make the action happen in front of hundreds of people, which cannot be ignored by the house, and we've just posted a score. If the mark's blown off in proper manner by your fine expertise, I'm sure we leave carrying the hard cash. It's an advantaged commodity to avoid any paper trail. The electrical and electronic equipment needed to pull off the scam is perfected. It's ready and waiting for demonstration at my place later."

Ed rose to speak, but A. D. waved him back down. "If you don't mind, let's get it all out on the table. Discussions will be best served when the whole of material has been presented."

Distraction was momentary. A.D. picked up where he'd left off. "The second scam I propose is way out of the ordinary and destined to tax the imagination. It's designed to be far more productive financially. There's substantially less physical risk involved, as well. If you will, visualize becoming manufacturing executives. As such, the job begins with surveying places to locate and speculating on sites to expand branches of a proposed factory into small, hungry towns of Arkansas, across Mississippi, and Louisiana.

Acting out the role, you'll approach local Chambers of Commerce and their industrial development committees, seeking buildings, or office space available to be rented. The image of stability and community dedication is furthered by accounts in the company's name opened at local banks. A portion of money squirreled from the previous scheme gets deposited," he outlined.

"To a point, some of what I'm about to say may sound like Greek. Bear with me, and I think you'll get the gist. First, orient yourselves that use of electrical power is the major key. A power company supplies electricity. We won't need any of it . . . What we must have is access to their lines and it's highly unlikely we'd get it on our own! Our game is to first acquire a legitimate front for an industry which purports a realistically, solid handicap. Excessive heat related to production becomes an energy by-product we can harness and sell back to the utility. To counter possible resistance put up on installation of a twofold electric hookup needed to make it work, we'll deal it off to the local movers and shakers who are to profit from the industry. Push may come to shove, but these people must fully grasp that our company cannot expand, nor compete, without the option to benefit from heat generated by production. Predictably, once conceived, the 'locals' should be able to prevail by applying pressure on the power company. In the process we must insist on a cogeneration contract being issued. As far as they are concerned, we're stymied without it and must scrap negotiations. Comply with our demands, and they corner an industry for their community."

Taking it two steps further, he disclosed, "In the name of progress, hopefully, a contract gets signed. The time allotted in one billing cycle is sufficient to deliver enough electricity for our future monetary needs. However, during those thirty days or so, the pretense of doing business as usual continues. Efforts are seemingly ongoing toward construction of factories. The townspeople can only have assumed that activity seen and equipment coming in is prelude to big business for their area. Short delays can be easily explained away to dispel concern . . .

"Downsizing effects within the utility industry are not well known to the public at large. But I see where it can contribute to our cause. For them to function with skeleton labor forces, everything has been turned over to computers, which are programmed to do the work of several thousand people. Thus, infusion of electricity into the transmission lines would be logged in, automatically recorded, and transferred to a base computer for processing payment. It is programmed to spot irregular trends and cannot pick up our action in one billing cycle."

Enthused, A. D. proposed, "If it can be pulled off, the 'take' expected from this baby will be sweet. So big in fact, why not exploit the same glitch with our own personal banking? One of us becomes a 'mule' taking, let's say, ninety-five hundred down to the Cayman Islands. We open the account in the same name chosen for our 'parent company'. Once the 'mule' is back in the States, that person sets up another account at an international bank in Atlanta. By phone, it then becomes possible to transfer several thousand back from the Cayman bank . . .

"Having established a record of transfers, between an offshore and a local bank, privileges are afforded," he explained. "We can automatically download from one bank to the other. The beauty of it is practically all cash proceeds can be moved to a Grand Cayman bank without our having to touch it. If all goes as projected, we'll have sailed out of the country, be present in the islands enjoying the fruits of our labor, and preparing to launch plan 3."

In conclusion, A. D. submitted, "These, friends, are the bare bones of the two lesser plans. Ed, I believe you have something to say."

Ed thanked him. "The first con to take a casino is classic, as I've said before. The mark, already stealing, doesn't have to be lured into attempted larceny. The third, a real scam, is also defined in that the gold market along with the silver market, diamond market, and other commodities markets are all manipulated for the benefit of the few. Now, this second scam I don't know about. It doesn't appear to be a pure con. Are you proposing we do an outright steal, without involvement of a more identifiable mark?"

"Excellent summation, Ed," A. D. ratified. "We've got to have unanimous agreement as to our purposes and goals for the sake of unity. Anytime something isn't clear, it must be put on the table for evaluation. You have voiced misgivings on ethics of the second con. I'd like to express my views on the matter because it isn't as immoral as you might think. The only swindle proposed is misrepresentation of who we are. Forget trying to focus on your friendly local power company. They don't exist anymore. A conglomerate of statewide local power companies, closely held elsewhere by a huge utility holding company, is target for our dealings. These entities are new, sanctioned by the U.S. Government to the exclusion of state regulatory agencies and to the absolute detriment of small consumers. Regardless of their pork barrel, we won't have to steal. We'll actually be producing and selling them generated electricity they don't need, and don't want, but must accept. It falls under terms of another federally sanctioned raiding of access to utility owned gas and electric transmission facilities. This 'boondoggle' wasn't created by us, and my sentiments are what's wrong with skimming a little of their cream!"

"Can it be summed up by assuming that we intend to steal from those already committing theft?" Ed persisted, slow to grasp the scope of his plan.

"Ed," A. D. bored down hard. "You must take something for it to be stealing! We'll actually deliver metered electrical power into their lines, which they'll be obliged to pay for."

Art Crissel intervened, "Guys, it's gotten down to nitpicking. Let's get the hell out of here before A. D. decides to make us go Dutch on the meal." Colonel Tom seconded the motion. The Association sauntered out of Vincenzo's into the night, leaving A. D. to handle settling up.

By the time A. D. cleared the door, his group was half a block away. No sooner had he strolled from the light in front of Vincenzo's than a pickup truck pulled to the curb. Four punks, two white and two black, leaped out of the truck bed armed with switchblades. A. D. backed up until he felt the brick wall while they went into a kind of hip-hop maneuver. Two of them jumped straight up into the air, followed by the other two. As they moved in closer, A. D. extended forearms into the air as if someone had a gun on him.

One of the four took a step forward, demanding, "Dad, cough up your green!"

At that instant, A. D.'s right hand dropped to his collar, followed by a sort of shrug. He pulled a straight, sixteen inch pruning saw, fitted with a thin metal handle, from under his coat. Within the split second of raising his arm to clear the holster, the kid made his move. A. D. brought the saw's toothed edge down on the kid's skull. Thrusting it forward, he ripped through an eighth inch of skin. Blood spurted profusely. Whirling aside, he caught a black across the cheek with the blade's flat side. Thinking he had been cut, the kid took off running west and, looking back, ran straight into Vivian. She immediately jerked him off his feet, shaking him like a dog subdues a mink. The Colonel went into a frenzy, crying, "Beat the shit out of him, baby. Show the asshole what it's like to be beat up by a woman!"

Vivian indulged. Slugging him into semi-consciousness, she brought him to his knees with an over-the-head twist of wrist. Using her left foot, she stomped his shoulder blade with her entire weight, breaking it effortlessly.

The other two toughs were no match for A. D. and his saw. They were cut and bleeding and in full retreat by the time A. D.'s group arrived to help. Wielding knives and chains, six more unloaded from another pickup at about the same time. Art, lighter and faster than his buddies, got there first to kickbox one punk into oblivion. Big Sam Thorenson came up as two others went for Art. He grabbed them by the nape of the neck, cracking their heads together. Two rabbit punches and they were on the ground. Suddenly, the hoodlum's task force had been cut in half. A few slaps from A. D.'s saw addled the remaining three. It allowed Ed, W. T., and Harry to restrain them from behind while Sam put them to sleep with his fists.

Loudly, A. D. commanded, "Run for it!" Everyone piled into the van. Deliberately, they slowly drove away from Vincenzo's and the scene.

A couple of minutes later, a lone customer coming out of the restaurant looked down the street in disbelief. Bodies were strewn up and down the sidewalk. Some were moving. Others appeared dead, and blood puddles were everywhere. Rushing back into Vincenzo's, he screamed, "Call 911! Get the police! There's been folks murdered outside!"

The patrol car, flashing blue lights, arrived in less than three minutes. Seeing the numbers involved, a backup request was radioed in before setting a foot on the pavement. "Also, get ambulances down here ASAP! Looks like there's been a gang war." was logged in at the police precinct and picked up by scanner hacks.

CHAPTER 3

In the headquarters an hour and a half later, officers began interrogations. The apparent gang victims had been given first aid in area hospitals and released back into police custody, except for the poor groupie who'd run into Vivian. It promised to be a long night. In lieu of no testimony from the elusive other party involved, the police were aware their efforts wouldn't be conclusive. Nonetheless, attempts began at trying to unravel the disturbance.

The bully of the pack, who wanted to act as leader, smarted off, "We ain't sayin' nothin' without a lawyer!" It was a provoking start to interviews.

"Listen, you educated idiots!" screamed the cop playing bad guy role to extract crucial information. "You haven't been charged with anything, so put it in your pea brains. We'd just like to know what happened. You've been taken to the emergency room and gotten patched up. Who'n 'ell do ya think's gonna pay th' bill? Santy Claus? Naw, course not! The state has to pick up the tab on deadbeats." Changing his tactics, he mellowed a bit. "Up until now, no one has come forth to charge you with anything. I've got a gut feelin' there won't ever be anybody that'll slap a charge on you. Come on . . . Cut the crap about a lawyer. Ante up so we can get this over with. Answer my question. What really happened down there on Markham Street?"

Two minutes of silence lapsed. Annoyed, the bad cop called to his Lieutenant, instructing, "Book 'em all with assault on each other. Book 'em, and hold 'em!"

The kid who had gotten his skull ripped open hollered out, holding his right forearm. "I think they broke my arm. I need a doctor!"

It caused a reaction from the good cop he'd hoped for. "Why didn't they find it at the hospital?" vexed, the cop demanded. "It means another trip to the emergency room."

"How would I know? I was hurtin' bad 'nough I didn't notice I guess. The way it feels now, I think it's broke. I'm tellin' you so's you'll get me some help," he lied.

Wearily, the good cop relayed it on to the guard in attendance. "Hold him separately. We'll have to get it checked out."

No sooner had the kid got out of earshot than he told the guard, "Tell that cop there ain't nothin' wrong with my arm. I need to talk to him, alone." Attuned that this kid intended to shed light on what had gone down, the guard steered him to a small room instead of taking him to a cell. Restrained by handcuffs in a chair bolted to the floor, he and the guard waited for the lieutenant.

Shortly, the good cop came in. Familiar with implications the room carried, he unlocked the handcuffs. Sitting across the table from the kid, he inquired, "What's on your mind, sport?"

"I want out. This gang shit ain't for me! It was my initiation night, and they ain't gonna lay the blame for their fuckup on me. I gotta run, pronto. And I gotta have a head start. I don't know for sure where I'm goin'. I'll tell you all I know if you can you get me a fifty-dollar stake and twenty-four hours head start."

"Let me ask you a question or two," the cop broke in. "Aside from the few nicks, a headache, and a bad haircut, are you able to do a day's work? If your answer's yes, I'll get you some cash, twelve-hour lead time, and a job where you can make it on your own. What about family? Got any that'll be affected by hate acts from the gang, or come looking for you?"

"Yeah, I can do a day's work. The answer's nope to your last questions. My daddy divorced Maw when I was five. She never remarried. All she does is work, slingin' hash. She's spent most of her time tryin' to raise and feed me. I'm sure I ain't been much for her to brag about. Lately, she's been livin' in with a fella and I don't blame her. I'm seventeen. Time to get off the tit, square up, and move on is the best way I'm figurin' it tonight," he refitted earnestly.

"Okay, here's the deal," the cop said. "I have a friend who's got a sawmill in the little town of Ola. He'll give you a job as a hand working at the mill. You'll be paid by the day until you're on your feet. I have one more thing to give you . . . Advice! Every little town in the whole United States is infected by drugs. It's the grease that moves the wheels of gangs. If you so much as buy a roach while you're up there, it'll just be a matter of time until you're dead. It's not enough to quit gangs and run away. You've got to be free of the traffic that supports them. If you're man enough, this is probably the only chance you'll ever get. If you're not, you'll die young, and the world'll never miss you. That I can guarantee," he pronounced with a fist to the table.

"I'll take the deal . . . Here's what went down," relieved, the kid recounted. "It was gang initiation night for the poor sucker in the hospital, another black, me, and one more white kid. The score was to be a simple roust on a customer comin' out of Vincenzo's. We was supposed to take his money, any valuables we could muscle, and make a clean getaway with the loot. Knockin' him in the head or cuttin' him up a little was okay, long as he didn't squeal like a pig and we didn't get caught. It was crazy, man. We jumped this old guy who'd just come out of the place, not more'n a half a block from its door. Ignorant like we hadn't paid no attention that the bunch halfblock ahead was buddies of his'n. This old geezer played us cool. He threw his arms up like we had a cannon on him and backed up against the buildin'. It sorta threw us for a loop, ya know, 'cause all we had was blades." His recall became animated.

"What happened next was unreal, man! From nowhere, ya know, the old codger reached behind his back, comin' straight up and out of his coat at us with a saw. Honest! I'd swear on Maw's Bible, and I got the marks to prove it! It was a honest-to-God, workin' saw. I think it had two sides to it, too. There weren't no way to take that saw away from him either. He had a two-foot reach on us, and we didn't have a chance." The kid detailed and ensnared more.

"Bigdoggin' it, I was closest. He come down on top of my head and sawed as he pulled it forward. I ain't believin' the blood that run down my face, nearly blindin' me. Scared me to death! What, I do remember was the old man spinnin' 'round fast as lightnin' and slapped that saw blade up against my black buddy's jaw. Man, Ole Red just knew he'd been cut and took off arunnin' like a scalded dog square into one giant of a woman. She musta been seven foot tall and really put the hurt on him, bad. I'm tellin' you I ain't ever heard of nothin' like it, much less seen it. Treated him like a rat bein' attacked by one of them terrier dogs. All the time she's doin' that, this sure 'nuff, little ol' fat fart was dancin' 'round and a eggin' her on."

Eager to have the cop believe him, he explained. "I seen every bit of it 'cause the old geezer had took me out of action in one move. His saw was too much for the four of us. But anyway, here comes his cronies. They got to us when six brothers finally decided to give us backup. Man, were they ever stupid. One of them old-timers could kick clean over his head and took out the first dummy off the truck. The other two 'would-be smarts' barreled over the bed of the pickup, reachin' for the little kicker, and got grabbed from behind by a gorilla of a guy. It sounded like a shotgun goin' off when he cracked their heads together. We're down to three guys by then, and they're dodgin' the old man with a saw, tryin' to make a strike. But it ain't over yet. Three more of his buddies come up from their back side, stoppin' 'em dead in their tracks while tha giant bozo beat the shit out of 'em. He scored so hard I'da sworn he broke their necks. Next thing I hear is the saw-slingin' feller ordering, 'Run for it!' They piled in a van I couldn't see by then, and left. That's it. I know you think I'm lyin', but I ain't."

The good cop punched a buzzer on the table, and a guard came to the door. "Take the kid to my office and sit with him until I get there." He walked out of the headquarters, got in an unmarked car, and drove to Vincenzo's. They had closed, and the front door was locked. Hurriedly, he walked around, entered through the kitchen door, flashed a badge, and asked for the manager.

A security camera had depicted entry of the officer. The manager met him at his office door. "May I help you, sir?"

"I hope so," the officer curtly responded. "There was an incident reported outside your establishment this evening. Did you serve a large party earlier? If so, who paid the bill?"

"As a matter of fact, we did," he contributed. "A gentleman came in yesterday to make reservations for this evening, requesting a particular table setup. I found it out of the ordinary and very unusual. He insisted on paying cash in advance, as I recall. Let me see. Those reservations were made in . . ." The manager paused, running a finger down the appointment book page. "Oh yes, here it is. Mr. Rob N. Hood was the name given." Throwing up his hands at the absurdity and disparity of the man, the officer stomped out.

The van slowly cruised down into the River Market and through older parts of Little Rock before entering Wilbur Mills Freeway to go west. Sightseeing preempted talk. Finally, W. T. couldn't resist. "A. D., I didn't know you were musically adept." The seemingly unrelated remark heightened the others interest. They waited, anticipating the byplay.

Preoccupied, A. D. shunted the remark. "I don't know what you mean."

"I had no idea you were a talented artist on the musical saw." A rumble of chuckles broke the quietness. A. D. didn't pursue the humor, and W. T deducted he wouldn't either . . .

Harry leaned forward, wanting mutual discourse on their parlay. "Hey! How did you like the way we demonstrated that we still have the moxie to meet the world, physically? Aside from a busted knuckle on Sam, I think we survived without a scratch. Maneuvering in that tight situation sure makes me a whole lot more comfortable with what we're about to take on."

Noting the positive intent of Harry's remarks, A. D. felt compelled to respond. Pressured, he soberly rejoined. "Tonight's occurrence could have permanently taken us out of business. If the police had arrived a minute earlier, our secrecy would have been compromised. There's a lesson here. We absolutely cannot operate identified as a group, nor can we socialize together in public again. Believe me, there'll be ample opportunity to enjoy each other's company in the future, in private, and without exploiting the privacy of a business relationship. When we get to the motel, it'll be time to hit the hay. By eight in the morning, be up, have an early breakfast, and be ready to depart for my digs."

CHAPTER 4

The van, loaded on top with luggage and crammed full inside with more baggage and seven passengers, rolled away from the motel at ten minutes after eight. A. D. retraced Chenal toward downtown until he could turn on I-430 loop, connecting to I-40 West, which winds northwest through the Arkansas River valley to Fort Smith.

Passing through the small city of Conway, he left the interstate and turned due north on U.S. Highway 65. Within minutes, scenery abruptly changed from rich, alluvial bottom land of the river valley to foothills of the Ozarks. As he sped around ever-tightening curves up the mountains, the use of seat belts suddenly became popular. Fascination with its spectacular view was tempered by sudden and repeated plunges of several hundred feet, first on one side of the road and then on the other. Nearly an hour of tension went by as the van wound its way upward. It was shattered by Vivian, sitting up front with A. D. "Do you have a woman?" she probed. Everyone stopped their chatter and craned to hear his answer.

"No, Viv, I don't. I was married once to a wonderful woman, Claire. She and I met in college, graduated, and got married the same year. I used my electrical engineering degree to pursue a career with a large electric utility out west. Claire was a schoolteacher and we were a happy, prosperous couple for five years. There was one exception. She desperately wanted children. Toward the end of four years, and no babies in the cradle, Claire insisted upon seeking medical advice. It turned out she was okay. Unfortunately, I showed up as sterile. We tried to hang on for another year, but it was over. My woman said she had to get out. We had an uncontested divorce, and I have no idea where she is today."

"But, A. D., that was years and years ago. This is now," Vivian held firmly.

"Yeah, and I have speculated time and again on such a curiosity. Maybe it's connected to having been adopted and never knowing my real parents. I could never find out who they were. Authorities were able to give me a biological mother's name, but records showed she didn't know who the father was. It's as if that genetic line is not to be repeated. Perhaps my belief may have emasculated me." He passed it off nonchalantly.

Vivian flounced in her seat, unconvinced. "I bet I could wake you up. I have marvelous powers of 'purr suaaasion', in case you haven't noticed." With that, she put her index finger in her mouth and sucked until both cheeks caved in.

"Cut it out, Vivian," reacted the Colonel. "You know the rules. You don't screw the help if you're the boss, and you don't seduce the boss if you're the help and want to keep your job. Above all, nobody screws around within their Association. Always take your needs elsewhere."

"Cool it, Tom. I was just trying to lighten him up," Viv soothed, a bit peeved at her tactics being so pitifully misunderstood.

Sam intervened, "I can tell you right now, I have regular needs for female companionship. Count me out, A. D., if I've got to become a hermit." The 'amens' were boisterous from Art, W. T., Ed, and Harry, who wanted it known their sexual preferences or needs hadn't changed.

Not losing focus, A. D. observed, "When I contacted each of you, and asked if you could travel extensively, it was assumed none of you had permanent type relationships that would suffer. The Colonel and Vivian have such a commitment, but they are both here and both needed."

"Guys," Harry chimed in. "If we're to make as much money as A. D. says, I can think of no better cover for what we'll be doing than to have a huge pleasure ship stocked with a staff for entertainment, including lots of showgirls."

"Catch your breath, Harry," A. D. joined in. "I don't find anything in such a notion which would be compromising to us. When you learn more about the power to be at our fingertips, the realization of a luxury cruiser is not only well within expected financial means, but it'll be of no threat to our security either. I confess, my field notes were incomplete on the subject of how the ship should be manned, and we'll take your suggestions under consideration at the next meeting."

"I just thought of something," Sam let out. "A. D., if you don't have a woman, are we going to have to do our own cooking? I'll tell you up front that I don't qualify for mess-hall duty. Tastin's my forte!" Everyone roared. The man of gargantuan size, had an appetite of equal magnitude.

"Now, there's an important question." Laughing, A. D. cited, "You will be happy to know that a wonderful black cook lives in at my place. Chances are, he'll permit sampling of the food. It'll remain to be seen, however, on how well he fares to outside input on preparation."

Sam, with a twinkle, commented, "I like a happy cook. Oddly, you say he's black though. I heard it dropped at the last pit stop we made that there are virtually no blacks in and around Harrison. Does he have a steady woman?"

Groaning, A. D. replied, "My, my, aren't we obsessed with sex today. As a matter of fact, he does have a woman. She's a fairly seriously retarded white in her late thirties or early forties. While I'm on the subject, you might as well have the whole nine yards on this man and his woman. He slowed to the speed limit, managing the snail-paced traffic through Marshall.

"Rabbit's a short male of undetermined years. He was farmed out of the penitentiary on a work release to cook in a hunting club during deer season for some local politician. His words were, 'I dissolved into the forest when the season was over'. Actually, he ran away and ended up hiding out on the property I purchased, where his prize talents have been discovered. The occult cunning and intelligence in him knew nobody would look very hard or be motivated to make an effort at finding him. The pens were overcrowded. Adverse publicity of political negligence, allowing a prisoner to escape on an obvious pork-barrel perk, worked in Rabbit's favor. He gambled on big stakes and won." Praise had crept into A. D.'s account of him.

"The real story on Lulu, Rabbit's woman," he related, "probably won't ever be known to tell. The name itself may well hold more fact than fiction to her past. I've deduced from bits and pieces gathered that parents are dead and, undoubtedly, were on welfare. They talked the State into tying her tubes when she was a teen and also managed a stipend to support her later in life. It's helped her to survive in their old farmhouse. Common talk around is of how she'd wander in the woods for days upon end." A few looks were exchanged as more was revealed.

"Not surprisingly, it was on one of those days she strolled up on my mountain and ran into Rabbit. His account is that Lulu mounted him in a frenzy, laughing and giggling all the while. My guess is two needs were satisfied, but he has been extremely good to her. He never lets her spend the night at the lodge with him. Apparently, Sam, he takes her back home, cleans up the cabin, and probably sees to it she has food to eat before he leaves . . . There are always some trade-offs. Strangely, Lulu is definitely more perceptive than when I first met her and, no doubt, keeps a cleaner person than she had been accustomed to in her adult life. Rabbit confesses to enjoying sex without commitment. He's indicated that for her, every time's like the first time."

A. D. decided to reroute the conversation. He needed to be able to concentrate on the road ahead. The next several miles demanded alertness and undivided attention while driving. Hoping to start an interaction among the bunch, he patiently waited for an upcoming stretch of highway. *If this lull lasts for another couple of minutes, I've got it made,* he thought.

Harry was about to crank up on more of the same when A. D. sighted his opportunity for a turnaround in small talk. "Look, guys and Vivian," he said, pointing to a road sign ahead. "Ever think you'd see a 'failed brake ramp'? Not bad for going down one of these dadburned hills, eh?"

On the outskirts of Harrison, A. D. pulled in at a Quickstop Station. The van's gas tank was woefully close to being empty. Vivian made a beeline for the restroom. Ed and W. T. were in hot pursuit, hoping to find a men's stall. The deli took a staggered hit on snacks and drinks as they alternated in and out to freshen up. On a whim, A. D. drove his charges through the downtown of Harrison, pointing out its historical structures, fine old homes, and churches. After the short tour, he headed north out of town on State Highway 7. Taking a cutback toward 65 North, he unexpectedly veered off to the right onto a barely passable gravel road. It curved and twisted for a short distance in a senseless contradiction of directions. Turning abruptly again, a set of tire tracks were followed across an open field to the edge of a thick grove of trees. Traveling not more than a hundred yards through these woods, the van lurched up on an asphalt road. A. D. threw the van into second gear and began to climb, circling up an otherwise pristine mountain. It crested, rounding a final blind curve on a tabletop plateau, which appeared to thrust out from the mountainside. Fenced, tree-bordered pastureland lay dead ahead. A complex of buildings that obviously had housed a sizable community at some time in the past dotted the landscape. In the distance, the mountain loomed on upward for another good half mile.

The entire panorama was so bizarre, alien, and unexpected to the eye that A. D.'s guests were stunned at its quaint magnificence. Before them lay two enormous structures and twenty-three small cottages resembling tiny houses built for the poor during the Great Depression era of the thirties. According to its shape, a church had occupied one of the larger buildings. The other seemed uniquely built to function as a lodge, and it's where A. D. parked the van.

Upon entry into the lodge, an observer saw the first level accommodations included a large social area, dining hall, kitchen, and rooms of modern hotel style and design. The spellbinding moment was broken by Art as he and the others stood entranced. "You've got some kinda digs here, A. D.! Why in Arkansas of all places?" he asked, unable to suppress his reactions.

A. D. softly touted, "In due time, my man. Follow me upstairs into a new address. Rabbit's putting final touches on a bite to eat. Then I'll attempt to tell all."

The lodge's interior reflected construction of rough-cut timbers and lumber, forming beams, flooring, and walls while the living quarters were paneled, carpeted, and had modern individual bathrooms. Disposing of luggage and making quick assessment of their accommodations, they were ready for the full tour. It climaxed in the dining hall at a massive table. Rabbit served the food. He retired to begin the dinner's menu. The late lunch aside, all eyes turned to A. D., questioning. "What's next?"

"This is not to be a presentation. I hope to make a brief life's summary to ease minds and make you more comfortable with the arrangement. What you see is for real. In the vernacular of the 'con', this is not a 'store' as you know it. And, I am absolutely not trying to scam you," he assured, knowing the nature of their interests.

"My corporate career had been compromised with the divorce. It placed me 'on hold', so to speak, for future advancement. The final eclipse occurred when my immediate boss's daughter chose me as a souvenir first and possibly as a husband later. I tried . . . It didn't work out, which was no surprise. The company CEO invited me to quietly leave. To insure my cooperation, a nice parachute was offered. Not a golden one, mind you, but adequate, nonetheless."

Distaste surged with the recount. "I sought to run away from the memories. Take my word, it didn't work either. I wanted to escape constant reminders of the lifestyle. It had to be a place where the parachute lasted long enough to find another way of making a living. The trip to Arkansas wasn't exactly an accident. I'd heard that north Arkansas, particularly the north central part, had become a haven for cults and the counterculture, with pot growers bold enough to farm their weeds in the National Forest. You may be asking why I didn't look you up and get back into the rackets. Let me tell you, I did consider it. It was rejected because, as you know, the world can spot a loser a mile away. And I was a loser! I could even smell myself!" Inadvertently, their thoughts of him having ulterior motives were being denigrated by the chain of events.

"Choosing Boone County was pure chance," A. D. allowed. "Thinking of buying a used house trailer to live in, I went to the county courthouse and inquired if any forfeited land was available for sale . . . There was, and they handed me a map on how to get there. When located, after several false turns, I was awed by a paved stretch of road leading to nowhere and by the extent of the structures you've seen. Why a local government would deed so much land to anyone for back taxes was beyond comprehension. Naturally, I wanted an answer," he interposed.

"At the courthouse, I received a rather hushed explanation. The land was developed years ago by a religious cult under the absolute and strict influence of a charismatic snake-handling, fundamentalist preacher who hated communism, yet practiced it in construction of his personal empire. It stood to make the real estate unavailable for taxation, since it had been classified as church property. Boone County had no expectations of ever receiving any tax revenue under the exemption. Over the years, the flock had grown to around two hundred until they simply vanished. No one confesses to knowing an exact date. The sheriff got nudged after none of the cult members showed up in town for a month. In turn, he and his deputies went calling on 'Brother Withers'. They were faced with a mystery. The entire commune population seemed to be away, and there was nothing to indicate foul play. Articles of clothing, food, and supplies were intact. Milk cows were seeking calves and offering milk-gorged udders. It was as if some unseen hand had wiped out humans and left the animals. Unfinished construction gave evidence that the disappearance had not been voluntary. They were never found nor heard from again."

Confiding on curiosities, A. D. enumerated, "In due course, a complicated court action turned the land over to Boone County, which promptly offered it for sale from the courthouse steps. An out-of-state couple made their land transaction through a broker. They had an ironclad promise from the county to pave the link between 'Brother Withers' road and the nearest other pavement within three years. Seemingly, the pair was well liked and spent money. To have inside conveniences, gravity-fed springwaters were diverted into a huge purchased tank, modernizing the lodge into what you see. More funds were applied into buying fencing and livestock and converting the old church to a barn. Two years later, they also disappeared without a trace. Once again the county took the land back, disposing of the livestock. By the time I came along, no one would even come up the road, much less consider buying the place."

The group's apprehension expanded as A. D. continued. "This ill-fated piece of property was the first thing presented to me by brokers and the county. It seemed ideal. I wanted the unlimited seclusion it offered. It went for a song, and so here we are. But wait! There's more to the legendary story. I know where they went! And I have a fair idea of what happened to all of those who disappeared!" he exemplified, kindling interest of something else that was strange.

"About two hundred feet above the plateau we're on, there's a sizeable cave in the mountainside. Quite by chance, I uncovered a carefully hidden opening into it. Just inside its entrance were two skeletal remains. Both had been shot in the head, suggesting a murder-suicide of the couple who had last owned the property. Going deeper into the lower reaches of the cave, a further search gave up multiple remains that had to have been those of the commune. Apart from all others and near an altar made of stones was a single frame of bones, which surely belonged to their leader. Alongside the bones was a dried snakeskin. It stood to reason that the old preacher had led his flock into such secret depths for some arcane purpose. My thoughts are, he practiced an intimidating snake-handling act. Only, on this occasion he received a fatal bite and had to kill the snake. True to form, he obviously was a control freak who forbade the flock to enter the cave except for special services and never without him. It would have been just like him to call for an act of obedience to stay and witness overcoming the Devil's test. It was pretty apparent they didn't know their way out. Remains of two or three turned up in tunnels coming out of the main chamber, as if searching for a way to the outside. As a whole, it seemed the total population had just sat down and waited to die. There were no signs of violence and none of cannibalism. It was the saddest thing I ever have seen or expect to see."

"Interesting stuff," Art relegated. "I suppose you've neglected reporting those findings to the authorities," he dryly speculated. His remark brought the others back to reality.

"You've got it right," A. D. answered with resolve and purpose. "Imagine the circus that media would bring in here. Why should I resurrect pain when it's finally become tolerable from losing someone? It would only cause more living hell for relatives and loved ones. All I found were bones. Their identity doesn't create life," he implored with conviction.

"Aside from all else, Art, local and state authorities have had two stabs at solving these mysterious disappearances. I am not obligated to inform them of anything, much less of our proposed operation where privacy is a mandatory essential. Later tonight, perhaps you'll understand why the importance, when I demonstrate the power available to execute our game plan. If there are no further questions, we'll parade by the kitchen and thank Rabbit for a fine meal."

Impressed with the attention, Rabbit drew up his five foot, five inch frame and, with great dignity, shook the hand of each guest. He obliged their compliments. "I cook Southern, as you tasted, but I can cook other things too. Let me know if you have a special request. Anytime!"

CHAPTER 5

Turning at the kitchen's door, A. D., rather unceremoniously, directed, "It's now time to visit my shoe store and try on shoes." Inside a storage room just off the great hall, he proceeded to outfit each in insulated shoes with two-inch soles, offering no explanation.

Vivian recognized the footwear had a later purpose. She tried to get a rise out of him, complaining, "These are the worst lookin' things I've ever put on. Couldn't you find something more fashionable for me to wear? And if you think man, you'll get over my head showing us you're another Einstein, you'd better add three more inches to the soles of your boots."

A. D. didn't ante to her bait. He was anxious to show them how electrical power could revolutionize the artistry of pulling off a con and refused to be distracted. For the most part, the guys were too intent on being fitted and experiencing the adjustment of walking in elevated footwear to harass him. It took a third try-on for Harry to be satisfied . . .

The church, converted from a barn to a laboratory, is where they 'stilted' from the lodge to survey operations. On one end of the building, A. D. had mounted a grounded antenna, roughly thirty feet high. On the other end, the wood-framed steeple contained a similarly grounded grain auger. Slowly, it spiraled down toward the earth. A raised, open platform covering six hundred square feet stood in front of the laboratory. Erected strategically about were various devices and gauges, appearing to be controls of some sort. Supported above by vertical framing, A. D. had fabricated a roof consisting of automatic garage doors that could be rolled down along sides of the structure, leaving an unrestricted view of the sky and surroundings.

The laboratory's interior was a maze of capacitors, transformers, rectifiers, and enormous waveguides, totally dumbfounding to a casual observer. Even W. T. elbowed Sam, mouthing, "Do you believe this elaborate setup?" Aware the tour had enlightened no one, A. D. signaled them outside to begin his orientation.

On the platform and speaking against a brisk wind, he raised his voice to be heard. "I see the setup inside didn't make much of an impression on you. Maybe I can change that! If you'll look around, you will see there are no electric wires coming up the mountainside, and neither are there any out here. Also, recall that the unit inside was entirely self-contained. Everything in that lab is running on a source of energy other than that supplied through a power company's lines." He waited for realities to materialize. Observing a state of wonder and awe being reflected, he guided them back toward the lodge.

"In here, your every comfort is provided by electricity coming from the unit just visited. Clarification is of more value than opening up to a discussion," A. D. advised. "What you have observed is no miracle. It consists of pumping electricity into the earth at approximately one hundred fifty thousand cycles per second. Thus, the precautionary purpose for the shoes you're wearing. As a further safeguard, the platform is insulated. These frequencies are being tuned by huge waveguides, which function exactly like smaller waveguides in a radio receiver. It corresponds to the earth's frequency in response to magnetic fields of the sun," he diagramed.

"Try to perceive that when in tune with the earth, our charge spreads around the globe to its exact opposite side, where a corresponding, opposite pole is developed. This pole 'broadcasts' a slightly greater amount of electricity back to our antenna and becomes available, adding to the charge. As the broadcast alternates back and forth, enormous potentials are developed at both poles. A prime example of what occurs can best be illustrated by observing a child on a swing. The child kicks off into a swinging motion. At the height of a swing, energy is applied by thrusting the body forward while holding tightly to the two supporting ropes. Each swing takes the kid higher until he nearly reaches the height of the extended ropes. In other words, force is cumulatively added to force." The comparison served A. D. an example by which to continue.

"As a consequence, the operation has to maintain a frequency with the earth, or the entire edifice comes crashing down. In that scenario, there quickly comes a time when excess power must be disposed of in some way that does not interfere with frequency modulation between the earth and the sun. The method developed to accommodate such a problem will be demonstrated tonight."

You could hear a pin drop as A. D. finished his dissertation and asked for comments. Beckoning to Ed, he cited, "Everyone here, including myself, defers to your judgment. Surely, you have at least one question."

"If I am confined to ask only one," Ed obliged, "it'd be more in the form of a statement. I know what I saw. I have to believe what you say is true. But my logic isn't cooperating to tell me why you haven't sold this invention to the power industry and taken its riches to live on like a king! To be frank, A. D., it causes me to be a little doubtful and suspect of your motive." Ed's assessment and his outspoken conclusion didn't go without notice . . .

"Well put as always, Ed," he commended. "Trouble is, it's already been tried by my predecessor rather unsuccessfully. My professed goal is to profit from his error. You will recall I told you up front, I'd rediscovered, not discovered, how to extract free electricity from the earth. The pioneer making its initial finding was a man whose name you probably have never heard. Back when, this father of the modern power industry, Nikola Tesla, was destroyed by his own invention. Tesla developed the patents for production of alternating current, and the generators were installed at Niagara Falls, where they still operate. Under sponsorship of financier J. P. Morgan, he sought to capture free electricity on a large scale and fabricated the machinery to use it. The cause of his downfall surfaced later. He died broke and ridiculed as a crazy eccentric. In death, threats to the power industry were buried, and he later gained deserved honors."

Obviously dispelled by Tesla's lot, A. D. refuted, "Ed, you couldn't pay me to go that route for all the tea in China. Today, the seats of power have shifted. Politics is no longer the agent for destiny of this world. In all forms, absolute power is held by those in control of the source and supply of energy and by those controlling communications. Between these two icons is where true power exists. Industrial might, consolidated through mergers and leveraged buyouts, crosses borders, negates sovereignty, and ultimately, personal identity. To tamper with that consolidation by introducing free electric power that 'every man' can have, is to invite annihilation. As long as it's confined to our use in operations to 'unbalance' the gold market, or to make the dice roll in our favor, we'll be relatively safe. Consequently, if it ever becomes known who reinstituted a source of free electricity, then you'd best get as far away from me as possible. My presence could become hazardous to your health."

"You speak of deferring to me?" Ed charged. "Well, I'll yield to the logic of what you've just related, anytime. It's cleared the last hurdle I had. I still remember the unproven stories of inventors, who brought out highly improved carburetors, purportedly cutting gas consumption in half. They disappeared, along with their inventions. You're right about ramifications if we're caught. In today's society, your man Tesla would not have been allowed to live."

Unleashed on the subject, A. D. took the floor again. "Tesla had a problem with excess electricity. He tried solving it in an unsatisfactory fashion. His solution was to blow it off in the form of high-voltage lightning bolts between two hollow globes in much the same manner as an extra amount of steam is released through pop-off valves in the tanks of steam engines. These discharges alarmed farmers in the surrounding countryside, who claimed their cows dried up and the hens had quit laying. Eventually, complaints led to serious conflict. Tesla's money was cut off, causing his ultimate undoing," he accounted, portraying the irony.

"In seeking another solution to his problem, I accidentally stumbled upon the most amazing phenomenon. Superfluous electricity can be used to warp space around an antenna and, I believe, subsequently around the virtual pole on the other side of our earth. Instead of lightning bolts between two antennas, space can be warped by shunting high voltage to an antenna in the shape of a spiral, which is turned in a downward motion toward the center of the earth. By manipulating the auger's rotational speed, coordinated with variations in the tension of high voltage, a semispherical 'bubble' can be created. The size and density of this curvature of space around the antenna can be regulated. I am working on the mathematics of relationships so the warp can be set and controlled on demand by computer. Tonight, I want you to see it in operation, manually. During daylight hours, I don't tamper with hard space warp up here on the mountain. Its effects might be visible, causing an undesirable inquiry."

Loaded with almost more than he could absorb, or to the point of being brain-dead, W. T. complained, "I need a drink." Harry stuck a finger up, joined by Art, who needed a breather.

"We're all over twenty one," Ed kited. "It's either appropriate to have a drink or drink to have comprehension. Before we indulge, and while it's still on my mind, A. D., tell me what turned you on to even seek a cure for Tesla's problem, much less the solution you found?"

"Careful, Ed. You know what they say about curiosity killing the cat. Truth be, however, I don't mind sharing my motivations on the matter. At the very time Tesla had been conducting his experiments, I picked up on another young man named Albert Einstein who was making a mark in the scientific community with his special and general theory of relativity. In that complete theory, space was sharply curved in the intense gravitational field of the sun. Experiments by astronomers, who set up their equipment at the equator during a full, midday eclipse of the sun, had proved Einstein to be correct. As a result, science had to learn to accept new concepts about reality. Mass increased to infinity at the speed of light, time stood still for clocks, and every measurement had to be qualified with the term, 'to an observer'. Einstein believed there was a relationship between electricity, magnetism, and gravity. He spent the rest of his life trying to construct a mathematical model of his unified field theory. He died unsuccessful yet convinced the theory was correct. His steadfast belief and the data compiled turned me on to explore in this direction," he conceded, pleased Ed had asked.

As an afterthought, A. D. reminded anyone still attuned. "My field notes aren't classified. You already have a copy of them." Excusing himself, he left supposedly to take up a thing or two with Rabbit before the evening's demonstration.

CHAPTER 6

Ed sat, staring into a drink. Emotions were on a second day binge. He saw the realism and promise of the greatest adventure of his lifetime! He felt the eyes focus on him. He sensed destiny had placed him in as pivot on critical points . . . Harry Annemann invaded his reconciliations.

"There are unexpected things here, which I don't like. I don't like the idea of anyone being electrocuted if we make a misstep. I don't like the possibility of us being wiped out by international forces because we've got so-called free electricity. And, of all things, A. D. wants to fool around with warping space! Now, that really scares the hell out of me," he emitted resentfully.

There were nods of skeptical agreement from those who could not avoid hearing his angry outcry. But not from Ed! He confronted him, poking holes in the inane analysis. "It's put-up or shut-up time once again, friend. Let's take it from back to front, Harry. You remind me of a true story about a prosecutor in New York state, who filed for an injunction against initial sale of Bell Telephone stock on grounds of fraud. 'Everyone knows that you can't send a voice down a wire.' Does that sound familiar, anyone?" asked Ed, including others listening.

"You and I are all suffering from a sensory and an information overload these past thirty or so hours. I can't personally advise you on how to live your individual lives. But, since you seem hell bent on turning to me, I'm going to tell you about my life and the way I've come to think. One thing's for sure. Each of us comes from a dysfunctional family. Living proof of it is in how we've chosen to pursue life," Ed reminded, spurring recollections.

"Here's some more fat to chew on. I'm an Arkansan. I come from a farming community just north of Pine Bluff. My paternal grandfather was a highly successful cotton farmer, blessed to have a good wife and large family, which he indulged with practically limitless cash. Results were, Daddy and every one of his brothers and sisters never learned to make or save a dime. All they knew about money was what and how much it would buy. Their spending was obsessive. When the depression of 1929 hit, Grandpa's holdings crumbled. My Daddy hung on to become a cotton buyer. At heart a gambler, the profession gave him a measure of status, yet the malady instilled so well at the family knee, he never quite overcame. The old adage, 'shirtsleeves to shirtsleeves in three generations,' still holds true. The notion of 'something for nothing' became my inheritance. It undoubtedly influenced me to flirt with the rackets and live a precarious, yet mundane existence. Years later, I woke up to a secret regarding my behavior. It, coupled with the idea of getting money without working, became a poisonous combination. Both my happiness and decision making process were messed up," he admitted.

Ed's logic bared realities. "One fine day, a stupendous revelation manifested itself. I'd been lying to myself. Not once or twice, but all the time. Here I was, in a profession that absolutely required living up to your unwritten word, yet I constantly lied to myself. Then an even bigger revelation dawned. I realized I could not quit lying to myself. I'd promise to quit, but even that'd be a lie. Finally, I learned the only way to control my destiny was to daily and repeatedly ask, 'Ed, did you just lie to yourself?' It's a routine I still use to locate the truth. Since prevarication is a human failing, have you given thought to how much you lie?" he asked, touching nerves.

"I don't mind telling you, you're liars and have been all of your lives. It hangs around your neck like a yoke. Survival has prevailed because you're canny and have had a certain amount of luck. If you cannot address the problem of lying to yourself, then you've no business pursuing the game. It'll be too fast and too demanding for any peace and comfort of mind. My reason behind telling you is that it's in the same context used for an alcoholic lecture at an AA meeting. One more thing. Surely you know, you can't share in a half billion dollars within a year and a half and put up nothing. Incidentally, age is catching up. Telemarketing is about the only pitch that's left before time pulls the plug. I don't have any control over it. What I do have control over, is the way I live the rest of my life. Make no mistake. This is a 'once in a lifetime' opportunity. I intend to live it to its fullest." Ed started to sit down, only to straighten back up. "Harry," he added. "If you decide to pick up and leave, stay the hell out of San Francisco. You might get run over by a streetcar!"

Eyes blazing, Harry stomped out of the room. No one seemed inclined to talk. They were lost in their own thoughts, complicated by Ed's challenge to Harry's damning attitude.

A. D., who had been recording in his quarters on a sight-and-sound tape, hunched forward. Stroking his jaw, he felt let down, self-debating, *Was it all going down the tubes?*

In character, thirty minutes later, Harry strode in. He faced up. "As usual, Ed, you have called a spade a spade. I am relieved. Deal me back in. It feels like I've taken a big laxative or had a good piece. My hope is I'm not lying to myself when I tell I'm in for the duration."

Tom, on reflex of the moment, did his thing. "Are we ready for a vote? With no objections, once and for all, now or never, those in favor of this venture, raise your right hand." Seven hands went up in unison, courtesy of Harry's far-fetched synopsis.

A. D. switched off the recording device. He lay down to relax before the evening's events.

The gang's humor at dinner reflected objectivity over the day's events. It was duly observed by A. D. A three-quarter moon revealed its radiance as he ushered them into the great social hall's sitting area. Mincing no words, he needed their undivided attention. "Among other things," A. D. began, "you've been indoctrinated on the principles of how electrical power is to be put to use in an unconventional way to pull off scams, be a protector, and produce wealth. Now, what you're going to see tonight will astound you! As you watch, bear in mind, it does not violate the world's natural structure. Also, recall that I stumbled onto the method for using excessively high potential electricity to warp space. It is not to say I wasn't looking for it, based upon Einstein's eternal belief in his unified field theory, unifying electricity, magnetism, and gravity, in one related equation . . . For me, it was pure serendipity to find the exact composition to warp space! That, my friends, is when I called you to meet in Little Rock." Pleased with the developments, his elation elevated.

"The discovery makes it ideal for our purposes. Not only does it absorb excess energy, leaving us free to stay synchronous with the vibrations between the earth and the sun, but it also provides a readily available shield from a hostile attack with minimum advance notice. Think about it! Installation of a modern radar system on that luxury cruiser, Harry, can insure that we will be impervious from attack. If you want calm seas and convenience without interruption from storms, it'll work too. So come on, slip into your boots, lace 'em up, and let's move outside. I want you to see for yourself what has me so consumed."

Arrayed on the lab's outer platform, A. D. pointed to the many gauges monitoring electrical forces. "These act as an energy readout. Now, take a look at the stars and moon we enjoy for the occasion. Be prepared tho, I'm about to turn them off as far as you're concerned. The curvature of space in the warp will be so unyielding that light cannot penetrate," he explained, adjusting dials. "It'll be diverted along the curved outer edges of a bubble I'm creating." Slowly, but surely, the moon and the stars faded from view. An awesome, inky blackness prevailed. A. D. gave them a few moments for it to sink in before enlightening. "There are no reference points in total blackness, except where your feet touch the surface you stand on."

Without warning, the entire plateau became illuminated by dozens of floodlights. The farthermost edges of the domed bubble were made visible. "Seeing is believing," A. D. predicted. "You are going to witness a demonstration of the effect curved space has on moving objects."

Rabbit, already walking out into the pasture, placed a small model plane on the ground while A. D. supplied, "It is a little over two hundred yards from where we stand to the property's edge. Concurrently, it is the same to the curved space forming this bubble. Watch carefully. The plane will be flying in a straight line." The plane revved up, taking off in a direction toward the plateau's edge, traveling at an angle of about fifteen degrees. Its speed increased until it struck the invisible wall, where it exploded and crashed.

Impacted by the display, Art was quick to single A. D. out. "I suppose you're showing us what would happen on the reverse side," he stated rather than asked.

"Yes, Art," A. D. affirmed. "In this next experiment, it involves the plane flying in ever-widening circles until it engages the curvature of space, again inside the dome. If we succeed in reaching curved space, and avoid a crash, you'll see the plane flies in circles without any radio input." All eyes were glued as the plane took off.

"Did you see the plane as it engaged the curved space's edge?" questioned A. D., guiding. "Notice how it's no longer flying at a forty-five degree angle to earth's surface. One wing is pointed straight toward the ground while the other one points directly upward. To the guidance system, it's as if the plane is taxiing dead ahead on a very slick, frictionless runway. Its forward momentum ceases to counterbalance the pull of gravity once it runs out of fuel." He had prepared them for the inevitable when an idea to magnify the event superseded.

"I've saved the best for last," A. D. elaborated. "It's possible the plane could be lost going out of the bubble, but I'm about to soften the dome's curvature of space." Turning dials with one hand, he pointed upward with the other. "Look! The moon and stars are reappearing. The plane continues to fly in a parallel position and probably should be brought in for a landing. For now, we'll let it fly to its destiny as a token of an unusual revelation."

Engaging them further, he solicited, "Tonight, what's left of it, I want you to think about the enormous advantage this technology offers. Most importantly, reflect on being able to observe objects outside the undetectable, protective shield, such as those on land, air, or sea, friend or foe, toting roses or explosives. These can all be redirected, or stopped by the produced curved space, which permits light and other electromagnetic waves to enter."

On a whim, A. D. decided to propagate. "Harry, even in the most ideal of conditions, I can't promise you luxury-liner entertainers who won't ever have reason to complain of being 'under the weather'. You can rest assured that only one conceivable condition is out there to foil our goals. Unlikely as the chances are, it'd probably be the result of an irredeemable human error made. Get a good night's sleep. We work tomorrow."

CHAPTER 7

Coffee in hand, A. D. invited his group toward the far end of the great hall, following breakfast. Double doors led into another area designed for recreation, including a small gambling den at the back. In addition to the usual snooker table associated with a bar, there were also professional setups to play blackjack, roulette, or craps. Spotting the gaming layout, multiple aahs and oohs erupted. "You've been holding out on us," W. T. feigned insult.

"A mere oversight on the part of your tour guide, I'm sure," A. D. returned. "Seriously tho, gather 'round and let's go over what I call the four Rs of a successful con. Categorized, I consider them to be research, routines, rehearsal, and resourcefulness. The research has been done, down to a scaled drawing of the casino's floor plan. Even distances in feet are mapped from one point to another. You will need to familiarize yourselves with the articles of supply required to either operate a crap table or interrupt its operation as the case might be, to establish a routine."

Going into inordinate details, he described fixtures, function, and protocol. "What we have here is a crap table wired to control the dice. Guts inside the table contain electromagnets weighing over two hundred pounds. On top you see three pairs of dice, two of which are fixed. One pair is rigged to stop on seven when the table is 'on' while the other pair ends its roll on snake eyes. The third pair is honest. A good stickman can move the dice around convincingly, keeping the pairs separated. For what it's worth, even crooked dice become honest when the table is turned off. Now," A. D. canvassed, "is there a stickman in the bunch to begin the routine?"

W. T. Farris tentatively raised a finger. "Off and on over the years, kickin' about to make a buck, I've done time on the tables."

"Then you know where I'm coming from." A. D. nodded, handing him the stick.

"I'm afraid I do," W. T. admitted, jockeying with the stick. "Show me the button."

"Hold up, W. T., I've got a weight on my chest as big as the one in this table." A. D. grinned sheepishly to avoid anyone's concern. "Furthermore, I feel as tall as you are, Sam. The ebb and flow last night and this morning's activity have to be embraced and recognized. I'm thinking it has to do with more of our manifest destiny surfacing. Why else am I cued in on two, unrelated subjects that need to be addressed?" The abrupt change in focus caught them off guard.

"Grab a stool and park it while I fill you in," A. D. insisted, bringing one out to sit on. "I'm not in favor of passing up anything that could be remotely beneficial to operations. However, when there's something that knocks you to your knees, as this one has done to me, it's time to incorporate a change in how business is done. Consider this. The realm to which sophisticated communication is used, for the most part, is being taken for granted by the general public. Not so for us. It'll become a valued key for resourcefulness. For instance, a miniature receiver, like the smallest hearing aid, will be worn by each. Such a microchip is capable of keeping us in constant radio contact and will enable every action to be coordinated," he said, referencing the fixed dice game as an example.

"The other blockbuster I've had," A. D. provided, "is that we cannot afford to clutter the airwaves by use of name initials. They can be confused for call letters or something worse. W. T. and A. D. are passé. The two of us must adopt another identity for this particular scam. What about it, W. T.? Do you have a real name to use, nickname or preference title that suffices?"

"Does a bird have two wings?" W. T. responded, citing, "As a kid, I hated both the given names, Werner and Theodore. They were the source of many a schoolyard fight. When my folks moved to Center Point, I traded them for initials at school and begged Mom and Pop to back me up. They did, but I never cared much for W. T. either. Didn't you call it destiny a while ago? This has to be mine. As of now, I am Theo Farris. Damn glad for the change, finally!"

"Hey, I like it!" chimed in Art Crissel. "Theo it is, and it fits you like a glove! How about you, A. D.? What's your new moniker?"

"It's not that big a deal for me. I already have two valid names, which I've nurtured down through the years. It's hardly the appropriate time to tell you how I came to have two legal, valid identities, so I'll catch you later on that story. I do think it's timely to mention that very soon it'll be mandatory to register a corporate status and secure a Federal EIN for the business. Since the paperwork for an EIN begins with a Social Security number, and my other name, James Freed Dacus, is on record there, it'd probably be advisable for me to retain that identity. Just call me Dacus from here on. Grab the stick, Theo, and let's show these folks how a 'juice joint' operates its little routine. The power is on. The button is in its customary place, and it's rehearsal time . . ."

Theo removed two of the three pairs of dice from the table and hit the button. The pair left on the table wiggled and rolled over with snake eyes up. He replaced them with a pair, which did not react when the button was punched. He verified the third pair. A three and a four came up. Next, he placed all three pairs back on the table and seemingly began to mix the six dice in a constant motion, using the stick.

Dacus passed around twenty chips each, and the practice game was on. It quickly became noticeable that the pair showing seven was the most important of the three. Theo could make a bettor, or bettors, win or lose with that one pair. If he wanted the dice to win on the first roll, he punched the button on a 'come out'. Up would come the seven. Anyone betting on the dice, won. Those betting against the dice, lost. By waiting for the point to become established, Theo could make the dice 'crap out' by bringing up the seven.

Two hours of play passed in a hurry. The power of a wired table to orchestrate payoff on the dice, and the almost infinite varieties of control available to the house, became familiar to everyone. Theo's senses, sharpened with the practice as well, prompted a point. "The house can use a 'juice joint' to grind out a percentage. It can also knock off an individual 'high roller' at will. But, Dacus, I don't know how you think it can be done to a stickman on a wired table. You'd better reconsider or have something else up your sleeve!"

"Okay," Dacus challenged. "We all know the sequence of a sting involves 'the story', 'the tip', 'the score', and 'blowing off the mark'. You've neither heard the story, nor do you know how we're going to control the tip to make the score, much less how we're going to blow off the mark. Here, Harry, slip on this belt with the blocks attached. Put a coat on over it and place this small metal disk in your left pocket. Using your right hand, feel the tiny button on the right side of your belt. Begin to practice pushing the button to the on-and-off position. Watch me closely because Theo as stickman is standing between us. When you see me lay a finger alongside my nose, belly in on the table and switch the button on," he instructed, demonstrating the moves.

"Art, in your role, consider the chips you're holding to be worth a thousand apiece. Place two of them on the seven in the 'come out'. You're aiming at a potential payoff of five to one, on first roll of the dice."

Wanting reaction time, Dacus slanted. "As stickman, Theo, what's your natural response?"

"My move, Dacus, would be to shove these snake eyes out on the table at him. The seven wouldn't be worth a damn on this kind of bet, but I could take him with snake eyes."

Dacus signaled to Sam. "Step up to the table. You're to be the bullish, spoiled, half-drunk sport accompanied by a brassy woman picked up at the roulette table. The two of you amble over to play craps. She's to goad you into betting heavily. You flash ten thousand dollars worth of chips, just to impress her, but you're a chickenshit bettor. She rides you about it in front of everyone. Seeing Art bet two thousand on the seven, her harangue escalates by calling you cheap. Ticked off, Sam, you place eight thousand on snake eyes at thirty to one and call her a loudmouthed bitch." Sam's casting triggered high approval ratings.

"What's the stickman's reaction in this instance, Theo?" Dacus asked.

"The stickman is blocked, but he does have an option. If he brings up snake eyes, the house is on the hook for two hundred and forty thousand in order to win two on the seven bet. All he can do is let the dice roll. The odds against snake eyes are thirty-six to one, and the odds against a seven are six to one. Any other number on the 'come out' will deliver ten thousand dollars to the house," Theo accurately assessed.

Dacus laid his finger alongside his nose, and Harry flipped the button on. In an instant, the dice quivered and jumped, rolling up *snake eyes*!

Theo looked at the dice. He palmed them to get a feel before exclaiming, "Well, I'll be damned! That's unbelievably awesome! You don't need me for a stickman. What have you got in mind for me? Play a passed-out drunk perched on some barstool?"

Before Dacus could respond to Theo, Tom and Vivian were crying foul play, "Are we left out of this one, or do we act like two poster dummies?"

"One at a time! One at a time," humored Dacus, amused. "Theo, you're to be the triggerman. You'll be guarding the stickman. Honestly, I thought training a triggerman would be an arduous task. Here again tho, we're blessed with serendipity. Your expertise as a stickman makes this operation a hell of a lot less risky. It is imperative to know when snake eyes are on the table. A tip from you on the come out, verifying the right pair is on the table after Art drops two thousand on the seven, is an absolute must. Confirmation from you, watching the stickman pass 'snake eyes' to Art, lets Sam know to drop his bet of eight thousand. The bipolarity of the electric field, causing the button under the table to trip, is manned by you and Harry. Its timing, as the dice roll, is literally at your fingertips," he emphasized the sequence's delicacy.

"Ah, Tom and Vivian, your resourcefulness is as gifted as it gets and equally essential to our ultimate success," Dacus humored. "Not only does the mark have to be blown off, he must be forced to pay off in cash, even though it's in violation of federal law. You're to be prominently located, betting at a roulette wheel nearest the crap table. Your signal to cue our team of 'law enforcement auditors' making the scene must be perfectly executed to blow off the mark."

Enlarging the scope, he consigned. "Next on the agenda includes hiring a temporary team who knows the ropes. We'll need four men and one woman to be temporary cohorts on the first scam that funds our nut. They'll have to be a special breed to function in the scam," he asserted, adding, "If you've got any ideas, let's have 'em."

"I've got a choice on the woman to pair up with Sam," Theo offered. "She was shill for the house where I once operated as stickman. The doll's good lookin', sharp as they come, and real versatile. She'll fit into the tempo of this con in nothin' flat."

"She certainly sounds like a winner. Come on, Theo . . . Give us the scoop on how well you know this person. Tell us more," Dacus prodded.

"Well, I met her at work in a Bossier City gambling joint. We pulled a night shift. She worked customers for the house, like I told you, and I was stickman on a crap table. She had a thing for more mature men, and we sorta' took up with one another in the daytime. Back then, her name was Maybelle Conner. Somehow, the name 'Maybelle' fitted her to a T. As I said, she's sharp. So much so that she soon made blackjack dealer in the place. Betting on the horses was among many loves, and she won at virtually anything I saw her take on. One day, at the track, she met this older man. He was a doctor and confirmed widower without children from Tulsa. Things happened. Maybelle married the prominent Dr. R. Bryan Barton and moved into his Tulsa society. Dr. Barton owned a mansion in one of the most exclusive subdivisions in the city. In the country club where her husband was a charter member, and being the vivacious woman that she is, Mrs. Maybelle Barton soon took up tennis, played in bridge clubs with his colleagues' and friends' wives, and hosted luncheons. She became an avid worker in charities and accompanied the good doctor to the Episcopalian Church on Sundays. They often took cruises, savoring both Caribbean and Pacific waters." His discourse was unfolding a bond that existed between them . . .

"Everything was peaches and cream until ten years later when Bryan keeled over and died of a heart attack. As a man with no heir, he had left the entire estate to Maybelle. She got the mansion, membership in the country club, and an estimated two million in stocks, bonds, and cash. But the minute the funeral ended, her position in Tulsa society got stripped. She was shunned at the country club and at church. No longer was she invited to play bridge, and no one showed up if she planned a bridge party. The isolation from high society came overnight," Theo cumulated.

"Maybelle said she grieved first, sulked for about six months, and then plotted to show them. She decided to shove society up their left nostril and turned the mansion into a whorehouse. And, she was smart. She had all the money she needed. Taking money from girls didn't have to be an option to operate. Instead, she'd set up a tax-free, charitable foundation to support and shelter battered women and wayward girls. It could be sustained with a grant from her own funds. To complete the charade, she separated herself from the mansion by moving into her lavish refurbished cabana near the swimming pool. An equally furnished office fronted her business. Before moving girls in, she invested a great deal in hidden surveillance cameras to cover action in the bedrooms. Every movement was monitored by Maybelle in the cabana. Even the hustlers didn't know their activities were videotaped. Maybelle built a library of tapes, involving many husbands of her former acquaintances and a fair sampling of the rest of high rollers in Tulsa area."

Theo broke into his own recitation of Maybelle's career. "I guess you need to know, if you haven't already guessed, Maybelle and I have been in touch with each other since her husband died. Being the former lover, she's shared personal problems with me, and I've been a sounding board for her present venture. Anyway," he continued, "when the inevitable pressure from wives and male prigs finally caused city hall to make a move, she received a call from the mayor. In her words, he opened with the old cliché, 'Maybelle, this is Mayor Clyde Burnes. How are you?', and she recoiled demanding, 'Clyde, you didn't call me to pass the time of day. Get to the point.' Enraged by his response, 'Maybelle, we have complaints, and I hope you noted it's plural. They're accusing you of running a whorehouse out at your place.', sent her on a tirade . . .

"Ball-bustun' him as only she's capable of doing, she proceeded to lay a grabbing hurt on him, divulging, 'If you're half as smart as you think you are, Clyde, why haven't you bothered to check up and find out that my house is strictly dedicated to charity? It's even supported by my own money, in trust. This is a home for abused women and homeless girls. I live in newly renovated quarters by the pool, not in the house at all. If you want to make an ass of yourself, go ahead. It won't be the first time you've been stupid, if you get what I mean!'."

Theo stopped, looked around, and grinned. "Okay, I just got carried away. The mayor surely got the message and a compromise was reached after intense negotiating, Maybelle set up a particularly naive preacher to run her charity. Ladies of the night were moved to a house outside city jurisdiction with bureaucratic protection. Her mansion was filled with truly needy females. The preacher received weekly, charitable donations from an estate out in the county."

"Sounds like quite a gal," Vivian commented, her appreciation evident.

"I may be prejudiced," Theo confessed, "but I think she's more than that. At any rate, she's bored where she is and would make a fine addition to join us in this scam."

Theo's resume of Maybelle met with total approval, and he was told to contact her.

CHAPTER 8

Scott Ballard sat in his office at the Lavender Peacock and tussled with realities. He was a certified public accountant who had done well. The decision to take his accumulated cash and invest in Mississippi gambling wasn't working, although it had indeed looked good. The damn casino was failing, and it wasn't his fault. It was in the straits because too many of them had sprung up recently. Why hadn't he realized that a state, unable to shake prohibition for nearly forty years after the Constitutional Amendment, couldn't possibly handle legalized gambling? In the end, it had cost him his wife. By trying to save his investment, it had also become necessary to abandon a lucrative practice. To salvage the Lavender Peacock, and as much as he hated it, he had to solicit a cash investment from the mob through old man Arnold Lipscomb. The small-time Mafia forced him to accept a wired crap table to suck in extra money and to hang on, promising one of the other casinos would fold, and their volume would boom again.

The odds sucked. Overhead had him strapped. Nightly, for the past week, tables had been idle and attendants spent more time talkin' than ripplin' cards or movin' the dice. Video poker and two-bit slot machines claimed as much activity as barmaids on the make or their no tips bitchin'.

Around ten o'clock, word was passed to him that a 'live one' had shown up, forked over ten thousand dollars to buy chips, but had headed for the wrong crap table. Quickly, Ballard recoiled, sending instructions to maneuver the sucker to the wired table.

Pretending to be loud and drunk, Sam got steered to the right one, on information it was the only crap table in the house with 'no limits' on bets. A very attractive, attention-getting brunette he'd met at a roulette wheel accompanied him. As they lined up at the table, she emphasized the obvious by molding her body to his, touching up against him, while clutching his right arm. "Gosh, you're so big and so firm!" she gushed. "Do you work out regularly?"

The stickman signaled to the pit boss. He stepped a couple of paces away from the table to make a whispered inquiry, "Is she working for the house?"

The pit boss mouthed, "She must be hustling for herself. I never saw the dame before."

"Well, that oversized guy she's with is my mark," the stickman bragged. "He bought ten big 'uns in chips. He's half drunk on his ass, and I think the woman's after his money. I'm goin' to take him as quick and clean as I can."

"Go for it," urged the pit boss. "You know how bad we need ready cash."

Unable to suppress a slight smile, the stickman thought to himself, *This rube is sure a gone*r. Turning back to the table, he noticed it had filled up considerably, hopefully by greenhorns loaded with money. None of the faces were familiar though.

Some of the nonentities at the table were strategically placed. Theo occupied a position on the corner to the left of the stickman, who was noticeably right handed. Harry took the corner at the other end, stationed on the stickman's right, while Art was just to Theo's left. Maybelle and Sam, alias 'Buddy Lee' and 'Greta', stood at the table's center, directly opposite the stickman. All others, waiting to roll the dice, were strangers to them. When the stickman picked up his stick, Theo glanced over to Tom and Vivian at the roulette table, letting them know the con had started.

The stickman shuffled his dice and shoved the straight pair out on the table. He wanted to get familiar with his customers. Each had purchased at least the minimum two thousand dollars worth of chips to qualify for playing at the high-stakes table. Initially, they were betting cautiously and conservatively, waiting for the dice to get hot.

Boosting things along, the stickman inserted the 'seven passers' dice into the game. He used the button to let those betting on the 'come out' win a little. To encourage heavier betting, he held off on using the seven with the button to crap out anyone, deciding to let nature take its course.

About thirty minutes into the game, Theo cued Art to start upping his bets. Buddy Lee held himself in check, causing Greta to begin needling him to bet more. He would good-naturedly up his bets for one round then drop right back down again on the next roll. Greta appeared to become disenchanted with her mark and started a play for Art's attention, irritating Buddy Lee. Suddenly, Art, stimulated by Greta's turn on, placed two thousand on the seven, at five to one odds. "Watch me win ten, baby," he boasted.

Responding immediately, the stickman shoved 'snake eyes missers' to Art. There was a mumbling around the table as action picked up. The word 'cheap' cropped up.

"Don't call me cheap, you loudmouthed bitch," Buddy Lee snapped as he shoved eight thousand dollars on snake eyes at thirty to one.

The stickman's eyes bugged out. He signaled to the pit boss and backed up two steps from the table. Theo caught Tom and Vivian's eyes again. The raid was on. Led by Ed and his officers, flashing badges, they commanded their way past two guards into Scott Ballard's private office. Slapping a court document on Ballard's desk, Ed said, "We know you're skimming the public by running a juice joint. You'd be advised to cooperate under terms of this search warrant." With authority, he instructed, "Men, there are five tables to be checked for wiring. You check the four out there on the floor. I'll take a look at his books and check the one outside this office." Pointing to his pager, he further instructed, "I'll call you if I need you." Addressing Ballard, he demanded records on activities for the last sixty days.

The stickman, and pit boss to back him, stepped to the table asking, "Are all bets down?" With a slight turn of his head, he questioned out of the side of his mouth, "What do you think?"

The pit boss mumbled, "You have no choice. Let it ride. Odds are thirty-six to seven to pick up ten for the house."

Art shook the dice, had Greta kiss 'em for luck, and rolled them the length of the table, hitting the far wall. Theo and Harry were in position. Just as the dice bounced off the wall, Theo turned the table on . . . Instantaneously, up jumped snake eyes!

The pit boss and stickman turned chalk white. Gamblers around the table looked at the dice in stunned amazement. Just as abruptly, Buddy Lee let out a yell. "EEEYOW! Nearly a quarter million dollars, baby!"

Greta excitedly grabbed Buddy's arm, engaging him and crying, "Ya wouldn't have done it, sweetie, if I hadn't egged ya on!"

Buddy caught her around the waist, picking her up in the air with one arm, and kissed her squarely on the mouth. "I'm not mad at you anymore, you sweet tart. Come with me, baby. Let's celebrate. You can have almost anything you want, honey. And I'm gonna put somethin' on you that won't rub off for two or three days."

The table was temporarily shut down, waiting for delivery of two hundred forty thousand in chips. Meanwhile, news of the huge win breezed throughout the casino.

The pit boss informed the stickman, "Stay put. I've got to go tell our man, Mr. Ballard."

"Be sure you tell him how it was. You were with me, and I was at least two foot away from the table when snake eyes come up. I ain't gonna be blamed for somethin' I didn't cause," sputtered a very apprehensive stickman.

As the pit boss reported in, Ballard tensed, reacting, "Say again!" before uttering, "How did it happen? How could it happen?" Disbelief wasn't the only thing affecting him . . .

"I don't know, and I was standing right there. What I do know is Jesse wasn't responsible! He backed off to at least two feet away from that table and couldn't have accidentally touched the button from where he was. It beats me what happened," declared the pit boss.

Eyes drained of expression. Ballard said quietly, tilting back in his plush leather office chair, "Describe it all to me. Every damn detail!"

"To sum it up, a two-thousand dollar bet was placed on the seven at five to one odds. Jesse, seeing an opportunity to pick up two for the house, presented the 'missers' dice to the customer. He had full intentions of turning the table on," recapped the pit boss, explaining, "but another bet went down, only bigger. Our prime mark, who had bought the ten thousand dollars worth of chips, got pissed off by this dame he'd picked up. By damn, out of the blue, he threw out eight thousand on snake eyes. That meant another one-roll proposition at thirty to one. You know, Mr. Ballard, Jesse couldn't afford to lose two hundred forty thousand to win two, so he called me. I advised him to let it ride. With the table off, the odds were thirty-six to seven that another number would come up. Jesse did as I told him, but the drunk beat the odds and won."

On cue in the adjoining office, Ed removed his glasses in closing the books and pulled a small plug out of his ear. Dangling the tiny receiver as he walked in, Ed flatly presented, "I heard every word of that. It confirms, you do have a wired table, right back here where you can watch it." Acknowledged, Ballard shrugged at his demand. "You and I need to talk."

Ballard nodded at the pit boss to leave before turning back to Ed, who had begun pacing the office. Ed continued a moment more, giving Ballard ample time to assess his untenable position. Leaning into Ballard's face, he appraised, "I'd like nothing better than to shut your sleazy ass down. But unfortunately for me, and fortunately for you perhaps, I happen to have a twenty-thousand dollar problem that's compromising me. In this instance it'd be advisable, maybe, for you to cover your ass as well as mine. You can do exactly as I tell you to beat this rap—or, I never said anything, and you're under arrest as of right now." Ballard became jelly.

Ed proceeded to issue commands. "Have two hundred forty thousand in chips taken to the winner. Tell the drunk he's to bring the chips in here. There's to be no paper trail. Contact your cashier to hand-deliver two hundred sixty thousand in cash to your office. Make sure he understands twenty thousand of it is in hundred dollar bills. You and I both know my men are out there on a pure snipe hunt. It should be of some consolation that you get a clean bill of health, certified by five law enforcement and accounting officers. It's a shame this couldn't have been done for my lousy twenty thousand, but you ran into a piece of bad luck. I can't wait, and I can't come back. Now, *do it*!" Ed demanded, unrelenting.

Composed again, Ballard walked out of the office, put an arm around his pit boss, and whispered, "Get a hold of Herbie to be on standby. When the big winner and his woman walk out of here asking for their car, let Herbie know. He'll take it from there to mount a beeper under the bumper before it's delivered to them. He's to get a monitor on the direction they're going. When I can get rid of this cop, I'll pick up on it myself. Oh, by the way, could you bring that winner to my office for the payoff?" Rounding a corner to the cashier's cage, Ballard personally left orders for the money to be delivered to his office in the next five minutes.

In the privacy of Ballard's office, Ed removed the pager clipped to his belt. Modified into a wireless cell phone, he transmitted, speaking softly, "Dacus, it's on. He's bringing the money to the office. If there's any funny business, I'm in contact with my men and will stay in touch."

Dacus sat on the general parking lot in a nondescript, one-ton refrigerator-bodied truck. It housed all of the electrical generating equipment required to expedite the sting by overriding the casino's power supply to the targeted crap table. He'd manipulated electrical controls from the cab, where scanners kept track of numerous radio channels. Fortuitously, he observed the bug being placed under Sam and Maybelle's car on the valet parking lot. He fought down a temptation to tamper with it, knowing there wasn't enough time for him to remount it under another car. Even if there had been time, would a blocked signal pose a greater danger to the occupants, on getaway? The numerous high-frequency transmissions he was using to coordinate all the swapping of drivers into different vehicles had to take priority . . .

As Dacus scanned through frequencies, searching out which one identified the bug, things were happening inside the casino. The Colonel and Vivian left, getting into their rental car on the general parking lot. The two drove off toward Memphis, where they'd meet up with Ed and his men. Behind Tom and Vivian, Harry, Art, and Theo singly sauntered out of the casino without stopping to cash chips. They came to their car from three different directions on the lot. Piling in, Harry was grumbling, "I hated leaving the money those chips are worth."

"Cool it, Harry," Theo tossed. "We've taken 'em for a quarter of a million. If we get away from here whole, we'll be damn lucky. You just don't mess with the mob unless you want the consequences of their vengeance. I can't believe you, or why you'll concern yourself about a few lousy uncashed chips! Guess you probably never heard what they say on Wall Street."

"No, what's that?" Harry snapped.

"They say,"—Theo obliging recast,—"the bulls make money, and the bears make money, but the hogs don't make nothin'." Still amused, he pulled off the lot and drove toward the preset rendezvous point. Art began changing his clothing in the backseat. For all outward appearances, Art had donned camouflage coveralls, maybe a little big, but there was much more than met the eye. The suit was insulated beyond even a space suit with molded boots. The glass visor helmet, sitting beside him in the seat, had a coupling seal to block all vibrations. It was housed in a round bag, resembling that which contains a bowling ball.

Sam grabbed up the large bag of delivered chips, hugged and kissed it, then wrapped an arm around Maybelle. They proceeded across to the main office, playing their role to the hilt. He left Maybelle parked outside Ballard's door. A guard standing nearby sized Maybelle up. He suggestively remarked, "Looks like you've scored tonight, honey."

"You've got a smart mouth, and your ears are too big," hissed Maybelle, blocking any advance with the insult.

Inside the office, Ed retired to a back room, not wanting to be present for the payoff. Using a peephole, he saw Sam enter. Ballard, faking pleasure, looked up from his desk, greeting, "Congratulations, neighbor! You are a big winner. There's been a slight complication that's causing us to pay you in cash. Do you have a problem with us giving you the real stuff?"

"No problem at all," Sam slurred. "Thank you, kindly."

"Would you like for me to count the money out?" offered Ballard.

Sam dumped the paper sack of chips onto Ballard's desk, almost losing his balance. "No need to count it, man. Just hand me the bundles, and I'll put 'em in this tote." The cash bundles were handed over. Sam riffled through them to make sure they were all money before stuffing them in the sack. As Sam and the money left, Ed beeped his men to the office. He walked out of the back room, confronting Ballard. "Hurry up. Give me the twenty thousand before they get here." The transaction was barely completed when Ed's fellow officers came in off the floor.

Ed approached his men with apparent irritation. "You mean to tell me you've found nothing wrong?" Receiving a series of negatives, he verified, "I have inspected the books and their back gaming table. Everything appears to be on the up and up. Shall we sign off and get the hell out of here? I deplore night work." The officers followed suit, signing their names and titles to an official looking piece of paper. Ed then dated and stamped it with the great seal of Mississippi, leaving behind a copy. "Cheers," he saluted, walking out.

CHAPTER 9

Ed and his associates, who had parked their police car near the entrance, pulled away. Observing Sam and Maybelle still waiting for their car to be delivered, Ed, noting a troubled look in his bunch's eyes, reassured, "Don't worry about Sam and Maybelle. This outfit's too smart to take 'em on right in front of the casino. We'll wait down the road."

Ballard had begun tracking as Sam and Maybelle finally departed from the Peacock. He used a very sophisticated computer program, which unrolled a detailed highway map depicting where their car was at all times. He had also assigned a car to follow the signal. The driver was ordered to maintain a distance of at least half a mile and to keep radio contact with the office. Ballard took due note of the tagged car stopping an unaccountably longer length of time at one intersection. He didn't know it then, but his quarry had already escaped. At a prearranged juncture known to be fairly isolated late at night, Sam and Maybelle and the money made their way into Theo and Harry's car. Art in camouflage, carrying a large round tote, piled into the tagged car they'd vacated. Ballard's vehicle, obeying orders to follow no closer than half a mile, missed any action of the byplay.

Art switched on the shortwave radio, contacting Dacus that the deed was done. Relieved, he assigned Art to keep the frequency open and to await further orders. Over the hailing frequency, Dacus announced, "All plans are on schedule. Proceed accordingly." He got a ten-four from Vivian, as usual, driving Tom. Ed and Theo echoed it, moving on to their destination.

Without warning, Dacus urgently instructed Art, "Go to semicode mode." Pausing for him to make the adjustment, he continued, "We're in the 'fox-and-hound' phase. Turn on the locator . . . Watch as I intersect ahead of you. See the tail about half a mile behind you? Pay close attention. Use code only. Your life depends on it!"

Theo, Harry, Sam, and Maybelle, with the money in her lap, headed south toward the Greenville Bridge into Arkansas. Vivian and Tom, and Ed with his team, separately ran the same road north into Memphis. Art followed Dacus through a few country roads until he finally settled on a state road. It ushered him over into Arkansas across the Helena Bridge with an ultimate routing to somewhere near Brinkley.

Ballard was tracking Art's vehicle on his monitor and staying in contact with his trail car. Unsuccessfully, he tried to explain the problem to old Arnold Lipscomb in Memphis.

Lipscomb was irate. "How could you be so stupid? What you're telling me is that a classic scam went down, even to the part about blowing off the mark with fake police, and you didn't even recognize it. I intend to get that money back! I am sending my heavy hitters, and you'd better not lose the bastards before my men take over," he sputtered, threatening. "Or you'll pay for your stupidity in a novel and unusual way. I'll see to it!"

Hanging up, Lipscomb paged his lead goon in the Tunica vicinity. The number to call back was his, prefixed by 911. It gave Lipscomb desired results. He laid out the hit as the four heavies picked up their violin cases and left.

Constantly flipping through frequencies since leaving the Helena Bridge, Dacus homed in on one right away. It profiled itself to be between Lipscomb and goons he'd sent to apprehend them. They'd latched on to Art's beeper signal, and Ballard's pursuit man was on his way back to Mississippi. For a good ten minutes, Dacus listened in after hearing what sounded like a report given to a leader, "We've picked up on 'em, Mr. A." The Mr. A. didn't disguise who was being spoken to, and the periodic interference caused Dacus to decide they had a mobile line open.

"Where are you?" broke in Lipscomb's impatient demand.

"We've passed through Marvell, going north. I think the next town of any size on this Arkansas map is Brinkley," relayed his man.

"Don't do a damn thing except close the gap between you. Then keep 'em in sight. You've gotta be away from any towns, and this may be the one. I want my money back, but I don't want survivors when you take it." Lipscomb then added, "I know those delta roads. They're straight as a string, and you can see for miles. Trail behind at least a mile because there won't be much if any traffic at this hour. Got it?"

"Yes, sir, Mr. A.," came the response through static. "Don't worry, we'll get it done!"

They had made known their location. Their intentions were never in question. At the speed he was traveling, any minute Dacus would be passing through the intersection of 79, exiting to Monroe or Clarendon. Slightly north of it, he'd make his move for a showdown.

South of Brinkley, Dacus turned off Highway 49, which led Art onto a road in fish farming country. "Code red," intoned Art's frequency, followed by, "Alert! Alert!" He squinted into the night, looking for Dacus's truck. "Swan song," Art radioed, braking in time to pull in behind him and park parallel to a fish pond levee. He grabbed his helmet and struggled to get into it. At the same time, Dacus met and handed him a gun. Keeping one in his right hand, he reached for a remote of some kind from his left pocket.

A sleek, black sedan skidded past and then backed up to stop behind Art's car. Dacus's police scanner in the truck squawked, "This is it, Mr. A.! We got 'em!" Wielding automatics, four goons unloaded, jumped the ditch, and started up the embankment. Dacus activated the remote. Instantly, they fell to their knees, out of control, with pain. One man fired off a round into the air as weapons were released like hot lead. They grabbed their bellies, groaning spastically.

Art and Dacus, unrecognizable in camouflage suits, moved from in front of the truck to where the goons writhed on the ground. They picked up three Uzis', placing them in the back end of the truck. Dacus threw the goons' car in reverse and backed it to the highway, with Art quickly following in the monitored car to bring him back for the truck. Dacus drove the truck down and disconnected certain wires in the sedan. Using their fourth weapon, he shot all the tires up. He and Art were ten miles or more down the road and rolling before the goons began to get any relief.

Finally, they managed to stagger into consciousness, became highly nauseated, and then found the agonizing cramps had not been without a cause. They'd filled their pants, and it was running down their legs. Utterly distraught, the leader shucked out of his, jumped in the ditch to wash off, and headed for the car. It had been moved, but the mobile wasn't ripped out. He dialed Lipscomb, wishing 911 was his out of state-area-code.

Lipscomb came on line screeching, "What's happening?"

"They whopped us, sir. We had 'em trapped up against a big pond levee out in nowhere. Soon as we come out with the heavy metal, somethin' put us on our knees. We musta' dropped the guns . . . I don't know."

"You what? You don't know!" shouted Lipscomb.

"Yes, sir" his number one man reported. "The pain was awful. Our guts was gripin' somethin' fierce and had us helpless on the ground, paralyzed in misery. I did see two somethin' or others, in space-lookin' suits, with helmets, ya know, pickin' up our guns. I think I remember th' cars a' bein' moved. Looks like they shot tha tires out, too. At most, it had to've been twenty minutes before the pain quit enough ta think. By then we found out ever' one of us had messed in our pants, and it's took some time to clean ourselves up."

"You what? Are you drunk?" screamed Lipscomb, outraged by the reports.

"No, sir, I ain't, Mr. Lipscomb. I ain't lyin', either," his man answered aggressively.

Calming down, Lipscomb asked, "Are you sure you haven't been injured? Your breathing sounds strange and irregular."

"No, I'm cryin'. I'm a big man, and I' been reliable too. You know that, sir. But these guys put me down in a way I can't swallow. Ain't been nobody big enough to make me shit in my pants! I'm sorry, but yes, I'm a'cryin'."

Lipscomb tried to console. "Get a handle on, man. You just lost your cool. You've also committed the no-no of calling my name over the waves. Pull yourself together! It sounds like we're up against something different. That battery pack on the mobile will let us talk. Meanwhile, we'll be bringing you tires, clothes, and some help. Do you have any idea where you are?"

"No, sir. All I know is that we are somewheres south of Brinkley on some state road in Arkansas. I believe we're alongside a dike, smellin' like dead fish." The connection went dead.

Lipscomb issued orders. Then he picked up the phone and called Ballard. He wanted everyone working at the casino quizzed to find out if anybody recognized a single one of the bunch that had raided him. Ballard was already home drunk. Lipscomb sat back in the comforts of his lavish office to reflect on what had gone down.

Art followed Dacus for about fifteen miles. Abruptly Dacus signaled, and they pulled off on a dirt road, traveling another quarter mile before stopping. Dacus got out of the truck, disarming the 'bug' under Art's car. Art, already out of his outfit, had a pair of coveralls on as Dacus crawled out from under the car. Changing into lighter, more comfortable clothes, Dacus suggested, "Art, let's drive west on these lesser roads to the White River. It'll take us north to Des Arc, where we can dogleg north and west on over to Clinton. We should be at home base before morning."

"I'm ready to be there now," Art asserted. "This is a one-night stand I could do without."

Crossing the Greenville Bridge into Arkansas, Theo, Sam, Maybelle, and Harry turned north on Highway 65. It traversed the state diagonally from Lake Village to Harrison and the mountain. They lost no time in heading home with the money.

Ed drove his recruits north toward Memphis until he came to a deserted crossroad. He peeled off left on a river road, coming to a secluded place where the five of them could remove police signs and apparatus to be concealed in the car trunk. Opening it, he stopped, realizing how much luck had entered into the scam. The Mississippi license plate, half wired on the back bumper, was gone. It left the Arkansas plate in full view on a rigged Mississippi police car. "Hey, guys. Come take a look," Ed summoned. "If anyone at the casino had seen this Arkansas plate, we'd be up to our ass in alligators by now. Better count blessings and hope no one is trailing us right now. Let's get a move on, what ya say?"

Ed drove straight to the rent-a-car center at Memphis International Airport, where Tom waited to turn in his vehicle. Waving to Tom and Vivian, who went inside to check it in, Ed settled up with his men, paying each twenty-five hundred, in one hundred dollar bills. Tom and Vivian finished and managed to squeeze into Ed's car for the short jaunt to the airport's main gate. On delivery of his charges, Ed left them, promising possibility of more work in the near future. Tom sprawled out, taking the whole backseat. Vivian sat up front as Ed made a beeline for Arkansas and home. Vivian spent time on her side, rearview mirror, just in case . . .

"The hell of it," Ed would say later. "We weren't so lucky. A guard at the casino had seen the Arkansas license plate and had scribbled down its letters and numbers."

That was only half of the hell evolving, tho. Dacus had recognized Lipscomb's name, knew of his dealings, and knew exactly what to expect next. Lipscomb, reputed head of a noxious mob in Memphis, also had a reputation in the rackets for being unreliable by those 'families' in territories bordering the one he controlled. He was especially despised by the Zallafino family in Louisiana, whose influence extended from Bossier City to New Orleans.

Arnold Lipscomb took pride in his reputation as a coldly calculating pragmatist. Normally he could could lie down and sleep after a screwup of this sort. However, there was something strange, and it became all the more disturbing to him.

He sat at the beautifully carved massive desk in his huge library of books he'd never even touched and poured himself a snifter of brandy.

Brandy in hand, he wandered to a window that looked out across his carefully groomed and landscaped estate to the lofty, fourteen-foot wall that surrounded it. He knew his enemies and knew them by name. After all, he had cultivated each one through his own avaricious desire for more and more wealth. Mentally thumbing, he discarded any thought that one of them could have done this, even though he had cheated and chiseled each at some time. No doubt, collectively and individually, they'd all like to see him dead.

Abandoning enemies for the moment, he returned to the desk. Quietly sipping his drink, he sat thinking. What was the thing he was trying to remember? Just beneath the surface of his conscious mind hovered a memory from long ago that related to this night . . . Bursting out laughing, he cackled, "Son of a bitch! I'll be damned! So that's what they did!"

He recalled a series of newspaper articles from the sixties, during which all of the riots and demonstrations were taking place over opposition to the Vietnam War. A scientific study had published its findings on successfully testing the exact vibration frequencies in ultrasound, which relaxed the human sphincter muscle, causing the bowels to unload. Prospects to control unruly and destructive crowds were very attractive. Who could riot and loot aggressively if they were subjected to crapping in their britches? In particular, two city police agencies in California quickly expressed an interest in obtaining such a device.

However, two drawbacks to the proposal, one serious, the other humorous, were so glaring the fluff of a feasibility study was avoided. To wit, the enormous amount of electrical power and the portable transmission of that amount of electricity required was a logistics problem. The most humorous objection involved the absurdity of having a large freshly purged and cleaned-out police squad on standby twenty-four hours a day to operate the device and manipulate a crowd.

"Try putting that one in a job description for them young rookies," one old flatfoot patrolman remarked. His comments received the city council's attention. It was a cold, hard fact no one would agree to work in a job that required a purgative or an enema every twenty-four hours. What city's budget could afford to pay the price, if someone was willing?

The logic of all previous events became apparent to old man Lipscomb. These people, whoever they may be, obviously solved a dual problem. They mastered how to produce enough electrical energy by portable generation to do the job. And they improvised a type of protection from the assault by wearing special clothing down to using a helmet, making it look like a space suit. Most amazingly, he assumed they had been able to electrically override and manipulate the wired crap table for a payoff without having to touch it. When the correct reasoning of these facts was inescapable, he promptly drew a conclusion, went to bed, and fell asleep.

Awakening about eleven the next morning, he was still comfortable with his decision of the night before. Convinced he was witness to an unknown and advanced technology, he concluded the only way to win had to be through stealth, trickery, and an element of surprise. Two very big problems interfered. Who in hell were they, and where were they?

An unexpected break came right after lunch when reports from the guards at the casino reached him. *Why had these unknowns been stupid enough to pose as state law enforcement officers, traveling in a dolled-up, white car representing the Mississippi State Police with an Arkansas license plate exposed?* he contemplated briefly. *They may have the technology, but they're still capable of unwitting mistakes,* he mused with a certain degree of satisfaction . . . He had the name of the vehicle's owner before sundown.

The more he thought about the ridiculousness of the license plate, the more convinced he became of the vulnerability of his quarry. He conspired to play it out to his own advantage, regardless of how the chips fell . . .

CHAPTER 10

Maybelle, an early riser when she didn't have to pull a night shift, was dressed and down in the kitchen at ten thirty the next morning. Rabbit, awaiting his first breakfast guest, asked her what she'd like to have. Ordering pancakes, bacon, and coffee, Maybelle went out to one of the vehicles, plugged in her mobile, and dialed from a roam signal. Reception clear, she talked with her people in Tulsa and instructed six personal choices of her girls to fly into Springfield. They were to be on a flight arriving at three o'clock in the afternoon. Returning to the smells of coffee and bacon, she asked Rabbit as he served the food, "I thought that tonight everyone should celebrate our good fortune, so I requested six of my preference 'ladies of the evening' to join the party. While there's still time in the day, can I order someone special for you?"

Looking away from the table, Rabbit answered, "No ma'am. Lulu and I have a thing going, and it suits us both. We don't need anyone or anything else. But I do have a favor to ask of you. Could I bring Lulu with me to the party tonight? I promise she'll behave and not be a problem."

Maybelle had to hold back quick tears. "Of course you may, Gallant One. I guarantee you she'll be well received, and both of you can have a good time."

"Miss Maybelle, what does gallant mean?" Rabbit asked, trying to get things in perspective.

"Rabbit, to me it means you're an understanding, very strong man emotionally, who can honor a woman and consider her feelings without concern of having to surrender his balls. If a man's got it, a woman knows it. Need I say more?" Maybelle complimented.

"No, ma'am. I thank you for it, and I like the way you said it, too." Rabbit's pride climbed a few notches as he poured more coffee.

Oddly enough, Art was the next to crawl out of the sack, even though he and Dacus had been the last to arrive at the headquarters. Rabbit patiently prepared his breakfast before inquiring, "Well, how did it go down in Mississippi?"

"It went great, thanks to Dacus," rejoined Art. "We took 'em for exactly the amount of dough we set out to get. There was a little trouble after he and I got on the road, and I'm still trying to figure out how Dacus did what he did. You should a seen those four thugs come at us, packin' the latest two-handled automatics. For the life of me, I don't really understand what I saw. Somehow, Dacus disabled them. He did something that stopped them dead in their tracks. Whatever it was made them drop the guns and stand there like they had egg on their faces."

Rabbit stifled a grimace. With a peculiar look, he gazed off in another direction. "I know what you saw!" he said with aversion. "I was a guinea pig in perfecting Dacus's experiments to cause someone to lose their concentration. I hate that damn machine! He'd put me in the pasture, buck naked, and turn the power on. I'd get the most terrible belly cramps and then shit all over myself. Time after time it was done. He'd measure out the distances where it was most effective. There's one thing I can say for him though. He went through it too while I ran the damn thing. Claimed he had to experience it personally to know how to get the best use of its power."

Art stared at him in disbelief, pondering, "Do you mean to tell me that taking a crap was all it took to make them drop their guns?"

"No. What, I am telling you is that a bad case of the shits makes you stop whatever you're doing. That machine does it to you, every time, believe me. When that brown buttonhole turns inside out, you're through thinking about anything else!"

Later in the day, Art cornered Dacus after he had gotten up. "Dacus, we were in a tight spot last night, and you knew it. Why would you take a chance with our lives by relying on a remote? One squeeze of their triggers was capable of ten to twelve bullets each. We did have the edge to shoot first. One sweep of their weapons would have taken out our vehicles, man!"

"Art, that ultrasound generator is a lot safer than a gun. You seem to have forgotten there were four of them, all heavily armed, and only two of us. What possible chance do you think we would've had with two pistols? That machine, as Rabbit chooses to call it, doesn't have to be aimed. It'll totally disable anybody and, more importantly, everybody. Besides, I'm not really into killing. It's not to say that I wouldn't kill in self-defense, but I'd suffer for it too much afterward."

Art was quieted by the rebuttal. Shaking his head in consternation, he took off walking.

Rabbit spent the rest of the entire day making hors d'oeuvres, dressing a salad, and preparing his menu of marinated beef and shrimp kabobs, with twice-baked potatoes for easy cooking that evening. The morning conversations passing through the kitchen were food for thought as he worked, topped off by the pending party.

Around one thirty, Dacus and Maybelle left in the van to meet Maybelle's girls at the Springfield airport and bring them back to the mountain. Driving along, Dacus chanced drawing Maybelle into a more personal conversation. "When Theo invited you here, I expected the two of you to become an 'item' again. What gives?" he pried.

"Theo and I, as you recall, have a wonderful set of memories that neither of us want to disturb. He and I have had our fling. I was just a kid of nineteen, and he was in his prime at thirty-three. It wouldn't be the same for us now . . . Not after these many years. Theo needs a younger woman, and I am bringing him one. As for me, to show you how sophisticated I've become in Tulsa society, here's an example. I believe a woman is like a fine violin. Nine times out of ten she gets a man who is a fiddler, and she dances to the fiddler's tunes. If she doesn't know any different, the fiddler's tunes can be fun. But I found a quality few experience. Bryan adored me beyond life, and it did something for me. I soared with him as if he were playing a Strad."

Maybelle retreated into her thoughts. Eventually, she broke the silence, taking up where she left off. "It will not happen to me again. Six months after Bryan died, realizing Tulsa society was shunning me, I took a trip to Acapulco. It was a place the two of us had so much fun together. The sadness lingered. A bitch of emotional stress clung like a leech, and shock treatment became a last resort. I did one thing which was good for me tho. I purchased the time of a young Mexican cliff diver. He was indeed young, handsome, muscular, and juicy. Oh, was he ever juicy! If I had what I needed, it would be another virile, young lover, whose sole intent was to satisfy. Theo will have what he needs tonight."

Dacus chuckled, enjoying the worth of her last statement, reflecting, "That reminds me of a story about two young women stranded overnight in a very small town. Inquiring at the rooming house where they were to spend the night, the two headed to the only cafe in town and ordered from its menu.

No one could miss the large round table full of good-looking young men and one older woman. Try as they might, by coy gestures, bold looks, or kicking of a leg, they couldn't get the attention of a single one of the young men. After a while, the older woman went to the only restroom. One of the young gals followed. Inside, she complained that she and her friend were unable to attract any of the young guys at the big table. The old doll confided, "Dearie, when I was your age, I gave it away for love. Later, I got wiser and sold it . . . Now, I'm buying it back!"

When Maybelle stopped laughing, she caught him off guard again. "Dacus, I have a proposition to make you."

He could not hold back a grin, nor his reflective response. "Hey, I'm not a good-lookin' Mexican lover boy for hire. What's the score, lady?"

"Shut up you ass and listen to me," Maybelle chastised. "I'm bored to death with life in Tulsa. There's two million in my semiliquid assets, aside from the house and property. I have traveled abroad and can speak Spanish, French, and German. I've got a valid passport and can move from one country to another legitimately. You already know my other qualifications, and I want in on an equal basis with everyone else. There's more too," she cited.

"Theo's filled me in on your next caper and the ultimately big one. If I read it correctly, you are envisioning an 'association' that has to stay together continuously for an extended length of time, even to being confined on a ship. You're as aware as I am of needs for variance from constant togetherness and have already okayed inclusion of showgirls on a 'spec' yacht for entertainment and pleasure. The six girls I'm bringing in here are actually a group of seven, but one is presently on the rag. These seven are true professionals. They're also musicians who, when tricks are slow, occasionally play a gig on a weekend. I know what's probably on your mind. My operation could not survive with the type of women generally associated with hustling," she aired, advising . . .

"Stereotyping pretty much categorizes the hustler who's screwed up in the head, on drugs, suffering from self-hatred, generally due to having been sexually abused as a child. This type gravitates toward the ruthless pimp or 'pimpess', as the case may be, subconsciously wanting endless same treatment. There's also the call girl with her hang-ups. For some reason or another, she needs to lead a double life. Exceptionally though, women of and for pleasure only do exist. I've screened each and every one of mine for this quality and can vouch for their habits and behavior. Sex is their motivation, a little booze and cigarettes their vices, but not drugs." Her passionate zeal had not eluded Dacus. He debated her depth but didn't have long to wait . . .

"As for hang-ups and from what Theo has told me, your sexual lockup comes not from sterility, but from losing a wife you loved. Bryan's death has filled me with nostalgia and has made me choosy. It sure as hell hasn't caused abstinence."

Maybelle continued to astonish him. "As an association partner, Dacus, I would bring the seven girls in as my employees, responsible only to me. It'll be my duty to control them as well. Your team must not suffer from any frictions, least of all that caused by jealousy. The association pays me, and I pay them. An existence of established personal relationships cannot be tolerated. Random, rotational schemes are the solution to assuring all parties are challenged, entertained, satisfied, and content. Especially of value is that, even though they know nothing about it as yet, these girls are ready to diversify. In their midthirties now, awareness is beginning to emerge that it won't be many years before they'll be too 'long in the tooth' for cathouse business."

It had crossed Dacus's mind on just how much Theo had divulged to this woman. Plenty, obviously, from the tidbits she'd been dropping. He decided to use her no-holds-barred approach to pursue one she'd left on the table. Bluntly, Dacus propositioned her, questioning, "Are you saying to me that you'll put two million into this venture?"

"I am not!" retorted Maybelle. "All I'm saying is, if the operation gets in a cash crunch, money can be borrowed from me. I certainly expect it to be paid back."

"Let me give it some heavy thought," Dacus countered, before being interrupted.

"I have one more inducement for you to consider," Maybelle imparted, dropping a bomb. "I'm referring to your plan to take the conglomerate which owns the power companies in three states. I suspect the scam only becomes operational if you can get electrical cogeneration contracts at ten or twelve sites. I assume also that you expect to achieve it through political pressure from the small town entities involved, right?"

Dacus didn't have an opportunity to answer. She had his attention and pressed on. "It just so happens, a certain top official in the holding company you intend to exploit is a frequent visitor to my house of pleasure. I have several tapes of him demonstrating his unusual tastes and whims. Of course, it'd be much better if he never had to be enlightened about the videos. However, their existence could pretty much assure the issuance of the cogeneration contracts."

The trip to Springfield was becoming surprisingly too short, Dacus thought. "Give me a little more time, Maybelle," he chuckled. Admiration, respect, and amazement at the insight of her business scope and unusual talents inundated further. Her candor to interject 'could' on prospects of getting the contracts signified an interest in contributions to the association, rather than bribery.

Notwithstanding his natural instincts and to always cover bases, Dacus proposed, pulling into the short-term parking. "Maybelle, let's tell your girls I have a company that contracts with a larger company doing classified research for the federal government. The employees and I are celebrating a breakthrough in technology we've just achieved."

CHAPTER 11

The men gathered around the lodge bar, just off the mocked-up casino where they'd perfected the first scam. Portable screens separated it from most of the great social hall, decorated by festooning balloons. A ring of candlelighted, four-top tables circled a small dance floor featuring a shiny, ancient Wurlitzer juke box. The bar was arrayed with Rabbit's hors d'oeuvres. Dacus positioned himself in as bartender. Joining them, Maybelle and her entourage, full of gaiety and laughter, descended the broad stairway from the upper level.

Taking advantage of the moment, Maybelle snatched it. "Rather than go through problems of introducing thirteen people to each other, we are going to have a lottery to find out who is paired with whom for the evening."

"Whom with whom?" cackled Art, somewhat exhilarated.

"Shut up, Art, or I'll leave you out," bantered Maybelle. She selected two hats from off a hat rack. Deftly palming a folded paper, she placed it under the headband of one. Into this hat, she dumped the billets containing names of the girls. Picking up the second hat, Tom and Vivian's name was discreetly tucked under the hatband which held the men's names.

"Now, by the authority vested in me as Secretary of Pleasure," she announced, "I shall select partners for the evening." Reaching into each hat simultaneously, she drew billets out pairing up, Ed is with Randi. Proceeding, she coupled Sam and Rosie, Theo with Julie, and Harry met Barbee. Seizing the buzz made by couples meeting each other, she slipped the two billets from under the headbands and put Eva with Tom and Vivian, stating, "Eva is the lucky one! She'll make double time tonight." Reaching once more into the hats, she pretended not to find anything . . . Impishly then, she brought out the last two slips, putting Art and Candy together.

As couples drank and smoked, talked and danced to big band sounds from the Wurlitzer, Rabbit eased in and set up a side table with the full buffet he'd prepared earlier in the day. He was satisfied it would please.

In the shank of the evening, with lights turned low and colored beams moving aimlessly across the room, an extra couple twirled onto the dance floor. Rabbit and Lulu, who had chosen to eat privately in the kitchen, had at last joined the party. Lulu was strangely beautiful. She positively glowed in the party dress Dacus provided for Rabbit to give her. Maybelle choked up and got misty eyed. Dacus, having observed Lulu since the first time she came to the mountain, looked on in wonder at the transposition.

Maybelle eased over to the empty bar, telling Dacus, "Look at what the power of love and respect for a human being can do. It's a miracle that's always available and seldom breaks the surface of our lives."

Dacus sized Maybelle up for a long interval. A mixed stirring of feelings that had become utterly foreign invaded before he disclosed, "I can remember Lulu when there was hardly any perception in those eyes. Her being was deep inside, and Rabbit is responsible for having drawn it out. She now shares an awareness of the world around her through Rabbit's eyes, and it's growing. No one can really know what her limits are, but she has not yet reached her potential."

The party flowed on for about another hour and a half when, one by one, the couples drifted upstairs and into the ladies' individual rooms. Rabbit and Lulu slipped out, making their way to his cottage. Meanwhile, Maybelle had seemingly disappeared. Pouring a brandy, Dacus shut down the bar and stepped out on the veranda. He seldom smoked. On this night he lit a cigar, and pondered the probabilities of the second scam. The likelihood of an impending problem with old man Lipscomb couldn't be ruled out, he knew.

Thirty minutes or so later, as the cigar burnt out to a nub, he came inside and climbed the great stairs to turn off a few lights on the second level. As Dacus reached the head of the stairs, he saw old Tom crouched down at the keyhole to his own apartment. Motioning for Tom to come to him, he asked in a low voice, "What're you up to, Tom?"

With eyes all shiny, and in a half whisper, Tom drooled, "I'm watching Viv work up Eva for our troika. Eva just pled with Viv that she's ready for me. Viv gave her a classic reply. 'Sweetie, I'm not getting you ready for Tom. I'm getting Tom ready for you!' This earpiece of yours is great for hearing what's going on in there. She'll have Eva walking on the ceiling before she lets me in."

Nonplussed, Dacus said, "Well, have fun." He shook his head and went back downstairs, forgetting to turn out the lights.

Later, much later, Eva wearily unlocked the door to her private room. Hearing the key turn in the lock, Barbee popped out of her room next door, traipsing in behind Eva. "I've been waiting up for you. If Maybelle rotates us according to the way she assigned rooms, I'll be next with that couple tomorrow night. What's it like?" Barbee asked expectantly.

Eva hesitated before responding, "Pour yourself a drink while I freshen up a bit. Then we'll talk." Taking her leisure in coming out of the bathroom, she poured a drink, standing with her back to Barbee. "I'm simply overcome with emotion," she faked a downer. Slowly, she turned around, sporting the broadest grin Barbee had ever seen on her face.

"No punning, bitch," recoiled Barbee. "Let's have it. What about S&M? Was there any?"

"You don't have to worry about S&M," Eva rejected. "That is a private thing between the two of them, which is probably occurring right now, if it's not already over. The thing is, you're in for a real ride. I can promise you that. Old Tom has unbelievable stamina. Once he gets his Richard up, it won't go back down. I accused him of having put a shot in it, but Viv said he wouldn't use them. The one time he took a shot, it didn't go down until the next day. He was miserable, couldn't pee, and it nearly made him sick, according to her."

"Why did you call his whanger a Richard?" queried Barbee.

"Because it's way too big to be called a mere dick," chirped Eva. "I think the size of it has something to do with his trouble in getting it up. When it's up, it's up for the duration, kid. Plus he's a master of timing with it. Just when you think you want to go, he'll withdraw to the teasing point and raise you to another level. Ultimate finesse!" she added, seasoned with deviltry.

"That's not his strongest asset tho. He absolutely has the most wicked tongue in all of creation. I thought Viv had done a pretty damn good job with hers, but it was only a warm-up. He's unique because he can actually touch his forehead with the tip of his tongue. Imagine that! At some point Vivian explained that ole Tom was first hired in a carnival sideshow, where he demonstrated the 'believe-it-or-not' art of touching his forehead with it. While I'm on the subject, you should know he and Viv conned me. She trussed me up with my legs almost over my head then tied me at the knees with men's silk ties attached to ropes anchored under the bed. I thought, 'My God, I'm in for a bad time'. Her little charade though amounted to nothing more than keeping me from seeing ole Tom remove his teeth," Eva confided.

"No doubt about it, he's a master of the 'don't come'. If I begged, he'd tease some more. I thought this is it when he asked, 'Are you ready for me to get your goody, sweetie?' All I could do was moan, 'Yes, yes'. There was more teasing and more begging before he came up with, 'What you really need is penetration, isn't it?' Not needing an answer, and knowing he'd brought me to the brink, he inserted his monstrous tongue. I've never experienced anything to equal it. Like rice crispies, I snapped and popped and couldn't quit. I climaxed three times before he'd let up. It's just awesome! I know now why he and Viv has been an item for so long. She is a large woman, inside and out, and I oughta know from what we did together, but he is well able to satisfy her. His problem is how to get off himself, and she's evidently an artist at it. They're a great team! You're in for a helluva joyride," Eva promised.

"Sounds like you had a rather fulfilling experience," Barbee surmised enviously.

"No punning, bitch," Eva copied. "We rode old Tom for an eternity. First, I rode his prong while Viv tailed his tongue. It seemed we'd swap back and forth for hours. He was still up and hard and relishing every thrust. It beats anything I've ever seen. After we were both worn out and satiated, he was still up and going, like a battery-operated rabbit. I'm here, exhausted, and Viv's, no doubt, taking care of his needs with her special cat of nine tails. Now, how was your John?"

"Aw, he's a nice guy. A little hesitant maybe. Really, I'd prefer that kind of guy to some smart ass who thinks he's a stud. I can say this though," Barbee confessed. "He didn't do me any damage, considering how worked up I am over the possibility of a coming night like yours."

Eva yawned and grunted, "Turn off the light on your way out."

"Well, you're not very hospitable," pouted Barbee in jest as she was about to leave.

"Tell you what. If Maybelle chooses you for old Tom and Viv, I'll come to your room afterward. We'll see how long your chat lasts," Eva half rebuked. Short with her remark, she appeased, "You'll be welcome to one of my new powder puffs."

Turning out the light, Barbee cooed, "Tootleloo, I have one of my own in reserve."

Brunch the next morning was scheduled for eleven. Last sips of coffee were interrupted by Dacus's announcement for an immediate meeting of Association members. Maybelle wisely gathered up her group as they finished eating, ushering them out on an extended tour of the estate.

Dacus rose to speak. He went straight to the subject. "Maybelle informed me that she would like to join this association. She comes with very impressive credentials. Aside from the fact she's every bit as skilled in the con as Theo related, she has two million in semiliquid assets that she's willing to lend the associate body anytime it's needed. The one provision is, it's expected to be paid back, with interest. Another attribute sorely needed, which neither any of you nor I have, is she's traveled abroad and is fluent in French, German, and Spanish. It is obvious to me her presence can only strengthen the organization."

Harry, as usual, couldn't wait to haggle. When Dacus paused, he complained, "This is a serious matter. It can't be decided without a lengthy discussion."

Dacus was in no humor to placate. "The party is over, folks. Whether you know it or not, we're luckier than we deserve to have pulled off this operation without someone getting killed or badly hurt. I take full responsibility for the inevitable showdown it later precipitates with old man Lipscomb. If there's more to it, I'll handle it without involving any of you. Just as surely as an army requires discipline and leadership in the trenches, so does this association," he instilled.

"Democracy is out if goals are to be met. A discussion and a vote would have hardly been appropriate facing off four goons ready to take out Art and myself. Knowing the facts as they exist, let's say we're here applying my inventions, executing my plans, and using my money up to this point. Expenses to date are in the forty to fifty thousand-dollar range, leaving two hundred thousand to be split eight ways between me and the seven of you."

Indignant, Dacus didn't mince words. "I am not willing to advance another step, unless I have absolute control. Not only am I claiming full reins of this operation, I want a unanimous show of confidence. Let's have no grudging, half-assed acceptance, because it's all or nothing. Anyone who can't accept it walks out of here twenty-five thousand better off. If you all leave, I'll give my twenty-five thousand to Maybelle, piss on the fire, call the hounds, and call it a wrap. I'm telling you flat out, as of now Maybelle just became a full partner!" He disregarded breath being sucked in and stolen glances made at one another.

"It's time to stop straddling the fence," Dacus stipulated. "Either you play the stakes as they fall or you're out. Anyone who can't take it, as is, step up here, look me in the eye, and say, 'El Paso'. I'll hand you your bundle and wish you well. We were friends before any of this went down. I'd like to depart that way. But, may God help any one of us who is so narrow and so greedy as to think these and all proceeds aren't to be divided up equally. Otherwise, what kind of mayhem is in the offing over a five hundred million-dollar scam?"

The other seven were stunned. They had never before seen this side of Dacus displayed.

Ed stood, without hesitation, declaring, "You've all previously heard where I stand. Not wanting to offend, Dacus, but I'm not about to say that I vote for you. I'm stating you'll have to run me off to get rid of me."

"Dacus, honey," Vivian rose, breaking the tension. "For the life of me, I can't imagine how of all people I could have missed it. I didn't know you had such a big set of balls. Tom and I aren't going anywhere." It caused chuckles and a smile from Dacus. Tom tugged on Vivian to sit down.

Harry, the thorn, got up repentant, admitting, "Aw shit, me and my big mouth. I need a keeper, and I oughta be happy to have someone who'll take me into their charge." He was the first of seven to step forward, shaking Dacus's hand, solidifying confidence of his referendum.

More than happy to oblige, Theo broke the news to Maybelle when she came back to the lodge. "Welcome, partner! And there's more," he greeted. "You wouldn't believe the outright transformation we saw in Dacus's personality. Or, maybe it wasn't a change! Maybe he's just kept it hidden or suppressed. Anyway, he's one tough-minded son of a bitch and grabbed Association members by their throats today. He laid the law down. I think all of us are more comfortable, knowing exactly where he stands and the way he really is. For a while, I've had a niggling feeling he'd have to tighten things up. Thank goodness it's behind us. Frankly, I'd feel sorry for anybody who gets in his way after this go down."

Small talk was scarce at the subdued evening meal. Dacus's statement had its impact, except for the women. Reflecting on a return to the same old grind in Tulsa the next morning occupied them. The men, mainly satiated yet unwilling to pass up a chance for a little more sex, made the first overtures. Sure enough, Maybelle rotated in a predictable manner, pairing Barbee with old Tom and Vivian. These three were the only ones showing any enthusiasm for impending liaisons.

Mostly, everyone was tucked in before nine o'clock. The men retired to their rooms by ten. Not so for Tom, Viv, and Barbee. Their session was another marathon, lasting into the wee hours. When Barbee stumbled to her own room, midnight had long passed. She attended to her ablutions, thinking that Eva would be coming in to visit. When Eva didn't show, she slipped on a robe and traipsed down the stairs to the bar, where she gathered up a bottle, ice, water, and a glass. She was gratified, totally worn out yet higher than a kite. It took a couple of drinks plus concentrated effort to settle down enough to douse the light and go to sleep.

Missing breakfast, Barbee cornered Eva to have coffee on the veranda. "Did you set me up?" She had to know.

"If my telling Maybelle that you hoped the rotation would place you with the two of them, then yes, I guess I set you up. I told the truth, didn't I?" insisted Eva.

"Oh, I'm not mad," Barbee assured. "I just asked the question because the whole thing was so different from how you had described it."

"Really! In what way?" Eva asked, curiosity aroused.

"As soon as Viv had me pinned to the bed, spread-eagled, with those silk ties and ropes, she body-covered me, tying my arms too. Next, she blindfolded me, probing all of my sensitive areas with a finely pointed feather. I got so out of breath from screeching, laughing, and hollering that I thought I'd faint. After an eternity it seemed, she finally jerked off the blindfold. I was startled nearly out of my skin. Viv stood there, in full costume of leather and metal studs, with a whip in each hand. I couldn't see the expression in her eyes because she wore a pair of black glasses that served as a very thin mask. When she cracked the whip hard, I damn near jumped out of my hide again!" Barbee kind of shuddered, anxious to continue.

"Guess what? The one who had dealt me misery with the feather was ole Tom. He had entertained himself with me while Viv changes to her dominatrix outfit. Having let me see again, Tom put his head between my legs and went to work with his tongue. He used the old hot-and-cold routine, where he'd cool his tongue off with ice water before switching to scalding hot coffee. It's a fact that the human mouth can comfortably stand a wider temperature range than a vagina. I was pulled, pushed, and nudged to the top of the highest mountain then cast off of a sheer cliff by the thrust of his full tongue. Falling through endless space, I encountered sensory explosions of color, sound, and feeling as I passed into oblivion. When I woke up, they both were gently slapping my cheeks with a cold cloth and holding smelling salts under my nose."

Dodging concerns, she recouped. "From here, satisfied she'd scared the snuff out of me, Viv removed her leather trappings. She whipped it on Tom's head while I mounted his 'Richard' as you call it, and began the 'back-and-forth' routine. I was already beginning to get raw when he finished me off with his 'coup de grace'. He had duly noted, with his feather, that I was super sensitive around my rear entry, so he secured me between his thumb and middle finger. Every time he squeezed my 'taint' it caused a reflex so strong that my pelvis ached."

"Wait a minute," Eva interrupted. "What are you calling your 'taint', gal?"

"I forget you're a city girl," Barbee giggled. "Back in the woods where I lived, the tiny space between places was called a taint, from 'it taint this and taint that'."

Amused, Eva recalled, "I thought that's called a twitchet."

Barbee laughed outright. "Well, it 'taint' a twitchet. Anyway, you'd think it'd be impossible to put that big thing in while he had me in what he called his bowling-ball hold. Not so! he did it all by himself. And how about the name he seems to have for everything. I don't know whether he told you or not, but, he called his Richard the 'redheaded, swaybacked, blue steel throbber' to me. I feel I should be using a walking cane for the next two or three days."

"Wanna bet they got their money's worth, even though Maybelle paid us double for the gig?" Eva calculated.

"I'm sure they got full value," Barbee agreed. "And, I think you and I together still left 'em hungry. I think too, they want it every night. Ole Tom evidently goes off once in a night, but I think he's probably good for every night. Of course, stimulated by him, Vivian is incredible."

On a roll, Barbee schemed. "You know, I could get used to this kind of life. I've worked in some grungy places with some lousy people. Certainly, working for Maybelle has been a step up for all of us. Even that has its downside at times," she concluded.

"Barbee, you've put it in focus. I've been thinking along the same lines. I like all of these guys, and then there's ole Tom and Viv for the way-out stuff. Variety, you know. Like a lot of things, it's beyond our reach I guess."

"Eva, Maybelle likes you a lot. Why don't you ask her if we could fit in up here?" Barbee suggested. "It can't hurt to ask!"

"I've already brought up the subject to Maybelle this morning," Eva shared. "She said, if all seven of us agreed, she'd consider it."

Theo and Sam hastily volunteered to take the van to Springfield airport and place the ladies on their plane back to Tulsa. Almost immediately after leaving the mountain, Eva and Barbee commenced harassing the guys to promote a return trip next weekend. "Hold it, gals," Theo corralled. "Whether or not you make a returned visit is really up to Maybelle, isn't it?"

"True," Eva confirmed. "We work for Maybelle, and yes she calls the shots. But it's like our musical gigs. You have to make a request to get us back. I've got another goody for you. We get a lot more repeat trade from bedroom performance than we do with our band."

Big Sam, sitting in the back, trying to hug all five ladies, rolled with the drum beat. "Which one of you plays a mean trumpet? I need someone to blow my horn."

"Let's rape the big ox!" shouted Candy. With that, they all fell in on Sam, giggling, pinching, tickling, and pulling his fingers, ears, and hair. Two were busy jerking his pants down, but not off. They took turns riding him and got him off twice before he played completely out.

"Now it's your turn, Theo," chortled one of the girls.

"Oh no, I didn't make any smart remarks," Theo blurted, trying to dissuade them.

Seeing he wasn't going to stop the van, Eva, sitting beside him up front, got her foot under his leg and put the break pedal to the floor. Theo managed to pull onto the shoulder. The rowdy gang dragged him out of the driver's seat over into the back. "This is on the house, Theo," giggled Candy, the instigator. Eva, still sore, stayed out of the melee. Barbee, in a similar condition, helped to subdue Theo, steering clear of any sex.

Theo barely got his clothes back on when Sam pulled into the Springfield airport. Parking the van in the short-term lot, they piled out and headed for ladies' and men's rooms in the main terminal. Assembled once more in the lobby, they promised to meet again, soon. The ladies boarded their plane. Theo and Sam recovered the van, drove straight out of town toward Arkansas and the mountaintop. After a short silence, Sam rebounded enough to ask, "Well, what did you think about the supposed rape?"

"It wasn't bad," admitted Theo. "Tell ya what . . . I've had more fun in the last two days than I can remember. They're a great bunch of gals. I don't care how sorry their music may be. I'd personally like to have 'em permanently on board the ship Dacus alludes about to Harry."

Sam seconded Theo's opinions, with motive of his own. "We haven't met the hooker called Cherrie, who insists on the French pronounciation of Cher'EE. One gal touted her as 'old deep throat', swearing she could suck a tennis ball through a garden hose."

CHAPTER 12

Dacus sensed an overwhelming urgency to remove his team off of the mountaintop before a most certain retaliation would come from old man Lipscomb and company. The air had been cleared by having the ladies there, and his 'go down' had smoothed frayed edges. Yet the pressure to act persisted into the night. Early the next day, he posted a notice for everyone to meet at one o'clock. Over morning coffee, Maybelle tossed her head at Ed. He welcomed her attention and came over, inquiring, "Did you see the note?"

Quietly she relayed, "Sure, and we need to go somewhere and talk before this meeting." They wandered out of the lodge and down to where horses were grazing. Leaning against a gate, Maybelle opined, "Your instincts about the second scam are correct, but I believe you've cited the wrong reason. Dacus obviously is too engrossed with something to consign any attention to it. For some reason I'm challenged to get my head into the matter. A real problem in his proposal is to pull off ten scams at one time, having each to come off simultaneously. To my knowledge, it's never even been conceived, much less attempted!"

Ed's head snapped up. "That's it!" he exclaimed. "You have touched on the very core of my dilemma. I've been trying to isolate the problematical irony ever since he presented it. Can such a series possibly be executed?"

Looking him straight in the eye, Maybelle explored, "Ed, aside from Dacus, you have the best mind up here. The plan isn't operational without precision. You and I will have to constantly stay in close communication and be in complete understanding to keep everything straight. Given the 'L' factor, the answer to your question is yes, it could succeed. Incidentally,

I have a question for you. Can you work with me in fine tuning the details to pull it off?"

Bemused at her intensity, Ed searched. "First, what in hell is the 'L' factor? Secondly, are you wanting an endorsement, or my input?"

"Ed, I must rely upon your expertise. Yes, and I must have your valued input, too . . . Endorsement? Really, Ed," Maybelle laughed. "I don't think so! I stand on my own two feet. It's nice to have, but! As to the 'L' factor, it's a metaphor for luck, not love. Now, can we get serious again?" The thesis she had for him unveiled muscle.

"The very nature of this scam is not workable unless you consider the part sex plays in it. This type mark even suggests potential blackmail for end results. I have certain talents that could be exploited if they are needed. Maybe a choice bit of slightly undisclosed information can entice your logic and put you more at ease. It's something Dacus and I have agreed on that doesn't need to be broadcast, just yet . . . How does having a sex video, with sound, of an upper management executive in the conglomerate controlling three power companies we've chosen as marks, strike you?" Maybelle threw in, regrouping.

"The tape alone assures cogeneration contracts can be awarded in a timely fashion. If it becomes mandatory, I'm quite capable of applying identical inducements from any level of these public officials. Men, in the age bracket usually involved in actively securing industry for small towns, are publicly known for having their dick in hand, on the lookout for my age as mature, youngish women to be pursued. It's leverage, Ed, to incorporate sex as a weapon for assuring quick compliance within political needs. Last resort, by all means, is use of blackmail."

Staring across the pasture, Ed absorbed the evolving terrain Maybelle had unfurled. "Your insight is awesome, my dear," Ed mulled. "And, your point is well defined and accurate. I hate to change the subject on you, but there is one point still bothering me. Under the law, the power companies must accept and pay for cogenerated electricity. What's the purpose of going to all the trouble it'll take to get 'cogen' contracts if we won't be in business long?"

"Being totally ignorant on the subject," Maybelle confessed, "I have already put a similar question to Dacus. He told me that power companies were compelled to accept all generated electricity from environmentally friendly methods, such as wind or solar energies provide. Therein lays the problem, Ed. The method Dacus uses does qualify. The but is, it must be guarded with our very lives, as you know. To get around divulging the method, we apply for a contract which specifies we'll sell them electricity from heat generated in conjunction with a product being manufactured. God forbid, should Dacus's secret method ever become known to the wide coalition of energy sources in production of oil, natural gas, and transmitted electricity. I shudder to think what the ramifications would be if it's even suspected that energy could be so readily available and so cheap. It's all the more reason to cover the ass. They'd be hard put to call for an investigation after the fact, with a signed cogeneration contract. It'll omit a fear factor . . .

"Perhaps, Ed, you'd understand it better if you read a printout of the 'The Tale' that'll be distributed at today's meeting. Here's a copy, and it'll clue you in before time. As I read it, we're to fake being executives in a company named Crown Alloys. Owned by a privately held investment group, it expects to profit from manufacture of a recently patented product produced under a technological breakthrough. It's projected to come on the market at one-half current price. Sale of electricity back to the utility is the key to success of the whole operation. None of us will be at liberty to discuss the nature of the product, because it's classified. Proving intent and reliability of the company can offset inquiries. On the front end, we come on strong that there are fixed things the group is willing to do. But, we are always assertive on first acquiring a cogeneration contract with the local electric company. Money talks, so bank accounts need to be opened in select towns. Then, we begin to make offers to rent existing facilities as part of the package. For appearance's sake, our company places enough money in escrow to pay for a three months lease, explaining operations will be slightly delayed, awaiting installation of fabricated machinery. Secure the leased construction site with hired guards to keep prying eyes away and we're in business, so to speak."

"Now I see! Oh, do I ever see!" exclaimed Ed. "I'm so glad the job has finally evolved into an effort, dependent entirely on the negatives of greed and lust, which had to be for it to succeed. Reminds me of a caper I once participated in that relied on a small group of people to do the right thing. They blotched it by doing the opposite. Needless to say, we lost our ass. Your version of this con at last makes sense. However, I wish there was some way to avoid the 'vengeance factor' resulting from blackmail," he adverted, expressing a concern.

Maybelle knew she had his alliance. "No difference, Ed. We're already dealing with a vindictive element from the last scam. That old bastard Lipscomb knows he has a 'little to none' chance of getting his quarter of a million back. I'd be willing to bet, however, it won't keep him from trying. If Dacus was stupid enough to hand it to him, he wouldn't be satisfied until he'd gotten even with the lot of us." *Hmm* escaped her . . . She'd opened a window, but closed it.

"On this next one, Ed, I'd be doing the blackmailing should drastic measures be needed. I'd be the lone target if there was any vengeance to be dished out. It hasn't occurred to any one of you that my position in Tulsa might have become untenable. Sooner or later, 'the house' is destined to be raided . . . Then, I'm finished. When it happens, lawyers will sponge up all the assets, putting me in business as a bag lady on the street. My house of ill repute has been a lot of fun, but it's time to consider shutting her down. I must leave, be truly gone, with every available liquid asset I own, to survive. Regardless of the odds, this new caper offered the best chance I had to look beyond living on the street, pushing a grocery cart." Her reasoning was almost undefiled.

"Another thought, Ed, to soothe concerns over pitfalls of blackmail. Think back. How many times have you blown off a mark by faking a killing in which he was involved, either as a participant or as the witness? Was that not a form of blackmail? Purposes for blackmail are much broader than obtaining money. Essentially, they involve forcing an individual to do one's bidding, by hook or by crook."

Ed shook his head in disbelief. "Maybelle, I don't ever want to hear any more lyin' crap from you about who has the best mind. I've got to hand it to you. It's just not right for anyone to be that knowledgeable, and that smart, and have the advantage of being an attractive woman."

"Cool it, Ed," Maybelle retorted. "My sole interest now is buy it, sell it, or trade it for influence and favors."

"I knew I was too old, too ugly, and too broke for you," Ed bewailed indignantly.

"Oh yeah! I'm the pope, and you lie," Maybelle chided. "Since maturity, I've always been a sucker for older men. The problem is, I am not remotely interested in any kind of relationship at the moment, no matter how casual it's intended. Too many other priorities I guess."

Ed sucked up his pride. "Okay. I've got the message. We'll be close friends and nothing more. Remember though, I'm looking to you for 'sense of direction' on this score. After all, you have the weapons and will be using them as you see fit. Let's head back for the lodge before we're missed and something inappropriate is made of it."

Maybelle had turned the side of her head to a light wind. "Listen. Listen to the guinea chickens! They're really upset, Ed. You don't suppose someone is out there, do you?"

"Nah," Ed dismissed. "It's probably a fox or a coon that has 'em all excited."

Maybelle's womanly intuition persisted. "I don't know," she wondered aloud. "Surely, as a country boy from Arkansas, you're acquainted with their usefulness in sounding an alarm when an intruder invades their territory."

Ed ignored her last comment as they walked, increasing the pace. Inside the lodge, they found Dacus looking for Maybelle. "There you are," Dacus confronted, flatly stating, "I need to talk to you, Maybelle." She followed him out onto the veranda, leaving Ed to his own devices.

Standing at its railing and looking across the valley, which spread out below the mesa, Dacus conferred. "I have got to clear the mountaintop of every person except Rabbit and myself. Can you come up with a plan that'll productively occupy the whole group for a week or ten days? Time is fast running out before Lipscomb will make his move. It's got to go down up here, where I have control. The only way to counter him is to make damn sure there's no potential for hostages. You'll have to exclude Art from plans, though. He needs to be in Harrison on surveillance to alert me of the old man's arrival and activities."

Maybelle quickly reacted. "There's no problem. Consider it done. If I can distract you for a moment, there's a world of details to be attended to before our next caper can be put into motion. There isn't one decent suit of clothes within the bunch that characterizes middle to higher level, corporate executive dressing. A shopping spree in Tulsa will take time for every male to be outfitted in suitable style. Vivian needs a professional hairstylist, suits, dresses, shoes, and a hat or two to be spruced up as the wife of a CEO. Of course, they'll all get polished and manicured, and I could use some of the same. I propose to use my credit cards for this buying bash. Before you say a word, let me explain. The whole proceeds of two hundred thousand dollars from the first scam can be absorbed in my bank accounts and dealt back through credit card charges and personal checks. How's that for instant laundering?"

"Are you putting them up in your whorehouse?" an overly anxious Dacus queried.

"Not on your life," asserted Maybelle. "My entire existence in Tulsa is very limited. Actually it's hanging by a thread. The situation, and my future there, doesn't relate to what's right or what is wrong. Demise for Maybelle is already predetermined by fact. I've thumbed my nose at the monolithic social order in that town for too long. In the end, and the truth be known, they'll crush me. No way, my Man, can we afford a raid to be staged on my house of ill repute while the bulk of our group is rooming in as guests." Virtue of her deep-seeded, shielding loyalty spoke for itself as she collocated. "Early on, I was afraid to let anyone know of my less than satisfactory existence inherited in Tulsa. Fear mostly influenced me to think I'd compromise chances of joining the Association. Now that the jack's out of the box, and as we talk, I realize it was not a premeditated move. It was strictly compulsive, lusting to be a part of the action."

Her sagacity intervened. "Changing the subject, Dacus, let me toss this at you. You've previously mentioned a second identity of James Freed Dacus, along with a valid Social Security number. Do you intend using it in obtaining an EIN to set up a phantom corporation for this second scam? Instead of forming a corporation, why don't you use the current identity and SSN of Arthur Dacus Mays, establish a limited partnership, and an EIN, whereby you'd hold all general partnership equity? When I get the casino money laundered through my accounts, I'll put it in the partnership, where you'll maintain absolute control. It seems a better way than doodling two hundred thousand back through credit cards. Whatta ya think? Would it work?"

"Your analysis of the difference between control and ownership involving a partnership setup is absolutely correct," Dacus agreed. "I'd forgotten the old time con used on doctors as the only holders of ready cash in hard times. The scam was to bundle timber and mineral rights into a limited partnership, selling the limited equity to doctors. The general partnership equity would be retained for assured control and ultimate disposal of all assets. A real artist in that game never stole and ran. He'd skim lightly enough not to be detected so as to milk the 'cows' again and again. Your ideas have just resolved a number of problems plaguing me, so it's a deal." Relieved, Dacus grasped Maybelle's hand in his, sealing the appreciation.

"One other thing," Maybelle provided. "I have four late-model automobiles in my garages. An expensive weakness of mine. While everyone's in Tulsa, these vehicles can easily be brought back and used in this next caper. If you think it's possible, let Art accompany me. Surely, you recognize it'll take the van to get everyone to Tulsa, leaving no transportation for Art to 'bird-dog' in Harrison. This way, he'd get measured for clothes and drive a car back by evening tomorrow. Keep your fingers crossed Lipscomb holds off one more night."

Dacus nodded his agreement. "We'll stay in touch on cellular phones with voice messages. Very soon, at the called meeting, I'm going to distribute 'The Tale' to each member. You already have a copy. Later, I'll relinquish the floor to you to describe the outing planned for immediate departure to Tulsa. If the meeting's short and you push on them, maybe you can be in Tulsa by ten o'clock tonight. I need Art back here no later than tomorrow evening."

Maybelle concurred, "It's a done deed."

The Association's meeting, brief and concise, was over before one thirty. Maybelle had her charges packed and leaving the mesa by three o'clock. Tulsa was six hours away.

As the van vanished across the mesa's brow, Dacus turned to Rabbit at his side. "I want you fully aware of the coming events to affect our abode. Very shortly, as early as tonight or in those to come, it'll be set upon. Expect it to occur in the middle of the night, led by old man Lipscomb and some of his 'soldiers'. He is vengeful and absolutely ruthless. The men under his command are hired killers. If you would like to leave here and go live with Lulu until it is over, feel free to do so with my blessing. There's no one left to cook for but me, and I'm self sufficient."

Rabbit sort of stomped his foot. "You don't know anything about me, and I'm smart enough to know you don't keep me around to play house jock. I left my fine, strong, and smart Mama and my good, hard working, but slow Daddy, 'cause I was just too smart for 'em. It led me straight to jail, where I graduated into prison. Finally, the second time around at 'the farm' convinced me it wasn't my callin'. I learned to cook. I studied, tryin' to educate myself. Lurking back there in my head, I knew I'd stacked the cards against me. I guess that's why, stupidlike, I ran away from deer camp. Now, ain't nobody left for me but you. My folks worked hard and died young. Whatever I've got is here. If I leave you, and they knock you off, I'm finished too. Forget what you just said, 'cause I ain't buyin' in."

"Okay, trusted friend," Dacus readily consented. "I know all about having nobody left. We belong to the same club, and its fraternal brothers are faced with a pending crisis. Sorry to say, it won't be anything remotely akin to other member initiation rites tho."

A mutual compact made, Dacus outlined his strategy. "Here's where things are for the moment. The mountain's clear, except for you and me. I'd planned for Art to be in Harrison to spot Lipscomb's gang. He'd warn me when they showed up. But now, Art won't be back till tomorrow night, and surprises I can do without. Set our motion sensitive monitor on the road. Make sure it's operational and absolutely reliable by tonight. Also, help me take this wire locator to trace underground lines I buried several years ago. We'll need to hide and position about three 'speaker mikes' in various places so I can talk to Lipscomb whenever and at whatever direction he comes in from. As soon as the sun goes down, I'll explain a 'double shell' which you haven't seen, and instruct you on how it works for future use."

CHAPTER 13

Arnold Lipscomb and his hit men arrived, registering under false names at the Maple Leaf Motel in Harrison. A small establishment, it was located right next to a Waffle House that was of no practical use to them. He'd forbidden eating forty-eight hours prior to staging their raid. Lipscomb, determined not to be outdone by the ultrasound machine again, had everyone on laxatives. There was little to no grumbling over these demands. Anything would be better than the recent demoralizing agonies. For added protection, Lipscomb had provided flexible latex shields to be worn over a set of Pampers plus earplugs, hopefully to further block the vibrations.

It didn't take Scotland Yard to locate a Mr. A. D. Mays, and more! Small town post offices and courthouses are notorious for gossip. The special soldier quickly discovered Mays had a private box in the Harrison post office and that he didn't pick up mail every day. Sometimes it could be as long as two weeks before they'd notice the box emptied. He also learned Mays owned property northwest of Harrison. From the courthouse, he got a description, was given directions, and gratuitously informed of the mountaintop where he resided being haunted and somehow badly jinxed. The soldier volunteered to folks at the courthouse that Mr. Mays had come into a very modest inheritance. His signature was sorely needed to settle a complicated estate problem back in the eastern part of the country.

Receiving the information impatiently, Lipscomb ordered the soldier to search out exactly which mountain then to hide his car before climbing to the top. He was to scout the terrain in daylight hours, sketch a map of the area, and return without being detected.

When the soldier reported back late in the day, first words Lipscomb uttered were, "Did anybody spot you?"

"No, Mr. A.," he assured. "Two people were down in a pasture with horses, and they didn't even look up as a bunch of wild chickens got to cackling. One off 'em two was a gal, and I think she might fit a description of the broad in on the take at our tables."

"I'd like to get my hands on that woman." A grim smirk formed on Lipscomb's face. "Were there any more people visible to you?" he asked.

"Yes sir, Mr. A.! From time to time, there'd be folks come out of a building. I saw one or two sittin' out on a big porch."

"Good!" Lipscomb said. "We'll take 'em by surprise tonight after midnight. Mays can't use that crazy ultrasound thing unless they know we're coming and have time to get prepared. It'll likely take capturing someone like that gal to get any money back. Then everyone dies!"

Dacus and Rabbit lost no time setting about to experiment with the double shell. Cheese, sardines, and crackers, washed down by beer, became their seafood fest for the evening. Dacus began by creating a shell over the entire mesa and hardened it to exclude light rays as Rabbit watched. Next, the mesa was lit up as he'd done the night curved space was demonstrated to the Association. Details complete, he and Rabbit descended the platform to enter into the heart and soul of the complex of machines housed inside the old church. Seating Rabbit at a monitor, keyboard, and joystick, he diagrammed. "You can scan the whole mesa or stop it at any place by applying the joystick. Once you're locked in on an area, use the network keyboard to erect a second shell of variable dimensions and degrees of hardness over the targeted subject."

He diverted with an example. "Somewhere in your native roots, it was the custom to dispose of a rogue lion or other animal by luring the creature into a trap with live bait, usually a goat. It's the same here," Dacus explained. "I'm to be the bait, which means you learn to set the shells. I'll be on the platform, ready to turn the floodlights on after you set a big shell over the whole mesa, the minute Lipscomb and his troops trip a sensor. Your job is to pinpoint him in the middle of a small tight, semihard shell. What you want is a shell hard enough to stop bullets yet translucent enough for them to see me and for me to see them. The computer'll do the calculating. All you have to do is direct it accurately." He retraced the steps with his finger.

"It's my intention," he made clear, "to lure Lipscomb far enough away from his cars that you can get a shell around the entire bunch without involving the vehicles. When you get it in place, I'll speak to him through a battery powered bullhorn. It'll seem a normal sound, but actually he'll be hearing one of the three wired speaker mikes we hid in the shrubbery this afternoon. Now, let's practice setting the small shell."

By nine thirty, Rabbit, who could be called a quick study, became proficient at setting the shells. The two then unfolded cots to sleep on in a corner of the old church, where an alarm connected to the motion sensor out on the road would be activated.

At midnight, Lipscomb assembled his gang, and they drove out of Harrison in two separate automobiles. He'd passed around copies of the hand-drawn map, along with flashlights for them to get acquainted with the layout, while en route.

Unloading after parking at the foot of the mountain, Lipscomb announced, "I haven't wanted to clutter your minds by giving details on our raid beforehand. Notice the arrangement of these buildings on the map. Our main weapon, aside from guns, is to make a surprise hit. Lots of people stay up 'til midnight, and this is why we won't be going in until a quarter to one. We're out here early because we don't want the cars being remembered at a particular time on the main roads. If any of you can't read the map, ask Lenny to explain it. After all, he's the man who made it, and he's the only one of us who has actually seen the place."

In less than ten minutes, unable to wait any longer, Lipscomb asked, "Are there any questions about the layout?" Not waiting for an answer, he started dishing out orders. "When we break the brow of this hill on top, let's leave the main road and see if we can drive along the edge of this sawed-off mountain. Lenny, park your wagon at the far edge over here and wait. The rest get into Leon's Suburban, on top of each other if necessary, to travel about a hundred yards inward to this big flat, open area. Leon, you stay with your vehicle. Everyone else comes with me to sneak in on these living quarters. I want each of you carrying a machine gun. I'll have my Uzi."

Organizing to move out, he unified. "Bear in mind we're all in this together. I have my depends on, the same as you. If the plan to surprise fizzles, be prepared for the pain. Program yourself to open fire at first twinge of a belly cramp. Maybe someone can take out that damn vibrating apparatus. These remarks have covered special contingencies. Listen for my orders. Obey them to the letter," Lipscomb emphasized.

"Right on, Mr. A.," they echoed, cocked and primed, ready for duty getting into their cars. Shifting into low gear, Lipscomb gave Lenny the signal to get started.

Three-quarters of an hour past midnight, the alarm went off, announcing the anticipated arrival of Lipscomb's mob. Rabbit hung a pair of night-vision binoculars around his neck, grabbed a night-scoped rifle, and positioned himself at the computer monitor. Dacus, appearing disheveled, wearing only pants and insulated shoes, sneaked around to climb the platform, laying a rifle and setting binoculars on the control bench.

The night sky was heavily overcast and a seemingly ideal condition for Lipscomb's purposes. Actually, it was far more advantageous to Dacus. Out on the platform, Dacus quickly spotted his quarry. Softly he spoke into Rabbit's ear through their mike intercoms. "They're here! One station wagon, with driver, is at the edge of the mesa. The other one is parked about eighty-five yards in, also with a driver. There are several thugs trying to sneak up on the lodge. Set the big shell and stand by for 'lights out'. When lights go out, I'll turn on the floodlights, which will bring into play the really critical part . . . The little shell must be laid down without them suspecting a thing! Be alert," he admonished.

As Dacus looked on, the gang stealthily entered one of the three designated areas equipped with a hidden speaker mike. Waiting until they were about thirty feet from the shrub, he called on Rabbit for 'lights out'. Immediately, inky blackness occupied the mesa.

"Don't move," Lipscomb ordered under his breath. "Don't make a motion. Let your eyes get used to the darkness."

Two minutes of blackness lapsed. One of the gang whispered, "I doubt I can ever see nary a thing up here. It's weird!"

"Shut up! Do as I told you!" hissed Lipscomb. A fear of the unknown gripped him and a bitter taste invaded his mouth. Suddenly, floodlights lit the entire plain, temporarily blinding them. Dacus, standing behind the lights, was only mildly affected.

"Set the shell. Set the shell, now!" Dacus commanded Rabbit. "Use position two for centering the shell. Let the computer take over. Set the shell, dialing in hardness limits to degree of six and a half to seven and three-quarters."

"It's done, done, and done," snorted Rabbit almost simultaneously.

"Rabbit," he routed. "Get up in the steeple. Keep your eyes on the two guys at their cars. Try not to shoot 'em while I maneuver Lipscomb and his main gang."

Dacus retrieved his electronic bullhorn but actually began speaking to Lipscomb through the shrubbery. "Welcome to our little community. What can we do for you?" The unexpected voice in their midst breached.

"You know damn well what you can do," erupted Lipscomb, collecting himself. "I've come to get the money you stole from me."

"Stole is a strong word," argued Dacus. "The way I remember it, you had a 'juice joint' set up to steal from anybody ignorant enough to play on the equipment. For that matter, you intended to steal eight of my big green bills."

Lipscomb went spastic. "You two-bit cocksucker. Nobody steals from Arnold Lipscomb and gets away with it!" Ranting, he stomped the ground in a frenzy.

Leon, seeing the antics of Mr. A. as a signal to come forward, made a move away from his car. It was too much for Rabbit, wired to react. He shot the guy between the eyes.

"Kill him, kill, kill 'em!" screeched Lipscomb. His men opened fire, aiming at Dacus on the platform. Programmed to obey orders, they continued firing hundreds of rounds, reducing themselves to hunks of bloody flesh from ricochets bouncing off walls of the compressed bubble.

Dacus looked at the withering piles and heaps of quivering, dying flesh. Unanticipated, his mind transfused a boyhood remembrance of seeing his stepmother kill a chicken in the backyard by wringing its neck. The memory, relating to how long it took the chicken's body to stop moving after being separated from its head, was etched in another time.

Rabbit, however, busied himself watching the other driver, Lenny, who'd strayed too far. Witnessing the bloody end of his group, Lenny forgot the car. He tried to escape by running down the mountainside, wanting to access the same path he'd traveled that afternoon when spying on the compound. In full flight, he bounced off the wall of the big shell, falling backward. Crawling on the outer slope's edge, he bumped into the invisible wall and panicked. *My god*, he muttered to himself. *I'm trapped. They'll hunt me down and shoot me like a stray dog!* Without warning, the floodlights went out. Gathering wits in the ordinary darkness, he decided to stay hidden below the mesa's plain. Feeling around on the layered rocks, he found no holes to crawl in.

In contact with Dacus through their miniature intercom, Rabbit reported, "The guy tried to run down the mountain but hit the wall. He's just over the pasture's brow along the fence line, about three hundred yards from its corner."

Dacus responded, "Rabbit, don't take any chances. I need you, and not just to cook."

"I thought we had that settled," Rabbit strongly reminded. "What I need from you right now is backup. Man the computer and give me 'lights out' if

I call for it, or throw the floodlights on when they're needed. While you're at it, how about transferring control of all floodlights from the platform down to the computer before you leave. I'll stay in touch."

Rabbit left the steeple, going to one of the small houses on the grounds, where he had ample feed stored for the horses and cattle. Picking up a couple of cubes of pressed grain, laced with livestock quality sorghum, he crept into the pasture. Sliding along the fence row, he slowly worked his way up to a horse feeding next to the fence. With hand extended holding a sweetened cube, he eased up to the horse, offering the sugary token. As the horse munched, he softly blew his breath into its nostrils, gypsylike. The horse then belonged to him. In a meandering fashion, keeping the horse between himself and the fence, Rabbit methodically worked his way up along the fence, keeping downwind from where Lenny hid.

Lying flat on the ground in weeds of the fence row, and just inside the shell wall, Rabbit wriggled under the lowest strand of barbwire to get positioned at the trunk of a dead tree. Countless trial settings of a shell wall, striking limbs of the tree, had killed it. Whispering into the intercom, he contacted Dacus. "Lights out, lights out!" Under its cover, as inky blackness enveloped inside the bubble, Rabbit shinnied up the tree trunk. He felt along until he could reach the upper half of the tree. Here, he called for floodlights. The lights, bouncing off the invisible wall, were blinding and disconcerting. Lenny spun around twice, looking for an adversary. Calculatedly, after a lengthy pause, Rabbit said, "Hey." Totally muddled, Lenny looked about, more for someone than to retrieve his weapon.

Aimed squarely on target, Rabbit ordered, "Up here!" In response, Lenny tried focusing dazed eyesight upward from ground level. Rabbit nailed him between the eyes. Dropping from the tree, he walked over to the body, placing his rifle next to the gun on the ground. In spite of his shortness, Rabbit was immensely strong. Capturing both guns, he passed them through the fence. Climbing over, in one tug he pulled the body under the bottom strand. Whistling for the horse, he lifted and laid it across the horse's flanks, picked up the guns, and began walking back. Coming out of the pasture, Rabbit led the horse to the piles of self-riddled remains.

Observing the approach of Rabbit, Dacus dissolved the inner shell from around the bodies of Lipscomb and his men so Lenny's could be included. Leaving the electrical complex, Dacus reflected on shortage of time. Looking up, Rabbit saw Dacus striding hurriedly toward him.

"Rabbit, there's a lot more to be done before the night's over. Let's move up to the lodge," insisted Dacus urgently.

"But, what about these bodies and that other gunman over there?" Rabbit balked.

"Later!" urged Dacus. Inside the lodge, he presented a chauffeur's uniform to Rabbit, complete with cap. "Before you unwrap the coverings, or touch anything, put on these surgical gloves and don't take them off," Dacus directed. "Our next move is to dispose of these vehicles before daylight. There's to be no traceable evidence left. You'll look very natural in uniform, driving each of these wagons. I'll precede you in the pickup to bring you back each time."

"What about the bodies? The buzzards'll be here for breakfast at daylight," persisted Rabbit, somewhat perturbed.

"Let's go, Man! I'll drive you to their Suburban. While you're checking out oil, gas, and tires on it, I'll retrieve the other body in my pickup and place it with the others. A very small, solid bubble, not visible from the air, yet adequate to prevent any escaping odors, should take care of the situation. If it's a little after daylight before we return from the second trip, it won't make any difference!" Dacus reassured.

Uncapped adrenaline flowed in both men. Dacus sped off the mesa in his pickup, followed by Rabbit in uniform with the black Suburban, spinning around hairpin curves going down the mountain. Reaching State Highway 43 cutoff, Dacus turned due west and intersected U.S. Highway 65, going into Missouri. A short distance across the state line, Dacus turned left on a road leading to a lavish resort. Proceeding about a mile and a quarter, he pulled to the side with the Suburban right behind him, motioning Rabbit to park on the edge of the highway. Dacus turned the truck around in the middle of the road, leaving no tracks. The speedometer in Dacus's truck indicated he had traveled thirty-one miles. They were back at the mesa by three fifteen and on their way again in five minutes to relocate the maroon wagon.

Dacus turned off on the same road, and Rabbit parked only a hundred yards off of Highway 65. No police were encountered in Missouri. In Arkansas, between Omaha and Burlington, Dacus and an Arkansas State Trooper passed uneventfully in opposite directions. The pickup topped the mesa around four thirty, with Rabbit dead asleep in the seat. Recalling what Rabbit had taught him about sleeping in a sitting-up position when you can't afford to stay asleep for eight full hours, he cracked the windows on both sides of the pickup and closed his eyes.

At six o'clock, Rabbit woke up. Getting out of the truck, he succeeded in waking Dacus. "I'm sorry I woke you. I slept all the way home," he apologized.

Dacus, still groggy, grunted, "Forget it. It's time to move. I'll get the four-wheeler and the wagon. You go get the large plastic leaf bags for these body parts. I don't want time wasted trying to identify separate bodies, but I do want old man Lipscomb's false teeth, glasses, and wallet. Come over here first so I can point him out to you."

When body parts, with the exception of Lipscomb's upper torso and head, had been collected and loaded on the wagon, Dacus unexpectedly injected, "I'm going down the mountain and bring Lulu up. I want her on the property, spending time with you. There shouldn't be any trouble, but it'll cover the bases, leaving the police with no one to question. Whether or not they'd know to ask Lulu about our activities is beside the point. I simply want her here. Suffice to say, about the time you've reached the cave's entry with these remains, I'll go after her."

As Rabbit entered the mouth of the cave, Dacus left, driving straight to Lulu's modest farm dwelling. He honked her to the front porch. She came out, greeting him with a smile. "Lulu, Rabbit wants to see you. He's busy and asked me to drive you up. Bring some things to spend the night." The smile broadened as she went into the house. Dacus saw her go out back of the house, feeding and watering the rabbit which Rabbit had caught and given to her. In a few minutes, she returned thru the front door, carrying a small bundle, and hopped into the pickup.

Lulu said nothing. The brightness in her eyes mirrored her happiness. Like clockwork, Rabbit had already returned from the cave and was putting up the four-wheeler and wagon when they topped the plateau. Only one more thing was yet to be done. Dacus told Rabbit to use the wagon, load it with barnyard manure and humus, and then haul it to cover that certain area in the pasture. The high organic content of the manure would quickly break down any traces of blood.

Lulu followed Rabbit through the final chores, asking him about the blood. He smoothly lied, sloughing off the question by saying, "A foal of one of the mares had broken its leg and had to be destroyed." Aping truth, he spieled, "Dacus doesn't want flies to build up!"

By eight o'clock, Dacus was in bed asleep. Rabbit, after a session with Lulu, was headed in the same direction. Consequently, Dacus was first up at noon thirty, hungrily going into the kitchen for nourishment. What he saw in the refrigerator killed his appetite for food, sending him to the bar for a drink instead.

Slightly after one o'clock, Rabbit showed up. Dacus accosted, "Rabbit, I asked you to save Lipscomb's teeth, his glasses, and wallet. Why in hell did you cut his ears off?"

Rabbit looked away to avoid showing amusement. "You reminded me once of my past ancestors in Africa, on how rogue cats or other animals were trapped, didn't you? What you failed to mention, or didn't know, is that when that varmint is caught, we cut his ears off and save 'em for braggin' rights." Making his point, Rabbit reached for the coffee.

Dacus was taken aback yet amused also. "Well, I'll be damned!" he muttered. Slowly, a thought began to generate and take shape. Dacus went to the refrigerator, took out the plastic bag with Lipscomb's ears and effects, and retired to the lab in the church. He carefully removed the ears with tweezers, immersing them in formaldehyde.

Going back to the lodge, he summoned Rabbit, giving no explanation, to follow him to the lab. "Rabbit, I want you to have the money in Lipscomb's wallet!" he enlightened. "Since I plotted his death, I considered it'd be bad luck for me to keep it . . . You take it!"

Rabbit picked up the wallet. His eyes grew round at the sheaf of bills inside. Eyes shining, he counted them twice. Still intent upon the roll, he blurted, "There's twenty-five hundred dollars here in one hundreds. That's more money than I've ever had at one time in my whole life!"

"Take it and hide it somewhere. You'll never be broke again." With Rabbit gone, Dacus carefully lifted the wallet, using a pair of tweezers. Gently, he placed it in a plastic bag. Reaching for the cellular phone, he called Maybelle. Receiving the recording "Your party is unavailable at this time" provoked him to cancel the connection. Defusing his short temper reflex, he placed another and left a message on her answering machine in the cabana.

Rabbit served them a meager supper. Dacus updated him that he'd be gone the next day and night, instructing, "Set the motion detector out on the road to sound off at your bedside. Expect Art and Maybelle's girls to come in tomorrow or the next day. It'll be during daylight hours though. At night, place a semihard shell just inside the motion detector for protection."

Rabbit mused, "Who else do you think would be comin' up here?"

"Damned if I know, but I do know one thing," Dacus added. "The way to survive is to not take any chances. So, don't cut any corners when you're carrying out my business."

Rabbit had no reply to Dacus's seemingly unnecessary shortness.

Early the next day, Dacus left for Memphis in the pickup. He carried an overnight bag and a small well-wrapped package. On the way through Little Rock, he stopped to call in reservations for the evening. In little more than five hours, he'd be back at the trendy and elegant Capitol Hotel. Dining at Ashley's would be a welcome treat, and he hoped for diversion in the bar.

Room service included first edition of the state's daily paper with coffee. The news was out. Abandonment of two larger SUVs, one black and one maroon, found off a Missouri state highway, spiked a police inquiry. Identity of the vehicles' owner, Arnold Lipscomb, had been made. There were no leads as to his whereabouts nor to the lieutenants under his command, who seemingly had vanished also. The Feds were involved. Disappearance of the nonindicted mobster from Memphis had captured the attention of national news.

The media's embroilment stimulated even more intense investigation by state and federal authorities. But there were no clues. A careful dusting of both vehicles produced no prints other than those of Lipscomb and his cohorts. All told, twelve men were unaccounted for. Each had criminal records, except for Lipscomb. He'd been charged with theft of property at the age of nineteen. Strangely, however, that indictment was dropped when the only prosecution witness couldn't be found. Now, Lipscomb was gone. Had he met a similar fate?

In regions surrounding Memphis, many within the rackets rejoiced. One in particular was the Zallafino Family of Louisiana, who had fierce animosity toward Arnold Lipscomb.

On the evening following the news release, Marcantonio Zallafino, the eldest of three, dined out with his two younger brothers in a small Orleans courtyard. "Do you know of any other families with a vendetta against the son of a bitch?" Before either sibling could answer, he had to insert, "I don't." Their discussion was interrupted as parties of vested interest felt compelled to drop by the table. Conversations were light and closely guarded without specific mention to news headlines. There was no mistaking that homage was being paid to the Zallafino Don. Toward the evening's end, Marc summed it up for his brothers. "I don't mind taking credit, but I'd sure like to thank whoever is responsible. That old bastard was due to die."

A package, originating out of Memphis, was delivered the next day to the Zallafino's private coastal resort. An alert guard on duty at the gate notified the main house of its arrival. Marc took the call. Immediately apprehensive, he cautioned, "Take the damn thing very carefully, if you please, and transfer it to a spot at the farthermost place from any buildings or trees."

Contacting a brother in town, he confidentially relayed, "I think we may have a bomb package. Round up someone who can take care of it. I'll see you when you get here." An hour and a half later, a two-man bomb squad arrived. Donning protective clothing, they made necessary tests from a safe distance, followed by a look at the contents thru portable X-ray equipment. Smiling and satisfied, they slowly unwrapped the package, laying it open . . .

Inside were several individual plastic bags. One contained a wallet. In another was a pair of glasses. A set of false teeth had been zip-locked in one, and a pair of ears floating in solution was in the fourth bag. The two bomb experts began to roar with laughter. At their display, Marc strode from the mansion to where they were on the lawn. He couldn't believe his own eyes either. Quickly he snapped, "Place Luthor in his pen for the present. Don't let anyone touch a thing. Get a guard posted, right here, right now!"

Returning to the house, he caught his brother leaving the office in town. "Send Ollie the Ex out here to dust for prints. Contact one of our 'friends' in the police department that we're going to need urgent, special service."

"Marc, what have you got out there?" asked Gitano, alerted by his tone of voice.

"You won't believe this! I have Arnold Lipscomb's false teeth, his glasses, his wallet, and his *ears*!" crowed Marc.

"I'll get right on it," Gitano replied. "Tell me first, how do you know it's Lipscomb's?"

Marc's eyes fairly danced with joy, responding, "I'd recognize those ears anywhere. He should've been able to fly on his own, little brother!"

The only prints found were those on the wallet. They were sent off through the NCIS for identification. The report came back verifying Lipscomb's and those belonging to a black male who had run away from a penitentiary sentence in Arkansas several years ago.

"You're not goin' to believe the person's name," relayed the detective on the line. "It's George Washington," he said, laughing hilariously into the phone.

"You're shitting me," exclaimed Marc in disbelief again.

"No, sir! However, the records do indicate this person goes by the nickname of Rabbit, if that helps you any," offered the detective.

"I do appreciate it very much. Feel free to call on me if I can ever help you," extended Marc, pleasantly impressed with the input.

Marc caught one of his battery of attorneys at home. He gave him the delicate assignment of finding out the history on this particular George Washington. By midafternoon of the following day, Marc had his answer. His attorney said the information was highly sensitive . . . Officially, it wouldn't have been released except for the fact that he got an old classmate on the phone, who could vouch for him. It seemed that Rabbit had been given an unofficial furlough to cook for a deer camp in Boone County, Arkansas. On the day he was to be returned to prison, he escaped into the mountainous backwoods and couldn't be found. The matter had been hushed up because the politician, though powerful in his own way, couldn't take any heat resulting from the spoiled, pork barrel perk . . . It stood to reason that the record was buried.

Marc got out a road map of Arkansas and one of Missouri. It became very obvious that Lipscomb and company had been done in by someone within a range of thirty-five or forty miles from the spot where the cars were found. And, it was within the immediate proximity of where Rabbit Washington had vanished. Yet, his unsolved mystery remained. *What was the connection between the two of them? Who sent the ears?*

CHAPTER 14

Ensconcing partners in a Holidome Tulsa amid sighs of relief, Maybelle summoned her grounds and maintenance man to deliver the Lexus over to the Holidome. Returning him to the poolside cabana, she went through telephone messages for the past sixteen days. A recent, pressing call from a friend caught her attention. Even though the hour was late, she made contact.

The caller was an employee at the county courthouse. He confided, "Maybelle, you've barely made it back in time to save your hide. If the sheriff's office gets a search warrant from the court in the morning, they'll be raiding your cathouse by this time tomorrow night."

"How is it, the minute I set foot back in town I've got deep troubles! What's happened with my deal for protection?" demanded Maybelle.

"It's all a matter of pressure, Maybelle. Somebody's developed more political clout than you put out," advised her friend. "That person is our appointed, ambitious County Prosecuting Attorney, the Honorable Bob Ed Gables. You don't follow politics very closely, so you probably didn't know he raided the midway at our annual livestock show last fall. Said he wanted to stop illegal gambling in the midway booths, for gosh's sakes! He'll do anything to gain enough name recognition to run for governor!"

"Is the house under twenty-four hour surveillance, yet?" Maybelle questioned.

"Nah," he replied. "They know what it is, and they know where it is. The sheriff won't stage a raid without a court order, so there's no need for a stake-out. The word I have is that the prosecutor's gonna make a move to get the order tomorrow, and 'course, the sheriff's gotta respond. Probably already knows everything about it."

"One more thing," quizzed Maybelle, getting sights set. "Is this Honorable Prosecutor kin to old Ross Gables by any chance?"

"Mr. Gables's one and only offspring from a miserably failed marriage," affirmed her unnamed liaison, who wished her well before he hung up.

Maybelle, no slouch at plotting or counteracting plots, was up at daylight, prepared for a long day. She drove to the Holidome at seven o'clock, exchanging her car for Dacus's van. Renting an extra room, she notified all associates that plans had changed and to be ready to receive ten extra girls in their accommodations. "I am assigning Eva and Barbee to Tom and Vivian's suite. Randi will be coupled with Harry, and Candy with Theo. Julie is to share your room, Ed, as is Cherrie in Sam's pad. Art, take care of Rosie. The other three have reservations in an extra room until their flight out can be arranged."

Going directly to her house in the county, she woke up the girls, alerting, "There will be a raid tonight. Pack your every belonging. We won't be back!" It took several trips in the van, but they vacated the house by noon. All of the lights were turned on and a continuous tape player put in motion for musical background, suggesting business as usual.

The girls and luggage situated, Maybelle asked Art, Sam, and Ed to drive with her to the cabana. Art and Sam wasted no time returning to the motel, one in the van and the other driving her Land Rover. Maybelle packed her remaining wardrobe and toiletries into the Jaguar and directed Ed to load all the recording equipment, tapes, and records into her Mercedes. She left him with an admonition. "Ed, I cannot afford for anyone to know what you're hauling. Lock the car securely until I can get back to you."

At the motel, Maybelle ordered a coke and sandwich from room service and promptly went to work on the problem of her three extra ladies. Explaining to them she had absolute advance notice of the certainty of a raid that evening, she gave each a bonus of three thousand dollars, then reserved plane tickets on the two thirty flight out to Dallas.

During the drive to the airport, they were interested in her intentions for the other seven girls. Maybelle filled them in. "I have plans for them I hope work out. As of right now, they are out of the cathouse business. The three of you have chosen to go to Dallas, and I think you've made a wise decision. Is there a particular reason for the move?"

Amy spoke for the three, "Wiggle business ain't what it used to be. There's too much free stuff floating around. Besides, we're all about over the hill for hustling. Our best bet is to take our savings, plus your bonus, and try our luck as whores, hunting husbands to steal in Big D."

Maybelle smiled knowingly. "Good luck!" she conveyed, compassionately.

Amy talked on, "It's not as if we had a choice. We're not attractive to younger men, and we know better than to hook a thirty-five year old that's never been married. Who'd want a mamma's boy? That leaves us the option of runnin' bars with others out there, trying to snare a husband. We think we've done our bit as the 'housewife's friend'! Stealing husbands never entered our heads as a consideration while in the business . . . It was a better deal to sell it piece at a time. We'd have to say it was fun while it lasted. They say nothing last forever . . ."

"I'm proud to have known you, gals," Maybelle told the three, depositing them and their luggage at the airport. "You've been an asset to me as well as to yourselves. The fact that not one is hooked on booze, drugs, or abusive pimps, is proof enough and will serve you well in a quest for a good man. Aside from that, you've reasonably assessed your predicament. I do believe you will come out well in the future. As I said before, I wish each of you good luck!"

Breaking a few speed limits getting back to the motel, Maybelle took the extra room she'd reserved for the departed girls. She dialed Ed's room, anxious to have a 'put' session on how to expedite details at hand. When he entered, she offered him a chair and began airing her thoughts. "You and I are involved in a mutual understanding on this next scam. It needs a jump start, and I've touched on a probable tactic to use if all else fails. In the Mercedes, there are hundreds and hundreds of video tapes. They are of prominent and semiprominent men in the act of having sex. My girls are unaware of this slight intrusion and must remain uninformed. All of you are depending on me to keep order amongst them in the future, so it is imperative they stay ignorant on the subject." She all but threatened harm if the confidence was violated.

"It was premeditated that Julie be at your disposal, with so much going on, Ed. She has a peculiar ability to remain oblivious to her surroundings, and for that reason she's generally happier than most of us. Most of the crap occurring in this world just doesn't touch her. It'll make your task easier to accomplish if there's no questions asked," Maybelle exerted, then redirected. "Now, the cargo we loaded earlier into the Mercedes needs to be rearranged. I want you to go down and make sure all the tapes are stacked, in numerical order, in the car's trunk. As you go through them, hold out the ones numbered fifteen and four thirty-two to bring up to me. While you're at it, bring me one camcorder, two blank tapes, and the two videos you held out. When I'm through making duplicates up here in the room, I'll get you to lock the camcorder in my Jaguar. For Pete's sake, don't forget to return my keys, or I'll be afoot," she said, dangling keys and primed with more.

on and a tape was playing forties and fifties music, but no one was dancing. The Prosecutor lost his composure, accusing the sheriff's office of leaking a tip. A deputy sheriff was obvious in whispering something into his ear. The entire raiding party promptly sped away, blue lights flashing, just inviting the press to follow.

Their search took them into a very exclusive section of town. The Prosecutor refrained from breaking down the door to his target, a guesthouse on a rather large estate. Instead, he politely knocked on the door. When no one answered, he turned the knob and walked in without a search warrant, followed by deputies and the press. The disarray certainly suggested someone had been hurriedly looking for something. One of the deputies spotted the video tape atop a kitchen cabinet and handed it over to the Prosecutor. Being visible in handling it for the cameras, he called a press conference for eleven o'clock the next morning.

Maybelle turned off the television. She said a silent, *Yes!* It had played out exactly as scripted. Gratified, she curled up for a contented night's sleep.

A haggard Bob Ed Gables hammered on the front door of Ross Gables's home early the next morning. Ross, in pajamas and bathrobe, answered the summons. Bob Ed brushed past his father and marched in, demanding, "Do you have a VCR in this house?"

"Certainly . . . It's over there," Ross said, pointing to a TV in the living room. "First, don't you want some coffee?" he asked, trying to figure out why all the stir.

"No coffee. Just look at this," snapped Bob Ed as he turned the television on and inserted a tape. As it came on, old Ross himself was starring with one of Maybelle's babes . . .

A broad smile spread across Ross's face he couldn't wipe off. "Well, I'll be damned . . . Where'd you get it? Bob Ed, I want a copy of that tape," he exploited selfishly.

"What?" screamed Bob Ed, inflamed. "Are you trying to ruin me, your only son?"

"Spit it all out, Boy. It's been a long time in coming and quite a while since you would admit to being my son," fathered Ross. "Your mother poisoned you against me even when you were a baby. You've wanted nothing to do with me until today. It's insane you'd march into my house with a video tape of me in a sex act and then accuse me of trying to ruin you. Once and for all, why don't you say it like it really is? I'm listening. Go ahead. Confession would be good for what ails you. Tell me how much you despise me!" Ross edified as a last resort.

Bob Ed was furious and cold. "You have always been a whoremonger. That's why mother divorced you. You're never satisfied. Now, you want to inject yourself as an impediment to my becoming governor. I hate you!" he grated disgustedly.

"Nothing's new, Bob Ed. You've always felt that way, because that's what your mother taught you. The world you perceive is the one she fashioned for you as a child. It never really existed. She's hurt you far more than she has me, and you're headed downhill. Without either passion or compassion, how could you ever know what people like to have or expect from a politician? If your opponent hadn't died five days before the election, you wouldn't be serving as county prosecutor today. So be it. Before you go, I've got something to say that you need to hear." He figured it would fall on dead ears coming at this point . . .

"Long ago," avowed Ross, "I woke up to where your mother was concerned. Disdain turned to pity. Finally, with eyes opened, I came to realize, no man existed who could satisfy her. It wasn't just me. Your mother never had but one orgasm, and it occurred the night you were being born. I can see her now, a beautiful woman in the face yet somehow genetically flawed. A woman in every other sense, even to the full bosom, but narrow in the hips like a man, she was not built to bear children or entertain men. I had to deal with my hurt for not being able to satisfy her before forgiving the way she'd treated me. May God rest her soul."

Ross admonished him, "In spite of the way you feel, we are yoked by blood to our mutual disadvantage. If I could speak to you as your real father, who unfortunately I am, I'd tell you to forget politics and go practice law. There are too damn many lawyers, going straight from law school into government service, without any knowledge of the real world. A lot of the crap in government comes from these jokers, who never represented a client, stood before a court and pled a case, met a payroll, or understood what a bottom line is. It's politics of perception only, not reality." He abruptly changed course, charging, "I don't expect you to have paid the least bit of attention to what's been said, but you'd better take heed to what I say now. To keep you from making an even bigger ass of yourself, leave that tape here! If you don't, much as I despise politics, I'll file and run for governor against you. Furthermore, I can promise you it'll be nasty. Now, git the hell outta my house, you uncouth, despicable brat!"

Bob Ed grabbed the tape and left, more irate than when he'd arrived.

The wonderful night's sleep behind her, Maybelle drove to Mercantile and Traders Bank of Tulsa, owned by her longtime good friend, Jack Rainwater.

An old and well established institution, the bank had been founded in the late thirties by longtime partners of a mule trading firm known as Cloudy Night and Rainwater. Cloudy Night was a full-blooded Cherokee, and Jack Rainwater, eighteen years younger, was half Indian. The financial success of their mule buying and selling enterprise had led them to decide to invest in the banking business. A closely held corporation, only 20 percent of its stock had been carefully offered as goodwill to select members of the Tulsa community over the years.

Old man Night had been dead fifteen years, and the estate was held in trust for the benefit of his heirs. Jack Rainwater, sole trustee at eighty-two, greeted Maybelle with a hug. "Still one of the prettiest women I ever laid—I wish—eyes on!"

"Still full of it, aren't you, Jack? Time hasn't dimmed you one bit," bantered Maybelle, easily returning the flattery.

Ushering her into his office, Jack seated her, inquiring as he claimed his chair behind the massive desk, "Where've you been the last couple of months of my life?"

"Aw, Jack, you would have to ask. Call it 'mainstream blues' for lack of a better term. I've got a few good friends like you, but the constant pressure from other sources gets to me every once in a while. Without being specific, let's say I needed an attitude adjustment and got it. It's left me a two hundred thousand-dollar problem. It has to be laundered, and I don't want any trouble. I've come to you for your personal, professional advice."

"Maybelle, do I look like I just came to town and fell off a punkin' wagon? You and I have been friends for years. I'll help you anyway I can, but you're going to have to cut the bullshit and level with me."

She paused, obviously meditating. "Jack, I'm not trying to put you down. I'm trying to protect you. If you had certain information, you might be vulnerable to questioning."

"I already know how to launder your money, Maybelle. What I don't want are any back doors opened that gives access to me," he counseled.

Shifting in his chair, Jack shuffled papers on the desk contemplating, "The world has changed in the last twenty years and most drastically in the past five. In its future, changes will be even more rapid. I want off this boat, and I intend to be free of it within a year. Mankind is not handling new technology well. High tech is shifting economic power into fewer and fewer hands. The piteous deinstitutionalization of honor at all levels in branches of government and industry has left society without any guideposts." The accusation caused him to quickly retaliate.

"I'm sure you remember, when we were warned by 'the few', that a shadowy group called the Trilateral Commission was hell-bent to deliver the world into international communism, it traveled under the milder guise of international socialism. Collectively, mankind is psychic to a certain degree, but not profound. The causative agent will not be international communism. Rather, it is international commerce. I am not, and never have been, an isolationist. I cannot forget that the poison pill to dissolve this government by treaty has been present in our Constitution from the beginning. The mere possibility of it being used revolts me," he scorned.

"Personally, my time is limited as a small businessman. I've been threatened with frivolous lawsuits for not selling this bank to an out of state conglomerate which is now a free-ranging predator in the twilight of relaxed antitrust laws. As you know, Annagail has been dead four years. My two kids have an independent lifestyle. They don't really need money. What I have left in trust is just a token to how much I love them. The trust for Cloudy Night's heirs is safe and secure. As such, I'm getting out within the year, and I do mean completely retired! I have enough money, placed elsewhere, to secure me comfortably." He'd indulged himself for the sake of insight.

"Let's discuss alternatives, Maybelle, while I'm able and still in business. Laundering the money isn't a problem. You might consider leaving the country in six months or so, and you should be prepared to live abroad. If there's an attainable option, I can help. Otherwise, there's a good possibility the government will find out about you and put you away on a perjury charge."

Maybelle shrugged. "Okay. Here's the story. I was a casino dealer when Bryan met and married me. I had other attributes as a 'confidence' woman which were given up before marriage to avoid embarrassment to my Bryan. His death left me ostracized, lonely, and very unhappy as you know. A few months ago, some past acquaintances who are old time cons contacted me. I helped in a scam on a failing gambling house in Mississippi, which was cheating customers at the crap table. The take was two hundred forty thousand. The mob has already come after us and failed to collect. It's precipitated the need to launder two hundred thousand of it. The other forty'll be used for expenses and in plans for executing another, more lucrative caper. It's expected to put us out of the country in less than six months."

"Now I'm comfortable," assured Jack. "Here's the scheme to launder your money. First, how quick can you get your hands on it?"

"Pretty fast." Maybelle alluded. "Before coming into your office, I just put the whole amount of cash in one of my lockboxes at this bank."

"Follow me carefully, Maybelle," somberly, Jack invited. "When you decided to make a whorehouse out of your mansion, I helped you set up a charitable trust. Later, when the heat got on and you moved your 'house' out in the county, you picked up a street preacher from somewhere and really turned the mansion into a home for abused children and battered women. You have been supporting the whole thing with excess cash from the transition. The history is already established for outlays of cash being deposited into the charitable trust. Moreover, the government doesn't look closely at cash in charitable trusts or tax dodges under Regulation 501c3."

Sold on the prospects, he advanced. "Here's the sequence. I've already told you my time is limited. I own two hundred acres, which I bought for ten dollars an acre years ago. I want you to buy the land for fifty dollars an acre, which satisfies my banker's instincts. Do not buy it under your name. Put it under another name and tax ID number. Let that account then sell the land for one hundred ninety thousand to the charitable trust. I will place one hundred ninety thousand of the cash in the trust so the land can be paid for with a check. Thus, voila, the money is laundered. The other ten thousand is to be handed over to the preacher for signing the check."

Maybelle's eyes were shiny. "Got it," she acknowledged. "Here's an EIN for Crown Alloys, formed through the name of Arthur Dacus Mays, whose SSN is written under the EIN. Hold twenty-five hundred in cash to open the account while I go to get the little wormy son of a bitch who'll sign a check."

Maybelle deliberately gave vague answers to the preacher on their way to the bank. "You're about to receive ten grand in cash for yourself. Don't look a gift horse in the mouth," she chided, letting him know not to ask why. "We'll discuss the future later today."

With the last T crossed, Jack called Maybelle aside and instructed, "Request cashier's checks to close your accounts. Clear bank attachments today, including your safety-deposit boxes. You should do it at every bank in town."

On the way to the mansion, Maybelle told the preacher, "The source of income for our charity has dried up. You don't have a problem with paying rent, but you'll have to scrounge up enough money for food and the utilities. With ten thousand in your pocket, you'll have enough time to mount a donation program for the charity's future. You know I picked you up out of the gutter. So consider this as your one big chance. If you screw up and these innocents suffer, you'll pay dearly. Don't think of dropping out of sight, either. I have ways to deal you won't like." The preacher was no sooner out of the car than she signaled to her grounds and maintenance man.

Inviting him to sit in the car, Maybelle reflected, "Nothing is permanent. I am finished in Tulsa. You've been a loyal friend and a very good workman. I know dislocation is painful. Here's two thousand I hope will smooth the way into another line of endeavor for you. Don't count on the preacher for anything."

Not so much shock, but the pained look hurt as he lamented, "Thanks and best of luck to you, too, Mrs. Barton. My displacement can't be any worse than yours."

Maybelle spent most of the afternoon closing accounts and cleaning out lockboxes in Tulsa banks. Foregoing another night in the town, she checked out of the motel room. A nine-millimeter pistol and an extra clip on the seat beside her, she set the Jaguar in motion for Arkansas . . . She'd been too busy to learn about Bob Ed Gables calling off his eleven o'clock news conference with the excuse, "Matters are still under investigation."

CHAPTER 15

Maybelle drove the hundred miles or so into Arkansas thru Siloam Springs. She continued another twenty miles on to Springdale, putting up for the evening at an upscale motel. There were no posted speed limits on the trip of her thought-filled highway. It had been bumper to bumper crisis traffic until her detour by Jack Rainwater's office. The stop allowed her to shift gears. She decided to place her money and assets in the industrially fat regions of northwest Arkansas, where all banks were strong and accustomed to large deposits and withdrawals.

Seeking out the largest banks, Maybelle selected two in Springdale and one in Bentonville, none of which would be particularly out of the way on her return to the mountain. With her personal money divided between the three banks, she then opened an account for Crown Alloys at First National Bank of Springdale. The cashier's check issued by Mercantile and Traders Bank of Tulsa set it up. All bank mailing addresses carried the PO box of A. D. Mays in Harrison for printing up personalized checks on the various accounts as well as those for Crown Alloys.

Cross, ill tempered, and tired, Maybelle reached the mountain by midafternoon. She found the bunch already partying at the bar when she walked in the lodge. Annoyed, she bellowed, "Hey, don't let this go on past dinner. I want everyone to sleep in his or her own room tonight. The delays in Tulsa have put us woefully behind schedule. Girls, see if you can help Rabbit get my things unloaded. The rest of you want to know where I'm coming from? Doctored passports and suitable wardrobes have got to be purchased.

It can't be accomplished if the lot of you are hung over from getting stewed tonight. You're on notice to prepare for traveling to St. Louis tomorrow."

Harry just couldn't resist. "Have you now appointed yourself housemother, Maybelle?"

Before Maybelle could react, Ed took the floor on her behalf. "Let's have a vote to placate Harry. I move that all of the girls be assigned to Harry's room for the night." Everyone except Harry put their hands up, approving the motion.

Harry, sensing he was being teased, slapped his hand on the bar, feigning outrage. "Oh no, you don't! You're not about to lay that one on me. I remember what happened to Sam and Theo. I'm locking my door as soon as we've eaten supper." The tension was diffused amid laughter.

Maybelle needed Ed to arrange for a quiet, private place to have a conference with her girls after breakfast the next morning. "They're wondering about their future, and who can blame them," she told Ed. "I have to inform, even counsel the seven on a one to one basis, if necessary. In the end, they must decide their own destiny. I'd much prefer not to deal with any two-bit qualms."

Ed sought out Association members individually, telling them of an upcoming meeting between Maybelle and the girls. He suggested a put session afterward to compare ideas.

Maybelle, her crew, and Ed sitting in, gathered in the lounge area with coffee in hand. Portable screens were moved in closer, making for privacy and snugness. Choosing to stand behind the bar where she could address and observe each one's response, Maybelle somberly rested her elbows on it, stating, "Unanimously, including Cherrie, you've solicited me that you're interested in residing here. As you know, whorehouses open and close at the blink of an eye. It's happened to us. We're here prematurely, looking at a forced change or a new direction in lifestyle. Time is marching on all of us, and it takes this sort of thing to bring it home to one's self. Reality is, you're confronted with the same decisions your sister associates are facing today in Dallas. Except, you have a couple of options they didn't have. For a certainty, there might be five good years left in the prostitution racket, but what then? Your former buddies chose to leave the profession and run the bars in Dallas with a single purpose . . . Entrap a husband before the money runs out. In the absence of hitting it big in the entertainment world, which isn't likely, about all you're qualified to do is tend bar or become a barmaid, should you decide to get out. Or, you can take stock of your ambition versus risk in the proposition of this Association. I lay it before you as an option only because what you think exists here may not be for real. A dream of leisurely living your time out in this place, servicing some older men, and playing music may be pure fantasy . . . And that's risky." It was a point well taken by her girls.

"Listen very carefully," Maybelle instructed. "I'm going to tell you just enough to make a decision but not enough to compromise any strategic plans. Everyone here except Rabbit and Lulu is a product of the old time confidence game. At your age, it's unlikely you'd grasp the full impact of what it implies. Old time cons had a code, and they operated under it. The code declared that you can't cheat an honest man. This was not so much proof of a high-minded impulse as it was a result of wisdom and caution. If Ed and I ran a confidence game on any one of you, the con would be that you and I steal from Ed. Now, if Ed winds up with all of your money as a result of your cheating actions, you're not nearly as inclined to complain to the authorities. The con banks on greed usurping honesty. Of course, the fact that Ed and I are in cahoots is a conspiracy and qualifies as a felony. Also, with the present state of communications, practically every conspiracy is interstate in nature, which can bring the Feds into it."

Aligning other matters, Maybelle related, "A format for many scams is patterned around businesses. They can become legitimate and productive, depending upon the expertise of an entrepreneur who uses some misdirection to achieve his means. The Association's next venture is business oriented and is expected to take about three months. It is the stepping stone to an even larger, more extensive transaction, and one very lucrative in nature, which promises traveling abroad in luxury, with enormous wealth anticipated for its investors. Since none of you have had experience to perform in the technical capacity it requires, in no way will you be expected or allowed to take part in any of the business functions. You're invited by the Association to continue as employees of mine. Duties to perform involve those in which you've the most experience.

Proffering, she asked, "Sound good? Well, it very well can be! Initially, if you choose to make this business journey, the residence is presently here. Specific terms entail bed and board perks and an agreed upon salary for you to use, squander, or invest. The qualifying clause to the deal is, if the first projected venture flops, we'd have to split and go separate ways. Nothing ventured, nothing gained, they say. Should it succeed, your world evolves into another universe. The Association stands to become enormously wealthy. I guarantee compensation for your work efforts to be adjusted upward, accordingly, so that you're afforded ultracomfort in retirement."

She alluded, further. "There is no real foreseeable danger in the proposed enterprises. The oddity to advise against is that we may be spending months together on shipboard later. It'd be wise to consider leaving here right now for another type of life if you're fearful of storms at sea or know that you suffer from severe motion sickness. Don't ever make the mistake of subjecting everyone else to your misery." Her interest covering eventualities, tightened . . .

"I see some heads nodding in anticipation of better things to come. Wait! Please don't commit yourself yet! Before a decision is made, you need to recognize certain secrets are going to come unavoidably into your possession. A shared confidentiality would be highly dangerous and inexcusable. Even though there won't be blood oaths taken, no one can be permitted to leave until the Association dissolves business relations at the end of operations. This definitely is not a judgment to be made or taken lightly. Give some heavy thought to it. Life's a gamble. Remember too, you are chance takers. Every time you spread your legs, you've been at risk."

A low murmuring arose among the seven as Ed and Maybelle awaited their reactions. Finally, out of the huddle, Eva eased forward as spokesperson. "How much time do we have to make a decision?" she asked.

"About the same amount of time the others had," Maybelle censured. "The place for purchases of clothes has been changed from Little Rock to St. Louis, mainly because top quality, fake passports are more easily obtained. Others of the Association and I depart this afternoon. If you want out, there'll be a three thousand cash going away bonus for each, and we'll drop you off at the Springfield airport on our way. I'll expect an answer in forty-five minutes."

Ed and Maybelle stepped out on the veranda. Precisely thirty minutes later, Eva joined them. "We couldn't decide, so we tossed a coin. We're staying," she reported.

"You what?" snapped Maybelle, almost beside herself!

"Oh, come off it, Maybelle! We didn't really do that. You scared the livin' hell out of us with talk about not being able to leave alive. I was just trying to be flip about it. Really, in the end, it was quite easy. Something like that old movie. You made a proposition we couldn't afford to refuse. The comparison between a future as barmaids or an opportunity to retire in comfort left us no alternative, regardless of the odds."

Mollified, Maybelle sighed. "The last few days have been a strain. Why don't all of you gals go enjoy the weather and get used to your new home. Ed and I have tracks to make."

Ed rounded up all members, sending them into a session chaired by Maybelle at the podium. "What went down in Tulsa, for the most part, is unfortunate in that it was time consuming and nonproductive," she reviewed.

"Consequently, we can't afford to waste any more time. Although Dacus isn't here, it's a must for us to move on. He and I have talked by phone. He's aware we're pushing to finalize details. Considering what has happened in the past few days, I feel sure no one's had time, or inclination, to study the spec sheet on the next caper. Get into it as we travel. Hopefully, an in-depth analysis of your characterizations can be formalized before we return." The closely fixed subject evaporated with her next remarks.

"Another thing that's occurred to me is that each of us has an investment in the operation. Being very circumspect about everything that's done from here on is imperative to protect our interest and the future. For example, the place where we buy fake passports could be raided while we're actively acquiring them. It'd be disastrous. Thus, the idea is to get in and out of there one at a time in rapid succession. And by the way, you will be happy to learn the girls have decided to join us. If there's no further discussion, let's get packed. Rabbit promises sandwiches and cold drinks by departure time. When you're finished packing, begin loading up because it's about five hours drive time to St. Louis."

The meeting adjourned, and five minutes later Dacus walked in. Finding Maybelle making notes and putting materials together, he wanted to be apprised of where things were. "We've been trying to make up for lost time," Maybelle obliged. "In a little over an hour, we're planning to be on our way to St. Louis, instead of Little Rock, to get the clothes and passports. Rabbit and Lulu are included, unless you have an objection."

"No problem. It's a thing that can't be put off. And, the sooner the better," Dacus assured, updating her. "In its original form, the tale is too complex. On my trip to Memphis, I changed the mechanics, making details simpler. In order for it to work, however, at least one 'factory' must be located very near a five hundred thousand volt substation. While everyone's gone, I'm going to scout out suitable sites that will qualify. When you get back here, I should have a new outline drawn up. The previous fact sheet is obsolete, and you may as well toss it."

"I'll let the bunch in on it after we're on the road. Off the subject though, Dacus," Maybelle queried, "if you leave and we're gone, aren't you a little concerned about someone wandering in up here and causing trouble?"

"I'm glad you brought up that factor. It's mandatory to maintain our electrical supply. I'll erect a soft shell to accommodate the buildup of excess voltage. This won't interrupt transmission of electrical signals, and its only side effect is nausea for someone passing through the soft shell. Whoever returns first should try to reach me on my mobile. If I'm not available, here's a remote to temporarily kill the shell. Once removed, be prepared to make entry quickly. Also, be sure to restore it by clicking the remote again. The last thing we need are lightning bolts discharging on top of the mountain, encouraging the curious." Summing it up, Dacus concurred, "Guess that about covers most things for now. Better luck with the retailers than you had with wholesale politicians on the last trip. Be careful!"

The entire gang, minus Dacus, turned onto U.S. 65 at a quarter after one o'clock, headed for Missouri and St. Louis in particular. Dacus shaved and showered, dressing as a casually attired businessman. Taking Maybelle's Mercedes, he drove into Harrison, stopping at a semioccupied strip mall in the seedy section of town. His interest was focused on an abandoned building which had once housed a pawnshop. Heavy metal mesh still covered the windows and doors. 'A For Sale or Rent' sign, with phone number, was displayed on the door.

For appearance's sake, at a nearby service station, Dacus called the number. Ten minutes later, the landlord showed up jiggling a set of keys. An inspection of the building's interior met Dacus's expectations. He noted electricity was still on, and phone jacks for two separate numbers were in the inner office, which meant no downtime in obtaining service. An agreement secured a six months lease. After issuance of the check, using his Harrison identity of A. D. Mays he took possession of the place. Deposits with the utilities by A. D. Mays, completed the accouterments for his *store*, with the exception of setting in a computer to send and receive e-mail. Leaving the 'For Sale or Rent' sign hanging on the door, Dacus locked up and made his way back to the mountain.

Preparing for the new day, he dressed in khakis and equipped himself with a laptop computer and map depicting those territories assigned to private power companies and others earmarked for electric coops. He set a shell and left in the one-ton truck used in their casino caper.

His intent was the careful investigation of a corridor in eastern Arkansas lying roughly between the White and St. Francis rivers. According to the territorial map, there seemed barely enough industry in the larger towns and cities of the area to have justified construction of high-capacity electrical transmission lines. Within this grid, he hoped to develop a network of small towns receptive to any form of commercial activity.

The first night was spent in Batesville. Exploration began the next day. Oddly enough, he found the ideal spot to set up his central factory. It was located just outside the little town of Garlington at an abandoned limestone mining operation. High-tension lines passed right along the edge of its property, and a large substation loomed less than four hundred yards away.

Partaking at the largest cafe in Garlington, he acquired the name of its mayor, chatted with the locals, and proceeded to spread rumors of an industry possibly interested in establishing there. It was fertile ground. He decided to move on so the rumors could reseed themselves. Like Johnny Appleseed, he sowed as he went, circulating his current story for the rumor hungry and collecting names of mayors, plus relating opinions.

Dog tired after five days, he correlated thoughts as he headed home. Culling through some twenty odd communities, he had ten potential marks in the small incorporated towns of Ambrose, Cork, Garlington, Glendale, Mossy Banks, Norwood, Parsons, Sunnydale, Ulster, and Walters.

The gang, already in from St. Louis, had few tales to tell. Spotting Ed first, Dacus hailed inquiring, "How'd it go?"

"Smooth," Ed replied. "Only one glitch, and Maybelle handled it so quick it made my head swim. The little fart who owns the photo shop where passports were made in the back room tried to hijack us on the price. Maybelle, having already recognized him, was ready with a counter, parrying, 'well, well, if it isn't Benjamin Goettz, better known as Benny the Dip. You know there's still a warrant out on you in Bossier City? That's not the worst of it tho. Mon Kee is still looking to get his hands on you after what you did to him. I bet you'll die slow, and it'll be bad when he finds you. Forget me! I've got no debts to pay in Bossier City or to Mon Kee. My advice is don't screw me up on these passports, or else . . .' Her way of twisting the knife worked," he attested.

"I think you're getting sweet on her," ventured Dacus to make conversation.

"Dacus, I admit she fascinates me to distraction, but I wouldn't want her on terms of 'for better or worse'. I think it'd be hell on earth. What I'd like is to break through that pragmatic, steel rationality, and find her soft side. It has to be there," Ed rationalized.

"You've been bitten, all right," counseled Dacus. "If you can't see it, then to use your own words, you're lyin' to yourself. By the way, tell the bunch we'll review my revised version of 'The Tale' in a couple of hours. See you then."

Seemingly refreshed after a short nap, Dacus presented his partners with renewed vigor . . . "Each of us has had reservations about this second caper. Fortunately, Maybelle put her finger on the problem when she described to Ed the logistics of pulling off ten simultaneous scams. It wasn't feasible, and

I had to agree. Time to think on my Memphis trip and being in the field this past week caused me to revamp the entire mechanical process. Here's the plan in a nutshell," Dacus assorted, emitting an ever-so-slight roguishness.

"We're looking at a one-site operation, plus the variables nine other sites can give us. Here's how it'll work. Essentially, there has to be ten towns in the same power grid. They exist! I've selected and made a list of those that meet the standards. Situated exactly to our purpose is the little town of Garlington. It's in a totally isolated location, less than a quarter of a mile from a sub-station which can handle high voltages and amperages. I want it earmarked as the prime spot. Every bit of the electricity we need to pump for virtually thirty days can be done at this one location . . . Uncontested, and before it's time to collect, I might add."

Art surprised himself, asking aloud, "Dacus, if a one factory set-up is capable of receiving and registering all of the electricity we can generate for the payoff, what's the deal on these nine other towns being included in your plans?"

"Pure con, my man!" Dacus gestured with a salute. "For lack of a better term, call it misdirection. These town halls will feed an industrial blitz we promote by pretending to begin building factories. Their strategic location within the power supply grid I mentioned doubles the chances for success in pulling this one off without too many complications. When we get our hands on a cogeneration contract from the power company, it'll be applicable to all ten sites . . . And, we'll need every one of them to draw from when the Garlington meter is read after thirty days! So much generated electricity will have been pumped into the power company's lines and registered that it'll raise all sorts of red flags to a meter reader. At this stage of the game, the last thing we'd need would be a confrontation on the why without a counter. I've got a story already made up which can waylay any meter reader's apprehensions," Dacus confided.

"In selling the package," he continued, "answer all questions of the townspeople with logic and reasonableness. For instance, relate the company owning these plants is newly formed and privately held. Such a statement shuts down a record search on history, structure, financing, or a list of officers. It'll give license to tell what we want told. Volunteer that the Crown Alloys group has an interest to locate and develop sites for manufacture of a relatively common, very essential product, the name of which cannot be revealed at this time. Under a patented technological breakthrough, it's set to come into the marketplace at one-half the cost of its nearest competitor. Wisely, to avoid harassing court cases that it may cause, the patent has been secured under a separate name. As a hedge against industrial spying and sabotage, you could disclose the company conceives all ten factories to be equipped and capable of completing the manufacturing process. However, in actual practice of producing a finished product, they intend to assign only partial steps of the process, one per factory, for security reasons." Capsuled precisely, he sought to renew.

"That, good people, becomes 'chew and spit' talkin' fodder. The hook is baited when genuine bank accounts are opened, under the name of Crown Alloys, in every town. These accounts can serve to pay modest expenses and be a source for escrow funds to cover short-term leases. We'll constantly emphasize secrecy as a buffer against the competition to protect our patent pending. In reality, we're shielding against too many inquiries while biding time."

Dacus presented his coup. "Believe me, if Crown Alloys is awarded a cogeneration contract, the hard part is over. The conglomerate's hasty and untested downsizing of industry puts us online instantly. To our advantage, their computers are programmed to spit out the money directly to a customer based solely on what a meter reader logs."

After a flurry of exchanged comments, Ed confirmed, "It's finally come into perspective. You've got all the wrinkles ironed out!"

Disregarding the logic, Harry needled, "What if all ten towns don't go along? That'll put the 'quietus' to our latest plan for one to defect, won't it, Dacus?"

The negative vibes on heels of progress brought Maybelle out of her chair. "If they don't go along, Harry, then you and the rest of us have failed miserably in our responsibility. After all, we are pros." Backing off, knowing she'd overreacted, Maybelle threw in, "If you can't get more positive, I might get so damned confused I'd skip you on the nightly rotation."

"I'll take care of his share of the sex," intoned Sam, the deep voice dropping a notch or two lower, endeared by the prospects.

"The hell you will!" cried Harry indignantly.

Art stood up, accosting, "Cut the bullshit. I believe Harry's trying to contribute something. If anything happens, we simply have to come up with plan B. What's so different in individual obligations here than from any other scam we've ever pulled off?" Undone, he sat down.

Impatient from tedious thoughts, Tom moved to adjourn. He suggested a card game to Vivian if they could find a couple of girls. Dacus handed out marked maps of the area and a list of the towns to those leaving the room.

Thoughts still racing, Dacus detained Ed and Maybelle. "Let's visit a moment on another matter. My role is to be nothing but a workman on the job. I never intend to be seen in anything other than khaki clothes. The rest of you will be fronting operations. When the time comes to pump electricity, I'll be present. You can count on it!" Dacus assured and reflected . . .

"That aside, probably the greatest asset we'll have is being able to leave the country as fast as possible. Plans are in the mill on this matter, which will take me away for a few days at a time. When it comes down to it, it may take more than a time or two to set all the wheels in motion. Along these same lines, Maybelle, when that nice check from the utility is received and deposited in Crown Alloys account, it's your baby. You're responsible for shuttling it down to the Cayman Islands. That means flying down fairly soon to mule in ninety-five hundred dollars and open an account for Crown Alloys. Remember too, you have to begin spending a certain amount of time exercising bank transfers to build a solid history. In the meantime, I'm absolutely sure of your competence and must rely upon the two of you to organize and direct the 'in-town' groundwork. Keep in mind later on, these plants must reflect beginning activities."

Maybelle winked at Ed. "That's easy enough. Guys traditionally handle taking directions better from a man. I'll devote my energies to window-dressing bank accounts."

Ed agreed, "Maybelle and I can work together. Go ahead and do what you've got to do lining out the next phase, Dacus."

CHAPTER 16

Weather in the South is generally unpredictable due to proximity of the Gulf. In fact, it's been said, "If you don't like the weather, stick around for a while. It'll change." Moreover, there's one thing about southern weather that's absolutely predictable. At some time in late August, a cool norther will blow in for a couple of days, reminding everyone that the fall season is on its way.

Around 8:00 a.m., Dacus pulled up to his new office in Harrison, lugging two computers and a space heater to go in its inner office. For the next few hours, he busied himself testing the modems, sending e-mail back and forth through one telephone number and then the other.

Satisfied both computers were capable of receiving and sending e-mail, he locked the office and drove up U.S. 65 to Springfield. Accessing that city's UPS processing center before closing time was no easy task. The enormous amount of traffic in and around Branson made it nearly prohibitive. It would have been faster to find an outlet in a Harrison business, but they wanted too much ID. Exhausted on return to the mountain by early evening, Dacus drank a glass of milk and quietly found his way to the bed.

The delivery of another package to the Zallafino Estate caused a mild sensation. To be on the safe side, Marc called out the bomb squad again. He contacted Gitano and Gilberto to remain in town until notified otherwise.

Unidentifiable by bar code tape, the package contained only a single message. Marc sent immediately for his brothers. He stared off into space as he waited, deliberating the contents of the note, "I have an honorable business proposal. Reply via e-mail to mountain@aol.com." It was signed by the pseudonym Mountain Man.

Marc handed the note to his brothers when they arrived and turned away so they could not read his face, intent on making a point. "Give me your opinions on this latest." He tossed over his shoulder, going over to sit down behind the desk.

"Do you think this is the same individual who sent the ears?" Gitano asked, taking on a reserved interest.

Marc spun around. His eyes were flat and without any sign of expression. "It's highly unacceptable you'd ask a question in response to a directive. I do not answer questions, I ask them. I've asked for input. Someday, one of you'll have to take my place as a Don. Who'll answer your question then? My decisions may not necessarily agree with what you believe to be true, but you'll learn and grow in experience from practice in analyzing a situation for yourself." Qualifying, he explained, "Gitano, you had an opinion but presented it wrongly. The merit for thinking existed. Now, do you agree or disagree that whoever sent the ears also sent this note?"

Gitano turned to Gilberto, who nodded to affirm. "Marc," he firmly professed, "we agree. There's a similarity in style and probably more to it than is disclosed."

"Can we also agree," Marc prodded, "that he, she, or it probably has another motive in retaining our attention because of something we have that's wanted?"

"It makes good sense to us," Gitano stanchly conveyed their accord.

Eyeing Gilberto, Marc stimulated, "Little brother, you must step up and take part in these discussions. It's not sufficient for you to glance and nod at your brother and to let him be your spokesman. Tell me, do you think this individual is potentially dangerous?"

"Hell yes, I think he's dangerous," lambasted Gilberto. "And notice I said, he! If he could talk, I betcha' old man Lipscomb would say the same."

Marc looked to Gitano, who concurred. "Yeah, he could be dangerous, even lethal, but I don't get the feelin' he'd be a threat to us. He's smart. Real smart! It might be beneficial to deal with him or to at least find out where he's coming from."

"Suppose we ignore him. Would that be a wise move?" Marc pressed for their interaction.

In unison, "It would not be advisable, any one-word way, shape, or form!" erupted from the younger brothers, questioning. "Why should we deny him access?"

"I've heard enough," stated Marc, pleased with their input. "Cool it and listen to me on what we're going to do. Use the office space in the old bayou warehouse that's got telephone access and move in one of those shelved 486s. Test the modem by e-mailing a note back to one of our other offices followed by an answer back to make sure everything's in working order. By the time you've finished, I'll have us a message prepared for Mountain Man."

Acting quickly, and with direction, Gitano and Gilberto sped away in separate vehicles to the downtown offices. They claimed a 486 clone with all the necessary accessories and put it in Gilberto's Montero LS 4x4 for destination on to the bayou. Anticipating a time lapse before the equipment would be in operation, Gilberto drove to the nearest quick stop for a cheap cooler, beer, ice, and snacks. He'd be prepared if a long wait occurred later on out there.

Marc grew impatient. The message, containing specific contents and instructions, was ready to transmit. Almost another hour went by before he received a call from the offices in town that the setup had been completed and was operational. He hurriedly faxed information to Gitano, who forwarded the e-mail content on to Gilberto. It's address cited, mountain@aol.com, and stated for transmit, "Interested. More details required. Respond. Olivebranch@aol.com."

Surprisingly, the brothers received a reply the next day conveying, "Will come to New Orleans at your convenience. A proposal to discuss. Must speak directly with Donald."

"Who the duce is Donald?" Gilberto asked, not computing its significance.

Indignant, Marc raised his hands in exasperation. "Wake up, little brother. He wants to speak to me, Don of the Zallafino Family."

Dacus came through the arrival gate at New Orleans International Airport, where he was promptly met by two trim, intelligent, and immaculately dressed men in expensive business suits. Spotting the manila envelope sticking conspicuously out of his pocket depicting a mountainous region, one of the men inquired, "Pardon me, sir. Are you Mountain Man?"

Nodding affirmatively, Dacus obliged and indicated the briefcase as his luggage. He was chauffeured to a small, very private chateau in the French Quarter between Bourbon and Royal streets. There a suite, facing an inner courtyard, was waiting for him. Addressing him for the first time since they left the airport, the spokesman advanced, "You will either be contacted in person very soon or through the phone in your room. If you need anything, room service is excellent and at your disposal. Have a good day, sir."

Maybe an hour went by before a knock at his door sounded. "Come in," Dacus called out. "It's not locked." He arrived to open it as the knob turned.

A short portly, semibald older man entered. The wisps of hair on his large head were neatly plastered down. A protruding lower jaw, plus huge hands, indicated a pituitary dysfunction at some time in life after long bones had fused. True to his physical condition, he spoke in a deep, booming voice. "I'm Gulliver Norton. I represent Mr. Zallafino as one of his attorneys. I am here at his request to learn the nature of your business proposition."

Dacus, poised on the balls of his feet, stood facing the older man who appeared to be in his seventies. "Mr. Norton," he invited, "would you be kind enough to place your briefcase in the bathroom and close the door?" Dacus further adhered, "When you have done that, you and I are going to strip-search each other for a wire. If you're not willing to cooperate, may I suggest you leave, now. Mr. Zallafino and I obviously share the same concerns about a government shill in the midst when conducting business."

Shrugging, Norton took his briefcase to the bathroom and returned. Dacus had laid out his opened briefcase on the bed for inspection. "Mind going through these first, sir?" he asked, before contributing. "You are fully aware I was met at the airport by two of your men, and I know they've reported my every possession in detail. Feel free to go through all drawers and closets in the room. I already have. We'll search each other when you're finished."

Norton made a thorough inspection of the suite, including the attaché case. Without a word, yet holding eye contact with Dacus, he began removing his coat, placing it on the couch. Dacus followed suit, handing his coat over as he reached for Norton's, going through the pockets and feeling of its lining for any abnormalities.

The strip search proceeded warily until they dropped their pants. It struck each one, simultaneously . . . They both were wearing jockey shorts, a rarity in men of their age. As Dacus turned to toss his trousers on the couch, Norton remarked, affected by the situation's humor, "Hmmm, nice buns, but don't expect me to call you darlin'."

"Thanks," Dacus grunted, then snickered. Norton laughed. Connecting, Dacus brought the contagion of laughter to a crescendo as both men collapsed, heaving, on the couch.

Dacus was first to regain composure enough to confide. "I feel better about you, Mister. A sense of humor and sabotage don't go hand in hand."

"I have to agree," joined Norton, putting his pants on.

Slipping into his coat, Dacus conveyed, "I have a message for Mr. Zallafino, but let's get acquainted and order something to drink." Deciding upon keeping the Harrison identity intact, he introduced himself. "My name is A. D. Mays."

Norton reflected a moment before responding, "No one calls me Gulliver. I don't know where in hell my folks got that one. I don't dislike the name but it's awkward and I only use it when I'm introducing myself to a stranger. Friends call me G. W., for Gulliver William. Please call me G. W., and let's not laugh any more. My belly's too sore."

Perrier water and a twist of lime in hand, they seated themselves at a small table looking onto the lush courtyard. "I'm not about to allege, G. W., that I've never done anything illegal," Dacus opened. "I can boast of never having been charged with so much as a traffic violation. My associates can make the same claim. The one exception is my only employee, whom I suspect has already been identified." The latter statement well confirmed his identity.

"My proposal to Mr. Zallafino," Dacus imparted, "is both honorable and legitimate. It has nothing, whatsoever, to do with any activity of 'operating' privileges in his territory. Rather, the proposition involves safe passage through his domain for certain bulky machinery items, legitimately mine, to a destination for later discussion. The journey entails fixed and stated services, and possibly goods that I purchase. The transaction won't require paper and ink for legal documentation. Therefore, the service of an attorney is redundant. I would not object to your presence when it's discussed. The deal itself hinges entirely on personal, perceivable eye-to-eye communication to seal the contract. Tell him that I am a reasonable man."

Norton rose and reclaimed his hat. "I have no idea what Mr. Zallafino thinks, or what his response will be. For the record, though, you're not at all what I expected, Mr. Mays."

Shaking his hand, Dacus reminded, "Don't forget your briefcase in the bathroom. Thanks, G. W., it's been by my pleasure to meet you."

Less than two hours later, the phone rang in Dacus's suite. "Mr. Zallafino requests your company for dinner tonight, sir," a refined voice invited. "If suitable to your convenience, the car will pick you up at five thirty this afternoon."

Not surprisingly, the same two who had met him in the airport arrived on the exact hour designated. They further informed him he had been checked out of the chateau and to bring along personal items. He would be an overnight guest at the Zallafino Estate.

The trip from deep in the French Quarter to the southern edges of New Orleans went swiftly. There was no input from his taciturn companions. The countryside subtly changed by the mile. A lone, Lafitte sign tipped him they had entered the bayou backcountry, haunted by the spirit of Jean Lafitte, pirate, smuggler, and bon vivant of this country's early days. They sped along over countless bridges. The roadways and banks were lined with massive trees, draped in Spanish moss, whose limbs extended to form arches across them. Dacus speculated, "Are these bayous?"

The answer came without expression or elaboration, "Down here they call 'em 'by-uus'."

Shortly, the driver took a right fork, off of the main road, passing through a grove of huge pecan trees. Set deep in the woods, an electric gate connected to untold amounts of fencing was opened and closed by remote. A couple of miles further, they pulled up to the enormous Zallafino estate main gate, complete with guard station and two uniformed guards. One of them stuck his head through the window on the driver's side, and the driver pointed to Dacus in the backseat. "We have a guest of the Don's for this evening." The guard looked at him and Dacus met the coldest set of eyes he'd ever encountered.

From the guard post to the main residence was probably another quarter of a mile. It was one of those antebellum mansions that dot the landscape of Louisiana and Mississippi. The wide driveway curved in a sweeping circle, touching the great steps going up to a columnar veranda. At the precise instant the car stopped in front, thick, heavily carved doors swung outwardly, revealing a neatly suited, grey-haired butler. He glided down the steps, opened the car's back door, saluting, "Welcome to the Zallafino Estate, Mr. Mays."

The mansion was traditional with two curving staircases leading from both sides of the foyer to the second floor. Dacus was ushered into a large room on the right, which in its heyday would've been deemed the parlor. Modernized, it had become an entertainment area, including an impressive, completely outfitted, ornate bar.

"Sir, can I make you a drink before I takes your luggage up to your room? Mr. Zallafino will be down, directly," offered the butler.

"Not just yet, thank you," Dacus exchanged, declining a drink.

The dark complexioned man striding into the room in a white linen suit appeared to be equivalent in height with Dacus, a fact noted by both parties. Dacus mused, *At least we won't be bothered by one-upmanship.*

"May I call you Antonio?" Dacus asked with a handshake.

"Marc is preferred," replied Zallafino, adjoining. "I see you don't have a drink. What is your preference, assuming you're a drinking man?"

"Do you have a pale dry sherry?" Dacus ordered, squaring the variable.

Accepted, Marc poured a glass of sherry for his guest and scotch for himself. "A. D., if I may call you that, shall we get certain basics behind us before my brothers show up for dinner? Let us not recount things I already know," he suggested. Highly curious of intent for the visit, he exposed. "For example, I have bothered to learn that you and your group are running a confidence racket. Recently you knocked off a Mississippi casino under control of a mob leader. Is your purpose here to launder money?"

"No. The money has been attended to, and it has nothing to do with Mr. Lipscomb. Rather, it is that groundwork has just been completed to implement an extensive endeavor. It should culminate within two months. On or before that time, it'll be imperative to quickly and quietly arrange for some machinery to be moved down into the Caribbean. It's not contraband. The equipment legitimately belongs to me. The motive in contacting you is dictated by your proximity to the sea and, of course, by your reputation for discretion. My proposal is to secure your services if the job can be expedited. Further," Dacus inserted, "as a favor, I would appreciate any advice you may offer regarding the purchase of a small ship large enough to contain my machinery and a crew of about twenty-five."

There was a long pause. Marc lighted a Havana cigar before reflecting on a proposition he'd least expected. "You're naive, A. D." Marc hedged for time. "You've bought the Hollywood version of us. True, we are secretive, you don't have access, and undoubtedly, you're thinking we dominate the coastline. We don't! It happens to be the drug trade's domain . . . Not even the U.S. government can claim that title. Drug traffic is far bigger than we are, and it's out of control. I pulled the Family out after the death of our father, who had come to hate it passionately, although he dealt in it. He'd transferred Gitano from a fine scholastic university where drugs were being promoted and sanctified by the intellectual nabobs teaching there. Both brothers, whom you'll meet later, graduated from church colleges."

Unleashed, Marc continued. "Certain Senators and Congressmen gave 'organized crime' a bad name years ago. I admit 'organized crime' is worse than no crime, which is impossible. But it's infinitely better than disorganized crime resulting from the unabated drug trade. We seem to have forgotten how the British kept a foot on China's neck for decades by promoting opium trade among its people." Dacus indulged Marc's seemingly unrelated declarations.

"Much as I despise communism, I'll take my hat off to the Chinese for disposing of their problem. Do you know how they did it, A. D.? They didn't just execute the dealers. They lined up all the drug users and shot them, too. It wiped out the market! Of course, we can't consider such drastic measures in this country. But our 'patty-cake, patty-cake' court system is ineffective to make a dent in it. It's purely foolish, even absurd, to think that drug education is the solution when its use is condoned, publicized, and subscribed to by the educational system itself."

Having absorbed Dacus's proposal, Marc reconciled, "Let me get off these damnable irritants. I'm sorry to have burdened you, but I must deal with it every day while at the same time guarding against some federal prosecutor making a political career off my ass. The bottom line is, you've asked for the impossible. No one, except a government entity, can guarantee safe passage to the Caribbean for you, your people, or your equipment."

A redirection of thoughts became apparent as Marc tended the bar, pouring Dacus another sherry, and relit his cigar. "If you're in the market for a small ship, I happen to have one. Not to bore you with history, my first wife died in childbirth. The second wife was quite expensively demanding. For her, I retrofitted a small vessel into a pleasure yacht. It's a hundred ninety feet by sixty feet in the beam. The superstructure houses guest quarters and entertainment facilities, leaving enormous cargo space in the hold. We had a zillion parties, cruised the Caribbean, but I had to equip and staff a small gunship to accompany us for protection. The cost was astronomical. When I beached the yacht, she filed for divorce and hauled off another bundle. I've decided pussy's cheaper by the piece than it is wholesale." His dark eyes were snapping at recall of the lush blonde.

"I've been restoring the old doll to mint condition, and I'm prepared to take a sizable loss and sell her to the first one coming up with two million. If it's in your league, I'll show her to you in the morning. Part of the deal is, you're on your own as soon as you leave my dock."

"There's two hours of daylight left," Dacus surmised, suppressing excitement. "If it won't interfere with dinner, perhaps we can go look at her now."

"Why not?" Marc consented, picking up on Dacus's enthusiasm. "Dinner can wait!"

They got in Marc's SUV and drove toward the dock, having to stop and unlock the cattle gates a number of times. Finally, they came upon a grove of ancient oaks, canopying a vast territory in their shade. Positioned on chocks in a deep, dry ditch rested the yacht. A mammoth, mechanical floodgate held back brackish water from the bay. Boarding the ship was by catwalk from the ditch's edge to the deck, but Dacus clambered down the side to examine the considerable keel. Getting Marc's attention above, he shouted, "Were you able to dock this baby throughout the Caribbean, or did you have to stand out in the bay?"

"We docked her anywhere we wanted," Marc recounted. "Most large cruise ships can be accommodated at all major islands now. However, if you travel to some of the more lightly populated islands, you may encounter problems. Nautically, five fathoms of water floats her."

Dacus found a rope ladder close to the fantail. After examining the twin screws, he climbed up to rejoin Marc on deck. They proceeded first to the wheelhouse, and then descended into the 'hold' where he examined the twin diesels which drove the screws. Dacus silently noted the amount of room in and around the complex transmission that enabled the helmsman to reverse one or both screws under the command, reverse engines. Leaving the engine room, the two boarded a lift and rose to the main deck. Continuing his appraisal, Dacus inquired, "Do you happen to know if this vessel was ever rigged as a sailing ship?"

"Yes, she surely was by one eccentric owner," Marc revealed, surprised he'd been so observant. "What cued you?"

"I noticed the wall, serving no apparent useful purpose, rising up from the bottom of the hold," Dacus divulged. "I believe it contains an extra keel that can be lowered in rough weather for greater stability, and thought I'd ask."

Marc, mentally thrown off balance by Dacus's knowledge, stared after him. Completing the tour, they entered the elegant mahogany-lined guest quarters and entertainment salon with stunning teak paneling, where neither commented. On the ride back in to the mansion, Dacus eased Marc's perplexity. "I can use the vessel. How much trouble would it be to get the specs on her? I'll need weight and space to compute capacity for my cargo," he explained.

They arrived at the mansion, still visiting. Dacus excused himself and was directed to his quarters on the second floor. The suite was simple, yet impeccably furnished in an antique style that would fetch a fortune. Dressing for dinner, he could barely control his elation. *This setup is perfect,* he thought. *My trucks can come in here and unload in absolute privacy. I can even test my equipment before we leave the dock. As for protection, I won't be needin' any.* Putting on a fresh shirt, his tie and coat, he sedately descended the stairs, suppressing a desire to straddle and ride the banister to the bottom.

Marc, Gitano, and Gilberto were waiting for him at the bar. Marc aptly handled informal introductions. He'd already briefed the brothers and included Mr. Mays was interested in his yacht. It made for benign small talk over a couple of cocktails before retiring to the dining room, where hearty, dry red wine and the aroma of Sicilian fare waited. Well coached in dining etiquette, the brothers kept their conversation light. Under Marc's guidance, over strong coffee and liqueurs, the meeting turned inquisitorial. Pointedly, he submitted, "A. D., how did Lipscomb die?"

"By his own hand." Dacus's reply was blunt, intended not to be pursued.

Ignoring it, Marc decreed. "Look! You sent the glasses, the teeth, and the ears. I must presume you sent them to introduce yourself because somehow you knew there was bad blood between Lipscomb and the Family. Why the coy bit, now? It don't hunt in my society!"

Dacus pushed his chair back to stand, addressing all three intently. "It was you who had known differences with Lipscomb, and rightly so. Since his disappearance, it is you authorities have been looking at—not me! Frankly, I don't believe law enforcement can ever get enough leads to pursue an investigation. But should they, you're still a prime suspect. Putting yourselves, or having someone put you in a position whereby you couldn't pass a lie detector test, wouldn't be advisable," he admonished, having cited the facts.

"All I intend to say regarding the subject is that he died by his own hand, and so did his men. They witnessed an illusion, assuming they were firing at a target other than themselves, is all I know. Short small men, such as Lipscomb, are suckers to their ego, easily deceived, mainly because of hatred toward mankind. I believe it is referred to as the Napoleon Complex. The fact remains, any more discussion would serve nothing but idle interest in nefarious details. Gentlemen," Dacus implored, "let me offer a toast to my hosts for delightful dining and good companionship. It's already past my bedtime. Can we call it a wrap for the evening?"

Rising from the table, Marc succumbed to having the last word, paying tribute. "You sure you're not Sicilian?"

"Truth be known, I'm not sure what I am, ethnically," detained, Dacus reflected. "I was adopted by the Mays family, who were in the rackets. Their game was to launder money for the so-called Dixie Mafia out of a small bait shop in Irving, Texas, during the late fifties. Their main pursuit in life was the old time con. That's how I learned. Sometimes I wonder what my genetic base is," he pondered for their benefit, mounting the stairs.

Amid goodnight wishes, the Zallafino brothers were gratified to have some answers and less mystery. However, one thread was dominant as Marc drifted into sleep. *Mr. Mays is much too complex a person to unravel tonight.*

At the crack of dawn, Dacus stepped out on the private balcony, raised both arms, and breathed in great gulps of the fresh, slightly salty morning air. The view was compelling. He dressed and started making a leisurely tour of the grounds. Abruptly, a guard appeared at his side. "I'm sorry, sir. You're not allowed to wander the grounds unaccompanied. Why don't you wait until the Don is up?" Thanking him, Dacus went in search of the kitchen, where a cook served coffee and offered to make him breakfast.

Marc came down the stairs at eight o'clock sharp to strong coffee, juice, and sweet rolls. Finishing the morning ritual, he looked up Dacus who was on the veranda with coffee and newspaper. "What's your pleasure, A. D.?" he greeted. "I am free and at your disposal."

"This gunship you mentioned, Marc, raised my curiosity. Any reason why we couldn't take a look at this vessel sometime today?" Dacus proposed.

The same tracks they'd taken the afternoon before were followed. Without turning in, they passed by where the yacht sat in drydock to a larger dock, extending into the bay. In its own stall rode an impressive catamaran, twenty by sixty feet long. Proudly, Marc interposed, "There's so much firepower aboard this baby that the long gun would turn the hull over if you fired it broadside. You'll notice also that nearly everything of weight is above deck."

Dacus went aboard, making a careful inspection. "What's her top speed?" he asked while prospects of acquiring it accumulated.

"I'll have to find that one out," Marc half apologized, again registering Dacus's shrewdness.

"I'm interested in this boat as well. The long gun would be extraneous," Dacus rejected its value, verbalizing only partial thoughts.

"Oh, but you'll need the long gun!" Marc vindicated. "Believe me!" he defended, ardently.

Inadvertently Dacus spat out, "I don't need, or want your long gun!" It ended the subject. Marc withdrew, once more struck by the man's peculiarities.

Sitting on the veranda afterward, Dacus expounded, "I like and am comfortable with what I've seen here, Marc. I'm very satisfied with the yacht's price, and the gunship has my attention. Although the long gun would stand to compromise our mission, you need assurance on my intent." He had arbitrarily assessed without contributing specifics on the long gun.

"Intentionally," Dacus allowed, "my people and I are not betting on the 'come'. Our endeavor is well conceived. Only the most unexpected, and unplanned-for set of events, could derail it. In other words, the scam would be forfeited early enough in the game that you wouldn't be left holding the bag. The closer we come to blowing off the mark, the more certain success can be measured. To sum it up, I must ask to be notified if you get an offer on the vessels prior to completion of our implemented efforts, which are promising."

Proceeding, he rendered the unexpected. "Another detail involves method of payment to be considered. I am sure you don't want to sell assets for money that must be laundered. It will not be the case. For the record, neither you nor I need any traceable threads that lead to either of us. With that in mind, I'd prefer payment be issued from a Cayman Islands account. If it's not satisfactory, then I'll arrange a bank transfer from another account before monies leave the States."

Marc contemplated long, finally disclosing, "The yacht can be sold tomorrow if I'd finance its purchaser. That's not my way of doing business. I'd have to say the chances of it being made available to you for the next sixty days are nearly 100 percent. I'll push on the crew to speed up repairs, making sure that it's seaworthy and completely renovated as quickly as possible. Having established terms, and based on conditions, I know you're anxious to return to your place, wherever that is. My men can deliver you to the airport, at your instance."

Dacus departed the estate at eleven o'clock to make a flight out. Marc sought the solitude of his tree-shaded gardens the moment he was gone. He walked and walked aimlessly, well past lunchtime and until his brothers' yelling brought him back to reality. Still preoccupied, he strode into the mansion and found them at the bar.

By early afternoon, Gitano and Gilberto, too distracted to function in the offices, had put communications on call forwarding and driven to the mansion. The butler didn't have a chance. They came bursting through the door, yelling for Marc to meet them at the bar. Their voices carried through an open window, amplified as if through a bullhorn.

Marc poured himself a scotch mist. He sipped slowly, all the time trying to absorb the guys' rehash while regaining his composure. Gilberto was showing no qualms in airing his opinions of the past twenty-four hours. "I don't buy the cock and bull about an illusion causing old man Lipscomb to shoot himself. It's a helluva story. Just as strongly, for some strange reason I'm havin' trouble that Mr. Mays didn't tell it like it was. He was different in a rather disconcerting manner. I bet his suit wasn't tailor-made, yet that's the problem. On him, it could have been . . ."

On a roll, he hyped, "Did you take in his universal accent? He could have been from anywhere. The 'mountain man' bit sounds like Colorado, or suppose it's a shill for flatlands. Fact is, I suspect he's a transplanted Okie or Arkie in from California."

"Okay, okay, time out, Gilberto. You're rambling now," said Gitano, trying to intimidate.

"Oh yeah, you just can't wait to put your two cents worth in. I got a whole lot more to say about our mystery man. Is it age before my good looks, bigger brother?" Gilberto agitated.

"Cool back. Pop another top and listen," Gitano insisted. "I'm interested in knowing how the man knew we had any previous dealings with Lipscomb, let alone the bad blood existing between us. Surely, he's not professionally in the rackets or our Internet would have picked up sooner on anyone with as much clout. Talk about an obscurity!" Imbued with the subject, he flirted for answers.

"The total of Mr. Mays's demeanor last night was fluid, exemplary, unaffected, solid, unpretentious, and on and on. The unusual was a vast intelligence literally oozing from the man. He didn't seem to lack for a single quality or how to use them all. I was impressed, but I happen to have a lot of untouchable reservations." Gitano checked himself. "Where are you, Marc? Tell us what went down this morning before he left."

Marc had gathered his wits during the back and forth rhetoric. "About eleven o'clock," he enlightened, "our guest got off. In that short three hours' time, he managed to cause a little more intrigue. I've spent the last couple or so hours trying to determine the whys and the wherefores. To be honest, I haven't made much headway. First, A. D. asked to see the gunboat. He went over it with a fine-tooth comb, wanting to know size, firepower, speed, the works, you know? Then he informed me, in no uncertain terms, he'd have no part of the long gun. After we came back here, he expressed his pleasure and satisfaction with what he had seen, only to begin laying out terms and conditions for the merchandise, method of payment, when, where, and which banks would be preferable. He covered it all, and I was left without one demand or opposition to make."

Surprisingly Marc conceded, "Your curiosity confirms my every conclusion. This has been an unusual encounter, and our guest is not an ordinary man. He is very powerful in a way I don't understand. He is totally self-assured. He comes across as absolutely truthful. He doesn't appear to need subterfuge. He is not venal nor does he seem to be vindictive, which Lipscomb surely was. In short, I'm convinced he's a straight arrow, accountable to his own word, but dangerous as a bolt of lightning in a summer thunderstorm to anyone foolish enough to stand under a tree."

Marc had no idea how truly he had spoken. As soon as he left for the 'john', Gilberto had to emphasize his apprehension to Gitano one more time. "I don't feel the least bit good about this. He has proselytized Marc like a flute player charms a snake."

Gitano was uneasy but not diverted. His instincts told him the man didn't pose a threat, unless threatened. He sensed that it could be one's undoing. "I tell you what, Gilberto, let's remain quiet, stay on the defensive, and keep our eyes wide open."

CHAPTER 17

Arkansas has always been a politically minded state. In its rich history, the fine art of rumor spreading was raised to its zenith. Unfettered by the burden of truth, they flowed to the State Capitol in Little Rock thru a filter of embellishment and innuendo at the Marion Hotel, the favorite watering hole of politicians, statewide. The potent mix of lounge lizards, con men, and politicians sucked up rumors like a sponge and spit them back out to the far corners of the state. Some daytime older residents of the hotel developed the art further by originating rumors to see how long it took them to travel to Texarkana, Blytheville, Fort Smith, Lake Village, and return. It never once involved over three days.

When city fathers brought down the Marion to make way for an ill-advised convention center, after the downtown was already dead, rumors lost their focal point. But Arkansas has never lost her taste for rumination on scandals, especially when they are garnished with prurient, or at least, malodorous details.

Now, the likes travel directly to the State Capitol, where they're processed and sent back to the state at large. Thus, it was . . . Rumors flooded the entire capital city about a big new company wanting to open factories in ten east Arkansas towns. Both the Arkansas Industrial Development Commission and the governor's office had been contacted by the company previously, but mills of the gods were grinding too slowly.

A siege of speculation and hope was fueled by senators and representatives from the regions where a company had solicited local sponsorship for its new industry. Senator 'Buster' Eades, whose district included both Garlington and Parsons, was particularly adamant in seeking aid from both offices. He refreshed the governor and his staff on their perilous status of just some of the administration's pet legislation in the upcoming session. Joined by two senators and ten representatives, whom he prodded with trades, Buster promoted the ante to a level whereby the administration had to exert pressure on the energy conglomerate in control to expedite issuance of a cogeneration contract with the company.

The government doesn't have a monopoly on bureaucracy. The negation of antitrust legislation by a corrupt Congress foisted an endless series of mergers, creating conglomerates, resulting in displacement and distress of sizable segments of the working population. It confronted the public with an unreachable, centralized system operated by computers and recorded voice messages. Naturally, any pressure from a state administration flowed like molasses through this virtually impenetrable morass of minimum responsibility within the utility holding company.

Complaints by foot-dragging politicians were not lost on Dacus's organization. The same was true of lesser public officials in the designated towns. Through Ed's contacts, he'd determined that even they hadn't sufficient pull among them to unseat a baulking jackass. Maybelle, for one, said to herself, *I knew it had to happen this way. Get ready, kid.*

Truth be, H. Thornton Joyce had led a sheltered life. His father, Harold but never Harry Joyce, and his mother, Boodie Quinton Joyce, saw to it. As they say in Oklahoma and Texas, Harold was "rich as a foot up a bull's ass" from oil and cattle, having also bagged a small empire in investments. Socially trendy, and per the status, their dominancy paralleled in public affairs.

Thornton, educated in private schools from the very beginning to protect him from influence of the 'hoi polloi', returned home to Tulsa. Groomed to become a banker in the finest schools up East, it would not be his destined career. With huge investments in the now world of proliferous conglomerates, his father placed him in electric utilities. Thornton quickly was assigned away from Tulsa by the corporate headquarters in Dallas to work his way up the ladder. Progress had been steady and sure with his father's backing. He had more than a little control over affairs of his utility companies. Yet, being aware he hadn't achieved the goal of his father, he feared corporate knives if Harold should die. Consequently, he pussyfooted on decision making.

Since puberty, the level of his testosterone posed a threat, better described as a menace, to him. He just couldn't keep it in his pants. Crossing over to the hoi polloi and satisfying his needs in cathouses became common occurrence. A golfing buddy, who happened to be a doctor, would fix him up with a shot of penicillin, right before or after exposure, even though he always wore a rubber to satisfy his protection obsession. Obsessive concerns, such as his, didn't weigh too heavily on chances of contacting another virus nor did it dampen his insatiable drive.

A 'momma's boy', he made regular trips to Tulsa to see Boodie and Harold, unaccompanied by the kids and wife, who couldn't stand his mother. On one of the trips, an old chum introduced him to the delights of Maybelle's place out in the county. Thereafter, trips home became all the more frequent, and he acquired 'house' nicknames of Horny Thorny and Juicy Joyce.

The secretary, sensitive to detecting the nature of most or frequent incoming calls to Mr. Joyce, touched the hold button. She used her speaker to ask if he was available to a Maybelle Barton.

"Yes, put her through," Thornton, stunned she'd have the audacity, authorized the call. He answered the hello politely guarded. "How are you, Mrs. Barton? What can I do for you?"

"Thornton, I have to fly into Dallas on another matter, but I need to see you on a business subject of utmost importance," Maybelle baited. "When are you free to meet for a conference with me day after tomorrow?"

Reluctant, unable to decline offhandedly, he was curt. The early lunch hour he set didn't affect her. "Fine," said Maybelle. "I'll meet you in the Airport Hilton dining room," and hung up. She kissed the cell phone, dropped it in her patio lounge pocket, and ran into Rabbit on the way inside. They kibitzed mostly about his and Lulu's antics together before she made herself scarce.

Maybelle put into action a devious and dangerous plan. Her thoughts were on fast forward to anticipate every scenario and execute it in the short time frame allowed. She coaxed Sam into a ride to the Springfield airport, where she pretended to board a plane. Instead, after he left, she rented a car and drove to the Dallas Fort Worth International Airport. By late evening, reservations were claimed at a motel in the sprawling airport complex, give or take sixteen hours before she'd meet Thornton. Using a pay phone outside, a room for tomorrow at the Airport Hilton was secured.

When Thornton arrived to keep the luncheon date, he fumed, "You would make me drive halfway to Fort Worth."

Smiling, Maybelle consoled, "I came in last evening to be with an old friend. This shouldn't take long, dear, and I'll be flying right back out of here."

Over lunch, she outlined the nature of business and the purpose of her trip, which only slightly interested him. "I am heavily invested in this privately held enterprise, and I believe it has great promise. We're in a slump presently, because your holding company, one of those damnable conglomerates, is stiffing us on issuance of a cogeneration contract." Thornton sat up straight, giving full attention as Maybelle continued. "I've bothered to study the structure of that utility cluster and your position in it. I happen to know you have the authority to issue a contract. And why not? It's politically expedient. The governor's office is for it, and so is the AIDC. There's also a majority in the Arkansas legislature beating the bushes to clasp this contract. For some reason, it's languishing, unsigned, in your corporate headquarters."

In silence, the formality of finishing the meal ended before Thornton rendered a response of retreat. "I just can't do it!"

Maybelle set fixed, resolute, eyes on him. "Now we're down to the quid pro quo. Pay the check and accompany me, because I have something you need to see."

Reaching the lobby, she indicated the elevators. "Get on. I'll show you upstairs in my room a little something I brought along," she directed.

Thornton recoiled. "I wouldn't be caught dead in a room here with a hustler."

Pointing to a television with VCR in the motel's large foyer, she countered, "Maybe you'd prefer to see what I have to show you right here in the lobby." Seeing Thornton's face go ashen, she quietly commanded, "Take this key and go on up. I'll be there in a few minutes."

A detour by the desk to ask for shuttle departure times, an in and out at the restroom, and a stop for the *Dallas Morning News* served as a diversion, masking the rendezvous. Within ten minutes, she entered the room to find Thornton breathing heavy and heaving over the commode. Hearing the door open, in a rage he came out of the bathroom and lurched toward her, all but screaming, "Why are you doing this to me, Maybelle? What have I ever done to you?"

Standing her ground, Maybelle got right in his face, not wavering an inch in spite of the foul smell of his puking. "You've never done anything against me, and you've damn sure never done anything for me or anyone else I know of," she flatly stated. "You'd like to think you dwell in another world, but this business of liking to dip your dick in my world without consequences ain't for real . . . You need to grow up, honey, and it may be right now. Compare it to a 'katydid' at molting time. When you feel like jumping out of your skin, you'll know what I mean."

The power button activated instant television on, and Maybelle turned to push in the video tape. Thornton couldn't take it when the action started. In a tantrum, he made a sudden lunge, grabbing her by the throat with deadly intent, only to find a pistol tunneling into the flesh of his chest. "If I have to kill you, I will, and I'll follow right after you," Maybelle hissed. The moment his hold began to relax, she thundered, "Now! Sit down!"

In his unsettled, disturbed state, she knew Thornton was unpredictable. *The slightest miscalculation precedes tragedy, old girl,* flashed through Maybelle's mind.

Eyes unfocused and shoulders slumped, he muttered, "Please turn it off. I can't look at any more," Thorton pleaded.

The 'please' gave explicit guidance of what Maybelle's next move was to be. With gun still being held on him, she eased over to eject the tape, turning off the set. Sitting down, rationally she began to converse. "I haven't asked you for the whole world, Thornton. All I'm propositioning for is a contract that's politically positive for you and the company in Arkansas. You don't stand to gain any clout by pissing off the political establishment there. So, what's the hang-up? Lost your balls?" Maybelle affronted, compounding gross indignity.

"Take me," she pawned. "The spoon was stainless, not silver, and only for a brief time did I experience 'the good life'. Times change, and circumstances are that I've gambled every asset I own toward a new stake with this venture. Your problem is you've never had to accommodate anyone in your whole sorry, worthless life. It's been all take and no give. Most certainly, you've never had to deal with a life-or-death crisis," Maybelle spelled it out. "Let me show you the other side of the coin, fella. If you don't turn out this contract for me, I go down . . . I'll take you and the whole city of Tulsa down as I go. I have tapes of three-fourths of your high-falutin' friends, cavorting in my establishment. You'll be 'persona non grata' in the company and back home, when the business community falls to its knees. All the financial structure holding your daddy and mommy together will disappear in dozens of divorce suits and other litigation. Understand too, if I release these tapes, there'll be no way to suppress them. A crazy son of a bitch in Tulsa named Bob Ed Gables, who's dying to run for governor, craves publicity. He would kill for the videos. It's your call. What's it gonna be, bastard? Life as you know it, or affluent suicide?"

Thornton reacted and, in a strangled voice, rasped, "God, I hate you, bitch! You leave me no choice. I'll get the contract signed and a copy sent to you as soon as I can."

His factious attempt to stall infuriated Maybelle. Catlike, she sprang out of her chair and in one leap, buried the handgun in the temple of a petrified

Thornton. "Any more famous last, lyin' statements you wanna make, you despicable weasel?"

"No! No! Wait! Wait! I'll get Gladys to bring a contract out right now and sign it here," begged Thornton, his composure destroyed.

"Oh, that won't be necessary," Maybelle smoothly blocked. Reaching into her large purse, she skillfully produced an envelope. "This is a contract prepared by the Arkansas Public Service Commission with the concurrence of the Arkansas Industrial Development Commission. It is valid and meets all requirements of Arkansas and federal law. There's a lady notary in the lobby who can witness our signatures. I already know you can legitimately sign. I'll be signing for Crown Alloys. As a major investor in the company, I function as secretary/treasurer. Pull yourself together. We're going down and attend to this right now."

Closing the door behind them, Maybelle obligingly committed, "When the signing is completed, and it's officially sealed, I'll give you the tape." She patted her purse reassuringly.

In a failed attempt to be amicable, Thornton said, "That's the last thing I want! What good would it do me? You have other copies, no doubt."

"You're absolutely right, but you have the secured benefit of my protection. I'd be remiss if I didn't see that nothing adverse happens to you. Fact is, you have saved a lot of dirty butts in Tulsa today. Know what? You oughta go home and meet your family again for the first time. Be most careful to watch out for your skin. It may split wide open any day because, like it or not, you've had to expand your horizons the past hour."

After the signing, Thornton never looked back as he strode to his car and drove away. Maybelle checked out, threw her luggage in the rented car, and made a call to the mountain, reporting, "Everything's in hand. Have someone meet me in seven hours at the airport lobby in Little Rock off I-440."

Dacus took the call. "I'll be there myself," he responded, detecting her lack of vigor.

When Dacus picked her up at the car rental agency, he couldn't wait to get a reverberating question answered. "Maybelle," he prompted. "You had a round-trip plane ticket to Springfield. What caused you to change your mind and drive to Little Rock?"

Exhausted and spent, she grunted, "Because I didn't trust either you boys or the bastard down there." Changing the subject, Maybelle asked, "Don't we need to stay over tonight so this contract can be recorded with the Public Service Commission tomorrow?"

Dacus was silent as he sped Interstate 40 toward Conway. "No," he said at length. "I want you to personally deliver the contract to Senator Eades. Call him first thing tomorrow and ask him to meet you at the cafe in Garlington. He'll get the mayor there, and you need to be ready for the local press. Play it down if he tries to make a bigger production, explaining you can't possibly stay. An early consummation of the contract has resulted in call of an important policy meeting involving directors of the company. As Executive Secretary, it is imperative to be present. You can follow up by saying how you deeply regret not being in attendance when he presents the contract for recording with the Public Service Commission, which, incidentally, will command a much larger press. Also, convince Senator Eades that it would be very helpful if he'd encourage their district superintendent of the power company to initiate the physical hookup at Garlington."

There was no response from Maybelle. Dacus drove on awhile before he said softly, "I want to know what the hell you meant when you said you didn't trust 'you boys'. Mind telling me who the bastard is, and where is down there?"

Maybelle changed her position, tucking a leg under her on the seat. The reply had an edge, "You'll have to wait till we get to the mountain. I don't intend to tell the story but once. I'll have a drink in hand when I do!"

A brief stop in Clinton for fast food put them at the lodge around eleven o'clock. Letting themselves through the shell with Dacus's remote, upon entering, they found everyone in bed except Ed, who had stayed up to hear the latest.

Maybelle wasted no time attacking the bar, followed by Dacus and Ed, forgetting the show he'd been watching on TV. She tossed off a jigger, neat, chasing it with a cigarette while mixing a bourbon and water. In passing by Ed, pouring a brandy nightcap, she compulsively brushed his cheek with a kiss and, giving a hug, gratuitously dropped, "Gads, is it ever good to be back here."

Walking to a game table, she put her drink down, stepped out of her pumps, and positioned another chair to prop her feet and legs in while waiting for Ed and Dacus to join her. "My 'here to eternity and back' has only been about forty-eight hours and it's forever etched, believe me. I'm shot. The nerves are fragmented, so indulge me," Maybelle began.

"Sorry about the 'you boys' bit, Dacus, but if any one of you men had known what I was about, you'd have tried to prevent it. I'd probably have been a homicide statistic in Dallas by now. Realization struck me there's only one way to get a signed contract and to have it secured without, inevitably, months of extended red tape. I didn't think we could afford to lose that much time. The odds were even, maybe stacked in my favor a little, to pull it off. Bear in mind, you don't run a cathouse successfully if you can't figure out the regular customers, their quirks, weakness, and foibles. Their livelihood often gives a clue to learning more about their natures as well."

A frown etched her brow, recalling, "Horny Thorny had been a regular. He held a perfect, rather guaranteed position of authority to provide a valid contract. Trouble is, the bastard's a pure chickenshit. He'd been raised with a silver spoon and perhaps platinum-threaded diapers and doesn't know the word 'oblige' exists or its meaning in an untenable situation . . ."

Maybelle pushed her glass to Dacus for a refill but didn't miss a beat of the step-by-step recall. "To make it work, I had to have some aces in the hole. The video was a sure bet. His reaction was not! I had to be on ready to command a recourse. Knowing him, it had to be one of lethal persuasion. Thus the gun and you bet, problems! You'd have put a stop on me just as surely as the airport security does with handguns. I finessed Sam, as well as you, and drove to Dallas, setting up the sting in the Airport Hilton."

The pause to light a cigarette and sip from her drink lapsed into minutes. Maybelle became engulfed in thought as she reflected on the minutest details which spelled out life-or-death essentials of her encounter. Dacus and Ed were lost in their thoughts, recounting the unwinding, unreal tale of her single-handed efforts to achieve their goals.

A faint, almost sob, from Maybelle exhaling brought Dacus around. Rising, he put his arm across her shoulder, reaching for the glass. "I'll get you another one. You're home, now." His compassion for Maybelle was unmasked.

"Yeah, and it's good to be here," Maybelle expressed, wearily insisting, "Let me finish while I can." Loosened from restraints of stress, it was a raw account that unfolded.

"Following lunch, my intentions were to invite him to the room, show the tape, and offer it in a proposition for a signature on the contract. Hell, he went berserk. First, he refused to come to the room until threatened with my showing the tape in the motel lobby. By the time he reached the room, he'd totally lost it . . . Threw up, grabbed me around the neck, and, in a fit, shouted paranoid accusations. Fear of my handgun cutting into his chest snapped him back to realization, I guess. Whatever, the son of a bitch was not through. He still had no intention of signing the contract and tried to put me off with the old cliché, 'I'll get it done later'. Well, I'd had it. I could just as easily have been incarcerated for murder tonight as I am drinking here with you. Thornton had no doubt about it, either."

Maybelle stood up a little unsteadily. Barefooted, she walked over to the bar to retrieve her purse. Reaching inside, she handed the contract to two dear, stunned friends.

Ed, overcome with what he'd heard, sputtered, "I'll be damned! I wouldn't have missed this incredible, firsthand reckoning of what went down with you in Dallas for all the gold in Fort Knox. Dacus, open that bottle of brut. We're gonna toast this gal and this occasion with the best champagne in the house."

Never suspecting but a mere fraction of the ordeal that had gone down, Dacus was tied in a knot of unspeakable, disjoined emotions. Ed's hail to bestow honors interrupted his trance. *Quit . . . Show them you've heard,* Dacus prodded himself, finally managing, "Ed, get those glasses out of the cabinet. I'll chill the champagne." Exercising fanfare, he twirled the bottle in an ice bucket, interacting. "These bubbles need released. Listen to 'em," he recast, popping the cork.

The three took hold of a stem each, holding the glasses together until parting to their lips. It was a silent toast, known only to each one. Dacus filled the glasses again, purposely overflowing them to symbolize an occasion worthy of extravagance. He and Ed individually followed, offering toasts to Maybelle for her uncanny ability of foresight and strength.

"Thanks, guys. My toast is to ya for being you. Excuse me a minute. I gotta go around the corner to the barstool. Oh! Let's use bourbon next time to do our toasting. The bubbles in this stuff are toxic as hell to my environment," Maybelle tipsily flipped.

Dacus began clearing the bar. Yawning, Ed said, "Think I'll call it a night. Anything else you want from me?"

"Not tonight, for Pete's sake. You could schedule an associational meeting for about midmorning tomorrow since you get up so early, anyway." In the process of turning the lights out, Dacus heard things dropping and some bumping about as Maybelle came out of the bathroom. Stepping around the corner, he asked, "Ready to go up?"

"If I can make it," Maybelle slurred. "Listen, about this thing for tomorrow with Senator Eades over in Garlington. Can it wait until another day?"

"Sure, it'd probably be better," he reasoned, considering circumstances. "Come on. I'll walk you up the stairs." His hand went out to steady her as she double-stepped.

"Don't humor me, dammit! I can make it," came her classic reply as she set one foot in front of the other, pacing off toward the stairs.

Dacus grinned inwardly at her gutsy fortitude and intercepted her on the bottom step. Putting his arm around her waist, he propelled her up without too many bobbles. When they reached her bedroom, Dacus opened the door and stepped aside.

Instead of going in, Maybelle curled around to face him. "Hold me. Hold me for just a moment. I need it desperately," she whispered in his ear. All too soon she released him, walked in, and collapsed on the bed.

Dacus pulled down the linens, loosened her skirt, and adeptly removed the jacket before maneuvering the bedding to cover her. *You're a helluva beautiful woman,* passed through his mind as he cupped her head in his hands. He kissed her goodnight on the forehead. Aloud, Dacus said with feeling, "Sleep well, Partner. You deserve it."

Ed summoned the Association as Dacus had suggested. All were present midmorning except Maybelle, who hadn't stirred. Dacus's words were sharp, pointed, and made with urgency. "Two events, one breaking only last evening, dictate the scheme will bear fruit much quicker than anyone thought. We've reached a critical juncture, requiring this now-leisurely pace come to a screeching halt. Every plot, plan, and all preparation previously initiated must now be put into action, focused, and fine-tuned to materialize. It must be completed in the next thirty-five to forty days. In case anyone wasn't paying attention," he repeated, "it must be wrapped up in the next thirty-five to forty days!" As impact registered, other phases followed.

"This is the first opportunity I've had to tell you, my trip to New Orleans resulted in being able to inspect a small ship. It's owned by a Mafia Don and is for sale. Not only is it ideal for our purposes but the price is within reach. That's number one, and secondly, Crown Alloys as of now possesses a signed contract for cogeneration of electricity, thanks to Maybelle. She literally gambled her life on getting it to make this caper feasible. Otherwise, we were looking at months of delay and possible consequences of charges for fraudulent activities to be slapped on us."

Toning intensity slightly, Dacus formed the network. "Perhaps you'll recognize where I'm coming from. The twin sisters of time and timing are essential ingredients of the profession. Conveniently, the time has been foreshortened drastically to our advantage here. The sequence of events in our game plan cannot be altered. Not one step can be altered, shortened, or omitted to accommodate the compressed time frame. Not the least will be dismantling and clearing out every shred of evidence on our activity and residency atop this mountain. Don't bank on having more than twenty-four hours to get it done in, either. In the meantime, which amounts to thirty-five or forty days while consumed to bring this scam to fruition, a ship must be purchased, equipped, and prepared for us to have in leaving the country."

He identified crucial criteria. "It'll require every spare moment of my time that can be mustered to assemble, deliver equipment, and get supplies needed for action, survival, and ultimately our success at sea. Somehow tho, I must find time for monitoring and supervising the pumping of electricity into the power company's lines from our generator. You must be ready to take up the slack or fill the niche to get everything else in place."

Sam squirmed in his chair. He stuck a finger up, and Dacus acknowledged it. "Hold it, man," Sam implored. "You're feeding my pea brain more nitrogen than it can absorb. I don't have a question or a comment. Just give me a second to catch up with ya." Unity of an accord mirrored in the countenances of others. Dacus caught Rabbit's eye for a glass of water, pleased that he was listening in on the meeting.

The reciprocal break opened up receptiveness to other factors Dacus felt needed brought to light. "Beginning right now, each and every one of us is expected to step up, taking on multiple responsibilities. As partners all, I would not attempt to tell you how to do these things. I have shared what I feel are some of my commitments. As professionals, I suspect yours will come on self-demand. It'll be important to have a sounding board to bounce ideas off and a focal point for direction. As such, it is only logical that Ed and Maybelle pick up on coordinating execution of these plans. Their roles of management in five each of the ten towns soliciting industry from Crown Alloys have already provided them with insight. They're familiar with what makes mayors, city councils, town gossips, and others click and which strings need to be pulled for promotional ease."

Projecting ahead, he programmed. "I foresee you forming two separate work teams. Without suggesting a how to do, let me emphasize a few essentials that may make the difference. First impressions are just that! Have large signs painted and put up at all sites. Mount magnetic signs on the pickup and van, rigging them as service trucks. For added appearance's sake, go by the laundry and get uniforms made up with Crown Alloys logo. While the signs are being printed, contract and build an eight-foot high, wooden privacy fence around the Garlington site." He included consideration be given to construction of an elevated guard station at the main gate.

"Senator Eades must be given his day," Dacus determined, "with an announcement flourish, filing of the contract, and ribbon-cutting ceremony. He should be encouraged to personally guide and prod the local power company into providing Crown Alloys access to electricity and installing a meter for measuring the cogenerated power we're to sell them. Lastly, money is no object. Placing ten thousand dollars from the Crown Alloys's account in a local bank of each town makes its own statement." Dacus singled out Tom and Viv, telling them, "I want to see you later."

Accepting the baton Dacus had handed over, Ed reacted, zealously. "You may be surprised that one of my duties as a youngster was surveying rice levees. You other four guys grab your hats and meet me outside to learn the art of a surveyor for later use. Dacus rented the equipment for us to use, not to look at. Oh! The meeting is adjourned," he added humorously.

Tom and Vivian, misput, joined Dacus on the veranda. Grumbling, Tom complained, "We're wondering if we're being left out. You didn't mention one thing that includes us."

"Not at all," Dacus assured. "Hopefully, it won't be necessary to drag out the 'CEO and his bride' scenario to push this gambit to its conclusion. What's needed from the two of you now is an inventory list of equipment needed to process the gold as we collect it from the sea."

Enthusiastically, Tom exploited, "Viv and I have discussed it at length. As you know, Dacus, electric ovens rely on the interruption of the flow of electrons, resulting in heat. Large ovens in use on shipboard would present a real fire hazard. We've concluded that sawing the daily masses of harvested gold into standard-sized bars could eliminate such a problem. For the scrap pieces, we'd recommend a small oven with molds of same size as the bars. I must tell you though, that processing a ton of gold a week boggles our imagination."

Matching their previous teamwork, Ed chose Art and Harry for one survey team, with Theo and Sam on the other. All four were quick studies. They leveled their instruments in short order, faking the act of surveying property sites with deceptive ease.

Savoring only a sandwich for lunch, Ed spent the rest of his day pursuing a fence contractor. He drove into Harrison to visit the local telephone office. Focusing on yellow pages for places in Springfield, Branson, Little Rock, and Memphis, which were readily available because of the large number of distribution companies located in Boone County, he made a selection. The very first call to a fence company in Branson proved to be most helpful. Their nearest branch outlet, located in Jonesboro, Arkansas, was between jobs. Ed called, requesting the manager, who was out. Leaving his number, he waited two hours for a callback, which produced an appointment to meet with the manager or a representative in Batesville at ten thirty the next morning. Elated, he locked up, driving in with the stereo tape belting out fifties music.

Spotting Maybelle on the veranda, he pulled up a chair and asked, "Have you talked to Dacus at all today, and are there any new developments?"

"Yes," she confirmed. "He wants me to move a hundred thousand from the Crown account in Springdale to the banks in our ten targeted towns. While this transaction is going down, he requested that the Association borrow a half-million dollars of my money. It's to be placed in escrow toward purchase of a ship in New Orleans, he said. His purpose, of course, is to seal the deal and proceed in outfitting her. I've agreed, but! Point is, Ed, attending to these matters puts me in the shorts for time to perform formalities with Senator Eades. What's your schedule, and would it be possible for you to take on the ribbon-cuttin' event? I'll let you borrow my skirt," she bribed.

Ed smiled. "No problem. You bet I'll handle it and get the Senator to apply pressure on the local power company to give us quick access, without your skirt or panties. Now, it didn't register with me until this morning, but how did you get Thornton to sign a contract with your alias on it? Didn't he know you only as Maybelle Barton?"

Maybelle looked at him keenly, parting, "You know we never work a scam without aliases, Ed. In this case, mine had already been established with Senator Eades. Besides, Horny was so befuddled that I had no trouble doing the old switcheroo used in the pigeon drop con. He never even looked at the contract he signed."

Ed just shook his head, marveling at her astuteness.

The evening meal was as fulfilling as the day had been productive. Contentment over accomplishments settled in with selections being played by the ladies. Maybelle was the only one not to have a drink. She substituted a glass of club soda with a slice of lime. During the course of the festivities joined individually by the bunch, Ed and Dacus in unison toasted Maybelle recalling portions of the evening before. A little unsteady and thick tongued, Eva took the floor toward the end of the session to pay regards. "Congratulations, Maybelle! The rest of the girls and I welcome you into our sorority. Each one of us, if you please, has bedded Juicy Joyce, alias ah-la Horny, numerous times, but you're the only one who's truly fucked him. Saluud!"

CHAPTER 18

The shindig for Maybelle had a history of about twelve hours when Dacus drove toward the Harrison Post Office. He took his mail into the office on the strip mall. As expected, both computers were up and running without an e-mail. Quickly, he prepared a message addressed to olivebranch@aol.com. It was brief. "Another meeting requested concerning ship. Can depart tomorrow. Please advise at earliest convenience. mountain@aol.com."

While waiting for a response, he took the other computer off Internet and inserted a floppy from his coat pocket. The previous afternoon he had spent a great deal of time starting a database. Hundreds of items relating to the ship's ability to perform in all eventualities were categorized. The database grew geometrically from memory and experience as he made entries. Every part for each piece of machinery and equipment got logged. He was reminded that Theo would probably be his man to benefit the most from such a list and made a printout. Three or four hours lapsed before familiar sounds of an e-mail message interrupted his thoughts. It read, "Come immediately. Same time. Same place. olivebranch@aol.com."

Not surprisingly, Dacus was met at the airport by the same two men as before. This time they drove him straight to the Zallafino Estate, where Marc waited, seated at a table in the garden gazebo. Standing, Marc shook his hand, offered him a seat, and anticipated the overture.

"Events are snowballing, which is good," Dacus cited. "Problem is, if one exists, it's time. Ours has been cut in half. To coordinate aspects of the caper's final leg, we must have access to the ship or make other arrangements. It is the reason I've urgently requested this audience. I'm here today, prepared to offer half a million in escrow secured in any New Orleans bank of your choice. Consider it as earnest money on purchase of the ship, providing it's agreeable."

"It's just not acceptable! My answer to your proposal is *no*!" Marcantonio declared, meeting Dacus's straight-on look. Only the sable edge around his green eyes deepened. "Now let me tell you what I want and my terms," Marc spat. "Because you're one of only two individuals in this generation I consider worthy of consideration to deal with on a handshake, I want no paper transactions with you, especially traced to a New Orleans bank! You are granted immediate admittance to the ship. Installation of your equipment and supplies are to be the escrow for full amount of the initial price asked for. The gunship, minus its long gun, is yours for another hundred thousand, if you want it."

Lifting a hand slightly, Marc indicated to the butler that he was ready for refreshments to be offered. These formalities attended to, he sat down to discuss particulars. "Surely, you recognize that under these terms, I still will not have received so much as a thin dime when you and your crew pull out of here." A nod, ever so slight, was made by Dacus to the comment. Marc sipped dark Louisiana coffee, tipped the cup to Dacus a bit as he replaced it on the saucer, and began setting forth his game plan for payment of the vessels. "One of my brothers and the two gentlemen who have brought you here, twice, will be on Grand Cayman when you arrive. Our dealings are to be consummated then and there. I want the full two 'mil' and hundred 'thou' in cash. It'll be delivered back to me on my private jet."

The pause, as both partook of coffee, could have been filled with sounds from garden creatures. Neither was attuned. Marc brought his hands together, extending fingers to touch and began looking at them while he made his point. "It may come as a surprise that I would want cash, hard as it is to launder money nowadays. However, sometimes laundered money is traceable in our complex technical age. This transaction will not be identifiable, and there's always a need for clean cash. How else is it possible to deal with politicians and the police? Now, do we have a deal, or do we sit around and quibble?"

Without hesitation, Dacus stood, and stuck his hand out. Marc grabbed it. They shook, looking at each other with steady yet probing eyes. Finally, Dacus committed, "Deal." A moment lapsed before he added, "There's a couple of more things to be put on the table. Unless you have some serious misgivings, I still intend to place a half million in a bank down here, mainly for the purpose of buying extra materials locally to outfit the ship. Is it satisfactory with you?"

"I have no objection," answered Marc, totally unprepared for the revelation that followed.

"The bank account will be opened under a name other than the one you know me by. It is my true identity. Here's my Social Security card, and my name is James Freed Dacus. As the many people come and go with me, you needed to know to avoid any confusion. They call me simply Dacus, not Mr. Dacus nor James Dacus, and not Freed Dacus . . . Just Dacus."

Marc gave a passive but inscrutable look. "Okay, what does it all mean? Care to fill me in on the purpose, or is it classified?"

Dacus sat back down and gestured for Marc to do the same. "We both know confidence men and women operate under different aliases for their scams. A. D. Mays and James Freed Dacus are my names. They are not aliases of mine! Useful to have in the profession? Yes! Arthur Dacus Mays is the handle given me by stepparents. When I was older, I pestered them until they confided my mother's last name to be Dacus and that she could not identify the father. Obsessed as youth can be, I obtained a blank birth certificate thru a friend of my stepfather and filled in the name of James Freed Dacus, adopting my birth mother's maiden name, much like the Spanish-speaking people do in Latin countries . . ." Marc waved him on, familiar with the custom.

"Impulsively, when I became a wage earner myself, I hired J. F. Dacus as a gardener and paid Social Security on his minimum wages. It established him as a living entity. The Federal Government down thru the years has him on record as an erratic worker living under the poverty level. I received a call from a government worker in Baltimore one day wanting to know the whereabouts of a Mr. Dacus, since he was not filing an annual income tax form, and I was shown to have been sole employer. If you've got a good story, stick with it. Mine became that Mr. Dacus was a distant relative, seriously retarded, and his salary was an act of charity on my part. I never heard another word, even though I continued to pay that Social Security tax from time to time . . . Relatively soon, A. D. Mays, no doubt, is going to be declared missing. He'll become part of a forty-year old mystery which surrounds a small mountain that devours its inhabitants. Dacus is not a successor to Mays. They are one and the same, but he'll come off as an entirely new player."

Marc gazed across the table and slightly shook his head. "I'm glad my brothers are gone for the time being. I need a breather to contrive a way to tell them about this one. They're already apprehensive of you. Changing the subject, it's the latter part of the afternoon. What's your pleasure for balance of the day?"

"I'd like to see the ship and take some measurements while there's still daylight. What are your workmen's hours? Do you think any of them will be around?"

"We'll have to go out there, take a look around, and find out," Marc replied as he motioned to be followed and strode toward his 4x4 SUV.

They pulled up to the drydock. The workmen were just getting ready to leave for the day. Marc signaled to the foreman. As he approached, Marc introduced, "Franco, this is Mr. Dacus. We have reached an agreement on sale of my ship, so meet the new owner. He has certain, particular requirements over and above those I have outlined. I want you to satisfy them as if I had told you personally. Okay?"

Franco grinned broadly, "Fait accompli, affaire Coeur, Mr. Zallafino." Turning to Dacus, he said, "Bonjour, monsieur. Comme il faut, sir, and bon gre to serve."

Marc and Dacus crossed the gangplank onto the deck. Stopping, Marc leaned against the ship railing and pondered their transaction. Dacus descended on to the engine room, where he proceeded to take measurements. Space for modified transmissions to convert the power source from two diesel engines into two electric motors, and back, was necessary. He found only enough room for the transmissions and electric motors. *An electric generator would have to be placed elsewhere and the power transmitted through wires,* he mused. Rather elated over finding that the project could be solved without major headaches, he returned to the deck.

"Ready?" Marc asked, making his way across the gangplank. They drove pretty much in silence to the mansion. Addressing the bar, Marc was a perfect host genial, and considerate. Their conversation could have been poured into a jigger glass. It took a couple of rounds before he opened a new avenue for discussion. "What I am about to say is in no way connected to or is a part of our deal. The ship's yours as agreed upon. It struck me though, you've made no mention of a captain for her. If there's one already in the wings, I'll stop here."

Checking Dacus's reaction, who returned an uncommitted gaze, Marc continued, "I have on my payroll, for life if he wants it, captain of the ship you're buying. He's got a few bugs on him, yet none are related to performance as a captain. His strong suits are reliability and loyalty. I know he'd be a happier man back at sea."

"What's the drawback?" he asked as an idle question, without much interest.

"He's got a record," confided Marc. "It hasn't canceled his license to captain a ship. He's a fairly small man who's very prickly, and it'll attract trouble. Word is, he was attacked by two men when leaving a dive and killed them both with an illegal switchblade. There's no telling how the trouble got started. Due to his size, and because there were two involved, he only got convicted of manslaughter. The sentence was ten years for each offense to be served concurrently. He put in a maximum of four years. "Marc contributed and included other particulars.

"Both haughty and also a sensitive man, the incident embittered his life. Sloan's never married and wants no permanent type of relationship with anyone, male or female. He's working for me under a lifetime offer, but I don't expect him to stay. However, he's extremely loyal to his word. Consequently, he's been wholly trustworthy."

Dacus, having trouble believing this one had dropped into his lap, commented, "I want to meet him. We haven't commissioned a ship captain yet. Set it up and we'll talk. His traits interest me. I consider myself and all of my people to be misfits capable of, but without the record."

Marc nodded, committing. "I'll be away this evening. A lady friend of mine and I had set a date before knowing of your arrival. The chef is looking forward to satisfying your palate after all the compliments lavished during the last trip."

"I thought you said pussy was cheaper by the piece," Dacus chided designingly.

"Don't worry, I'm keeping book on it," retorted Marc as he went upstairs to dress.

Ringing the butler, Dacus sent a message to the kitchen. "Tell the chef that I'm really a light eater, and he can fix something to suit his own fancy. I'll be in my room when it's ready."

Breakfast aside, Dacus was ambling onto the veranda when Franco pulled up with his workmen. He offered a ride, since they were on their way out to the ship. Dacus watched the routine get started before asserting himself. When Franco turned from his work detail directions, Dacus led him to the engine room, commenting as they arrived, "I intend to install transmissions and electric motors as an alternate to the diesel engines."

"Au contraire, why ya wanta replace le diesel power?" queried Franco.

"No, no, I used the term 'alternate' to describe their function. It may be necessary to shift from one power source to the other in midjourney, so to speak."

"I no ask raison d'etre of le vessel, mon ami," Franco elucidated. "Le tout ensemble is befuddlin' ta le Cajun. Á propos, one guy au fait, on dit, gotta helluva business. Makes da deals, ever'ting from da entrepot. Par exemple, massive, petit equipments used par sea vessels, wires, maybe radar and more gear. Pour le merite, he clean, okay. Au reste, dere's vraisemblance, he get big pla' pour le drug smugglers pour le materiels. N'importe, ya need see le materiels."

"Let's see what he's got. If it's the way you think it is, he won't ask questions, 'cause I don't have answers to volunteer. Sure sounds like a perfect setup to shorten the stroke for me."

Nick Runshang's place, ten acres wide and two acres deep along the shore, included nearly a thousand feet of dock. His yard was dotted with acres of dismantled machinery, rolls of wires, chains, dry-docked ship hulls, and the like. The hub of his complex was a huge building, serving as warehouse, repair shop, and office. Franco parked, and they began browsing the yard. Turning momentarily toward the bay, Dacus spotted something very interesting berthed at the dock.

Hands cupped, Dacus gave a low whistle to Franco and started for the dock. Catching up, and taking due note of the section where they were headed, Franco commented, more than asked, "En effet, ya wanna see in le submarine, yeh?" Dacus smiled, appreciating the guy's sharpness.

Stepping aboard to walk over to the open hatch, they discovered the ladder was lighted all the way down to the bottom. Accepting an open invitation to descend, the interior could be viewed from end to end, as all watertight compartments were open. Drawn to the engine room, Dacus saw immediately what would solve his problems. He'd mentally overlooked something he should've remembered from studies in college. The generation of submarine power from one source, for alternate use in another, was produced and stored in huge batteries which, in turn delivered DC current to run the motors. Nice! The only thing needed to reverse a DC motor is to reverse the wires feeding it. A magnetically operated switch reversing polarity with the push of a button eliminated any need to look for cumbersome transmissions. Having seen enough, he left the sub, followed by Franco, and headed for the warehouse.

The owner, found in a small inner office, waved them in, pointing to worn leather chairs. Standing, Dacus asked, "Do you sell submarine parts?"

"Nobody wants submarine parts as such. What do you want with submarine parts?" Nick pried with a question.

"I need them to form backdrop for a display of potted plants," fired back Dacus. "They must be shiny clean and operable or it's a no deal."

"I'm sorry I asked," replied Nick. "Which parts interest you?"

"I want two electric motors and drivetrains, including mounting plates and housings for the leakproof driveshafts and propellers," answered Dacus. "Oh, and I also want to buy a supply of sub batteries, if they'll still hold a charge."

Rising from his chair, Nick walked them out into the huge warehouse, where they climbed aboard a lift truck and were driven toward one of the far walls. Stopping at a designated spot, he joined Dacus and Franco on the elevating platform to be lifted up level with a high storage bin. Nick specified, "We don't get many calls for these parts, so they're not kept on the floor."

It only took a perfunctory look by Dacus to know he'd uncovered a treasure. Exercising restraint, he inquired, "How much?"

"You can have the lot as is for fifteen hundred. Or,"—Nick slipped a pad in on the quote,—"if you want it all to be in operating condition, I'd estimate cost at between twenty and twenty-five thousand. We're fabricators and machinists, and all of the equipment would be guaranteed."

Decidedly, Dacus responded, "The price is no problem. What's policy on taking a check or checks from a local bank where you can call to verify they're covered?"

"What bank?" posed Nick suspiciously.

"Name one," countered Dacus, curtailing him.

"The bank in Lafitte's fine by me." Nick backed down lamely.

"I'll be back in an hour with a check. You don't mind if it's a counter check on this short a notice, do you? I'll make arrangements for you to call and verify my liquidity. Now, how long will it take you to turn the job out on the two motors, drivetrain assembly, and batteries?" queried Dacus, imparting he expected a rush order status as part of the deal.

"About ten days," was Nick's idle reply.

Franco hauled Dacus to the small bank in Lafitte. The transactions finalized, they were back at Nick's within the hour. "Give me a figure," exacted Dacus.

Nick tucked his head down and grunted, "Ten thousand for starters suit you?"

Dacus patted his pockets for the counter checks and realized he had left them in Franco's truck. While he was gone to get them, Franco seized the opportunity to tell Nick, "Don't ya fuck'm aroun', mon ami. Entre nous, in le town, he got distingue liaison!"

"Yeah, who are these powerful allies?" Runshang tried to bully.

"Voila uno way to learn. Screw 'im 'roun' an' it be suave qui pent. Maybe too late par care if ya play'm pour le sucker. Ma foi, voila no francs par Franco, no douceur. En effect entre nous, it be advice pour ya, Nick," Franco wisely and strongly asserted the consequences. He added, "Au revoir," going out of the door to wait for Dacus.

En route back to the Zallafino Estate, Dacus quizzed Franco about the waterline on the hull of the boat. "I see you've scraped and repainted the hull. By any chance, do you have a mark of where the waterline was?"

"Oui, oui, fait accompli," alertly contributed Franco. Hand and finger motions were more descriptive than words, of how he'd spray-painted over the tape first applied to the waterline, then removed and repainted. He exuded pride over having had foresight that a preserved waterline might be needed as he pointed to a permanently marked line, asking, "Why ya wanna know?"

"Maybe you noticed there's an alteration to the hull whereby an addition to the keel can be lowered mechanically. This dates back to when it was rigged for sailing," Dacus explained. "I intend to place a ground wire, which must be above the waterline, thru that part of the hull housing the extra keel. The wire strung outside of the hull proper will be encased in a length of double strength pipe, coated inside and out with a quarter inch of durable plastic."

"Je ne sais quoi?" Franco threw his hands up.

"Surely, Franco, you do know what it's for! I shouldn't have to diagram the whys and wherefores of a ground wire. After all, I'm expecting you to help me rewire the ship!"

There was a note for Dacus at the estate guard post. It informed him that he was being waited for at the mansion. Marc and a smaller, neatly dressed man conversed at the steps. As Dacus approached, Marc made introductions. "Mr. Dacus, meet Captain Sloan Barnett. Now, gentlemen, if you will excuse me, I have things to do and you have things to discuss."

Briefly, they sized each other up and sat down. Dacus opened conversation. "May I presume you're interested in becoming captain of the ship I have just bought?"

"I am interested enough to have questions," replied Barnett. "I am familiar with the ship and heard something about your considering some sort of modifications to her. What's the general purpose of these changes?"

"Captain Barnett, let's say I fully understand your personal position. I am here to assure you that this ship has no destiny in drug trafficking or in any other illegal activities. It'll be a working ship. One outfitted to function in the capacity of service that I need. For all practical purposes, she'll come off as a pleasure craft, complete with female entertainers. I don't mind divulging that the nature of our work will be covert, but it absolutely will not be illegal."

"How about a crew? Would I have authorization to hire my own?" questioned Barnett.

"The ship's complement presently will consist of myself, eight partners, the seven females, a cook, and his common-law wife. We will be functioning as her crew members and staff."

Stupefied by the outrageousness of what he had just been told, Barnett tried to respond with realism. "I've never heard such a crock of shit. Without my own crew, I'm not interested in becoming your ship's captain."

"I respect your position," Dacus counteracted. "Thank you for your time."

Interested, yet not inclined to be outdone, Barnett wasted no time interjecting, "It strikes me that you're confusing demands of a captain with those of a pilot. If you want a pilot, and forfeit incumbent responsibilities of a captain, let's talk in those terms."

It was Dacus's turn to be taken aback for a moment. Bluntly he began, "I've been told you suffer from a difficult personality trait. Could it be you've gained from trial and practice of the past? Just now, you presented me a mental and personal flexibility this job unconditionally requires. And, based upon what you have shown me, I'm prepared to give you a contract. It'll specify you as the ship's pilot for a year and a half at a hundred and twenty thousand per year. Irregardless of time spent, you'll still be guaranteed a hundred and eighty thousand dollars. We'll renegotiate if time exceeds terms in the contract. One stipulation is made. The contract is null and void if you discuss with anyone the purposes and activities of the association owning the ship. Is that entirely clear?"

"You bet. Not only is it clear, it's vivid. You propose to buy confidentiality as well as duties of service. Let's see. I said I'd consider becoming your pilot. I am strongly contemplating the idea, but not without some reservations. What type of security for my safety can be warranted in a nonnarrated, undisclosed venture?"

"Absolutely zilch. None!" snapped Dacus. "You know better than to ask such a question, as many times as you've put out to sea. If I said yes, you'd know damn well I was lying. I can only assure you of one thing. You'll be safer as a pilot on this vessel than you ever were as captain of the same ship."

Barnett stroked his jaw and stared at the horizon. "You have made me a mighty tempting offer. One that needs to be sorted out in the mind. What say I give you an answer in the morning?" Excusing himself, Barnett skirted around to enter the mansion, reporting directly to the Don, which Dacus had fully anticipated him to do.

Marc sat quietly and impassively waited. Barnett cleared his throat, searching for a proper beginning thread. "I don't know about this, boss. Seems I won't be captain after all. When I mentioned getting a crew together, can you believe I was told that occupants of the ship, amounting to nine partners, seven entertainers, a cook, and his common-law wife, would function as the crew? I'd be stripped of any authority over such a motley lot. Naturally, I declined. I'm a ship's captain, not a seagoing baby-sitter." Marc was suspect of his two latter statements.

Barnett managed to feed an ego, relaying, "The man thanked me for my time out there. He'd effectively dismissed me when I countered. I made him a proposition that I'd be willing to serve as pilot but not to expect me to take on duties or responsibilities of a captain."

To influence Marc, he boasted, "Mr. Dacus stunned me by offering an unheard-of eighteen months pilot's contract at ten thousand a month, guaranteed. That ain't hay, you know."

"Uumm," Marc mused. "That's unsettling to hear, Sloan. It's frightening, in a sense. How can you operate within the law and pay that kind of money for pilot services on a ship so small? Too good to be true, don't you think?"

Turned on to tell all, Barnett threw a punch. "I asked for some sort of security pledge and was told none existed except for one. He guaranteed me I'd be safer on his ship than I ever was on yours. That's a hell of a statement, boss. How do you read it?"

Mr. Dacus becomes more and more curious to me ran thru Marc's mind. Aloud, he said, "Interesting indeed. I don't see how you can afford to pass up such a lucrative opportunity. You're damn lucky if one like it occurs once in a lifetime. Eighteen months or even two years is nothing. Think you'd consider coming back to work for me when your stint is over?"

"Mr. Marcantonio, what gives you the idea I wouldn't be back to assume my lifetime position here? For that matter, not only would I not accept the man's offer, if you ask me not to, but I'd tell 'em to take it and shove it if my job's not waitin' for me when I get back," expressed Sloan.

"Oh, don't worry about it, Sloan. Your job will be intact," assured Marc while adding a few specifics. "These peculiar circumstances though do justify the need for a condition that's never been mandated. If I understand correctly, there is an element of confidentiality attached to the contract's term. Of course, I wouldn't expect you to violate it. When the tour's over and you're back on my payroll, I'll be most interested in what you have learned about Mr. Dacus on this extended journey. In some mysterious way, he's perilous. He's powerful, inexorably so, and there has to be an explanation. If you come back unprepared to provide me information, you'd best have stayed far away. Consequences of breaking a contract with the 'Family' are well established."

"I got the message, sir. I'll take him up on the deal. Strange, how in less than an hour he's cast a feeling I'm caught between the devil and the deep blue sea. Dammit!" Sloan fumed.

"A piece of advice, Captain," Marc unleashed. "Never call either of us a devil to our face."

Dacus rang the butler, politely asking the Don be notified he requested an audience. Momentarily, instead of having Dacus ushered in, Marc showed up on the veranda. "What can I do for you?" Marc inquired. His unexpected curtness tipped Dacus that Sloan had made a snide report.

Dacus let it pass, responding, "I have need to contact my people thru the same Internet connection that you and I use for sending communications."

"Surely." Marc changed his tune to congenially agree. "I'll have someone take you there. I think Captain Barnett is free. Would you mind if he drove you?"

"Actually, I'd welcome an occasion to visit with him on a more casual basis," alluded Dacus, aware of the motive.

"Give me a second and I'll arrange for him to be out here in ten minutes," enjoined Marc, leaving to inform Sloan of an errand he had been commissioned to run.

The ride to the outskirts of New Orleans was punctuated by Dacus's quizzing of his chauffeur. "Captain, from your experience in the Caribbean, what can you relate to enlighten me about the hurricane season? Tell me a little of what's expected concerning ships traveling in them."

With a glancing look at Dacus, Barnett declared, "A hurricane at sea is as close to hell as you'll ever want to get. My first experience in one came as a young seaman on a death trap ship, if ever there was one. It was a converted Liberty ship, which had been mothballed at Newport News, Virginia, after World War II. Years and years after the war, I'm told she was purchased and put back in service by a private, commercial group to move cargo."

Recalling, he descanted, "Those ships, built as transports, sat relatively high in the water without the weight of a load. Broad in the beam, they were extremely slow at eleven knots per hour and had no keel for a counterbalance, offering damn little security to the sailors aboard. With no cargo, we rode out that hurricane for twelve hours in the shallow seas between the tip of Florida and Cuba. Word was that a tilt of forty-five degrees would put the ship on her side. The bridge called out forty-four and a half all night long. The good Lord must have been with us 'cause not a soul was lost. We had plenty of casualties though and returned to port the next day to replace crewmen who sustained broken bones and head wounds." He stopped short to digress.

"I'd signed on to bring cargo from South America to the States. I stayed aboard until the mission was complete but vowed never again to sail the Caribbean in a vessel that slow, and that big, with no keel. The Devil's Triangle is an overdramatization of Caribbean tragedies, but the fact remains that erratic weather develops more quickly in the region than any other location of the Atlantic. I'd rather take my chances in the Cape of Storms than in the Caribbean."

Having taken in Sloan's recount, Dacus urged, "Tell me, what's your opinion for the key to protecting oneself under those conditions?"

Barnett, absorbed in his element, held forth. "I'd consider it a duty to keep a continuous monitor on position of the ship at all times. It'd include projected locations every fifteen minutes, based upon compass direction and speed. Other than that, the ship ought to be equipped with the finest radio transmission facilities money can buy. Every piece of navigation and communication equipment better be reinforced with equivalent backup sources. Take my word, it's useless, not worth a damn, without a continuous monitor on radio transmissions twenty-four hours a day."

Dacus interrupted, "I'm with you on the communication needs. I'll also assure you ours will be equipped with the finest radar and sonar technology available. Not only that, we'll have special equipment for intercepting both public and private satellite transmissions. What I need to know from you is if hurricanes develop circular winds from seventy-five miles per hour and upward, how fast can one travel in a straight line compared to its circular velocity?"

"All I can say is damn quick in a Caribbean atmosphere with shallow seas of warm waters giving it an extra push," he emphasized.

Their discussion ended as the car pulled up and parked near the warehouse. Dacus lost no time in typing up an e-mail message to his Harrison office. "Man the phone at 4:00 p.m. daily, unless otherwise directed by e-mail." Turning to Barnett, he explained, "My office takes advantage of the convenience of fax messages, voice mail, plus computer printouts. Checking in once a day for updates generally is sufficient with my 'in-and-out' secretary."

Barnett, having observed the hour for checking in, asked, "Wanta wait here till four?"

159

"No," replied Dacus. "I'll be calling in from a public telephone. I have a hunch Internet messages aren't being monitored, but I wouldn't make bet that other of the Zallafino phones weren't tapped. I'm not about to expose a phone conversation between my place and here to a potential tap. Enough said. Can you find me a pay phone by four o'clock?"

"Yeah," said Barnett, driving away, adding, "Ya know this Cajun country could be my kinda haunt. All this history tickles some part of my brain. Up ahead is a bar and grill whose origin is built into its walls. It's like a trip way back into the past. I've had lunch there several times, and the food is always good. There's an old fashioned phone booth in it that will let us wait until time with a cup of coffee, gumbo, sassafras tea, or name your pleasure."

Inside, the bar was dimly lit by beverage signs and attended by several roughnecks perched on the stools. Dacus and Barnett sat down at a table next to the phone booth. The bartender came over and took their order, which was for two coffees. Returning, he socked the cups down and loudly announced, "This is cash-and-carry. That'll be two dollars."

The activity, as if rehearsed, gave the toughs at the bar their cue to stare. Each had the identical look of *fresh meat* in his eyes. At five minutes before four, Dacus stood up and stepped into the booth. Dialing the number resulted in a busy signal. Just as he began a redial, the largest bruiser, a big skinhead, appeared at the bifold door and ordered, "Out! Outta th' box, Andy."

Buying time and assessing the situation, Dacus pretended simplicity, looking up at him from a seated position, correcting, "My name isn't Andy."

The tough placed his hand on his hip and prissed, "Oh, my apologies, Amos. I never ever shoulda mistooken you for Andy." Pausing in front of the door, he commanded, "Come out befo' I yanks you thru thet keyhole."

He should have paid attention. Dacus had turned himself, still seated, to the half-open door and eased his left foot behind the heel of the skinhead's right ankle. The swift force of Dacus's right foot and leg pistoned against the punk's right knee decked him flat on his back.

Dacus, instantly over him, landed a foot in the groin. When his knees shot up to his chest, like a folded suitcase, Dacus drop-kicked him in the balls. In short order, the tough wasn't so tough anymore. The groan matched a sickly green on his face. Insult adding to injury wasn't over, yet. Dacus just as quickly dislocated fingers on both hands, by bending them backward before either of the other punks could react to get off his barstool. The tough passed out.

Dacus moved a tiny switch, just inside his shirt, under the tie. Catching Barnett's eye, still seated, Dacus motioned in a diagonal toward the front door. Turning his gaze to the bar, where the other two punks seemed glued down, he walked directly up between them. Just as he got within reach, they both grabbed him, one on each arm. Touching knees together, Dacus completed a circuit to hit both with more voltage and more amps than a cattle prod. They convulsed and stiffened every time he completed the circuit. When they became so out of it that his arms were freed, Dacus grabbed them by the back of the neck and repeatedly slammed them facedown on the bar, littering it with blood and teeth. Looking over at the bartender, he noticed him staring at the phone booth. With three giant strides, he gained entry into the booth, jerking the receiver and wire from the phone set. At the front door, he turned and threw the useless receiver at the bartender.

The door to the car was open and waiting. The moment Dacus got a foot in it, Barnett pulled away from the curb. "Dammit, Barnett!" Dacus complained. "So much for your choice of a coffeehouse. Man, don't you know I can't afford to have my name appear on a New Orleans police docket, even if it's for a minor infraction? It'd be as hard as hell on your boss. Think about it! Get me away from here. Go to a place serving food with fast turnover crowds like Bennigan's, Shoney's or whatever, and let me out. Then go directly to the mansion and explain the circumstances. Tell him to have someone else in another set of wheels come pick me up."

As he drove, Barnett had to offer Dacus an explanation, "The only other times I've been in there was for lunch, and there was a different crowd at that time of day."

"I'll buy that," Dacus humored. "No one's blaming you for what happened in there. The fact does remain that it's an incident that never should have occurred, and I cannot be connected with it. If the police have this license plate and pull you over, tell 'em you picked me up at my stranded car on the side of the road. You were just being kind by taking me to a phone to call for a wrecker. Say that I jumped out of your car at the first stop sign and took off."

"There's not a chance the police have this license number. I flipped the plate up before you came out the door," Barnett said, trying to recoup. "Besides, they wouldn't believe that cock-and-bull story you fabricated."

"That's very comforting, but it's not a certainty. Nothing has changed. Drop me off. Have Marc send another driver and vehicle for me," Dacus demanded.

Barnett had a sick feeling in the pit of his stomach driving from the guard station toward the mansion for a meeting with the Don. His dread was compounded when the butler ushered him into Marc's office instead of seeing him at the bar or, at least, at one of the side tables.

Marc, reading a document, motioned for Barnett to have a seat. After a moment, he dropped the paper and inquired, "Have you come in here to talk about Dacus?"

"No, sir. We got a problem. Dacus is about eighteen miles from here. He wants to be picked up by someone other than me and in a different vehicle. There was an incident this afternoon involving Mr. Dacus and three other people. He cannot afford to appear on any police roster, he said. Neither does he want the car associated with you in any way."

Marc handed Barnett a pen and slip of paper, saying, "Write down the place where you left him." He picked up a phone with an enormous mouthpiece, which muffled the voice, and dialed his two lieutenants. He instructed them to meet Dacus at the address. Turning to Barnett, he commanded, "Now, tell me what this is all about."

"Well, sir, we went to the warehouse first. When he had sent his e-mail, making a four o'clock appointment, I asked if he wanted to wait there until time to make the call. He said he didn't want to talk on one of your phones for fear of them being bugged. I wound up taking him to a little bar and grill where I had eaten lunch several times, because I'd remembered an ancient phone booth in there. It seemed like a good place to have a cup of coffee. Only problem was, there were three punks at the bar, who eyed us pretty good but didn't make a move till Dacus went into the phone booth. The biggest one hassled Dacus through the front doors of the booth as soon as he got inside and threatened to jerk him through a keyhole if he didn't get up and out. I don't know how, but Dacus, sitting in that booth with the doors pulled back somehow used his feet to put the big bastard on the floor. Fast as lightning, he was up and out of the booth, stomping the guy in the groin and then kicking him in the nuts, ending the discussion, I thought."

Marc's mental agitation increased as Barnett continued. "Dacus was far from through. He broke all of the guy's fingers in two more swift moves. Without a word, he directed me to exit through the front door and miss going by the bar, where the other two punks seemed frozen. He headed straight for the bar, messin' with the front of his shirt. I can't describe the look on his face as he strode toward them, just before they each grabbed an arm, one on either side. In that instant, they locked their arms in his. He moved some way, almost a jig, and they began doing a St. Vitus dance or having an epileptic fit until he quit whatever he was doing. He finished 'em off by bashing their faces against the bar, with teeth flying and blood splattering into two puddles. The bartender was petrified in his tracks, and Dacus wasn't missing a beat. Walking back to our table, he poured a glass of water over his bloody hands, stepped up to the bartender, and wiped them on the guy's apron. Returning to the booth, he reached inside and jerked the receiver, cord, and all out of the phone box. Tossing the receiver to the bartender, he leisurely walked out."

Trailing off, Barnett backtracked, "I'd run out to the car, flipped over the license plate, and got the motor started so we could get away from there in a hurry."

Marc gave Barnett a strange look and advised, "Stay close, where I can find you." To himself, he pondered, *I don't believe we've seen near all there is to Mr. Dacus. There is something implacable about the man. I gotta wonder if anybody, or anything, gets in his way for long.*

Dacus thanked the two lieutenants and went to his room to freshen and change clothes. They in turn reported to their Don, uneasy and bemoaning, "Sir, no one told us your man wasn't using the name Mays anymore."

"That bit happened the first night in on this trip," he rectified. "I'm sure the man didn't give it a thought, and neither should you. Forget ever meeting Mr. A. D. Mays, and address the man as Mr. Dacus hereafter." The lieutenants waited for Marc's further orders . . .

"Tomorrow, I've got a job for the two of you. Sometime during the peak lunch hour, visit the joint where Barnett took Mr. Dacus. Later, I want you to go again around four in the afternoon. Look the clientele over and tell me if there are two different crowds hanging out at different times of the day. Find out from Barnett where the place is but don't divulge why you're asking and do not let him suspect you're on surveillance of the place."

The lieutenants gone, Marc proceeded to the bar to wait for Dacus, who came downstairs some ten minutes later. "I hear you've had quite a day," commented Marc.

"Yes, you could say that and probably be putting it mildly," reflected Dacus. "Guess we all have a dark side. Mine is a particular problem for me. Today I was pushed to my limits. A lot of effort is expended in suppressing it. This afternoon I lost control and could have easily wasted three people with these hands. I'll spare you the details."

Conferring, he directed, "More importantly, what happened was hazardous, downright dangerous to the both of us, and shouldn't have occurred. I cannot afford to become incapacitated, especially not at this time and least of all by involvement with law enforcement. It'd prove to be fatal, a certain death of all plans, canceling everything, including purchase of your ship."

Dacus had finished his recount with a hint of exasperation. Marc couldn't determine if it was irritation with himself or anger at something or someone. He fiddled with his drink, clearly recognizing nothing more would be said. "Care for another drink?" Marc tempted.

"I don't believe so," Dacus declined. "My nerves are jangled. I need to eat light, drink light, and go to bed early tonight. Tomorrow I must catch a plane out of here. I'll be back in about ten days, however."

"Which way are you headed?" Marc asked benignly yet with a purpose.

"Why do you want to know?" reflexed Dacus, inadvertently distracted.

Marc chuckled to break Dacus's state of mind. "I'm offering to take you in my private jet to wherever there's a landing strip big enough and long enough to accommodate setting you down."

"Good. It'll beat the hell out of commercial flying," enthused Dacus as much as he could. "St. Louis or Dallas, preferably St. Louis, would be perfect for me."

Marc sensed that there would be no more conversation on the subject for the evening. He ushered the two of them into the dining room. They ate in virtual silence, holding unnecessary small talk to a minimum.

The next day, Marc's lieutenants reported to him at two thirty in the afternoon. "You're a little early to make a full report, aren't you?" noted Marc, slightly irritated.

The designated spokesman made it brief. "There wasn't any reason to stay for the late afternoon crowd. The place was seedy and the food worse than lousy. Customers, if you'd call 'em that, were grifters, already drinkin' dinner."

"Have any idea what Barnett's game is?" Marc posed.

The other lieutenant opted, "I've always thought he was a brick short of a load. Yeah! I think he was lookin' for a good excuse to cut someone. I'd bet he's carrying a knife in his boot. Probably thought he'd get by with exercising his devious hang-up and enlist your legal team for assistance if it didn't work, claiming he was protecting the customer."

Dismissing his men, Marc leaned back in the chair and closed his eyes. *This musta' been what it was like for Papa, only more of it*, surfaced. He decided not to share the information with Dacus who, no doubt, could take care of himself.

CHAPTER 19

Just before sundown, Ed was stretched out on a chaise lounge, gazing toward the horizon from the deck of the lodge and reflecting on events of the past five or six days. The high wooden fence at the Garlington site would be completed in a couple of days. Senator Eades had promised access for pumping electricity into the power company, which according to him would be physically available before the weekend. It precipitated reflection on what his next move should be . . .

Suddenly, a large rental truck topped the plateau, rolled into the driveway, and out stepped Dacus. "Welcome, stranger," tendered Ed, swinging his legs off to stand in greeting.

"Let me make a pit stop, put up these clothes, and we'll get together shortly," rejoined Dacus. Twenty minutes later, Dacus was seated on a bench outside, avidly listening to Ed describe the nature of progress made at the plant.

"Sounds like I got back just in time. Man, you've made some master strokes! For one that didn't want to fly, this scam is moving on! Where's Maybelle?" he quizzed.

"Banking is my guess. To be perfectly frank, I really don't know where she is. Maybe in the Caribbean as we speak. One thing I do know, the only time she's called in, it was to say she was hooking up with her old banker friend, Rainwater. Supposedly, he's steering her through intricacies of offshore banking and making fund transfers out of this country."

With a twinkle, Dacus couldn't resist commenting, "At eighty-two, that Indian's getting a little old to hunt, wouldn't you think?"

"In my opinion," Ed compounded, "age has nothing to do with it. Maybelle's made a statement she'd use sex as a tool or ploy to perfect our goals. My only problem with it is the fact that I'm not smart enough to figure out how to get in on the action."

Dacus laughed out loud. Soberly he redirected, keying on current demands. "I never expected such rapid development of the project. It would appear I need to be in two places at once, which means we must adapt. After supper, let's discuss these particulars. You, or someone, is going to have to take my place for long stretches of time, pumping electricity at Garlington. And it'll be my business to teach you how to become proficient."

An added dimension of solidarity existed throughout the meal. It's amazing how success either purifies or destroys the mind. To purse the matter, Ed and Dacus strolled to a table in a well-lit corner of the entertainment center. Ed secured a notepad and pen while Dacus brought along their coffee. The men, even Tom, drifted over picking up on something new afloat. Sam interceded, "Would it hurt if we listened in? The more we get involved, the more need there is to understand details in case of problems."

Glancing over at the ladies, who were eyeing selections on the jukebox, Dacus suggested Sam tell them to keep the sound down and invited, "Pull up tables and chairs, guys. You're right! The more you grasp on operational specs, the better our chances."

Dacus welcomed the class assembled around him, citing, "Though this is impromptu, your enthusiastic approach is reassuring that our ultimate goal can be successfully accomplished. Friendship didn't get us this far . . . Keep in mind it was team smartness while I lay out more variables we must take into consideration. The broad 'up tempo' of this scam has become such that everyone will need a double at some time or another. Regardless, by being ourselves we've done a pretty good job of faking it—up until now, that is! Relative to this, I must be away getting us ready for takeoff at the very time pumping activity is required. Some one of you will have to pick up the slack, doubling for me. Ed seems to be the logical one to function in my absence. Without a doubt, odds for our success multiplied tonight." Their display of interest and willingness to learn every aspect of execution couldn't have come at a better time, and he explained why.

"The value for any one of you to understand operation and machinery service used in capturing electricity never occurred to me before. For the moment, Rabbit is the only person qualified, other than myself. I do consider it unwise to visibly involve him in the field. In an emergency, he can be used as a consultant via cellular phone from the jobsite. Simply put, the equipment to be maintained consists of variable capacitors, or waveguides, transformers, shunts, a 'jillion' sensors, and both DC and AC generators powered by other electric motors. Everything is fused to protect the equipment. There'll be at least one spare on site for every functional part brought in from our warehouse."

Scoffing anxiety, Dacus promoted, "Sounds like Greek, doesn't it? Could be, except for the fact that there'll be a computer from an independent electrical source monitoring each component. It even scans individual parts for weakness, alerting potential failure. Essentially, all anyone's required to do is comprehend and read what the monitor is telling you, being able to locate a spare part, if needed, and seeking help on installation. I'll be around for about ten days, which gives ample time to have units installed and operating nearly a week before I'm due to leave. Whadda ya think? Any volunteers?"

"Sounds like a helluva responsibility," surmised Ed. Dodging a blatant lie, he rationalized. "I guess I'd give it a try, if worse comes to worse."

Theo reared back in his chair, teetering on its back legs, didn't ante. Instead, he watched the others debate their doubtful ability to tackle the job. Not wanting to apply himself, Art shunned the notion he'd be capable and pleaded ignorance with Sam. Harry vowed there wasn't insulation made for him to touch it with a ten-foot pole. It left the door wide open for Tom to rattle their cages. "I'm an expert at using electricity! I'll even profess I haven't the slightest idea on how to go about making it. Betcha even I could read that monitor!"

Dacus applauded, "Nothing ventured, nothing gained, eh, Tom? And probably Maybelle's synopsis exactly. The rest of you shouldn't write it off or put yourselves down. Surely, it can't be that big a deal to follow a well-orchestrated script in which the lines may be wires and the notes become fuses. The outcome is just as rewarding as slight of hand and misdirection, polished to perfection," he exposed, slightly miffed yet bent on altering attitudes.

"This is now. I'm home and one contented yahoo with where we are. Tomorrow's another day. Tonight, I intend to savor it all. Early in the morning, unless there are plans cooking I don't know about, we'll compile and examine the whole lot of things required on the job. It wouldn't hurt to get the larger items loaded before dressing in attire that fits the job status we've each assumed. Ed and Tom don the business suits, and the rest of us will sport our new logo work uniforms. By noon, we should be able to start hauling the generation equipment into Garlington. As of now," Dacus warned rakishly, "it's my turn to get a rise out of Vivian. Telling her Tom has ordered 'his' and 'her' chastity belts for them to wear oughta do it."

Art licked his lips, lifted eyebrows about three times, hailing, "Shall we join the lovely, so lovely, ladies?" His motive was twofold, preferring to spark another type of energy.

Amid giggles and laughter at Sam's jokes, the jukebox got louder as the bar became a rush hour event. "Anybody know where we are on the love wheel, tonight?" asked Tom.

"Dacus is the scientist. He can figure it out for us," teased Harry, looking around for a hat.

"As W. C. Fields used to say, 'I'd rather be in Philadelphia,'" quipped Dacus, handing him a bar bucket and suggesting he use ice cubes for billets . . . "It might cool 'em off!"

The distance between Harrison and Batesville is such that a trip from the mountain could be made in a little less than two hours. Following Dacus's morning briefing on equipment, in situ, Ed loaded the Mercedes wearing a newly acquired business suit, a hard hat for effect, and a handful of Crown Alloy checks signed by Maybelle, under her alias as Grace Latham Campbell, Executive Secretary. He set out, cocked and primed, relishing his role.

Arriving in Batesville just before one o'clock, Ed inquired about the most desirable motel accommodations. He was touted to the White Water Inn down by the river, where the White River Water Carnival holds forth every summer. There, he checked the rest of the gang and himself into separate rooms, under proper aliases. It created a mild flurry of attention with the number of guests checking in during the off-season.

In the restaurant, noon rush was over. Grabbing a tray, he started through a rather depleted buffet. Suddenly, he was nudged from behind and, turning, found himself face-to-face with Senator Eades. "Well, Senator. This is indeed a providential surprise," he exclaimed.

Eades propositioned, "I have a table by the window, viewing the river. Bring your tray and join me when you pass through."

Sipping iced tea, Eades addressed Ed's alias, remarking, "The other day, Mr. Baker, I told you that you'd be completely hooked up by the weekend. Well, I was almost correct. Full electric power will be available, I've been informed. However, cogeneration access has been delayed."

Ed put his fork down, frowning. "I thought you understood, Senator, the importance to have both access to power and a working, metered, cogeneration hookup with Arkansas Rivers Power Company at the same time. We are, at the moment, in the process of transporting generators in to test that hookup based upon the information you'd provided. This throws one hell of a monkey wrench into the schematic. It'll probably nullify the contract for twenty-five million being negotiated for fabrication of individual machinery that's to be housed at all ten plant sites."

Holding Eade's feet to the fire, he made a scorching accusation. "In fact, if we cannot have actual access to the power company, as contracted, then it's advisable to put a stop on operations." Reflecting, Ed fortified, "It was with great effort and priceless influence from both you and the governor's office that a cogeneration contract was obtained with the holding company controlling Arkansas Rivers Power. I foresee a lawsuit looming, based upon the above contract, which, I'll remind you, is already recorded with Arkansas PSC."

Trembling, the Senator stood, sputtering, "Take it easy, Mr. Baker. I'm going to move heaven and earth to keep from losing these plants. Believe me, when I get off the phone, I intend to be satisfied. Mark my word, we'll know something soon."

Having presence of mind to use a phone booth, he told a secretary at the power company, "This is Senator Eades calling Tracy Cross."

"Uno momento, Senator. I think I see him coming down the hall," cooed the secretary.

Tracy came on the line. "Hey, Buster, you're breathing heavy. What's got your blood pressure elevated? That White Water Inn waitress got you excited?"

Lampooning the trite by ignoring it, the Senator, wielded, "A major crisis . . . One that has to be solved this afternoon. You know about the Crown Alloys group, which is poised to bring industrial plants into eastern Arkansas, more than half of which are in my district. And you're aware there's a signed contract between them and your holding company, Central Amalgamated Power, recorded with the Public Service Commission. Problem is, I promised these people they'd have electricity and a hookup for cogeneration by the weekend. Not so, I've learned! The meter that would register their cogenerated power hasn't been installed. To add insult to injury, delivery on the damn thing's been delayed. I'll compound it one further for you, Tracy . . . A Crown Alloys spokesman tells me their twenty-five million dollar contract on purchase of specialty equipment to outfit all ten plants is out the window come Monday without having at least one site on line, namely, the one at Garlington. He went so far as to spell out the ramifications."

"Buster," wailed Tracy, "you know a big corporation like ours doesn't move that quickly. You're a master at gilding the lily . . . Why can't you placate him?"

Inflamed, Senator Eades whipped, "Aren't you CAP's lobbyist? There is a legislative bill pending, worth millions, and very dear to your collective, conniving hearts. That bill is presently before my Senate committee. I guarantee it'll never see the light of day if you bastards screw me out of these industrial plants for my district. Tracy, I've liked you ever since we served together in the legislature as freshmen, but I'm dead serious. Two things. You have the job of handling politics for the company, and you're the one who'll take the heat if that bill dies. Die it will, too, if you don't get off your ass and see to it the company lives up to its obligations."

The strong declaration delivered, Eades issued a deadline. "I can be reached through the desk at the White Water in Batesville. You have 'til sundown to put up or shut up!"

"Be reasonable!" Tracy shouted into the phone. But the line was already deserted.

Returning to the table, Eades said, "Mr. Baker, I've given the power company until evening to provide access by the weekend. I trust your company can indulge the time."

"This is very troubling," mumbled Ed. "I and a portion of the crew are checked in at the Inn. I'm expected to meet some of my people out at the site in half an hour. We'll return later for the night. You can look me up then."

Ed hadn't been gone over thirty minutes when Senator Eades was paged by the desk. A clerk pointed to a house phone nearby. Tracy came on the line, relating, "We have just completed an emergency conference by phone. A supervisor has been dispatched from Searcy to confer with you at the jobsite in Garlington around four o'clock. His whole purpose is to satisfy both you and the company involved. In return, we want guaranteed safe passage for our bill!"

"You've got my word the legislature will be in accord with me," assured Senator Eades. "In the meantime, Tracy, I'm driving out there. I'll coordinate timing to be present when the supervisor arrives to get a firsthand analysis of what he says. Talk to you later."

Meticulously, Dacus packed the balance of equipment into the rental van. He put his one-ton truck with refrigerator body through a trial run, even though generating equipment had worked perfectly during the Lavender Peacock scam. As a last act, he removed the Oklahoma license plate from Maybelle's Jaguar and mounted it on his one ton-truck. Loaded, another pilgrimage began. They left the mountain at five-minute intervals. Dacus, being leadman in the big rental van, was followed by Sam and Theo in the truck. The Land Rover, occupied by Art and Harry, had their survey instruments and tripods aboard.

Finding Ed involved, talking to the foreman of the fence and guard shack crew, Dacus flashed an ID card and drove through. Ed nodded and continued talking to the foreman without needing to introduce anybody. The briefing finished, Ed strolled over to Dacus still clipping his ID to a shirt pocket. Between clenched teeth, he mouthed, "We have a little problem."

In a low and guarded voice, Dacus ventured, "Tell me."

Motioning to be followed, Ed walked toward the interior of the abandoned limestone quarry. "I was informed this afternoon by Senator Eades that there would be electrical access by this weekend, but the hookup to generate would not come until later. How much later was never discussed, because I put the power play on him regarding the twenty-five million dollar contract. He immediately dialed up someone at the power company and apparently had his own pressure ploy. Told me he'd issued an ultimatum. They have until sundown to assure him the hookup's made within the time frame."

Seeing dust of another vehicle approaching, they began walking back. "By the way, everyone has reservations down by the river. I guess we'll know something by 'check-in time' tonight," Ed told Dacus.

The gang from Harrison rolled in like clockwork, fanning identification, getting parked for unloading, and donning hard hats began spreading out. Senator Eades arrived moments later to witness their display, etched as a formidable workforce. Lowering his window, he waved Ed over to the car. "Mr. Baker, the power company has obviously reconsidered its position. They'll have a supervisor based out of Searcy here around four o'clock. He'll make a jobsite assessment of your needs, and in my presence, incidently."

Ed hailed Dacus over. Turning to Eades, he introduced, "Senator, I want you to meet Stanley Claybaugh, our resident electrical expert for the company. Call him Stan. Stan, this is Senator Eades." Dacus shook hands without comment.

Eades summed up the newcomer, thinking to himself, *I don't know a damn thing about electricity, and he surely doesn't know a damn thing about politics.*

Sensing an awkward period in the making until the power company representative arrived, Ed extended an invitation to Eades. "Let me give you a tour of the place to become oriented. I'll try to lay out a description of plans Crown Alloys has for its development later."

His expedition underway, Ed had the Senator on a classic snipe hunt. Dacus seized the opportunity to ease over to his group and instruct, "Make yourselves busy. Stay completely out of conversation range from the Honorable Senator, Ed, and me. Be actively present at a distance, but not involved, and definitely not intrusive."

They immediately obliged by doing what they do best, appearing to be absorbed in a legitimate activity. Dacus, alone, wandered about yet with a marked direction, assessing the facilities, carefully keeping a distance from Ed and Eades. He would stop occasionally, as if to eye the level or distance of a subject and maybe step off a few feet, fulfilling the misdirection.

Only minutes late, James Brady sped onto the complex. Alighting from his company car, he hurriedly sought out the Senator. "Your Honor, I'm at your service," he announced, spitting tobacco juice on the ground.

Making introductions, Eades presented Brady around. "This is Mr. Baker, official of Crown Alloys." Motioning to Dacus, he involved, "James, this is Mr. Stanley Claybaugh, their electrical technician. Now, gentlemen, meet Mr. James Brady of Arkansas Rivers Power Company."

Before other formalities could occur, Brady spat again. Turning to Dacus, he engaged him briefly, prying, "Stan, are you an electrical engineer?"

"I don't claim to be." came Dacus's noncommittal answer, downplaying his status.

Brady engaged Ed more professionally. "Exactly what do you need, Mr. Baker, and when?"

"Sir," Ed intimidated, "our terms were to have electrical power plus a cogeneration hookup facility operable by the weekend. Monday is deadline for the test run to seal whether or not my company is favorably inclined to invest a considerable sum of money for construction of custom machinery or to abandon the project, entirely."

"Well, now I get the picture. If I was a Michelangelo, I'd paint one. What you've proposing is a physical impossibility," blocked Brady. "There's not a cogen meter in stock anywhere in this region. Least of all, can we get one in here and have it installed by Monday."

Dacus smoothly interjected, "Mr. Brady, take a look at those two poles over there. Is that what I think I'm seein' on one of them?"

"Hmm . . . Be damned! That's a cogen meter on one pole and a transformer on the other," exclaimed Brady lamely. "You've got it all right, Mr. Claybaugh, but I'll bet my boots it's not operational after who knows how many years."

"I'll make it work," vowed Dacus encouragingly. "Bring a crew in here tomorrow morning. If luck's a lady, all she needs is to be cleaned out of some spider nests and have the contacts polished. I've brought necessary equipment to independently generate the current for a test of pumping power into those lines. We'll see if we can't make it work."

"Thought you said you weren't an engineer," confronted Brady, his confidence assailed.

"My words were I didn't claim to be one," calmed Dacus. "Just put me down as a tinker and a handyman. Oh, one more thing. Initial construction can be started by using the existing transformer you have on the other pole. In operation tho, it'll take an enormous amount of power later. You might as well requisition a much larger transformer now. The facilities located here near that substation are ideal," Dacus said, pointing. "Sure would make things easier if the other nine sites had the same setup."

Leaving, Brady asserted he'd have a crew on the job between eight thirty and nine in the morning. Relieved and ready to get back to town, Senator Eades handed a card to Ed. "My home phone number is the printed one," he enlisted. "Written in is the Country Club's number, my second home, and I'll be there after seven tomorrow evening. I'd appreciate a call at the end of your day to bring me up to date. After this doozie, hopefully, I can sleep tonight."

Utility trucks, manned by Brady and his workmen, arrived earlier than expected the next morning to find a beehive of activity. There were two survey teams in separate locations on the property. Dacus, from atop a refrigeration storage unit on a one-ton truck, was tackling toilsome restoration of the cogen meter. The gang of fence builders hammered and cursed, unaffected that Ed stood nearby. They were hell-bent on finishing the job by day's end and getting paid.

Brady, prepared to install a huge transformer, pointed his crew in the right direction. He began watching Dacus out of the corner of an eye. By midmorning, he'd plotted a course of action to uncork what the guy was made of. At noon, when everybody was pulling out a sack lunch, he got a Coke, wandered over, and sat down next to Dacus, jawing, "You're damn good at what you do, and seem to know what's needed to fix most anything. Stan, if you're not an engineer, how'd you learn to do the stuff you're doin'?"

Inwardly, Dacus gloated. *This con is practically over*, he thought. In his guise as Stan Claybaugh, he rambled, weaving Brady into his confidence. "Oh, I ran away from home and became a roustabout in a midsized carnival. It was hard work with damn few rewards. Even as a kid, I knew I didn't want that abuse to be my life's future. The cuffs were a helluva lot harder than at home. I got a break when the old man, who was in charge of electricity for the carnival, took a likin' to me and decided to make me his apprentice. For the most part, we generated our own electricity except in those cities that were in the business of distributing and selling power to their citizens. Goodwill gesture, or case of have to, we'd hook on to a city's power and pay them for the week's run. When the old man died several years later, I'd learned the ropes and was able to take his place, thinking myself as having a career." Brady's buying it, allowed him to elaborate.

"Over the course of the next several years, carnivals were bought, sold, upgraded, and consolidated. I became the electrician for an affiliated group of them. My headquarters at the largest one, naturally, was near the company office of its president. He had a pretty young thing of a wife who'd put some moves on me. Dumblike, I went for it. Fine stuff, but I wound up making tracks for my own safety. The old man was very powerful, and I'd incurred his hatred big-time. Ever since then, I've bummed around, rebuilding alternators, generators, starters, and hiring on where electrical work could be had. Just sorta transient I guess."

"How did you wind up in this job?" pumped Brady, sold on his story.

"An old friend! Way back, when I ran away from home, another kid came along. Major difference was, he had neither the resolve I did for leaving home nor the fortitude for the kind of life out there. We hung together awhile. Maybe a couple of years later, he decided to go home and try for an education. To make a long story short, his business career took off, and it's been spectacular. He's a heavy stockholder in Crown Alloys, where it seems there's an absolute need for secrecy concerning a newly patented process. It required a person, with no vested interest, in charge of all electrical matters, some of which are an integral part of the process. Results were, my old friend looked me up, put the friendly persuasion to me, along with his strong encouragement, and I took the job. Their secrets were secure. He knew it, and I knew my future would be solid."

James Brady put things on hold, blurting, "I suspect I'll be looking for a job, 'round about the time this plant goes into operation. Downsizin's far from over. I got too much time in for the feather merchants to keep me on. Middle and lower management is bein' wiped smooth out. It comes to mind, my best bet is to do everything I can to help you, 'cause this section of the state needs help. It's dyin' on the vine as it is. Ten industrial plants would make a whale of a big influence to turn the local economy about-face. Maybe, out of it all, I can make a half-decent living when I'm put on the street." Reflecting on Dacus's tale prompted offering the positive . . .

"Before day's end," he predicted, "you'll have electricity thru a transformer big enough to deliver the size load you're after. When and if you can make the cogen meter work, I'll read both meters, punch you into our central computer, and you'll be in business."

Rethinking, Brady cautioned, "One more thing. You know contract meter readers have been hired to, what's the word, usurp career employees. Cheaper, of course, and sort of like a cleaning service that comes around regularly to groom offices. Fixing, or having the care to preserve ain't a part of it. Why else? You're not pickin' up the tab for any insurance, paid vacations, pensions, or the like. Don't get me wrong, these people do a job. Problem is there's really not any responsibility to, or for them, and they damn sure aren't inclined to assume any. The corporate big shots of my company and the meter reading company have now made another move to cut costs. They transferred a duty of the actual meter reader to be done by our computer. It's made things easier I suppose. A meter reader keeps up with only one figure, the one he reads. Using the network computer in his truck, he transfers the reading to their central headquarters, and the deed is done. Simple, eh?. But the meter readers are mad as hell and I don't blame 'em. Less time's involved, so more of 'em will surely be laid off to decrease payroll."

Exultant, Dacus returned to working on the meter. His thoughts raced, It's all mechanical from here on in! The company employees have come to hate the establishment. They're operating as individuals, not as a proud company team, and meter readers are also pissed. Life is sweet!

Progress during the afternoon exceeded expectations. Final hookup of the transformer was achieved and power made available. An hour later, Crown Alloys's generating equipment became ready. Dacus geared up and tested the cogeneration meter, which worked perfectly. Its reading was in agreement with the monitor reading on the generating equipment.

James Brady read both meters, went over to the crew's truck that housed a computer, and inserted his handheld device, which in turn moved the information to the mainframe in Dallas. "You're now a new customer listed in our computer," Brady professed. To himself, he happily mumbled, *My ass is safe with the bigwigs for a little while longer.*

Dacus met with his gang as soon as the power company crew left the site. "We need one more good night's sleep. Again, let's take everything in with us to the motel where there's a little security. Starting tomorrow night, this place must be guarded twenty-four hours a day until we leave. Harry and Sam will work as a team. Art and Theo are to become another. One guards at night, and the other becomes a day watchman. The other team will work the next day in the same manner. You'll only be working every other day, except in emergencies. That leaves Ed and me to rotate shifts on the generating equipment. If you're ready, let's load up everything portable, secure the place, and head for the motel." He disconnected his generator setup from the cogen meter, and they were gone in fifteen minutes.

After an obligatory call to satisfy Senator Eades's egoism, Ed phoned Dacus's room. His itch to discuss things was put on hold until after Dacus had showered . . .

Knocking, Ed came into the room, exerting, "I think it'd be a bad idea to discuss business over dinner, or at the bar, for that matter. I feel pressured with entirely too much information. I need an outlet, a summary, or something from you to arrange and put things in perspective."

As he combed his hair, Dacus relayed, "Let me finish dressing." Actually, he wanted to organize his thoughts. It had been a fast and productive day for him too. Sitting down to put socks on, he conceded, "Granted, I agree with you that our business shouldn't be hacked in public. Whatever's discussed between us, pass it on to the others in private. Grab your coat, Ed. We'll drop by the bar for a drink to go and take a walk down to the riverside gazebo."

Situated, Dacus disclosed the insight he'd gained. "This day has been very revealing. The power company we've known is slowly destroying its image by the misuse of computers. And it's not just only the utilities. It's an epidemic spreading throughout the industry. For instance, car dealers are now separated from manufacturers by computers. If there's a mistake in a shipment, or it's not on time, no one hears but the computer, which assumes zero responsibility. Any facet of industry that can legally merge to dominate a segment automatically turns to downsizing."

Fallout of the system evidenced, he proposed how it could be used. "The missing equation involving today's shift of structure in industrial management is mankind, itself. Brady hates the power company because of what he conceives they've done for the sake of money. Can you imagine his reaction when ten plants don't materialize, and he learns we've screwed the power company royally? Let's hope he blames downsizing and boasts of having known us. Incidentally, Ed, he said a new contract between the utility and the company providing meter reading service is in the works to cut its current staff of readers by 30 percent. They're mad as hell and looking for another job."

Dacus chuckled, put his glass to Ed's, and asked, "Now, what's this about your concern of being overloaded on today's occurrences?"

Disregarding his intention to fill Dacus's ear, Ed had trouble believing what he'd heard and demanded, "Are you saying the scam is over?"

"It is over, for all practical purposes," assured Dacus, firmly. "We've conned an industrial development commission, public service commission, governor's office and the legislature, along with a multitude of others. Central Amalgamated Power is conned through the coercion of one of its senior officials. Consequently, Arkansas Rivers Power Company had to follow suit.

For the next six weeks, everything is mechanical, except, of course, the general one of keeping up an image as representatives of Crown Alloys. Four weeks from now, the meter reader doesn't need to be conned into getting him to read the meters. From that moment on, Ed, our objective is in the tender loving care of computers . . ."

"I share every bit of elation that you do, Dacus," Ed united. "Particularly since I picked at and stirred controversy with it from the very beginning. Call me a true believer and willing to do anything I can to see it through. Let's face it tho," he confessed. "I'm not mechanically minded. There's no way I can fill your boots out in the field, unless it's with lead. I'd be scared to death of botching the operation and spoiling our chances of bringing this one to sweet fruition."

Dacus had listened patiently, fully comprehending his valid concern. "Tell you what, Ed. It's time to replenish these drinks, and at the bar this time. Go by the desk first and reserve a conference room for later while I make a pit stop."

The customary bar chitchat aside, they moved to a table overlooking the river in a mostly vacated lounge. "Cheers!" Dacus saluted, intent on derailing Ed's misconceptions of himself. "Seriously, I can tell from the look on your face what you're feeling. You haven't let anyone down, least of all me. Forget it, man! Time and again, we've turned to you for good judgment. Once more, hard as it's being on you right now, it prevailed. I'm to blame for arbitrarily appointing you to an ill-suited task and am fully aware that if push came to shove, you'd have given it your best shot. Deferring to your better judgment reflects character as reason to withdraw, so don't give it a black eye. I fully respect your insight. How about one more before we join the others for dinner?"

The best of White Water's menu was ordered and served. Business was set on the back burner while tall tales and jokes flowed more than the wine, and often more colorful. Over coffee, Ed announced, "We've reserved a private room for the evening to make revisions in planning. It shouldn't take long to evaluate things. However, if you'd like another drink, go by the bar on your way, and bring it with you to the meeting room."

Dacus kicked back in an oversized executive chair at the head of a massive table. "Well, fellow Associates, this is where we are tonight," he opened to wrap up events. Every facet of the day's operation was expounded and detailed, item for item, even greater than that which he had related to Ed earlier. Pausing, his demeanor visibly altered as a conclusion materialized to be pursued . . . "Ed," he revealed, "simply is not comfortable that he possesses enough mechanical capabilities to pull off being in charge of operations in my absence. To honor his decision, and oblige his concern, it's time to draw from plan B that Art referred to earlier. I've no qualms about Ed's qualities and recognize that they'd be put to better use supervising work at the ship,"

Blackballing, he fingered, "Theo, you played it pretty cool at our round table discussion the night before we left to move in on the job. We know you're not totally ignorant on the subject after having wired and rigged a few crap tables and roulette wheels in joints where you've worked. How about you taking over as acting electrician? If you can hold our equipment together for three days, while I take Ed to New Orleans to introduce him into that scenario, it'll work."

Rested, and with renewed direction, the whole gang of six converged on site at eight o'clock. Pulling up to a concrete slab, previously used as floor of a building, Dacus opened the rental van's back doors and lowered a Tommy Lift to the ground. The entire morning was occupied with unloading from the truck and placement of the heavy pieces of equipment into precise positions on the slab. While they worked, Dacus provided key pointers, answered questions, and lectured as to the uses and purposes of each item. When all heavy pieces were in place, Sam bid them adieu and left for the motel to get four hour's sleep before his night shift began.

Establishing the hookup became time consuming. It was after six before cogeneration was brought into operation. Even though they were steadily meeting goal after goal, Harry had to find fault. "No one's said a word or made a move to put the tent up to protect all this equipment."

Ignoring the agitation, Dacus very kindly consoled, "Don't worry, Harry. We'll get it up tomorrow. You're forgetting there's already an oversized, very soft shell cover in place, and I'll be here all night. If it starts raining, it's time enough to put the machinery under a small hard shell and keep the water off."

Signaling the others to join him, he outlined, "Listen, it'll take the next two days for me to adjust everything to deliver maximum charge into the power lines. After that, Ed and I will drive to New Orleans. I should be back here in three, four days max. If there's any trouble, or problems with the equipment you can't solve, try to reach Rabbit on my cellular phone."

Sam unloaded the coffeemaker, a fresh five-gallon chiller of water, and their hot food from the motel. Preparation for the night's duty was wrapping up when the others departed. Two uneventful days later, Dacus and Ed left, headed to the mountain, and ultimately the ship . . .

CHAPTER 20

In Harrison, Ed and Dacus's first agenda was to return and settle for use of the rented van. They then drove to Dacus's office in the strip mall, transmitting an e-mail. It announced his arrival at the Zallafino mansion the next evening accompanied by a partner.

Homecoming was not exactly as expected. Least of all was it mundane. Hearing the car accelerate along the incline, Randi came up from the pasture barebacked on the mare. Windblown and exuberant, she ran to meet them, planting a slightly sweat-salted kiss on their lips. "Gads, is it ever good to see you, guys," she said as she gave a little hug. Reaching into the car to retrieve something to carry inside, her whimsical nonsense flowed on. "Guess what! We've got a whole lot more pussy up here than when you left!"

Pussy meant only one thing to Ed at the moment. He almost bumped his head on the trunk lid, straightening up to ask, "How? Where are they? Who brought them?"

Randi giggled. "Sissy, the cat in the barn had seven kittens about three days ago. You gotta see 'em. They're darling!"

Dacus laughed, slapping his thigh. "I can't believe you got suckered in on that one, Ed!"

Stepping onto the veranda, they were greeted by Julie from behind an easel. Preoccupied with putting finishing touches on a landscape, she only cooed, "Hello, sweeties."

Rosie, curled in the big wing back close by, lost all inspiration for writing poetry upon hearing the car roll up. "Whistle, whittle, Yucatan. What'll ever take the place of a man!" was scribbled across the notepad she tossed aside to get in on the welcoming party. The big shirt she wore covered bare essentials and exposed sharpely long legs.

Tom and Vivian, reflecting moodiness of feeling neglected, began making their way out to the front entry. They couldn't help but drop a few special effects of facial distress for Dacus's benefit. It was preempted by a noisy hoopla gaining momentum outside.

Coming up across the knoll from a flowing stream below were Barbee and Cherrie, stark naked, hair dripping, and skin glistening with water droplets, holding only their shorts and tees in front as they ran. The little outing to wade and turn stones for crawfish had become a splash party after getting totally wet from slipping on mossy rocks.

Unable to concentrate on technical aspects of a latest-best seller she was reading, and a little disgusted with all the fanfare, Eva slammed the book shut. She slid off the couch, lit a cigarette, and greeted, "Hi, guys." In the next breath, seeing Barbee and Cherrie, she cried out amid laughter, "What the hell! We got a nudist camp going now?"

The two reached the veranda and slipped into a side door to get bathed and dressed. Eva pushed an auburn curl back, inviting Ed and Dacus to enter. Ed popped his head up, sniffing. Looking at Dacus, he asked, "Do you smell what I do?" An aroma led them toward the kitchen, where Rabbit was anchored. The expression on his face left no doubt his domain had been invaded. Smells of fresh baked yeast bread filled the nostrils, and a rum cake rested on a pedestal. Lifting a pot's lid on the stove revealed fish chowder simmering. Ed couldn't resist opening the oven and received a whop on his rear from Candy's tea towel. "Like the smell? Try tasting, or do you wanna lick tha bowl?" she said with another flip of the towel.

Tired, but refreshingly pleased with such a display of accord among the bunch, Dacus and Ed quickly moved personal gear into their rooms, washed up, and were back to pour a drink. They toasted toward all four corners of the room. Vivian, catching the gesture but not its purpose, inquired, "And who may I ask are you saluting? These four walls or something beyond?"

Still standing, Dacus nodded. "In a minute, Vivian. All ears here need to be tuned in on this one. Someone roust Rabbit and his helpers out of the kitchen so it doesn't have to be repeated."

Perking up, Tom became an esquire inquiring, "Lulu too?"

"Sure, if she wishes," consented Dacus, "and get Candy out of Rabbits' kitchen."

Rabbit and Candy joined them, without Lulu. Vivian helped Dacus, who saw to it that everyone had a drink of choice in hand. He raised his glass to arm's length, proclaiming, "Here's to electricity that's been pumping into power lines at Garlington for the past two days! Here's to the next twenty-eight days when the meter's read, plus a few more days for payment to be made by a bank transfer to our account!" Among the cheering, Ed, Tom, and Vivian clinked glasses to Dacus's in an elated toast. From the four, the sound of glass clinking against glass swept around the room. It was capped off by someone's sobering thought voiced . . . "That's five weeks from now!"

"You've heard it right!" Dacus said, breaking their trance. "This scam is ahead of schedule. In those few days we were gone, Ed took on Senator Eades, threatened to pull operations and slap a lawsuit if he didn't cure a major delay presented that could have derailed Maybelle's efforts. As I speak, our guys are rotating shifts around the clock on site to maintain its status. Here at base, there's more than a full share for each in the offing to make things work. The countdown has begun, and the number of days is established for putting final touches on departure," he imparted.

"Tom and Vivian, you know in depth the criteria of our Association. Rabbit, your role defies definition. Capable ladies, you are by no means totally in the dark on affairs. The sequence is manifest when a hired meter reader takes a reading off our two meters and logs it in to the utility. The guys and I are out of there and on our way back here. The instant an automated transfer of money to our account occurs, not a minute can be wasted in clearing the mountain."

Excited to be included, and a bit overwhelmed at Dacus's urgency, a couple of the girls chorused, "Where's Maybelle, and when's she due back?"

Ed fielded the question. "I'm the last one to hear from her. She's banking, getting ready to move the money offshore to Georgetown, a tax haven on Grand Cayman. Your guess is as good as mine. Maybe she's in Miami, Atlanta, or in between. Regardless, we'll get her here."

Eva fully grasped the future's promise of fortune. She didn't interject her usual bitch of, "We're not doing tricks, so we're not makin money," and refrained from comments.

Later, Dacus interrupted idle chatter. "It's good night for Ed and me. We expect to leave on the drive to New Orleans before daylight. My plans are to spend one day acquainting Ed and showing him what's involved. I'd like to fly back in to Springfield the next day and get a lift on into here. Tom, how about you checking in at the strip mall office to see if any changes in plans are on the computer. Here are the keys. And, Ed, before I forget it, where are the signed Crown Alloys checks Maybelle left with you? I'll need them while you're out of pocket. Just as soon as your name's added to the Association's bank account in Lafitte, you'll have money available. In the meantime, it eliminates 'signed checks' lying about."

Dacus chauffeured Ed late afternoon on the last leg of their trip. He pulled up to the gate set in great oaks leading to the mansion. A guard stepped to the Mercedes's window, recognizing him. Acknowledging, Dacus returned, "Hi, how ya doin'?" He introduced and justified their presence, relaying, "Meet Ed Bemis, and I believe we're expected."

Ed had been agog for most of the miles they'd traveled through the backcountry. He was quietly flabbergasted as they tooled up the circular driveway in front of the mansion. When met by a butler opening his car door, he lost his voice.

Dacus explained that his partner anticipated only the one night's stay and indicated those items needed. The butler took their overnight bags and ushered them up the massive stairway to separate rooms. He informed Dacus that Mr. Zallafino would not be available until morning.

The walk up and back downstairs loosened driving fatigue, and Dacus steered Ed toward the bar. Ed observed everything. He listened to small talk between the butler, doubling as bartender, and Dacus. After a perfectly timed interval, they were escorted into the dining room to a served, sumptuous Sicilian meal. The butler uncorked a bottle of dry red wine and served up two glasses before setting it on the table. He extended, "If you need anything, ring the bell."

Savoring last tastes of the vintage wine, Dacus rang for the butler, requesting brandy and a cigar. Obliged, he and Ed strolled out on the veranda to recap things. Absorbed with the clear night, Ed remarked, "Absolutely fabulous. I could get used to this lifestyle in a New York minute."

"Patience, man. Give it about a year and a half. By then, you and I, and all the rest of the Association, may have more than you think you're seeing here," Dacus predicted.

"Everything you've told me thus far," Ed surmised, "has worked out exactly as you said it would. Not only do I take your word, but I might hold you to it."

Dacus beat Ed up and out by ten minutes. Considering options to pursue, they walked outside to find Marc seated at a table. He nodded genially. "Welcome, gentlemen."

Dacus made the introduction. "Mr. Zallafino, meet one of my partners, Ed Bemis. Ed, this is Marc Zallafino. If it's satisfactory, we'll continue using first names." Ed and Marc shook hands, and the three seated themselves.

Marc, a perturbed look on his face, cited, "We have trouble, Dacus. When I learned you were coming back early, I sent Franco to find how much progress had been made to renovate the machinery you'd bought. He reported nothing had been done. He also told me he'd previously warned Runshang not to screw you around. This became known only yesterday. First impulse was for my people to call on him, but I thought better of it until you could be consulted."

"What did you have in mind?" Dacus asked vigilantly.

Marc chose his words carefully. "I already know what you personally are capable of doing when affronted. There is, however, the transaction between you and me involving the both of us. You're going to sail out of here. I have no reason to relocate, and I want to keep it that way. To ignore the situation puts the Family's reputation at stake. I'd prefer you stay out of this one. Let me handle it my way."

Dacus deliberated momentarily. "Fine, Marc. I respect and honor your position. By the same token, I have a condition. Allow Ed, as an unknown staying in the background, to go along with your people to make a report of what he sees for my evaluation afterward."

Marc credited Ed. "Do you have any objections to going along? If not, you'll be advised to carry a gun. My men will get you one."

Politely, Ed vetoed the weapon. "Thanks anyway. I'm not too handy with guns. I'm much more comfortable using my knife for protection."

Satisfied, Marc instructed, "Be ready to move out in an hour. Dacus, perhaps you might want to brief Ed on the place and the man, Nick Runshang. It's time I left to round up and brief my lieutenants and the soldiers who'll be carrying out the hit."

An hour and a half later, he addressed his troops, telling them how far to carry their intimidation. "Rough him up any way you want to. I don't want him crippled so he can't work. The best method of getting Runshang's attention," he opted, "is to destroy something of more value than the ten thousand Mr. Dacus has already paid."

The lieutenants responded, reassuring Marc it would be a measured and calculated effort. Ed was invited into their vehicle with a hand motion. Dacus took due note of an extra lieutenant he had not met. A monster of a man, the fellow stood at least six foot eight and probably weighed 350 nonfat pounds. His head matched his body and appeared to be as big as a bucket. Before getting in the car, he popped the trunk open. Removing his sport coat, he carefully folded and placed it inside. Without the coat, all he had on underneath was a tank top, exposing massive hands and muscle bound arms.

Accessing Runshang's shipyard, the car with the three lieutenants and Ed proceeded to the office parking lot. Not far away, the soldiers parked in the middle of a machinery yard and dry dock area. The two well-dressed lieutenants lured Nick out of his office on pretext of being interested in one of his boats. The big lieutenant stayed put in the car.

They walked to two boats parked side by side. One of them asked Nick the smaller boat's price then that of the other. Nick quoted twenty-five and thirty-five grand. "Perfect, I'd say," replied the lead lieutenant. The other lieutenant signaled to the soldiers. Fifteen piled out of the vehicles with axes and baseball bats, simultaneously proceeding to destroy both boats. Hulls were chopped full of gashing holes, windshields bashed, and outboards destroyed.

Nick screamed, turning red with rage. "What the fuck ya think ya doin'?" Before he could react to attack either of the lieutenants, Ed and the big fellow had moved in from behind. Nick found himself hoisted high in the air by two huge hands then promptly dropped on his heels.

"Phew-wee," rumbled the giant. "You stink. You never had a bath?" Grabbing Nick by the collar with one hand and holding his nose with the other, he proceeded to single-handedly drag him straight for the open bay.

Nick panicked, begging and yelling, "I can't swim! You'll drown me!"

Nonplussed, the giant ripped clothes off Nick and, raising him high above his head, threw him into the bay. Nick came up sputtering in waist-deep water. At the same time, two soldiers had stripped off, jumped in, and grabbed both of Nick's arms while another soldier handed the giant a stiff scrub brush and squirt bottle of deodorant soap.

Squealing like a stuck pig, Nick provided the background music to be methodically scrubbed from head to foot, especially the more sensitive parts. The music stopped. A soldier harassed Nick in terms more penetrating than stings of bristles. "You're surely going to die. It has to be the second time for you to be clean in your whole life." Shoving him ashore in newborn apparel, he was told to finish the job he'd contracted on the submarine equipment, or else!

The giant towered over a nude Nick. "You die slow, swine, if you don' finish tha work. I see to it. We be back tomorrow and every day ta come till it done. Unner'stand?"

After the Mafia's soldiers left, Nick ordered clothes from town. He sent an employee in to pick up and deliver them. Wasting no time, he called a steady customer, Rafael Mendoza, plying him with implications of what had happened. "I need protection," Nick solicited.

Mendoza asked suspiciously, "Was man who scrub you giant hombre?"

Nick scorned, "Yeah. Whazzat to you?"

Mendoza swallowed hard. "Ya crazy sumbitch. Ya done cross Zallafino Family. We don' get along. If ya t'ink we get inna gang war for ya, ya mo' loco."

Nick cajoled, "I wanna come see ya, monsieur."

"No come, Nick. Ya steenk. Talka business on le phone, an' maybe we no have to have ya business." The phone went dead. A televised evangelist never converted anyone quicker.

Back at the Zallafino Estate, two lieutenants filed their report. Ed briefed Dacus, privately. "These guys are very proficient," Ed related. "The worst thing that happened to him was losing two boats. According to his figures, it amounted to sixty thousand dollars. I personally believe he doubled what he said he had in them. Even at that, thirty thousand is three times more than you're out. In my opinion, if the son of a bitch didn't get the message, he's even stupider than he looks or smelled before they got through with him."

Dacus interrupted passionately, "What we're out is *time*. To hell with the money!"

Ed rationalized, "He hasn't been personally hurt, yet. A scrub bath with a stiff brush, soap, and cold water, peeled off the top layer of his thick skin. We'll see what tomorrow brings. It's his move. Lose more property, while having his pain tolerance stretched, or . . ."

Dacus changed the subject. "It'll work out. If it doesn't, we'll cross that bridge when we come to it. For now, we mustn't waste a minute in orienting you to all you need to know, and it's terribly important I speak with Marc."

Marc had just completed a debriefing of his troops when Dacus and Ed showed up. Dacus opened, commenting, "It's unfortunate half a day has been taken up messing with this sorta crap, although it had to be. Two things, Marc, now that time's limited and I must leave in the morning. Can you be available to intercede for Ed so he's able to take it from here? And, what kind of deal can I strike with you to ride your jet to Springfield?"

Marc shot a glance at him, allowing. "You sure hop around a lot. How would it suit you to buy the jet fuel as pay for the trip?" he bargained to keep Dacus from taking issue on price.

"That's more than fair," affirmed Dacus. "However, there's a little more to it than just me as a passenger, which might change your mind. You may need more money because I'm making a purchase down here to be transported back."

"What's the cargo?" asked Marc, less than interested, fully expecting it to be a woman and her baggage or something insignificant.

"Canisters of helium, to . . ." Dacus never finished.

"HELIUM!" Marc exploded. "Have you lost your mind? What sane person would go up in a plane loaded with an explosive gas? My pilot is no daredevil as you seem to be. I'm certain he won't consider flying it, nor could you persuade me to condone such risk."

"Ah, settle down, Marc. Helium is an inert gas," Dacus clarified. "Sure you're not hung up, mistaking it for hydrogen, the flammable, explosive gas that'll blow you to bits?"

"Oh yeah. What's it for anyway?" queried Marc, regrouping to be civil.

"Let's say I want us to leave the country with a little more money than what the boat's worth. To insure it, I intend to make use of cryogenics," Dacus explained.

"That's Greek, Dacus. Speak English," Marc rebuked. "What the hell is cryogenics?"

"Low temperature physics," defined Dacus as if it were an everyday discourse.

"Nuff said, please. Plane's yours. Anything else?" conceded Marc, shaking his head and wishing he'd never been so asinine as to react with such poor judgment.

"As a matter of fact, yes, there is." Ed needs a decent motel within ten miles that he can check in that's within distance to coordinate affairs."

Marc brushed him aside curtly. "Ed's welcome to be my guest. After today's event, it'd be suicide to put him up in a motel."

Dacus raised his right index finger, pointing out, "Probably true since neither you nor I know the security of your phone lines. It's simply not good business if my people talk to me from any of your phones. It's fine for Ed to stay. Truth is though, he and I need to be able to talk on a phone that's unlikely to be tapped. Any suggestions?"

Marc lit up, recalling, "There's a run-down motel on the edge of Lafitte that's perfect. Its heyday is over, but rooms are still maintained. No reason Ed can't check in there, explaining he'll be in and out, and pay a week in advance. He can come and go to the place with my lieutenants, and y'all can talk at designated hours. The rest of the time I'd like Ed here where I know he'll be safe just in case he's associated with me from the Runshang incident."

"That's a winner!" enthused Dacus momentarily. Pressure mounting, he cited, "Only now I must find time to show Ed through the ship and detail a few priorities. Also, on my list is to find and order as many canisters of helium as the plane will transport."

"Let me worry about the helium," Marc tendered. "We can settle up in the morning, and I'll even delay dinner for the two of you this evening."

"I owe you," declared Dacus. "Come with me, Ed. Gotta neat ship to show ya."

Shadows lengthened, as did Dacus and Ed's stay on the ship. Gitano and Gilberto drove in from a tennis tournament to learn guests were expected for dinner. The butler inquired if they were going to dine. Making an affirmative gesture to him, they sought out Marc. He watched their demeanor as questions were fired at him about the new guest.

Finally, he'd had enough and insistently ordered, "The man is not to be interrogated. Don't ask him one damn, business related question! You got it?" They nodded grudgingly.

Marc humored them. "It'll be much easier to outline pros and cons later. This is another time when you will learn. Use some discipline. Observe, listen, and trust me for who I am!"

Brotherly reaction prevailed to debate their cause, tho. "Get real, Marc, you still don't know anything about the man who calls himself Dacus," Gitano argued.

"Anyone," Marc solidly rebuked, "who can place half a million in a Lafitte bank, with a cashier's check, is no sleaze bum." It was the quietus for the two, who backed off.

The bar became the gathering place as usual. Marc, Gitano, and Gilberto dropped family subjects to catch up on personals of wine, women, song, and tennis. Dacus and Ed didn't show until dark thirty, apologizing for the tardiness. Marc made introductions, leading everyone to the dining room. Small talk dominated the conversation until Gitano couldn't resist sqeezing in a question. "Sir, how'd you like the ship?"

"The description I got didn't justify her qualities," commuted Ed, catching Dacus's eye. "She must've been great for leisure cruises in your younger days."

Unable to contain himself, Gilberto used the old cliché to pry. "You sure look familiar to me." Marc cleared his throat, glaring warily at the two brothers.

Smiling, Ed smoothly disclaimed the likelihood. "Oh, I've a nondescript face. So common, in fact, some folks think they've met me before." His remark strained their small talk.

"Something's awkward!" Dacus interjected. "I'm not exactly sure what it is, but I'm going to do my dead level best to make it go away. First up, Marc, you and I have made a one on one, eye-to-eye handshake deal that couldn't be more binding if it had every existing legal tie wrapped around it. Secondly, you have two interested brothers, both present. I have eight partners, equally vested, and one of them is seated with us tonight. Third, there's the unknown, and it loses the mystic if you can relate to it," he detailed, sensing a need to correlate principles.

Dacus further disclosed, "I've been associated with seven of these eight people for about twenty-five years. The rackets are our lives. I want you to grasp, as firmly as we're aware of, how fine the line is existing in bonds between an old time con and a Mafia family."

"You mean there's only nine of you?" Marc interposed, acutely surprised.

Disregarding Marc's instructions, Gilberto took the kid gloves off, questioning, "What about your man, George Washington?" A grain of salt falling from the table could have been heard thru the still lull that followed. Marc was too stunned to react.

Dacus, wine glass at his lips, sipped then extended the glass to Gilberto. His chuckle broke the silence. "You have Barnett. I've got Washington, and you're one up on me. An audience by this Family would never have been granted to me without your access to national police records establishing the identity of my employee. A chance I took, no doubt, to set the first meeting. Not totally an unknown one, however!" he prefaced foreknowingly.

"Let me go further, while we're on the subject of police files. There are seven other employees of our Association, and Washington's 'live-in', all of whom you will probably meet down the road. Of the Association partners, not one of us has a police record. It's been immaterial to run a check for past petty infractions of the law where the other seven individuals are concerned. You know the importance of these statistics without my telling you."

Reorienting, Dacus pledged, "A drastic change in original planning puts Ed here to stand in and represent our organization in my absence. It is not intended as an ulterior motive to betray a confidence. Rather, it is that he faces the task of learning and implementing unfamiliar technology. He will require latitude in exercising judgment for decision making that'll expedite our goals to materialize in a shortened time frame. It does not include being subjected to a quiz panel every night or time for racketeering in your turf! If you've got any more questions, put them to me now. I'll either answer or tell you it's none of your business.

There was a long pause before Marc responded, "One question only. Did you not tell me once you left my dock your activities would be strictly legitimate?"

"No!" Dacus recoiled quickly. "I never told you that! Once we were sailing, I said our activities would be strictly legal. A true relationship between legal and honorable does not even exist. Any relationship, between legitimate and legal, is purely coincidental. There will, however, be no police in pursuit as we leave." He let previous comments speak for assurance.

"Don't get me wrong," he asserted. "Our mission after departing your dock is to pursue another intricate caper, but it is legal. It'll take roughly a year and a half to complete before we're home free. Except, 'home free' is a misnomer in that we can never return to the States due to the purely fraudulent nature of the scam we're in the process of pulling off right now."

Dacus mellowed. "Incidentally, one more card's to be placed on the table. I propose you be paid in full prior to departure. When we sail, I want every one of my people on board the ship. Our paymaster is a beautiful, very savvy middle-aged woman. She's in charge of all offshore banking. If arranged, she'll fly round-trip with your people to Grand Cayman in a sunup-to-sundown operation. You'll have your money before we leave the dock, and that way, my entire crew can be under my protection."

"A shrewd undertaking, and I approve of it," authorized Marc.

"In the morning," Dacus threw in, "I'll have an e-mail message prepared to one of my partners so he can meet me with a truck large enough to handle the canisters. I'd appreciate your getting it sent from your warehouse computer. Ed and I have a little more talking to do and beg to be excused. Tomorrow promises to be a long one for both of us."

Marc and his brothers stood also. They bade the two visitors good night and retired to the living room. Marc snapped the end of a Havana, lit up, and accepted a brandy the butler poured. "Did you get the significance of Dacus's statement?" Marc asked. "He wants to have all of his people under his protection. Those are strong words."

"Which ones?" uttered Gilberto, a bit sullen. "The only significance for me is I wish he'd never sent those remains of Lipscomb's or showed up here."

"He's dangerous beyond any profit he can possibly bring the Family," mouthed Gitano. "What's in for us, Marc?" In his opinion, sale of the boat had been a losing proposition.

"I'm not nearly as afraid of him as I am of you, two one-track-minded, spoiled brats. There's more to life than a tennis match," lectured Marc, dismissing Gitano's question. "We've all lived too soft. Presently, you're only steps removed from assuming quality leadership. Repeatedly, my father stressed how important a responsibility we have to large numbers of other families totally dependent upon us. We cannot, and will not, survive if our word isn't worth a damn," he vowed.

"My word is out! Today's move against Runshang seals it before the world. Begin thinking like a patriarch!" He chugged the drink, mounted the stairs, leaving them with his wrath.

In preparation for departure, Dacus handed Marc a sheet of paper addressing mountain@aol.com. It read, "Go to town. Rent a truck like the one I turned in a few days ago. Meet me midday at Springfield's municipal airport, on the private side."

Seeing Marc scan the message, Dacus noted, "Marc, I beg of you not to send Barnett on this errand. I have a feeling he could screw up a two-car funeral if he's out of his territory."

"Don't worry." Marc laughed, projecting. "He's too spastic to type even his name. By the way, arrangements have already been made to load the plane with forty canisters. The helium will be on board awaiting takeoff before you arrive."

CHAPTER 21

A panoramic view of Springfield Municipal Airport had shrunk to one private runway when Dacus finally spotted a big rental truck. The jet taxied to an off-ramp, leading to a fuel supply depot, where the truck was parked. At the last dying whine of engines, Dacus deplaned, angling across the tarmac toward it.

"Put that 'girlie' magazine in the glove compartment, Tom," Vivian told him. "Dacus is on the ground and headed over here to meet us."

"Shit, Viv! When did you become 'Miss Goody' Two Shoes? What gave you the notion Dacus doesn't appreciate looking at a pretty woman? Don't go straight on me now, gal!"

Both doors of the truck cab opened with Tom and Vivian clad in jump suits, hopping down. Dacus didn't have a chance to speak or express surprise at Vivian being there. Inadvertently, she had yanked Tom's chain, and he was on a tear. "Viv thought she needed a change and wanted to come along. After the trip, I'm not sure who needs the change!" Tom avenged. "When we left, the whole idea was we'd have time on the drive back to get our ducks in a row on the gold-processing stuff. Now, all she wants to do is tell me how and what to do."

Tom's outburst sparked humor Dacus didn't know existed. He dared not commit and looked at Vivian who shrugged. He changed the subject arbitrarily. "Tom, let me go inside to arrange for someone to load the truck. Then we'll scoot."

Inside the hangar a shop dolly on large casters was offered, but no assistance. As he pushed the dolly toward the plane, the pilot stepped around to open the cargo bay. "Here, I'll be glad to help. I want this load off . . . Gone! My baby's dragged her tail all the way," he grumbled.

Dacus got in the truck Vivian had pulled over. He checked the hydraulic platform lift. It worked. He backed into position, and the four went to work unloading the plane. In a matter of forty-five minutes, the pilot had it airborne and they were headed for the mountain. Curious, Tom asked, "That stuff we unloaded, Dacus, what have you got in mind to use it on? Looks like you didn't plan on running out of whatever it is."

"I anticipate a real heat problem, Tom, trying to pump as much electricity as we need into the power company lines, especially in the limited time that's available. I intend to cool the connections on both sides of the co-generation meter with liquid helium, which is what's back there." Dacus reconsidered, "Just take my word for it, man. Explaining the mechanics of it would consume the balance of our trip. Besides, I thought you had an agenda to talk about."

Anxious to expound on his subject, Tom agreed. "Viv and I have put together a want list. It includes every conceivable piece of equipment needed to process gold. With only a few old catalogs to go by, I hate to tell you, but it looks to be at least fifty grand."

"Tom, indulge me," Dacus inserted. "Means nothing. None of us have ever dealt with such large sums of money. You haven't broken the fifty year old, penny pinching habit on today's comfortable income. It's time to bite the bullet and go cold turkey on your 'Depression days' stigma. Wake up and be ready for the twenty-first century and what our budget reflects. The ship and gunboat cost a shade over two million. Outfitting and stocking them adds an estimated quarter of a million. Plus, probably seventy thousand to get you set up," he predicated.

"Compared to first projections of a six to eight million nut being required, it's looking pretty good. I expected to pay a helluva lot more for a ship. Who could have known Maybelle would be in with us and good for a half million dollar loan in a pinch? Incidentally, there's four hundred ninety thousand of it yet in a Lafitte bank. Here's the kicker, Tom. If my use of cryogenics is successful on this job, we should net close to three million. Without a doubt, operating money seems unlimited to manage on such a scale, including what it'll take to harvest the gold. Nothing, but nothing, has gotten away from us, believe me!" he assured.

One-track-minded, Tom aired, "I have a few comments based on what you've said. There's the matter of you seeming to be sure fifty tons of gold can be harvested from the sea in a year and a half, at most. I don't question your grasp of the science involved. I do think, however, there's a woeful shortage of planning in how to accomplish it. In order to be done right, we'd first need to set up on some uninhabited island. Cost might increase another couple hundred thousand to gain mobility for transfer of equipment from the gunship to the shore and then out onto a location. The worth, I guess, could be reconciled in weight of gold." He turned away, unsettled as Dacus's last remarks penetrated.

Dacus nudged Viv, chiding, "You and Tom have stewed over not being involved in the present job. My, my. It's a far cry to move from a quarter million dollar scam to one that promises a three million take. What's next? Well, how about hundreds of millions the two of you'll bear ramrodding the heavy end of an entire operation? I'd suggest you not devote a minute more in underestimating our Association's impending need of your services. It's really counterproductive. Prepare a materials list, regardless of cost, and begin making purchases. The amount you spend is incidental. If a concern exists, it is for tonnage and displacement of these items versus the ship's capacity to accommodate them."

Vivian wrapped an arm around Tom's neck in obvious joy. "That's it, gal!" Tom reacted, squeezing her leg. "The man's shot holes in our procrastination. He's even squelched our belief that we're not as solid a link in the Association as anyone else. Dacus may call what he's done for us this afternoon 'a kick in the ass', but I'm here to tell you it's been a helluva boost!"

Their truck broke the plateau's plane. Rabbit could be spotted running across the grasses toward them, frantically waving. As they drew closer, it became apparent he held a cell phone high in his hand and was yelling, "It's Maybelle!"

Dacus hopped out of the truck, taking the phone. "Are you all right?" he inquired. "Where are you anyway?" he let fly, his control already having been tested.

"I'm peachy," she provocatively declared. "You'd better make lots of money to transfer overseas. The skids are royally greased."

"When'll you be home?" he asked, a little impatiently.

"Is wherever you are supposed to be home to me?" she teased.

"Yes, dammit!" he countered. "When, Maybelle?"

"Day after tomorrow," she ardently committed.

A time determined, Dacus elaborated, "I'll be at the Garlington site on that day. I want you to drive over, in order for us to discuss a few things. But, wait a minute. The Mercedes is in Louisiana, and the Jaguar's license, unfortunately, has been borrowed to use on the one-ton containing all the generation equipment needed for the job."

"Oh, no problem. I have a dealer's tag for just such an occasion." Maybelle impishly suggested dealing from the bottom of the desk.

"What'd it cost you, kid?" Dacus accosted, leading her on.

"Just a little time," she said gaily, and Dacus could imagine that twinkle in her eyes.

There was a pause. He signed off, "See you soon."

Vivian had scooted under the wheel, bringing the truck on up to park it for the night. Dacus welcomed a chance to stretch his legs. He and Rabbit walked along the road before cutting through to the lodge. Dacus pried, "Rabbit, whatcha got cookin' besides Lulu and fending off women? I'm hungry for your kind of fixin's."

Amused, Rabbit jested, "I didn't think you ever got tired of a steak. You'll have to settle for down-to-earth, country vittles."

"Serve it up as soon as you can. I think I'll go to bed with the chickens tonight. It'll leave you free to do your thing," Dacus joked in return as he detoured onto the veranda, stopping to watch an extraordinary sunset developing.

So much for wishful thinking. He'd relished the thought of Rabbit sitting across the table and having an exchange of old stories again. His early meal was disrupted with everyone deciding to eat. Tom sat down opposite him and instead of being exhausted from the day's activities, he seemed ready to boogie. "That session this afternoon was better than an aphrodisiac. You know the girls are a little lonesome, Dacus. No, *lonesome* ain't the right word. They're gettin' plum stir-crazy without enough male potions. I'd take the whole lot of 'em on, here and now, but . . ."

Leaning over Tom, Vivian chirped, "We need to celebrate a bit to unwind. Nothing like a challenge to turn ya on! I've already talked with the gals, and they're gung ho for a party."

"Me too," Tom drooled, already engulfed in fantasy.

"Oh toot, Tom! We've been talking 'bout brushin' up on the tango, gettin' in practice for the limbo, playin' calypso music, drinkin' rum punches, and, you know, a specialty kinda party. I wonder, Dacus, if you could spare a little helium to blow up a few balloons I've got stashed that'll brighten things up," Vivian gushed excitedly.

Less than enthusiastically, Dacus agreed. "Sure. I bought extra. Don't use but one canister, though. Do you have everything else needed?"

"Yeah. Tom hasn't forgotten how to perform his second job with the carnival. Aside from the freak show, he was an expert at filling and tying off balloons," Vivian expounded.

Retiring, Dacus praised Rabbit's food. The hand that grasped his shoulder implied far more to Rabbit. Dog tired, sleep came, even as music announced foreplay beginning.

The party went as planned, minus balloons. Tom had picked the first canister he came to in the truck. It was empty. No pressure existed in the cylinder. Easing back to the kitchen, he found Rabbit to ask if Dacus had left an early morning wake-up call. Receiving an affirmative nod, Tom asked that he be given one at the same time, dropping, "He needs my help!"

"I'll take care of it," Rabbit said, not connecting to Tom's concerns. Instead he posed, "Do you think anyone will mind if Lulu and I joined the party for a while?"

"Mind?" Tom spouted. "Why would you ask? You are as important a part of this organization as anyone else. Don't get bogged down thinking you're not, either. Vivian and I have had the blues, fretted, and fumed, all because of thoughts we were being left out. Not so! We got the message today on exactly how hard the work's gonna be to hold up our end. By the way, why don't you play dance instructor to that crazy bunch of females in there trying to do the limbo? See ya in a bit, and don't forget me in the morning."

Coming to the kitchen after his wake-up call, Dacus took a step backward to find Tom had beaten him to the table, coffee in hand. The distraught look on his face revealed he had a major, pressing concern. "There wasn't any helium in the tank I picked out. I got afraid they might all be empty and thought I'd better tell you as soon as you got up."

Dacus's chin dropped to his chest. He stared at the plate. When he raised his head to speak, it was an unfocused gaze that went beyond Tom. "I don't have many options left without helium. What I've been attempting is to pursue the least dangerous, most certain method for pumping maximum amounts of electricity into the power company's lines. If those cylinders are all empty, that option is gone. It'll mean setting up to try use of another alternative that's not nearly as reliable and much, much more risky."

Anxious for answers on the helium supply, Dacus hurried Tom thru breakfast. "If we find there is no helium, I need you and Rabbit to help me off-load the useless canisters and load up other selected pieces of equipment."

"Say they are empty. What're you going to do to get the money back?" Tom asked as they walked toward the truck.

"Absolutely nothing," stated Dacus. "Time's precious. I can't afford to waste any of it speculating on the might have been to the detriment of what has to be done. Besides, I'd already decided if something like this happened that you'd be the one to notify Association members."

A fast check on five of the forty helium canisters confirmed suspicions. "Well, Tom, I hope you're ready for this," Dacus began. "Maybelle is due in tomorrow. I'd suggest you be present when she arrives. It's hard to know the kind of reception her 'man-hungry' gals are going to give her. Their attitudes have changed somewhat, and there may not be much of a scene. Nonetheless, that'll be first up on your list. Next, as changes and plans are being altered this morning, I'm leaving Maybelle a personal note for you to hand deliver. Yesterday, I told her to meet me in Garlington. That's off! She is not to come. Make damn sure she heeds and understands it. Finally, follow these instructions to the letter. In case the thing blows up and I don't make it, everyone must scatter and take cover, including Rabbit and Lulu. The command is not a cause to worry, but rather one for survival. Don't forget. Ed must be contacted to tell him the score. Leave an e-mail message for him in Louisiana by way of the place in town. Do not, and I repeat, do not discuss anything remotely personal. Agree upon a time and place the two of you can talk by phone later."

Stunned, Tom eyed Dacus as never before. "I can't speak for the rest of us, but I'm not interested in you sacrificing yourself for me!"

Dacus smiled, relaying confidence. "You're forcing me to reveal one of my many hidden weaknesses, Tom. I'm a sucker for a dare or a challenge from anybody, or anything. It could well be my downfall someday. Until then, I don't expect to die. To innovate in the presence of extremely high voltage, of necessity, bears some degree of risk. Forewarned is forearmed . . . You've been briefed to react in case something happens. Nothing more! Now, round up Rabbit. We need his help in relocating these useless canisters for something of value."

All forty tanks were stored in an outbuilding. The truck was moved to Dacus's power center in the old church building. With the use of a dolly and a hoist, he, Rabbit, and Tom loaded four transformers, an equal number of capacitors, along with more insulated boots, coveralls, and elbow-length latex gloves. As a final act, he folded up and laid in the cots he and Rabbit had used the night Lipscomb, and his gang invaded the mountain.

Upon entering the White Water Inn coffee shop and spotting Harry, Dacus demanded, "If you're here, who's on duty at Garlington? Who has guard duty at the place tonight?"

"Sam has it today. I'm to be the night owl. Sit down and cool your heels," Harry invited. "They're about to put out a noon buffet, and you can join me for a bite to eat."

"Thanks but I've got food Rabbit prepared, and it's probably better than what's here." Declining, Dacus added, "I'll see you at six."

Sam and Dacus worked the entire afternoon. Unloading, they positioned the extra pieces of equipment in precise sequences, each of which was carefully aligned and measured by Dacus. Silently they toiled until at last, Sam quizzed, "How's it goin'?"

"Faster than that vehicle coming in," Dacus obliquely responded. Seeing it was Harry, he yelled, "What the hell are you doing here at this hour?"

"When it registered you were back with the big truck, it crossed my mind, such as it is, that changes were going to be made. I wanted to see everything in plenty of daylight."

"Good idea," assessed Dacus as Harry joined them. "Let's go sit over in the shade, and I'll bring both of you up to date," he said, motioning to Sam.

"Without rehashing all the circumstances that brought us to this point, just know for now I've come up with a means to get the job done in a matter of days rather than the two or three weeks proposed. There's far more uncertainty attached than I'd like to see. Nevertheless, we're going for it, perilous as it may be! The task at hand wouldn't even be possible if we weren't within spitting distance of that substation over there."

"Wait a minute," Harry interrupted. "You're puttin' out more than my pea brain can handle. I can always understand a need for money, but why has the time factor changed? What do you mean by perilous? How's all the extra gear you've brought in going to help? It was working fine before, wasn't it?"

Dacus threw his hands up. "See if you can comprehend this. The transmittal of electric power across country is done by high voltage and low amps. Amps are major causes of heat in conductors. Heat in the conductor is of a prime concern for me, considering the norm is to transmit at five hundred thousand volts and approximately one and seven-tenths amps from point to point, applicable only when distance is hundreds of miles apart." He stopped short, detecting their intensity in trying to absorb what had been imparted.

"Guys, I have no problem in duplicating the power company's large generators which are capable of producing eight hundred thirty six thousand kWh power at twenty two thousand volts and thirty eight amps. The bank of transformers needed to boost the voltage to a half million and lower amps to one point seven, is always located as close as possible to the source of power. That, fellows, is the fly in the ointment, and it'll be dangerous," Dacus lamented with cause.

"The engineers, who constructed the substation, never visualized having to accept current in the same increments produced by the power company itself. Certainly, not at the distance you see. Take a look. There's an octet of transformers poised to move current from this direction. The 'iffy' factor is the length of wire between us and them to accept the large amount of heat we intend to put into it. I've put a slide rule to the problem. Without the cooling element of helium, there's practically no margin of safety."

Sam stood up, reaching for another bottle of cold water. "What's the game plan, Dacus? I know you've got one in reserve."

"In the next three or four days, our stake can be increased to three million, minus value of what's already been pumped. Odds reduced to zilch will override the risk on success gained. I'm going for this one, alone!" stolidly, Dacus outlined. "Right now, we're disconnected from the power company and have ceased to deliver electricity for a couple of reasons. It's mandatory that all equipment be dropped down to air temperature tonight before cranking it up tomorrow. I need a full night's sleep under my belt to be ready for the start. When we begin, everyone on the premises is to back off at least a hundred feet from any section of the transmission equipment. If she'll hold for ten hours, it should be safe. The sweet part is, once started and successful, we'll be able to deliver three million dollars worth of current into the power company's line in just sixty hours!"

Harry erupted, "Sixty hours! You call it dangerous? I say it's impossible, hazardous as hell, and you're a lunatic!"

Dacus cut him off. "You've been in the rackets all your adult life, Harry. Only suckers bet against the dice on a comeout. Why do you refuse to live life according to what you know? Lighten up for your own sake," unconsciously he counseled, needing to move on.

"Sam, let's wrap it up. I'll ride in with you and leave the truck here. Remind me to enjoy the sack time tonight. I won't appreciate it enough until I've slept on that cot I brought along. Theo and I'll see you early, Harry."

Harry had to have the last word. "If we're not pumping electricity, why in hell must I stay around out here all night?"

"For appearance's sake," Dacus shot back without emotion.

It was ten thirty the following day before Dacus was ready. He moved about, flipping switches. Theo interrupted, posing a question. Pointing to a circular object, about forty inches high and two feet thick, he asked, "You made an addition yesterday. Is it what I think it is?"

"If you think it's a rheostat, that it is," said Dacus, verifying the item in question.

"Well, it's the biggest one I've ever seen," marveled Theo.

Dacus sought for a simple explanation. "We've got a logistics crisis. In order to move on and get out of here, certain things have become apparent. Available access to the substation is complicated by the distance from our power source to their step-up transformers. I'm geared to start off by choking production down to 80 percent through the rheostat. If all goes well, then I'll tiptoe upward to maximum capacity. In essence, we'll be out of here in three days."

A human calculator accustomed to years of mentally figuring odds as stickman and croupier, Theo reasoned, "If all goes well at 80 percent of capacity, what's the purpose in screwing around with trying for a hundred percent? It only runs you up from sixty hours to seventy-eight at high production. An extra eighteen hours can't possibly mean that much to us. Without you, it damn sure would mean nothing."

Dacus stopped dead in his tracks. "That's it! Thanks, Theo. They say two heads are better than one. Ever since I discovered there'd be no helium to cool conductors, I've been buried in an obsession to make the thing work and overlooking the obvious."

By six o'clock in the evening, when shift change occurred, operations were still running smoothly. Periodic trips up a ladder to read the cogen meter confirmed that 668,800 kWh or 80 percent of their capacity to receive, was being delivered to Arkansas Rivers Power.

Art, deciding not to dine alone, ordered up full dinners for two to go. Sam, Harry, and Theo could rehash over their hash in town. He'd eat supper with Dacus. On his prompt arrival, Dacus suggested, "Let's put the food aside until later, Art. There's plenty of daylight left for me to show you the new apparatus and explain what's to be monitored."

Dacus stirred as crow calls announced daylight. Putting shoes on, he strode across to get a full report from Art and hot coffee. It had held steady at 80 percent capacity thru the night. Refilling the cup, he set out to verify conditions for himself. Mentally he noted that in four and a half hours, a full day of high generation would be completed.

Shift change brought Sam in with breakfast, topped off by the sweet smells of success, as the clock continued ticking. Finished, Dacus sent Sam on an errand. According to Dacus's brief instructions, he drove back to Batesville in the big truck and waited for the lumber yard to open so he could purchase a list of items. At a pay phone around the corner, he used coins to call Tom that all was proceeding well. Loaded, he detoured by the White Water Inn coffee shop to secure a bag of doughnuts. On second thought, he ran to his room for a fifth of whiskey. He really wasn't sure whether it was for comfort to Dacus while camping out at the site or for a celebration later.

By the time Sam returned, most concerns of malfunction could be dismissed. The two of them began construction of a four-legged, elevated platform, exactly five feet square on top. It was mounted on lock-type casters, complete with a built on ladder to access the top level. All a meter reader had to do was climb the contraption and, standing on the platform, easily read the cogen meter. He'd be able to stand there while transfering the data to his portable handheld computer calculator, go down to his company truck and plug into the live computer network. It would deliver the information to data processing, a control center for both Arkansas Rivers Power Company and its owner, Central Amalgamated Power.

Stepping back to view their handiwork, Sam shook his head. "Mind telling me what this crude contraption is going to be used for?" he ventured to ask.

Dacus smiled. "It's to make things easier for the meter reader and a requirement to be provided by us. Then too, when he comes, I want to be on the platform with him to observe data correctly recorded. By building the deck five feet by five, it'll give just enough space that I can stand up there, seeing both the meter and what he punches into his computer calculator."

Sam speculated, "The thing's a little shaky to hold two people, don't you think? Want me to reinforce it with a couple of two by four cross pieces?"

"Nah, let it be. At most, it'll only be used about five minutes," Dacus disclaimed, not inclined for Sam or anyone else to guess he had a deeper and darker purpose. By keeping the structure unsteady, a devious opportunity could present itself . . .

Leaving Sam to monitor the equipment, Dacus took off to wander through a distant part of the property where he had spotted something of interest previously. What he found amounted to a steel casing enclosed in a concrete collar and was sunk into the ground to an unknown depth, except for eight inches left above ground. Discreetly, he turned his back toward Sam on the far side of the lot. In his left hand, poised over the top of an obvious old well, he held a sizable rock. His right hand cuddled a stopwatch. The time lapse from release to splashdown below clocked one and one-half seconds. It meant distance to water in the well would be approximately one hundred feet.

Dacus ambled around before rejoining Sam. "I'm going to crawl into the truck and catch forty winks before Harry comes on duty. I don't expect to get much sleep tonight," he commented. "Harry has a nervous tendency to overreact, and I'm afraid he'd panic if anything went wrong."

As Dacus entered the cab of the truck, shutting the door behind him, Sam tapped on the window. "Why don't you get in the back and stretch out on your cot?"

Rolling the window half down, Dacus confided. "Let me share a physical curiosity with medical proportions. Rabbit taught it to me the night Lipscomb and company came to hit us. Mind you, it comes straight out of his culture. If you know you're not gonna get a solid eight hours' sleep, napping for shorter periods in a sitting position is the way to go. It has something to do with the position of your organs. I find it works and will refresh me."

Exhausted, Dacus had crashed, sleeping hours longer than intended. Finding Harry peering at dials with a flashlight, he confronted, "Why didn't you wake me up?"

"I've been trying to live up to what you expect of me. Besides, far as I can tell, things have been running smoothly," assured Harry.

"I see," Dacus said, relaxing. "Well, you know the old adage that even a blind hog'll pick up an acorn every once in a while. By the way, didn't you bring some chow in here for me?"

"In my book, we've already picked up a bucketful of acorns, to my great surprise I might add. Yes, I brought sandwiches." Harry pointed to the cooler and waited.

Dacus rechecked dials before pouring a scotch and water. He picked up a sandwich, proposing, "What say we play a little gin to pass the time?"

"Wanta wager money or acorns?" Harry bantered in better-than-usual form.

Into the third day, Art noticed Dacus was becoming groggy and slightly smelly. "I don't know how you're holding up," he surmised. "Maybe a break would do you good."

Dacus agreed, "When Theo comes on at six this evening, I'm going to the motel with you. I've got to have a bath, a hot meal, and a full-sized bed. Be back out with Sam in the morning."

After briefing Theo at six o'clock, Dacus eagerly headed into town with Art. The Inn's restaurant was deserted except for the four of them. While steaks were being prepared, Dacus chose the time for a summation. "Guys, the hard part is over on this leg of operations, if . . . If the equipment for pumping holds up and proceeds successfully through the night, we ought to be able to break camp by early afternoon. Which means it should put us back on the mountain tomorrow evening at a decent hour."

Both interested to know how things had gone during the night, Sam drove Dacus out to relieve Theo the next morning as first light showed in the east. "Any changes?" Dacus asked, sensing something amiss the minute he stepped out of the truck.

Theo immediately beckoned Dacus to follow him. "Take a feel of your monster rheostat, Dacus. It's been steadily building heat the last hour," he said, logging a problem.

Dacus felt of the rheostat. He strode to the platform, climbed the ladder, and in one step was at the cogen meter to get a reading. Back on the ground, he announced, "At this moment, we've pumped roughly two million, nine hundred thousand dollars worth of electricity. A shutdown now is better than a meltdown later. The equipment is worth more than the gamble to make another hundred fifty thousand dollars."

With that disclosure, Dacus walked over to the complex and began shunting electricity. Using painstaking care, he slowly shut it down. Nodding to Theo, and handing him his motel room key, he instructed, "Gather up the other room keys and check everyone out except yourself. Round up Art and Harry, and send them out here to help load up equipment. Get some sleep. We'll pick you up on our way through Batesville around noon."

Dacus was the last to leave the site. Stopping just outside the gate, he locked it for the last time with the oversized padlock.

CHAPTER 22

An unconscious, mental countdown had begun for occupants on the mountain after Sam's brief call to Tom. Concentration was totally skewed to attempt anything other than basic essentials for the next thirty-six hours. Anxious for the motorcade to arrive, yet fearful of the consequences if it came too soon, they waited . . .

Slightly after four in the afternoon, the crew pulled in front of the lodge. Meeting them, Maybelle, the 'Ladies', Tom and Vivian, Rabbit, and even Lulu stood quietly as the guys got out of the vehicles. Maybelle looked to Dacus who broke the silence, shouting, "It's next to the last scene of 'Act III' on this one! Enough electricity has been recorded in Garlington to bring us a hundred thousand shy of the three million we were shooting for. All that's left is to go down in about two weeks and wait for the meter reader to show up. When he punches numbers into the company's mainframe, it'll trigger our payday anywhere from a few days to a couple of weeks later . . . Are you ready to become millionaires?"

A high decibel scream burst from the gals. Everyone began kissing and hugging. Shared embraces held forth like a huge, family homecoming. Maybelle ran to Dacus, grabbing him. "You're something else!" she said, overly emotional, laying her head against his chest. "We've been worried to death ever since Tom told us of that hellish new problem."

"Party time! Let's do some celebratin'," broke in Rabbit. He solicited help from the ladies. A spread of food was quickly laid out to tempt every palate, designed and arranged in an array to mimic a French chef's. Rabbit put finishing touches on setting the table as the gals split, rushing upstairs to freshen up and search for the party dress of choice. Two had already gone by Maybelle to say they were indisposed for the love wheel, but an idiosyncrasy of nature wasn't keeping them from making the scene.

Tom and Vivian deliberately moved to don party apparel early and took over as bartender and barmaid. They were hyped beyond normal energy levels by the turn of events. In fact, Vivian took pains to tell everyone when serving first beverages, "Tom and I are high as a kite, and we haven't had a drink yet. Dacus's dream is coming true for all of us!"

Dacus meandered toward the kitchen, finding Lulu all dolled up and Rabbit in a suit. "Why don't you come on up front with the rest of us?" he encouraged.

Rabbit answered for them both, "We'll get there. Small talk's awkward . . . Who needs it tonight? The two of us kinda like doing our own thing . . . Like helping serve everybody, eat alone, and come in later to dance. Our greatest times are when we can dance together in the presence of friends, feeling we're a part, and not have it spoiled with talk."

Dacus agreed. "I know where you're coming from, friend."

Catching everyone gathered at the bar, Maybelle made an announcement. "I'll not do my hat trick spinning the love wheel until later in the evening. I'm with Rabbit. It's time to celebrate and make it our best party yet, even though Ed can't be present."

On cue, the gals sprang into action to fulfill an idea to surprise. In preparation, they'd hidden their musical gear in a walk-in closet at the head of the stairs. Without warning and in a single move, they lifted their skirts to ascend the stairs, filed into the closet, grabbed their musical instruments, and came marching back down playing the old Depression era tune, Happy Days are Here Again. The selection gave way to hand clappin' and erratic gyrations.

In the spirit of the event, Sam loudly exclaimed, "Behold, Maybelle's Seven Belles, more fondly known by us guys as the Seven Bellies." The commotion attracted Rabbit and Lulu, who couldn't resist joining these festivities before the dance.

Tonight, a different and strange tension gripped the crowd. No one except Maybelle had ever experienced the possession of large sums of money. Adult caution and decorum was unhinged at the notion of nearly three million dollars, plus an apparent certainty of much more to come. Candy, as bandleader, unexpectedly heralded, "Come on! Get wicked! We're doin' the 'Bunny Hop' so bold and struttin' you may not recognize it!"

By the time the first "left foot, right foot, hop, hop, hop" sounded, Sam had grabbed Maybelle from behind to make her parade marshall. Theo, Art, and Harry quickly followed. In step with the music, out came Vivian from behind the bar. Tom double-stepped to the rhythm till he had her by the waist. Another trip around the dance floor and Lulu caught Rabbit's hand, putting him at the rear of the line. Dacus sought shelter behind the bar.

Candy caught Dacus's eye, crooking a finger at him. He shook his head. She crooked it again and pointed to the floor beside her. He couldn't refrain from the appeal and moved in beside her. Pointing to the bongos, she shouted in his ear, "Take my place while I go to the bathroom."

Hesitantly, he lightly slapped the bongos. It felt good, and the beat was compelling. Absorbed, he became one of the band. Candy, after a fast trip to the john, attached herself to the tail of the bunny hop line. This triggered an abandonment of the bandstand. One by one the girls left, squeezing in between the guys or to bring up the rear, leaving Dacus on bongos for rhythm.

Something primitive, buried deep in the collective psyche of the human spirit, responds favorably to rhythm dancing together. Stamina of the dancers governs how long a dance lasts. Three more complete turns around the floor had everyone out of breath. Dacus ended the Bunny Hop by changing the beat to Shave and a Hair Cut, Six Bits. Dacus, Vivian, and Tom returned to bartending, mixing, and pouring drinks. Maybelle took charge of music on the jukebox, selecting a menu of slow, big-band tunes before heading over to the bar. Covering the hand she laid on the bar with his, Dacus asked, "Got a minute to talk?"

"Sure! I'd even drink to that if you'd pour me one," she tossed.

Reaching for a cigar, he poured himself a brandy, mixed Maybelle a bourbon and water, then ushered her out to the veranda. Soberly, Dacus tipped his glass to her. "It could wait perhaps, but for starters I need to know the pathway for our money that you've set up," Dacus prompted. "Then I have something else to tell you."

"First of all," Maybelle obliged, "Jack Rainwater took me to banks where he was known, thus giving instant legitimacy. He has chosen the First International Bank of Tennessee located in Memphis for making the transfer to Georgetown in Grand Cayman. The money from Arkansas Rivers Power will be deposited to our Crown Alloys account in the Springdale Bank. From there, I'll use a PIN number for transferring the bulk of money to Memphis. As soon as a transfer from Memphis to Georgetown is made, Jack and I will fly to Grand Cayman and redeposit the money into four other banks. Jack alluded it was for insurance from whatever."

"How large are the sums you've already transferred back and forth between the States and the Caribbean?" asked Dacus to confirm his estimate of funds held.

"Just under ten grand. Remember we started off with cash," Maybelle reminded, inquiring, "Now, what do you have to tell me that's taken us away from the party?"

Dacus put his arms around her shoulders, whispering, "Just a little something that may complicate the process. There's one other move I'm gonna make. It could raise our take on this caper from a hundred thousand shy of three million to a mere twenty-nine million."

"What!" Maybelle softly cried out, whirling around. "What do you mean twenty-nine million? No way is the money pathway complex enough to handle that much green. Neither can it be done quickly, much less inconspicuously. It means getting in touch with Jack at once."

"I recognized there might be a problem," offered Dacus. "That's why I'm telling you tonight. If my strategy works, it'll be the product of misdirection and a peculiarity of calculators in conjunction with a computer system. The odds are highly in favor it can be pulled off. By acting now, Jack's given time to figure a way to maneuver the volume of money advantageously. Except for him, no one's to know of this possibility. Should it fail, we're still out of here successfully, and our people won't be left speculating on what might have been."

Maybelle looked up into a cloudless night and exulted. "I feel so alive! So lucky! I guess I was born to be a con. Even in marriage to Bryan, life with his friends was a sham. I didn't do too well at it, or Tulsa society wouldn't have shunned me," she smirked, knowingly. "Bryan is a forever love, but here I'm in my true element. I love this entire company of friends in one of the many ways I loved my man. Above all, I treasure having a family for the first time."

Dacus looked down at her with compassion. "You are so right! The fluid of this large family is becoming thick as blood kin ever professed being."

"Enough of sentimentality," Maybelle scolded. "I'm gonna do the hat trick and head for the bed. Jack is such an early riser that I must be at your office in Harrison by dawn to catch him before he leaves from his place in Georgetown."

Taking a hat, Maybelle dropped five names into it. She toasted, "Here's to you that do and to you that don't . . . Never be guilty of a won't!"

Dacus strode to Maybelle's side, reminding everyone, "Tomorrow's the last day to sleep in, so fend for yourself at breakfast. Enjoy your pleasures tonight because it'll be nothing but work, work, work until we clear this mountain and get on board the ship."

The party continued to swing as Maybelle and Dacus broke away to their separate quarters. In parting, Maybelle pouted. "You sure know how to put it on a gal. You gave the gang all night and half a day to sleep in. I might get five hours!"

At midmorning, Maybelle returned from town, seeking out Dacus. She found him in the kitchen with several others. Preparing some dry cereal with milk, and getting a cup of coffee, she slipped into an empty seat next to him.

"How'd it go?" offhandedly Dacus inquired, displaying only minor curiosity.

"I've got a meeting with Jack at two thirty this afternoon in Memphis. If it doesn't interfere with plans, I'm taking the Jaguar," she casually returned, implying it was private. "Before I get out of here though, gotta minute for a short session?"

Dacus made small talk as she finished. The two then ambled out and down to where horses grazed in the pasture. Once secluded, he anxiously asked, "Where do we stand?"

"Jack says that no problems exist here in the States as long as we stay under ten thousand dollars in cash, whether it's withdrawals or deposits. Otherwise, bank transfers in any amount, even out of the States, are not factors legally as long as it appears to be a straightforward transaction. A matter of concern though," Maybelle emphasized, "will be handling of money on arrival in Grand Cayman. Once money gets overseas, SSN and EIN numbers are useless. There, PINs and individual familiarity with a particular bank are extremely important. Most of my personal money, which could be used to create PINs for overseas transfers, is in Springdale. If Jack chooses to go to Springdale with me on this matter, do you have any objection to my bringing him by the mountain?"

"Why not? I'd like to meet him," enthused Dacus.

"So much for your concerns. Now it's my turn to be filled in," pried Maybelle. "Explain to me how you think you can screw a utility company's computer system into paying ten times as much money as was actually delivered in electricity to them."

Reaching in his shirt pocket, Dacus pulled out a hand calculator, relating. "Calculators and computers are much alike in some ways yet different in others for very complex reasons. Watch as I punch in numbers from one thru zero. The 'one' is displayed first on the far right side of the screen. As numbers are added, the one moves to the left to accommodate the next number. Every time a number is added, the result is virtually ten times larger than the previous number. For an example, I place the number five in the machine. Adding a zero brings up the number fifty, which is ten times five. Another zero produces five hundred, which is ten times fifty, and so on. The removable, handheld piece of a computer used by a meter reader records numbers in the same sequence as this calculator," he noted, pressing the clear symbol.

"Follow me closely," Dacus insisted. "Sam and I have built a platform of a specified height for reading numbers on the cogen meter. I plan to be on that platform with the meter reader when he's punching in the numbers. I'm very much interested, of course, to know the results. The instant he enters the last number with a remote, I'll electronically set off an underground charge that causes a helluva rumbling and a lot of noise. Hollering earthquake, I'll use my feet and legs to make the platform shake and sway, bump his arm, grab the computer piece out of his hand, point to the stairs and ground below, and yell, 'Hurry! Get down.' On my way down, I can punch in an extra number. Any number except the zero for misdirection gives us virtually ten times more money before the device is handed back to him on the bottom step."

Maybelle was bug-eyed. "Dacus, how'd you ever think up such a scheme? They're gonna have to screw you into the ground when you die," she predicted. "Or, maybe you have a way out of that one, masterful escape artist Mr. Houdini!"

"Not hardly," Dacus denounced with a sly grin of appreciation.

Realizing the time, Maybelle gasped. "Let's get moving. It's already going to be a push for me to make the Memphis airport by two thirty."

Dacus rounded up the troops at noon. Particularly, he wanted to address his plans to Rabbit in the presence of the other men. "Our first priority is to have everything placed in the cave that can't be housed on board the ship," he detailed. "I'll begin tagging those items, which go to the cave. The rest of you can make preparations to start hauling."

Rabbit took off with the first load destined for the cave, but he quickly returned, telling the others to hold up. Finding Dacus, he unloaded, "The bodies of Lipscomb and company are ripe. It'd gag a maggot in there. We gotta have something, or we can't stand the stink."

Dacus groaned. "The cave's got to be used for hiding so much material, and I don't have a plan B. Rabbit, bring me the Harrison telephone directory unless you have an idea."

Thumbing thru the yellow pages, he told Rabbit, "I'll be back in a couple of hours." Hurriedly jotting down phone numbers and addresses of a dive shop and farm supply store advertising quicklime for sale, he set off in the pickup.

Loaded with a ton of lime, five diving helmets, and the diving gear complete with wetsuits and canisters of oxygen, Dacus parked the pickup under a shed. He assembled Rabbit and the men to discuss the dilemma. "In the cave, we have a problem with odor from all those decaying bodies. On such short notice, I've bought diving equipment in place of gas masks, which aren't available up here. The lime's to scatter over the rotten pile. In the morning, Rabbit and I'll attend to spreading it. Meanwhile, if you're going to practice using the helmets, don't waste the oxygen-nitrogen mix. We can buy more, but, an extra trip to town is a slowdown to operations we can't afford."

In her Jaguar, Maybelle with someone else was spotted approaching the lodge at late evening. Dacus hurried to the kitchen to tell Rabbit. "Maybelle's bringing a friend in. I'm assuming they'll want to eat after introductions are made." Rabbit nodded, interested in checking out the guest as everyone else seemed to be doing.

The girls started squealing and descended on Jack as soon as he walked in. Poking, tickling, and pulling on him in their inimitable fashion, they began chanting, "Sport! Sport! Rainwater! Yea, the fifty-nine-and-a-half-minute man!"

Showing his pleasure, Jack played coy. "Shucks, y'all know I'm not that good. Besides, you can't fool an ole fooler. I've been with every one of you gals more 'n once."

Eva gave him a nudge, embellishing. "Jack, you're half-savage. You know it—we know it! Why, man, you just get so carried away that you lose all track of time. It's a shame they didn't put you out to stud sixty years ago to breed up men ready and able to really satisfy the women."

Flippantly, Candy interrupted, "Let's all crawl in the sack with Jack tonight. It's one way to make sure once again, don't you think?"

Maybelle jumped in to put a damper on their shenanigans. "Not on your life!" she objected. "No way are we gonna jeopardize the health and stamina of our international banker. Jack, pick yourself a babe for the evening. There will be rainwaters, I mean 'rainchecks' in the Caribbean."

Jack bowed in acquiescence. "Okay, if you say so. What about it, Candy? You seem to be turned on for fun and games," he said, pulling her into a big bear hug.

Wiggling supportively, Candy assented, "I wanta start off on top, Jack."

Agreeable, Jack added a 'but' . . . "Fine. But, what say you let me meet these other people first? A little food under the belt will be helpful for me to keep up my strength."

Following a couple more rounds at the bar and Candy's provocative moves, Jack succumbed to desire. Knowing full well old Tom would be keyhole peeking and listening outside her door, Candy proceeded to put on a sound-and-sight expo that would swell any man's glands . . .

Sure enough, sometime later Tom rose up from a crouched position at the keyhole. Eyes all shiny and drooly, he had to find Vivian. Leaving, Tom heard Jack tell Candy, as the bathroom door closed, "An Academy Award performance, dear, for sure!"

Meantime downstairs, Dacus, beset with passion not to leave a stone unturned, motioned to Maybelle at the bar. They walked to one end to confer. "I don't want Jack to know about the cave," Dacus cautioned, "and I'd rather the women didn't get too aware of it either. Turn off their curiosity by telling them the terrain is very rough and that Rabbit's seen some fair-sized copperhead snakes up there. Also, what are the chances of you getting Jack out of here early tomorrow so the guys and I can start work without raising a red flag?"

"I understand, and I'll handle all of it," assured Maybelle, thinking ahead. "You should know we'll probably be headed for Georgetown from the big new airport north of Springdale. I'll use my money from the Springdale and Bentonville banks to spread out and make the bigger transfers. We can settle between ourselves later. And by the way, where does your source of energy originate? I'm bushed and calling it a night." On a devilish whim, she needled, "By chance, do you suppose there's a plug-in connector to tap such a source?"

"Good night," Dacus reflected, ignoring the implication. His right index finger stroked the side of his nose and ran the outline of his moustache, watching her go up the stairs.

According to his customary habit, Jack was up and out of Candy's apartment before she woke. He even beat Maybelle to the kitchen for coffee. As a consequence, they were winding down the mountainside at slightly after eight.

Talk was sparse until Maybelle informed him of the twenty-nine million to be managed. Nonplussed, Jack evaluated, "Now our two worst enemies become suspicious banks and time. A draw amounting to this sum will alert the power company to a glitch, and it'll be a horse race . . . An interesting challenge you've presented me with to start the day."

"You've gotta understand, Jack, that Dacus does his homework. He is convinced the power company has shot itself in the foot through downsizing and reliance on computers. He says the computer can only spot trends, and a one month's billing cannot provide the history to program in a trend. Therefore, it makes damn good sense that it'll be sometime before a live body guru detects an irregularity," countered Maybelle, omitting further disclosure of details.

Jack recognized Dacus's feasibility study to be sound. He settled in for the hour or so drive to Springdale and the Northwest Arkansas national airport.

Dacus had Rabbit leave a note in the kitchen that the gals were in charge of meals for the day. He handed Theo a list of items to be ready for transport with help from Sam, Harry, and Art. Donning the diving gear, Dacus and Rabbit loaded the buggy and four-wheeler with lime and cautiously followed the tortuous path up to the cave. Three times they made the trip and used nearly half the lime to seal off decaying body parts emitting the rank odor.

Getting credit for unused lime wasn't worth the speculation idle loafers in the farm store might attach to its usage. Dacus decided to have the balance unloaded in an outbuilding, leaving him free to make a run back to town for ready-mix, bagged concrete from the lumber yard. Meanwhile, a fly didn't stand a chance of lighting on the five man task force carting subject materials to the cave. Dacus was pushed on his return to keep up with the tagging. Around five, Harry's ass dragged from the arduous day and let it be known. "The next trip I make will be to cart this carcass to the nearest bar for medicinal purposes. You can forget aspirin. What I need is liquids, taste, and calories!" Including Rabbit, they commiserated and moaned their way to the lodge. Refreshed by a shower and in sweats, the guys kicked back around a bar table for Dacus to outline tomorrow's itinerary. Rabbit came in with hors d'oeuvres the gals had fixed and was pulling out a chair when Dacus entered. "If you're ready, I guess I am," he said, sitting down.

"There are yet a few things to tag and be moved to the cave. It'll take me and someone else to bring in a rental truck from town to begin loading items destined for the ship's site. My plans right now are to leave at daylight day after tomorrow with the first load to Louisiana. Theo, how about you going along to bring the truck back for its next load because I must stay there and get started on readying the ship," he explained.

"And, Theo," Dacus briefed, "you'll need one of these other guys to come down with the load you bring so the way there is mapped out. We'll continue rotating one of the two drivers until there's nothing left up here but the bare bones of our mountain operation. Those items which remain will comprise our final trip load. The rotation also allows me more time to remain on the ship. She needs to be put afloat, cruise a part of the bay, and the equipment tested. Having added help from each driver who stays at the ship puts us that much closer to departure."

"Dacus!" Sam commandeered, soliciting. "If I make the next trip down with Theo, could a driver with me on the return trip be one of the gals?"

"Absolutely not!" snapped Dacus adamantly. "None of them are going to the ship until this place is buttoned down and we're leaving here for good."

Tired, Rabbit went for a basic. "What if some things are too big to manhandle getting them through the cave's entrance to the tunnel?"

"Then they'll have to be cut into smaller pieces, using either a saw or a cutting torch. We're destroying evidence, not saving something for the future!" directed Dacus . . . "Once and for all, clearly understand the underlying purposes for the way we leave this mountain. First and foremost, anything related to our use of free electricity must be removed or destroyed. Not one single clue about our energy source can be left behind! For deception, the kW generator powered by a diesel engine will be plugged into this complex as its apparent only source of power. Everything else that's in operation right now comes along with us," he reiterated a second time.

"Furthermore," Dacus continued, "keep in mind it'd be very helpful if our departure paralleled those of the previous two sets of inhabitants. Where circumstances of the other occupancies seemed to be controlled by a quirk of fate, our vanishing off the face of the mountain will be by calculated deception for the same effect. In other words, our disappearance from up here must appear to be beyond our means to resist." The assessment met with nods of approval.

"In essence," Dacus touted, "the stigma of strange phenomena attached to the mountain by Boone County officials and residents is reinforced by another unexplained vanishing. Moreover, an inevitable investigation by the sheriff's office should take an oblique position on it due to similarities of the other two cases. We'll provide a logical flaw in the fence that gives the livestock an opportunity to escape and roam the mountainside, as previously related. As I foresee it, only one set of fingerprints could be of consequence. However, that door is closed to scrutiny. When every 'jot and tittle' is completed to perfection in this deception, authorities will encounter an eerie, void scene, no foul play, no clues to pursue for the disappearance, and identity of the occupants a befuddling mystery, not worth the time to open a case file . . ."

Probing so he could answer, Dacus asked, "What does it all mean?"

"It means we have succeeded! The money's assured to fund the ultimate scam, and we're presently going to wipe the slate clean for smooth sailing!"

On their way to rent a truck bright and early the next morning, Theo and Dacus detoured by the office in Harrison. The e-mail transmitted to Ed apprised him of their arrival in Louisiana on the following evening, bearing a truckload of supplies for the ship. Due to Dacus's obsession with having three spare parts for everything, the full-sized box transport truck was easily filled to capacity on their return. The balance of the day was devoted to working on, as near as humanly possible, a fail-proof deception.

CHAPTER 23

Theo wasn't nearly as enthralled as Ed had been when he and Dacus sped through bayou country toward the Zallafino estate. Though never introduced, Theo recalled working for this Mafia Don's father years ago at a joint in Bossier City. Reservations began to surface . . .

Supplying identity at the guard station, Dacus presented Theo, another partner. They eased through the gate, driving on to the mansion. Ed, having been notified of their arrival by the guards, stepped out to greet them. "Welcome to paradise. A butler will be here momentarily to get your luggage and take it to separate quarters upstairs. Leave the truck here. Someone'll park it. Morning's soon enough to unload it in a storage building on the premises. Fill me in, guys."

Dacus couldn't wait. "Are the submotors installed?" he asked expectantly.

Ed shook his head, allowing, "Not quite. Final installation for completion is set for tomorrow. It's being attended to under the direction of Franco. When finished, the dry dock can be flooded from the bay to determine if there are any leaks. After that, the next move is in your hands, man. Not to mention I'm damn glad to be relieved."

Dacus stuck his fist in the air, whooping, "Yes! We're almost back on schedule! When we come downstairs, I'd like to hear about Runshang over a drink."

Standing at the bar, Ed's discussion was preempted. Dacus made introductions. "Marc, this is Theo Farris. Theo, meet Don, Marc Zallafino."

Marc took in Theo, who returned the gaze. "I have seen you before, Theo."

Theo nodded. "I recognize you, too. I once worked as stickman at a small gambling place outside of Shreveport. My ultimate boss was your father, Don

214

Zallafino. I never met him, but I do remember you shooting dice at my table on occasions."

"That's it!" exclaimed Marc, slapping the bar. "Now, I remember! There was a beautiful blackjack dealer I tried to make time with, but she was keeping house with you and would not give me the time of day. Did you marry her?"

"No. Not so lucky," Theo related. "She met and married a classic gent who was a very well off retired Tulsa doctor and widower with no children. When he died a few years ago, she became one wealthy woman. Hold on though. I don't want to leave that remark sounding the way it does. She was crazy about the guy. But without him, high society wasn't her style. Results were she got bored and you'll be surprised to know where she is now . . . In our Association, she's the treasurer."

"Are the two of you back together?" Marc pressured, enticed.

"Rots of ruck, as the Japs used to say," countered Theo. "She's not interested in even a casual relationship for old time's sake. Her only professed connection with sex now seems calculated, or so it appears to me. I've known her to give it away to carry out a scam on a mark. I've heard she's even paid for the attention of a few young Mexican cliff divers. She's one helluva gal who operates on a different level from other women."

"I think you're trying to tout me off her," challenged Marc with revived interest.

Theo remained calm. He played it cool. "All I know is that I'm too old for her now. Chances are that you're a far cry from an eighteen year old, Latino-lovin' hustler. Be my guest tho. She'll be here in a week to join operations," checked Theo.

"I want to know about Runshang," interrupted Dacus.

Ed complied, defusing an uncomfortable situation. "He has produced in a timely manner, but he's madder than hell. To make sure we haven't been sabotaged, Franco's broken down and examined every item, which is why we're a little behind schedule and won't be ready for a trial run till tomorrow sometime."

Marc picked up on turn of the conversation, inserting, "Runshang is under our constant surveillance. You're not dealing with a businessman. He's an ignorant, mean son of a bitch who, if he had a big enough purse, would ruin New Orleans. I fully expect he'll have to be eliminated."

Reacting, Dacus tipped Ed. "This calls for a change in plans. I want Theo with me when the ship is launched. As soon as the truck can be unloaded, you need to head back for another run. With Rabbit's help, Ed, load the truck and bring a partner back so he can learn the way in. One more thing, set up rotation so Harry is the last man down here. I don't care how it's done. Draw straws or pick numbers out of a hat. Just rig it for Harry to be last, but don't hurt his feelings. I'm sure, too, you won't need reminded to get laid a couple of times while there, either."

A beatific expression crept across Ed's face. "Not on your life, brother! I'm bankin' on it!" Attuned to the change in plans, he queried, "Tom's not in this rotation set up, is he?"

"No," Dacus replied. "He's not up to doing his part on that long a drive. Nonetheless, he and Vivian must be brought down soon to make their purchases of equipment."

Marc listened to their exchange with intense interest. "Sounds like you and your partners share equally in affairs, profits included, if any. In the end though, you are the boss, Dacus, aren't you?" Marc needled for a reaction from the two partners.

Dacus was noncommittal. "Unquestionably, he is boss," Ed sanctioned. "We're operating on his ideas, with his technology, and his seed money was used before we made the first dime. Why wouldn't he have the final word?"

"Count on it," Theo drawled, adding, "Personally, I was getting scruffy when he contacted me. This organization has revived every one of us, I believe. Challenge is the spice of life to a con artist. To have it back and to be poised for the greatest scam of all times, with the exception of politics, is a plus in anyone's book."

"I take it you don't care for politics," Marc deduced, trying to get a rise out of Theo.

"It reminds me of the clap," Ed smarted. "The little fun you get from catching it is not worth the long-term cost. Somehow I'm sympathetic. We're all brothers under the skin."

"Whazzat mean?" slurred Marc, cut off and feeling his drinks.

"I perceive no difference in politicians and con artists," Dacus delineated before either could reply. "Each has a different identity for every occasion . . . All phony!"

Their byplay was interrupted by the butler announcing dinner. The meal was eaten in silence. Marc no longer felt the need to entertain, and the two travelers were worn out.

Before anyone stirred at daybreak, Dacus and Ed drove the Mercedes down to examine progress being made on the ship. Following a painstaking examination, Dacus decided, "You'll be held up for a while, Ed. No matter how long it takes, contents of the truck are going to be directly off-loaded onto the ship. Every bit of it is ready for placement. My hat's off to you, partner."

"That's fine," replied Ed as he turned back to get in the car, placated by Dacus's apparent approval of the work. Joining Theo at breakfast, the two brought him up to date on plans to move materials from the truck onto the ship. Asking for coffee to go, Dacus and Theo hopped in the truck, suggesting Ed bring the Mercedes. To avoid conflict with Franco's work schedule, they hurriedly drove back to the dock.

The arrival of Franco and crew produced an on-the-spot jam session about how to work together without getting in each others's way. Franco offered to take his men and move the bulky items on board while Dacus would direct each large item to designated spots. The resulting coordination was spectacularly quick, and Ed departed for the hills in less than an hour.

By day's end, Franco had completed his work and was ready for the launch. Dacus and Theo still had another two hours to go. With Marc gone for the evening, they decided to finish, grab a late supper, and retire early.

Dawn breaking and reinforced with coffee, Theo drove Dacus to the ship for testing equipment before Franco and his men checked in. Five minutes after Dacus started the small diesel kicker motor, he'd built up enough electricity to turn it off and run on the excess. Without prying spectators, he set a minimal shell and curved space so hard they were in total darkness. Satisfied, he dissolved the shell, methodically shut down his equipment, and motioned Theo ashore.

On the way back, Theo reflected, "I've never seen you do that in broad daylight. Tell me again how you curve space to form a shell. What sets its size and density?"

"My reply would be inadequate, because I don't know," answered Dacus. "Remember, I told you that I stumbled on the method for curving space by broadcasting excess electricity from a revolving antenna. It resulted from a motor-driven auger, turning as if it were boring toward the center of the earth. I know no more about the nature of this phenomenon than about the nature of electricity itself—which is zero! But," he urged, "what you and I must determine is whether or not creation of a shell, hard enough to divert wind force, will slow down the ship's progress to detriment of our cause."

Theo nodded. "If you intend to test it this afternoon, Franco's gonna be aboard. What's your game plan to mislead him?"

"Say nothing to Franco. I'll distract his interest with some refined mumbo jumbo," Dacus disclosed as they approached the mansion for a break.

Returning to the dry dock, Theo parked near the bay side where Franco was wrestling several empty fifty-five gallon drums welded together. He had a couple of extra ones inserted at a right angle. Watching, Dacus gathered that Franco was rigging a relift when he installed a device in the latter drums. It's the same principle used to irrigate crops from ditches at a rate of eighteen thousand gallons per minute. *Innovative!* he thought, struck by the physics.

In three hours, the ship was afloat in the lock. Franco did a careful examination of the ship's interior below the waterline. Convinced she was sound, he okay'd taking her out. Heeding Dacus's orders of no passengers, Franco placed his men on standby at the gunship with radio contact in case of an emergency.

Gates to the lock creaked open. Franco eased her out. Below deck, Dacus started his generation equipment and commenced broadcasting electricity to the other side of the globe and receiving same in return. When there was a large enough surplus, he seated Theo at a computer to monitor data of the entire system then climbed up to the wheelhouse. Just before entering, he turned his head toward his left shoulder and spoke low to Theo, testing the same miniaturized communication system used in the Lavender Peacock scam.

"Mon Capitan!" Franco exclaimed as Dacus stepped inside. Quizzically, he pointed to the forward deck outside where the auger was slowly spiraling. He touched his head, shaking it from side to side to say that he didn't understand.

Dacus explained, "Oh! It's a fabricated radar antenna." Walking to Franco manning the wheel, he instructed, "Increase your speed to its limit and take a reading." It was twenty-two knots, Dacus noted as he eased in the auxiliary submotors, raising speed to its maximum. The ship had smoothly accelerated to a fraction over sixty knots. The wake behind was tremendous. Franco's eyes grew to the size of saucers, and he was holding on to the wheel as if for dear life.

Given a full minute, Dacus signaled Theo to set a soft shell four hundred forty feet in diameter. Correspondingly, the speed dropped slightly, even though both propeller sets continued to churn as furiously as before. Theo slowly hardened the shell, first to test diverting the wind, then harder for density enough to deflect bullets. As a result, the ship's full velocity rapidly dropped, leveling off to thirty knots.

Looking up, Dacus saw Franco rocking back and forth on his heels, gripping the wheel, white knuckled. His face pallid, the eyes were jumping two and fro. Grabbing the wheel, Dacus ordered, "Lie down on the deck, man. You're about to pass out." Undone, Franco promptly threw up. Over their private intercom, Theo heard, "Reset the shell to deflect any wind and come to the wheelhouse." Seeing the situation, he took the wheel. Dacus directed he steer a straight course, while noting and logging the compass heading.

Stripping to the waist, Dacus picked up Franco, carrying him to a bathroom below. Getting a motion sickness pill down to abate the nausea, Franco slowly stabilized under a tepid shower and was led to an above waterline stateroom to recover.

Entering the wheelhouse, Dacus took the helm, sending Theo below with specific instructions to be augmented by further communication. As instructions unfolded, Theo was to set a shell, retaining the same degree of hardness, while he doubled, quadrupled, doubled, and quadrupled its size again. It factored in a trend of the ship's velocity for Dacus as more space became included in the shell. All variables considered, the ship's speed would be effectively cut in half to a maximum of thirty knots.

In a final test, Dacus disengaged the two original propellers, observing speed had dropped to twenty knots. Noted, he reversed the ship one hundred eighty degrees and had Theo to drop the shell. He killed the auxiliary system and aimed for the dock. Assisted by Franco's men, he slowly backed the ship through gates into the lock. The vessel was tied and secured from both sides.

Pale and shaky, Franco rose and dressed in his clothes Dacus had washed. Walking down the gangplank, he saw one of Marc's lieutenant's, dreading what it implied. Delivered to the mansion and on to the threshold of the office, he stood, tremulously waiting.

Marc came courteously to the door, ushering Franco to a chair at the side of his massive desk. "You don't look so good, fella." Franco dropped his eyes. Proselytizing, he continued. "It's come to my attention that you're a well educated man. You don't feel well, and I have a slight hearing problem. I want you to drop the feigned Cajun dialect and speak in plain English. I'll direct the questions. You give me simple answers. Later, if you have something to add, we'll include that also." Franco, averting his eyes, nodded in agreement.

"Would you say the ship's virtually leak proof?" Franco nodded affirmatively, again, to which Marc asked, "Does she operate well?"

Raising a hand, Franco spurted, "He ran that ship up to sixty knots, which is about seventy miles an hour, using both his systems. It was the beginning of hell for me. Holding the wheel at that speed is a two man job in anybody's book!"

"Why? What do you remember went down next?" Marc probed, eager for answers.

"I don't know," bewailed Franco. "Dacus did something, but I don't know what."

Franco's pallor caused him to change tactics, sympathizing, "You look terrible. Is there anything I can possibly get for you?"

"I could sure use a martini on the rocks with three green olives and a tablespoon of olive brine added. It feels like all the blood has left my head. That might help, sir."

Over the intercom, Marc ordered two drinks made alike and remarked, "I've got to try one of those, Franco." When served, they remained mute, sipping in apparent oblivion, until he finished his martini and set the glass down. "Saluud, friend. Are you ready to delve a little deeper into what Dacus's purpose of such a maneuver could accomplish?"

"I am feeling better," Franco rendered. "But I sure could take another one of those." "This won't take much longer. Let's wait. Right now, I must grasp as much of the details as I can while it's still fresh on your mind," Marc inspired. "Try your best to describe what else happened. Then we'll indulge in another drink."

"Whatever Dacus did," Franco disclosed, "the ship's speed fell back sharply, even though both sets of propellers were running at maximum RPMs. I recall Dacus mentioning a gyroscopic guidance system that would take the burden off the man at the helm. Either it wasn't installed or something strange went down, 'cause I had to 'horse' that wheel. Marc took this as a clue.

"At about that time, I started feeling real sick from some kind of surges of force. My eyes felt like they were jumpin' out of my head. If I looked down at the deck, it curved away and made me feel like I was a goner. From nowhere, Dacus showed up, took the wheel, and told me to lie down on the deck. I did, but not before upchucking all over the place. It was as if his partner had been signaled to take the wheel. How, I don't know! Dacus was tending to me like I was a baby, even to washing my clothes. Thankfully, he put me in a bed above the waterline. He's a kindly enough man. Whatever it is he does is different from ordinary reality. It's confusing to me, and it's messed up my mind. I don't ever intend to leave the dock with him again! I've worked on scows around the mouth of the Mississippi and shipped out on tugs in the intercostals waterway without gettin' seasick. I've even ridden every ride on the biggest midway. Still, nothing compares with what I went through today . . . No more," Franco ended it, shaking his head.

"I suspected something bizarre to go down. For it to be absolutely clueless, however, wasn't expected," pensively, Marc reacted aloud.

"I've done all I can do," apologized Franco. "Perhaps if you took a ride, you could judge for yourself something I mighta missed."

Marc shrugged his shoulders in exasperation. He motioned for Franco to follow him around to the bar. They sat at a table nearby, drinking martinis in silence. He tried to assimilate the information he had received by musing to himself. The key phrase Franco came up with, *Whatever it is he's doing, is different from ordinary reality*, had Marc stumped. Mind afloat, he recalled someone had once speculated on the reaction of Ben Franklin if he could take a ride on a jet today. Would a comparative link exist? It was generally believed during that time a human couldn't survive speeds faster than a horse could run. Anyone'd be profoundly shocked, possibly temporarily upset . . . What had impacted Franco had him possessed.

Out of the blue, Franco blurted, "I did see something unusual! Dacus had what looked like a simple grain auger mounted on the forward deck. When I asked about it, he described it as a homemade radar antenna. I thought at the time it was a barefaced lie. I don't have a notion as to what it really had to do with anything or what I was up against."

Abruptly, Marc picked up a phone, dialing numbers. Addressing Franco, he advised, "I've mobilized my lieutenants to take you and your crew home, including the vehicles. Why don't you take a day off to recover?"

Franco responded, "One more for the road in a plastic cup?" He sat the empty stem down, making a half salute, and helped himself.

Marc was grateful for the peace and quiet after Franco left. He had no concerns about Gilberto and Gitano showing up. They had practically abandoned him over this very thing. Drawing from the past, his mind set on the painfully explicit method of rational thinking his father had taught. *Never fall into the trap of ignoring a third, or even a fourth possibility had repeatedly been emphasized. Dad had despised what he called linear thinking, defining it as up-down, right or left, us or them, good versus bad, etc. That would be helpful, now,* registered.

Redirecting focus, Marc sorted through Franco's report. *He'd related how Dacus, using the auxiliary system, boosted the ship's speed to sixty knots. As a result, Dacus did something else which caused the speed to keep falling off. Yet, the engines of both systems never slowed down . . .* Reasonably, his thoughts questioned, why?

Suddenly a supposition dawned. *For the ship to slow down using the same amount of power, it had to be pulling or pushing something extra! But what? Whatever it was must have distorted Franco's equilibrium. The effects made him*

221

deathly ill. Thinking back, the words of Dacus relating deaths of Lipscomb and his men, echoed. *All I intend to say regarding the subject is that he died by his own hand, and so did his men. They witnessed an illusion and assumed they were firing at something or someone else.*

It surely wasn't done with mirrors, Marc contemplated. *They wouldn't have fired at reflected images of themselves.* He descended into a melancholia, chasing the puzzle around. Gradually, other niggling references surfaced to be analyzed.

Dacus has never made idle comments. There was a reason for him to say he wanted his entire crew under his protection, when he sailed. It could only mean he has the wherewithal to deny access to anyone or anything on that ship. He apparently was testing today to see how it executed and the ship's response. A few of his crew could succumb to motion sickness!

Marc summed it up for himself. *Dacus is exercising thru an undisclosed technology. It can be manipulated at his own volition. He is in complete charge of every eventuality. Now, I know why he didn't want the gun on the catamaran! I wouldn't be guilty of ever putting my men in a position of being an adversary to him . . . Woe be it to any one who does.*

After a shower, Dacus and Theo nonchalantly sauntered down the stairs, fully aware Marc had already picked Franco's bones and was about to try to pick theirs. Marc eased behind the bar, cordially tempting, "What'll it be, gentlemen? How about a different kind of martini?" hoping to distract intent and loosen disclosure reservations.

"Have you just made a proposition to me that I can't afford to refuse?" affected Dacus.

Appreciating his stance, Marc grinned, imparting, "More or less, but not really."

Dacus poked Theo. "What say? Let's be sports and go along." Theo nodded he was game.

This arrangement was not in Marc's best interest. He'd just finished a third martini and was about to have another while his guests would be having their first. "How did you like the way your ship performed?" asked Marc, wanting an opening for discussion.

"It exceeded my expectations, so much so," Dacus hyped, "that I'm interested in investing in the most sophisticated electronic communicating equipment on the market. It must be capable of picking up satellite transmissions concerning weather and other governmental subjects. Through your connections, I'd like for you to inquire about the best there is. While you're at it, check on cost of descramblers for government transmissions."

"It could be very expensive," persistently, Marc censured.

"Everything has its price," qualified Dacus, nonplussed.

"Do you plan to fight the government?" reacted Marc.

"Get real, Marc," said Dacus cuttingly. "I turned down your big gun. Everything I'm doing is defensive. I suspect there are certain unethical interests who'll be affected by our next caper. Not for an instant would they hesitate boring in at some level of government to make a statement and try to wipe me out!"

"I didn't figure you to be paranoid," accused Marc, caustically rebutting.

"Paranoid, maybe. Practical, yes. Surely you're not too young to remember the CEO of one of the largest corporations in America making his timeless statement that the business of this country is business. Remind me later to tell you the story on German War Bonds after WWII."

Piqued, Marc abruptly changed the subject. "Franco was pretty sick and shaken up when he came by. Got an idea why?"

Dacus was ready. "Franco suffered some sort of unusual trauma. It's my fault. Without adequate warning, I boosted the ship up to sixty knots causing the wheel to jerk him around quite a bit. Every time the ship yawed, he had to fight against the veer from side to side. It's well-known, Marc, a percentage of the population suffers from motion sickness. He's obviously in that small class. I intend to have plenty of little pills on board to counteract such misery and regret his discomfort. Basically, all I was doing was testing the limits of the ship and charting numbers. It's doubtful we'll ever have need for that kind of speed again."

Marc knew he'd been outmaneuvered and slickered. He punched a button under the bar, and the butler appeared with a tray of hors d'oeuvres. Whispering into the butler's ear, Marc excused himself, assuring the evening's entree to be choice.

Removing a place setting, the butler explained Mr. Zallafino would be having dinner in his room due to an urgent, incoming call expected, and that he would see them in the morning. The food, superb as always, didn't hold a candle to the ship's performance. Dacus called for brandy and cigars, and he and Theo retired to the veranda.

"Well, what do you want to know?" Dacus invited.

"The hell of it is," Theo admitted, "I don't know enough to know what to ask. When you outlined the details to us in Little Rock, it seemed so simple. Complicated as it's been, everything has turned out up to now, and exactly the way you said it would. But it struck home today that none of us has ever lived on a ship at sea. Some big adjustments have to be made there. The reality of life on board the ship undoubtedly will be far removed from calm seas and picturesque sunsets. Tell me what's on your mind."

Dacus pulled on his cigar, exhaling a long plume of smoke. "We're on the verge of something so vast, and so big, it boggles the imagination. A day or so ago, you yourself described the upcoming gold mining scheme as the greatest of all times. Today, life at sea became a factor for you. By far, it's easier to talk about the 'take' than it'll be to actually pull off. For instance, who wants to consider having to work their butts off now? Or, the time constraints put on us later. After all, there's just so much of 'father time' left for us to think and work before 'guiding fathers of the gold market' catch on to the fact their market's being tampered with. Think about it! The five hundred million purse I've promised myself and all of you won't be a tragedy if cut a little short of goal. Collectively and individually, I know what a 'boot' it'll be to pull this one off . . . Clean, and without the sign of a ripple!"

Vigor spiked Dacus's sageness. "What's known after today's outing is we have control over storms at sea. Our prosperity can be further insured with hi-tech radar and sophisticated technical equipment capable of eavesdropping. By covering all bases, we become invulnerable, not only to the elements but to any kind of invasion by air or the sea."

"Yeah." Theo yawned loudly. "It's been an eye opener. Marc's the man to secure the fiber, cables, black boxes, and satellites. The rest I'll digest while I'm sleeping."

Dacus rousted Theo out early to begin a tour of the estate looking for potential storage to house incoming equipment. Around midmorning, they straggled to the mansion in time for coffee. Still nursing a headache from the previous evening, Marc mustered. "Please join me. Find what you were looking for?" he inquired, fingering his temples.

"Yes and no," Dacus assessed. "Things are pretty much at a standstill. Franco and his crew are off for the day. I'm flying out at noon, and Theo's in limbo until Ed brings in another truckload. I guess I need to know what the chances are of hiring Franco and his bunch to unload trucks coming in here. All items are pretagged for identity to warehouse."

Reaching in his pocket, Dacus drew out a signed check for fifteen thousand dollars, payable to Runshang. Handing it over to Marc, he solicited, "I'd appreciate your getting this check into Runshang's hands. For the record, you'll note it specifies paid in full."

"Runshang claims he's owed for two boats." Marc attached, eggin' him on.

"Yeah, and the son of a bitch is a slow learner, or awfully dirty again," damned Dacus.

At the airport, Dacus directed Theo to keep in touch from the motel room on the same daily basis Ed had followed and elevated communication to a priority level . . .

CHAPTER 24

Delayed by weather on the flight and fuming over poor visibility, Dacus touched the base of the mountain rather late in a blinding rainstorm. To complicate matters, Rabbit had set a hard shell above the plateau to shelter the complex. But in so doing, the diverted rainwater poured off its outer edge and down the mountainside, creating rushing gorges and threatening to wash out the roadway. Dacus found a foot of racing water under the car. Using his remote, he quickly dissolved the shell, replacing it with a much larger one to encompass the whole mountain.

The change triggered a sensor in Rabbit's bungalow. He dashed out on foot to access master controls in the old church. Seeing headlights, Rabbit dissolved into the shadows, easing through them along the buildings. Aware of his intent and having detected the glint of metal reflected off the pistol, Dacus stopped. Rolling the window down, he shouted, "Don't shoot, Rabbit! It's me—Dacus."

"Are you early or late?" wailed Rabbit, somewhat agitated.

"The bubble idea was great," Dacus deferred. "Problem is, this storm is too much for it. You've made a real stroke, though. Otherwise, the plateau would've been a nasty slophole by daylight with the downside being no roadbed left. Talk about manifest destiny! It's exhibited at every turn in the entire operation . . . What about Maybelle?"

"Maybelle got in here late afternoon. She went to bed right after supper," relayed Rabbit.

Dacus yawned, "Get in. I'll drop you off on the way in. In the morning, I need you to tell Maybelle I want to talk to her. Let her know it's possible I may sleep a little late. Oh yes, and when did Ed leave?"

"He's not gone yet. Said he was totally beat after the trip up. Tomorrow morning he plans to load and leave out kinda early. It's one reason for a hard shell tonight," Rabbit informed, backing up his decision.

Dacus greeted both Maybelle and Ed already at breakfast the next day. "Morning. This is a real break for the three of us to be able to confer. Maybelle, how about telling me first what kind of shape we're in for banking."

Looking quizzically because the projected twenty-nine million was still a secret from everyone else, including Ed, Maybelle hedged. "Everything's done that can be. All of my money, excluding the half million in the bank of Lafitte, has circled the Caribbean, been transferred back to the States, and is now sitting in the Caribbean again."

"Exceptional," reacted Dacus. "Ed," he briefed, "I'd left word for you with Theo in Louisiana to initiate a call in here to the Harrison office between five and five thirty every evening. You can be assured the phone will be manned during that time to receive or relay messages. Only in case of emergencies should calls be originated from the Harrison line to me in Garlington. Daily communications, less traceable, is a must from now on until we are on board the ship."

"Why're you going to Garlington now?" asked Maybelle.

"Because, when those meters are read, it's imperative to know they're recorded. Should the company fail to log in the first thirty-day period, it'd open an investigation of the account and consequently, a can of worms. Rumors of more downsizing are of a concern to me. The meter reader could come several days early if he's being laid off. I'd rather be safe than fingerprinted. Don't forget . . . Stay in touch."

Excusing himself, Dacus left to catch up on lost sleep. Urged on by thoughts to move, it proved to be a short nap. Soon he was up testing each item in the one-ton. With one short conference to brief Rabbit, Dacus departed for Batesville and Garlington. A quick check in at White Water Inn left almost three hours of daylight at the site to his advantage.

A shudder of premonition passed through him. The oversized padlock securing the complex's gate showed evidence of tampering. The keyhole was scratched. So was its U shaped bar, as if an attempt had been made to gain entry by use of a hacksaw.

Once inside, Dacus reconnoitered the grounds. Along the property's back side, exactly behind an old, once occupied outbuilding, a section of the new fence had been torn down. Coming back to the tent that had housed his generating equipment, he found its empty interior trashed. Crushed beer cans, broken rum bottles, and needles strewed the concrete slab of the tent's floor.

He involved himself by lowering a dynamite charge into the well, located away from operations. It was a simple task, requiring no decisions or thought. As he worked, his mind retraced what he'd learned regarding the intrusion and more importantly, what to do about it.

Concentrating on securing dynamite at the well's bottom and installing a fuse cap with a device to be triggered by radio waves, Dacus postponed turning to the new problem of intruders. On the one hand, it could be assumed happenings at night were none of his concern. Conversely, an event instigating a police investigation could prove to be sticky. Particularly, at a time when he was laying the groundwork to con a meter reader to record a false number from his computer into the power company's mainframe.

Beset by thoughts of a possible encounter, Dacus pulled out extra items stored in the truck and assembled them in the abandoned building. He started off by boring a hole in its roof to mount a grain auger antenna for materializing shells. A surplus of generated power, made available for transmitting to the outbuilding setup, was needed to energize a new and separate unit of electrical power. This detail addressed, he created a large very soft shell to absorb excess power and yet not disturb transmission of electricity from substation to the grid. Satisfied after setting and dissolving hard shells inside the huge soft shell, Dacus left in the one-ton. Using the damaged padlock, he locked up and drove into the comforts of White Water for a waiting period and to prepare himself if sound waves had to be used. He'd noted a full moon and surmised activity, if any, likely would occur around midnight.

At eleven fifteen, he made it back to the complex. Hiding the truck, the gate was opened and false-locked behind him. Armed with pistol and a handheld camera, he took a concealed position from a vantage point where he thought a gang might center activities. He patiently waited, guessing one o'clock to be the latest show-and-tell time.

Slightly before eleven forty-five, twelve young men in leather roared in on motorcycles. As they passed through the fence's hole, the loud hum of electric motors in the outbuilding was drowned by noise of their engines. With precision, they unhitched a trailer from one motorbike. A terrified girl of eighteen or nineteen was pulled out, along with a sturdy breakaway table.

While the table was being assembled, the girl, stripped of clothing, was bent over at the waist and then stretched facedown across it. Arms extended, her hands were bound and lashed to metal tie-downs set in the floor. As fearful panic gripped her, she cried out, uncontrollably shaking, "Why'd ya have to ruin my clothes? Stop it! Oh! . . . You're hurting me!"

One of the handlers sneered. "You won't need 'em, cunt. You're our sacrifice to the great god, Pan, tonight. That is," he driveled, fondling her buttocks, "after we're through with you."

Dacus reacted. The unfolding development left little to regard for rationale, much less the consequences! Safeguarding success of the scam ceased to be a factor. A simple case of scaring off a bunch of vandals had changed everything for him in a matter of minutes . . . He had to save this girl from satanic death at the hands of these deranged bastards and avoid a murder charge from killing any one of them.

In an ostentatious display, the gang began a lineup on their motorcycles, three abreast, three deep. Facing the altar, they waited for two others who were bringing in gear to front the column. Pulling into formation, one arranged battery-powered floodlights to illuminate the exposed girl. The other mounted a camera on a tripod, exactly between the restrained girl and where Dacus was hidden. Switching on the sound, he waved a doo-rag to the rear of the tent where their so-called Disciple of the Devil sat astride his cycle, obscured in darkness. The arena set and signal given, one by one, the gang performed brutish sodomy rape on the girl. In anguish she screamed out, pleading, "No, no, not that!" until collapsing into painful semiconsciousness.

Amid his and her agony, Dacus analyzed an untenable position. He needed to set a shell, one of precision that isolated the ten spectators, giving him a chance to deal with the rapist over the girl. But, how could the extra man, hidden in the shadows, be factored in? Plus, a problem loomed on precisely setting a shell without access to the computer . . . Shutting out the disgusting scene before him, Dacus exercised his only option. He visually estimated the distance, allowing space only for enough leverage to maneuver in.

As the eleventh man's last thrust of ejaculation was evidenced, the gang leader swiftly emerged into the spotlights. The helmet off, an eerie light reflected in his eyes as he moved to shake the spent girl, whispering audibly, "Hey, Marlene, it's Beau. Wake up, Marlene, it's Beau."

Falteringly, she became responsive. Without opening her eyes, she mumbled, "Beau? You gotta help me." Her eyes fluttered open to see Beau hideously standing over her. Reality instinctively hit! She grated, "Beau, you did this to me!" Voice dropping, she searched. "And I thought you liked me." Tears flooded, drowning painful emotions.

"You have a nice little pussy, but then, so does a hen," Beau giggled, inserting himself into her with a hard thrust.

"Chicken fucker!" she sneered, expressing the only thing holding her together—rage!

"Listen, dolly," Beau snarled. "You're nothing! You came from nothing, and this fuck's for nothing. After the sacrifice ritual tonight, you won't even be missed."

A blind, uncaring wrath boiled up in Dacus, tipping him over the edge. Impulsively, he set a totally hard shell around the unsuspecting eleven, whose outer edge barely missed Beau's butt by a foot and a half. No light could enter, nor sound could emerge, as he shrunk the diameter of the shell by six feet, scrambling the guys and bikes in darkness.

Beau, fatally distracted, pumping away on the girl and juiced from watching the orgy, was unaware of the man behind him. Dacus reached between the bared legs of Beau, grabbing his balls in a crushing grip, yanked him off and out of the girl. No sooner cleared from her and the scrotum still in a dead grasp than Dacus activated the switch pad under his shirt and touched knees together. It sent an electrical charge through Beau's body with the intensity of a cattle prod. Two such charges were sufficient to put him out of commission. Just to make sure, Dacus yanked him up by the hair of his head, placing a rabbit punch behind the right jaw. Turning, he rotated the tripod into total darkness and, untying the girl, loudly instructed, "Stay put. I'll be back a minute."

Retrieving the tape and camera, he rushed outside thru the false-locked gate to secure them in his truck. He reentered a disarrayed scene, carrying a folding cot and blanket. Erecting the cot several feet away, Dacus moved it over by the table. Gently he lifted the girl, now in a curled, fetal position, onto the cot. Around her shivering body he covered her nudity, tucking in the blanket.

Standing at midpoint between the girl and the shell, Dacus calculated. Instantly, the existing shell was dissolved. Another one, hard enough to shut out sound waves but soft enough to see thru, encompassed only the girl. Recovering, the gang was becoming pugnacious, which compelled Dacus to drag Beau in closer beside his buddies. Clicking a remote, he activated the sound wave machine and simultaneously stepped back for a shell to secure its effects. It stopped the punks dead in their tracks, grabbing bellies and falling to their knees. He moved to a less aromatic position to let his own gut ease off before dissolving the shell. Ire consumed him. Raising his voice above the din, he shouted, "You bastards are obsessed with shit! How do you like it wallowing in your own? Have some more. He upped the intensity while moving back for another shell and its protection. Like worms dumped on hot dirt, they writhed.

Leaving the area in search of fresh air, Dacus stood afar. He killed the ultrasound waves, dissolved the shell over the girl, erecting a new and larger one over the gang. A flashback of grueling detail caught him momentarily off guard before taking the cell off his belt to punch in 911.

Within thirty minutes, police arrived, requesting reinforcements on the spot, overwhelmed by the awful smell. Dacus had killed the shell surrounding the twelve in favor of a huge soft, innocuous one stretching for miles. Tiptoeing in, the top cop demanded, "Whatta we have here?"

Dacus surmised, "Who knows? Whatever? It's upset their stomachs, don't you think? Before this happened though, I can tell you the whole lot of them raped that girl over there. Eleven of them corn-holed her! As far as I could see, the last one put it to her conventionally. They made a lot of hoopla about later sacrificing her to some god."

The rookie cop put in his two cents worth. "I recognize most of these guys. They come from some powerful families. The stink here ain't nothin' compared to the one that'll come if they're brought in and booked on obvious charges."

Unexpectedly, the top cop all but ran to the car. He dialed a number and in a muffled voice spoke to the other party on line. Walking back, he winked at his partner.

Time for reinforcements to arrive stretched out. Dacus approached the officers to call for medical assistance. "Who's gonna pay for it?" they asked, putting him off.

"Either my company or I'll pay for it," snarled Dacus.

Seeing neither cop make a move to call an ambulance, he brushed past them going to get his truck. During the short interval, a backup police vehicle wheeled in thru the gate. Out stepped a portly older man dressed in a khaki uniform, wearing a badge and cowboy hat. "Wal boys, you're out of your territory. This property is in my county of Braddock."

"Sheriff, how were we to know? The dispatcher said come here from a 911 call received," whined the rookie cop.

Clearing the gate, Dacus was halted. "And who are you, friend?" interrogated the Sheriff.

Turning the ignition off, Dacus asserted, "I'm presently supervising operations here. When I arrived today, a section of the fence on the back side of the property was torn down. The place itself had been slightly trashed, so I figured whoever it was might return tonight. As you see, they did. To my way of thinking, I could've handled the situation. Seein' as it is, presence of that girl complicated things. They'd everyone raped her before a fight broke out between two of 'em. It wasn't anytime 'til the whole gang began throwing punches at each other when suddenly they seemed to get sicker than dogs. You can smell for yourself."

"What I see is a bunch of sick boys, all of who I know personally. Far as I can tell, you could've raped that gal and these boys caught you. I'm releasing them on their own recognizance and holding you and the gal for questioning."

Incensed, Dacus walked over to the girl, picking her up, blanket and all. Holding her with one arm while opening the cab door of his one-ton, he heard the sheriff holler, "Stop him!" to the two disgruntled cops standing by.

The top cop rebelled. "Sez who! You said we're out of our territory. Stop him yourself!"

Dacus backed his truck out of the compound, threw it into park, jumping out to lock the gate behind him. He drove in reverse another fifty yards in darkness before turning around and exposing the license plate. The rookie ran up to the gate, finding it locked. "Son of a bitch has locked us in!" he yelled, reaching for his cell phone. Seeing the Sheriff shake his head to negate and signaling, *come here*, the rookie left it clipped on his belt.

"Don't be stupid. Let 'em go. I'm out here to cover up a helluva mess, if I can, and confuse things by claiming to have jurisdiction. Y'all hop in my car. We'll find that hole in the fence." Halfway around the property's perimeter, they found a section out and discovered it was wide enough to allow passing of a vehicle. The sheriff directed his force, "Rouse the fellows enough to move 'em onto their motorbikes. Tell 'em to get the hell out of here."

"Your jurisdiction? Your duty, Sheriff," they reneged.

"Like hell it is! I lied, doin' a favor for a friend. Do it now or I'll call my friend and explain the problem you're causin', obstructin' justice." Driving back to the gang's proximity, he stopped, bellowing, "Now, get out!"

The rookie cop quartered his last snack apple with a knife and, holding two pieces to his nose, approached the liveliest looking kid. Motioning him to where breathing became easier, he repeated what the sheriff said, "He knows you 'no-goods' and is releasing you, provided you clear the premises on the double." The youngster fully understood, passing the word on to his buddies. They dared not fail to comply in spite of nausea or their embarrassing predicament.

Reaching in his vehicle, the sheriff pulled out a battery powered bullhorn, roaring, "None of you, young shits, are smart enough to pour piss out of a boot with directions on the heel. My advice is blow your nose, wipe your ass and GO HOME, NOW!"

Dacus touched the outskirts of Heber Springs about the time everyone had vacated the complex. He drove straight to Cleburne County Hospital, carrying a blanket-wrapped girl into the emergency room. The first repugnant question of whose financially responsible never failed to offend . . . Nonetheless, Dacus curtly crafted, "Crown Alloys, the company I work for." He brandished a blank signed check in its name to be drawn on First State Bank of Garlington. One intern recognized the company's name and a lot of scuttlebutt about ten plants to be built. A hurried, whispered conference ensued, and Marlene Wooten was admitted.

During examination, the uncontrollable shaking recurred. An intern in attendance looked to Dacus, pressing, "Listen! I need details to know how to treat. Tell me what you can."

His reply was short and to the point. "She has been gang-raped by twelve young bucks. Eleven put it to her in the anus, and one went straight stuff. During all this trauma, she had been tied and staked across a table and repeatedly told she'd be sacrificed to appease some unheard-of god later in the night."

A doctor entered, checking pulse and blood pressure again, declaring her to be in a mild shock. He ordered a shot to ease her down. Within an hour, the doctor came into the waiting room, advising results of an examination revealed excessive amounts of contusions in the rectum but no breaks in the tissues and no laceration of the vagina found. As routine procedure on such cases, DNA samples collected from the semen found were preserved in the lab. Dacus nodded, requesting, "When she's more responsive, be kind enough to tell Miss Wooten that the man who brought her in will be back early afternoon."

He checked in at the first motel he came to. He left a twelve noon wake-up call at the desk, went to his room, and collapsed. With five hours' sleep and a deli sub in hand, Dacus toured Heber Springs. Finding an outlet dealing in cameras and photographic supplies, he entered. Meandering through aisles of materials, he kept an eye out for a person in charge when a short man inquired, "May I help you?"

"I notice you have developing booths for amateurs. Can you give me the particulars on this type of service?" Dacus solicited.

"Oh yes, these are available, and cost is per tabulated prints made. Anyone other than our regulars are required to pay a small setup fee," the clerk cited.

"Reasonable enough," commented Dacus. In two hours, Dacus had paid and left with forty-six of the most damning imaginable records of the night's events. He crossed the street to a bank, where he rented two lockboxes, one large for the camcorder and another for negatives of the prints.

Returning to the hospital in time for visiting hours, Dacus located Marlene in a semiprivate room. She was alert, hollow eyed, and distraught. "Marlene, I'm the person who saved your life last night and brought you here for treatment," he introduced.

"I'm not goin' to trust anyone ever again," she mumbled lackadaisically. "Why'd you bother, mister, whoever you are?"

"Trust me, young lady," Dacus chastised. "My compassion is why you're here. You were gang-banged into oblivion on company property under my charge. You were even set to be sacrificed to a pagan god later by a bunch of perverted joy seekers. You needed a friend then, and it makes it even more so now!"

"Why would you want to be a friend after all that?" she tentatively asked.

"Circumstances! I was forced to choose between being a friend or standing aside, doing nothing while they tortured, mentally crushed, and slowly killed you. I'm no murderer or parasitic leech on another's self-image, which in my opinion is the seat of one's soul. I'm far from perfect, honey, but there was only one choice to be made last night."

Compulsively she blurted, turning away, "I wanta see every sorry one of 'em in prison."

Dacus restrained himself to keep from barking. Using composure, he laid out the facts. "It won't happen, so forget it. The police have those boys' best interests at stake, not yours. Our judicial system is a joke in these matters. You will be prosecuted, not the guys. Try to bring charges against these bastards and you'll disappear. Believe what I say and let me help you. For the present, stay here. It's the safest place. Promise you'll let me do what's best?"

"Oh sure, I trusted Beau and look what it got me," she sobbed.

"I haven't been in your britches, missy. I'm too old and not the least bit interested in having any kind of an affair," he sternly imparted.

Slowly she turned her face from the wall and softly acknowledged, "I really have no other choice. You were there to help me and kind enough to take 'em on, and get me to this hospital. It's more than I could expect from anyone else I know." She grasped his big hand as he came closer. "Thank you for wanting to help. I'll do my best trying to do what you tell me. Say you won't hold it against me if I question it though."

"I'll be back in a day or two," Dacus appeased, in leaving.

Wasting no time, Dacus made White Water Inn around five thirty. Seeking messages at the desk, he also requested a six o'clock call in the morning and specified not to be disturbed. A stout drink poured, he dialed room service, before stripping for a shower.

Maintaining a vigilance for Dacus's truck, Senator Eades had just missed him. Inquiring at the desk, he was informed Mr. Claybaugh had already retired, asking not to be disturbed until his wake-up call at six. Eades went home to an uneasy night, vowing to be back early morning.

Dacus came through the lobby at six thirty, expecting an encounter with Eades sometime during the day. Eades sat waiting. Nodding to each other, they went to partake of the breakfast buffet, anticipating the chess game ahead. Senator Eades cautiously opened conversation. "We have a very serious, maybe volatile situation here."

"Why do you say 'we'?" probed Dacus guardedly with motive.

"The stability of our community is jeopardized if these boys go to trial. Each one comes from a very prominent family, a sum of which constitutes the political and social structure of this area. You're an employee of a company doing business out there where a so-called crime occurred. What makes you think you don't have a part?" Eades retorted, becoming defensive when Dacus remained noncommittal.

The Senator ranted on in suppressed tones, "The girl's a nobody. Her mother spends more time in the drunk tank than on the streets, where she used to hustle before gettin' too old. The father's an unknown. Hell, she left high school about halfway through and screwed most of the young bucks in this neck of the woods. She's not worth the trouble that'll afflict the whole county if a rape trial were held."

"Have you ever seen a rape?" Dacus was triggered to ask.

"No, can't say I have, unless I'd committed it," half bragged Eades. "I mean, I came up at a time when no from a woman could mean maybe, which could mean yes, too. A lot of physical effort was expended by both parties before anything conclusive ever got established, as I recall."

"Come on, Senator," Dacus insulted, relating to the irony. "I'm a little older than you, and I've lived through those same times. You know, and I know, the woman is always in command. It has forever been so because of her nature and the primitiveness of man. Any male failing to understand it is a loser in relations with women. What makes you think virginity's a criterion for rape, anyway? Who the girl's mother is, or has been, or that previous sexual liaisons may have occurred, is no excuse for rape. Ultimately, rape or no rape rests on an act being committed against the will of a potential victim or by permission of a subject."

"Let's quit sparring, Mr. Claybaugh. You're a witness. We don't want a trial. We're prepared to make it worth your while to disappear. How does forty thousand in cash to leave the state sound?" the Senator willy-nilly flourished.

Answering in his guise as Claybaugh, Dacus feigned. "That's about what my annual salary and bonus amounts to, leaving out the background it takes to get another job this good. It's not to say we can't deal, sir, once terms of the camera factor I failed to mention are tabled . . ."

"What kinda camera?" snapped Eades, deflating further.

"The gang must've wanted a porn. One of them probably swiped his folks' camcorder. Anyway, I have the equipment with an undisclosed tape showing exactly what went down, complete with sound. If you and I are to deal, it'll be in two steps. First step involves duty to my company. Secondly, I want a meter reader to read and get the month's activities recorded. Before resigning, certain commitments are due the company on this location's activity. Once that's satisfied, we'll discuss a number equitable to move me."

Eades was visibly upset, and Dacus increased the pressure. "Do we have a deal to try to deal?" Dacus asked. Diverting his eyes, Eades nodded affirmatively.

"Okay, then. Get a meter reader to Garlington, today. I'm not interested in staying around a minute longer than necessary," Dacus demanded, deserting Eades at the table.

In ill humor, the meter reader arrived on site, noting time to be three thirty by his watch. Piling out of his truck, he ventilated, "I'm about through jumpin' thru hoops for you hotshots."

Dacus rebutted, "I'm no hotshot. I take my orders from higher-up, just like yo do. I'm nothing but a peon puppet, jigging to strings being yanked!"

The meter reader eased off. "Sorry! I'm caught in the latest downsizin' wave and completely out of sorts. It's my last day on the job. To make matters worse just recently, I bought a house in this forsaken, damn part of the state and won't be able to sell it. Here I am, with no job and plenty of payments to be made. My credit's about to crash!"

"I understand," Dacus sympathized. "My job's not safe, either. C'mon, let's get this over with. Something's got me feelin' plum spooky."

"Whatta ya mean?" anxiously asked the meter reader.

"Oh, I don't know. It's an eerie feeling I get coming on to the property. Maybe someone died hard here. Or maybe something's waiting to happen. I dunno. By the way, the name's Stan Claybaugh," said Dacus, sticking out his hand.

The reader shook Dacus's hand. "Glad to meet ya. My name's Otha Hargrove." He walked to the meter recording customer usage, punched numbers into his portable computer calculator, went to the truck, and transferred information to the mainframe in Dallas.

"Where's the other meter?" he quizzed, peering around.

Pointing to a pole, Dacus stuck his finger upward to indicate its height. Lastly, the platform with crudely built steps was pointed out.

Otha went over, leaning up against it. Feeling it sway, he jumped away, complaining, "This table's too rickety. Why didn't someone put a crosstie in?"

Effortlessly, Dacus bound up the ladder. Stepping atop the platform, he reinforced, "It's fine. Two of us have been up here before. Come on. Whatcha say? Let's get it behind us 'cause I need to be on my way. Neither is it wise for me to ignore these increasingly urgent, strange vibes I'm getting, man."

Not relishing the idea of being abandoned, reluctantly Otha mounted the table and punched in figures displayed on the meter. The instant his finger left the keyboard, Dacus set off charges in the well, rocking the platform in sequence to the explosion, yelling, "Earthquake!" Otha, flinging an arm out in an effort to steady himself, allowed Dacus to retrieve the calculator in apparent concern he'd drop it. Pointing below, Dacus shouted, "Keep your eyes on the ground and go for it, man!" While Otha descended the still-pitching ladder, Dacus verified the reading then punched in an extra number . . . The 4. Reaching the ground, he hurried Otha, extending the calculator. "Here, get it recorded. Let's get the hell outta here! Do you reckon the New Madrid fault is fixin' to erupt bigtime again?"

Pale and unsteady, Otha inserted the calculator, sending its data. Dacus ran to his truck shouting, "Burn rubber!", while motioning to be followed, and peeling gravel. Making a sharp turn, he led them down side roads for about five miles without having gone more than a mile off the main road. He stopped in a wide tree-shaded spot. Waiting for him to pull up, Dacus had a bottle in hand. "Can you handle a drink 'neat', man?"

Otha immediately shucked concerns. "Hell yes!" Dacus passed him the full pint. Turning it up, Otha handed it back a moment later with nearly a fourth of the bourbon gone.

Taking a swig, Dacus reflected, "Now I know why I've been so uneasy. The place has been mined for years. No telling how many caverns are under the mined area we were on. Just think, we could've fallen up to eighty feet and been buried alive if there'd been another tremor."

"I'd rather try out for a job as stuntman in a carnival than read any more meters," Otha vowed. The two sat in the shade, killing the pint before accessing the main road. Dacus waved as Otha exited onto the pavement. He drove off in the opposite direction until Otha was out of sight then retraced his tracks back to the site. There was ample time to dismantle equipment in the old outbuilding and load it into the truck. For appearance, he relocked the gate.

Dacus, feeling a great burden lifted from his shoulders, walked into White Water Inn. He was ready to add to the half-pint and devour a thick, juicy steak. Dining aside, he had two drinks at the bar and retired to his room, where he pulled out a fifth, and proceeded to get stinko.

Missing breakfast, he slept in. The Senator paced the foyer, nervously biding time. Eades's survey of his bunch had found the father missing a camcorder. An urgent meeting of interested parties had produced an agreement to try matching whatever demands were made for money.

Waiting, Eades signaled the minute Dacus hit the lobby. Over coffee and toast, Eades was presented a deal. "I want a hundred sixty thousand dollars, and not a penny more or a penny less," Dacus firmly bargained.

Eades bristled. "You're crazy! Stark raving mad to think you can get that kind of money!"

"No," replied Dacus. "You just hope I'm crazy. Those daddies are going to hire lawyers to defend their sons. That'll cost one hell of a lot more than I'm proposing. If each one came up with twelve and a half thousand, that'd be a hundred fifty thousand . . . Pennies in lawyer fees! Since you obviously foresee benefits from keeping this quiet, it might be you'd decide to supply the other ten thousand as contribution to being politically correct."

Senator Eades swelled around the neck, turning red as a beet. "God, I hate you, you bastard! You'll play hell trying to extort money out of me!"

"Who's shaking you down?" Dacus calmly jabbed. "Seems your profession's the culprit responsible, and you should be comfortable with it by now. A shakedown began in the weehours the other morning when calls from your financially and politically powerful friends waked you, attempting to cover up a nasty crime." He pushed back, letting Eades squirm.

"I despise myself as much as you do. I've joined with you in a conspiracy to circumvent the law," Dacus glibly lied. "You're in conspiracy with the fathers of these punks. You're also in a separate conspiracy with me on concealing, and eliminating, a potential witness to a mass crime. When you offered a bribe to leave my job and the state, I considered it. We became co-conspirators in a criminal act ourselves. If you decide we can't deal, because a kidnapping occurred, I'm able to go to the Feds with my evidence and my confession and cut a deal for amnesty. They'll even put me in the witness protection program. The current practice of forgiving a criminal or two to convict other criminals, by both the state and federal governments, is a disgrace. Common law on corroboration has been overturned, but I'm not above using it."

"You're a phony," accused Eades. "You pose as an electrician. Yet, you'll quote the law to me like a lawyer. Who the hell are you, anyhow?"

"I doubt you'd wanta know," returned Dacus. "It's immaterial at this point . . . To move on, here are two photographs out of forty-six. One's of a gang member in the act of raping. The other is of Beau Baxley, double-crossing boyfriend of Marlene Wooten, assaulting her in front of the same camera. You've got twenty-four hours to come up with the money. Don't act stupid, or I'll take my chances with the courts."

Dacus rose, abandoned the Senator, and left White Water in his truck. Eades sat stunned, trying to collect thoughts for the problems destined to come. Deciding, he dialed Angus Baxley from a phone booth to give him a new update. "I've just seen a picture of Beau screwing that girl from behind. It sure doesn't look to be a love match with her head yanked back and him ahold of her hair. To make matters worse, a twenty-four hour deadline's been called to come up with a hundred sixty thousand to squelch the affair."

"That's not possible!" Baxley yelled indignantly.

"Don't tell me you guys can't fork over thirteen thousand three hundred thirty-four apiece. Whatta you think it'd cost for lawyers in a case like this? Certainly, not for that piddlin' amount, any more than it'd be to bet the horses. Get everybody to the same spot. I'm on my way."

They met in Baxley's spotless show barn. Eades chaired the meeting. "It's down to the wire, fellows," he began. "My first reaction to a counterproposal was resistance. The problem was, I got hit between the eyes with ace evidence. Here are two pictures out of forty-six claimed. In this one, Beau has mounted the girl from the rear. She's tied across a table, and he's jerking her head back by grabbing her hair. On the same girl is Roy Smithers, Jr., only he's not pulling hair." The pictures were handed to Angus as he continued.

"Claybaugh described the rest of his material. It included forty-four other pictures, identifying each gang member, as they separately rode the girl while comprising their own cheering squad. He professes to have the missing camcorder and its undisclosed video with sound, showing the entire sex ceremony. Assuming he's got this kinda physical proof, plus a pathology report of DNA, he's holding more than one ace. If testimony of the girl as victim, backed up by sight and sound and Claybaugh as witness, ever gets to trial you're all finished. Why? 'Cause dogs wouldn't piss on any of you or your families!" Eades lambasted.

Larry Hall butted in. "I refuse to be shook down."

Senator Eades lashed back. "What's the difference, Larry? You're a pay-off man, and a 'cheapass at that'! Successful only with those who don't know you well enough to measure your depth. Those in the know just laugh it off. Insulting the preacher by trying to buy him with a twenty-dollar bill during a handshake at the church door is no secret either."

Directing attention to the other eleven, Eades patted his own back. "Luck's about used up, if there ever was any. Our first break came when Archie Pinkston, and that rookie partner of his, answered the 911 call. Archie, having sense enough to call me, kept the state police out of it. I was able to get my buddy, the sheriff of Braddock County, to pop in and claim jurisdiction so as the boys were released on their own recognizance. Fellows, forget contemplating having enough influence to corrupt the county sheriff's department or the local contingent of state police on this one. They'd hang you along with the boys!"

Angus took the lead. "As a group, we're bound together by one occurrence. It involves each of us. Why not take a majority vote and act accordingly? All in favor of the hush money, raise your hands." A solid majority of eleven hands prevailed. "All opposed?" intoned Angus.

Larry stuck a hand high, dissenting, "I'm not paying!"

Angus menaced, "Larry, in the country club, there's a blackball policy. At our next meeting, you're out!" Among shouts of approval, Hall stomped out, ending the session.

In the bank next morning, there was increased activity around safety-deposit boxes. Some were counting their cash when Larry Hall appeared, sporting a bruised cheek. "What happened to you?" Roy Smithers harassed.

"My wife voted your way. The kitchen was no place to tell her about the money. She threw a skillet, hitting me upside of the head and tongue lashed me for not helping our son. Next, she picked it up again and come after me for losing our membership in the country club."

"Bully for her!" Smithers added insult to injury. "Say, Larry! Where'd you get off on the idea money would buy you class? Ain't you heard? The only sure thing it'll buy is a one-way ticket on the next bus going through town."

Coming up on one o'clock, all twelve men, along with Senator Eades, met outside Baxley's barn. Angus instructed Beau to stay clear, because Claybaugh would be arriving to get the money. Neither Angus nor his wife had an inkling of the monster they'd bred. Prior to meeting time, Beau hid in the hayloft with his idol, Billy Don Varner, a twenty-five year old thug. He convinced Varner lots of money could be his if he'd intercept Claybaugh's truck and make the hit.

The transaction between Eades and Claybaugh was visible to the two above through peepholes in the loft floor. To them, it looked like megabucks. The last bill counted, Senator Eades swore, "I never want to see you again."

Dacus looked him squarely in the eyes, reciprocating, "Granted, Sir. The feeling is mutual! As I go, step outside with me and pick up the camera and pictures."

Varner was turned on. He shinnied down a rope behind the barn into a scope of woods alongside a road where he'd parked. As the one-ton came thru, he couldn't see a girl in it and decided to follow at a discreet distance. All the way to Heber Springs, he trailed the truck and on out to Cleburne County Hospital. When the truck drove in at the hospital, he passed on by before backtracking, seeking a circumspect place to park for continued pursuit.

Dacus checked Marlene out. The office ventured to mention the DNA samples. "Correct me if I'm wrong," Dacus responded, "but aren't you to protect them as if a court case were imminent? I am only a friend and cannot discuss it."

Reserved, Marlene stepped into the truck. They were silent as Dacus sped toward Rose Bud. The population and terrain were not adapted for carjacking, so Varner lay back. Dacus, already onto him, took an abrupt left in Rose Bud. The road to Searcy became virtually straight, causing Varner to lag back.

Just outside the little town of Joy, Dacus noticed the pavement turned south toward Lake Barnett. Varner followed, seeing cluttered house trailers now and then, isolated enough to make a move. He revved up his speed. Dacus watched, knowing a hard, unbanked S curve lay ahead. Varner increased speed dramatically. Dacus waited to brake for the curve, hardening a shell around his one-ton and expanded it into space where there were no houses. Trees bent and some fell. Nonetheless, Varner met his fate. He tried to slow for the curve too late, only to encounter the shell at ninety-plus miles per hour. His pickup veered left, flipped a couple of times, and crashed into a tree, bursting into flames. Marlene had been on both sides of other high-speed chases and adjusted her side mirror, preparing for an impact. Voicing a natural reaction at seeing the wreck, innocently she asked, "Don't we need to go back?"

Laconically Dacus responded, "Nope. We've dodged the bullet of a premeditated hit, motivated by money and power, intended to do away with witnesses. I haven't the slightest notion who has followed me from the outskirts of Batesville. But whoever it was, they're beyond help. Understand, this very incident is why I warned you against the hazard of filing a complaint. Dead people don't talk, and consequently they can't be a threat. Surely, it makes sense to you. How about rotating that mirror up to reflect the sky and getting yourself ready to meet a new life?"

Making a sharp curve to cross Lake Barnett and a left onto State 31 through Floyd to Beebe, they joined the freeway into North Little Rock. From downtown, Dacus drove to the Riverfront Hilton, registering himself and his niece in adjoining rooms. Bathrooms were priority after the drive. Meeting in the hallway, they wearily sought the dining room.

Back in his room at nearly nine, and even though it begged good reasoning, Dacus adhered to a niggling whim. He dialed the Harrison office and was startled out of his wits to hear a female on the line. He stammered, "Uhhm, I musta dialed the wrong number."

"To whom did you wish to speak?" came the unexpected formal reply.

"Is Tom your husband?" Dacus speculated.

"He is. Who are you?" Viv faked, recognizing him.

"Viv? What in the world are you doing at the office this hour of the night?" Dacus's antenna skyrocketed with anticipation.

"Maybelle's beside herself. Where have you been? She hasn't been able to contact you. Around noon today, some kind of a big transfer occurred at Springdale. She's outta here in the morning, headed for you know where, and desperately wanted to reach you before leaving. You've got her cell number. I'll 'phone-sit' ten minutes longer, just in case you fail to get an answer," relayed Vivian.

Maybelle was lying on the bed in her room, staring wide eyed into the dark, when the phone rang. A poorly disguised voice on the other end galvanized her emotions with the preposterous question, "Is this Mary Bell Sickhim?"

"Dammit, Dacus. Where've you been?" she fumed.

"That's the second time in five minutes I've been asked where I've been. It's been hell, and I've been there. We almost lost it all, Maybelle," Dacus lamented. "A dozen rapes on one victim at the generating site, two attempted murders, and a fatal car wreck have been interfering with our con and my time."

"Well, tell me about it," prompted Maybelle, still agitated.

"Not on a wireless," cautioned Dacus. "Priority first, dear. Right now, listen carefully. I presume you've told no one what's on the piece of paper found in Springdale today. Get Jack. Take all the time necessary to enter pieces of it in as many 'like' places as possible. Jack'll be able to determine the most appropriate ones, exempt from reciprocity to Uncle Samuel's access for information. With claim to a 'deed is done', I'm buying some very specialized communications equipment, for peace of mind." Confident she'd decipher his charade, he depicted more.

"As a matter of fact, stay put when you get there. Do not travel commercially. When the plane comes for you, be ready to board with at least seven pictured pieces of paper instead of the two previously decided upon . . . Understand? Also, jot down this number. It's a direct line and doesn't go thru a switchboard. Ed'll be there daily, between five and five thirty, in the evenings. You'll be informed of the plane's flight itinerary and any other essentials. Absolute coordination is required to formalize the current countdown. I promise to be more accessible in taking care of our business. Ask Viv to let everyone know I'm in Little Rock on business and will be back in two days, three at the most. Be the sergeant on movement of materials down south."

"Gotcha, Colonel," summarized Maybelle. "And, I haven't told anybody anything!" Relieved, Dacus quickly fell asleep while mentally programming the next day's schedule.

The shops opened at ten. He escorted Marlene in and out of boutiques. Completely outfitted, she was ecstatic as a thirteen year old. Years of gritty survival and neglect faded temporarily, and out rushed an exuberant young lady.

Over lunch, Dacus began to educate and inform. "We'll spend the rest of today and tomorrow on a 'crash course' to prepare you for a new start. Please absorb what I'm going to say. It's important to remember every word said, since you won't have me or a textbook to reference."

Dacus bared the harshness first. "To dwell on the ordeal solves nothing other than to take into account what's required to survive. That being someone wants you dead! The person who tried yesterday didn't succeed, but others may follow. It means, too, you can never reveal or discuss with anyone who you really are, your history, or breathe a word about your recent encounter. Assume, but never forget . . . You don't know that person!"

Interrupted by glasses being refilled, Dacus mellowed. "If the resolve is there, and I think that it is, meeting the challenge for a new identity may be easier to handle than the one about to be presented. Do you think you can learn to manipulate a hundred sixty-one thousand dollars for living and educational expenses?"

Marlene's fork clattered into her plate. "Wha . . . What do you mean? What's the gig with giving me that kinda money? The clothes I could accept as more of your kindness. But, money? Thanks, but no thanks! I'll make it fine."

"There are no strings attached," Dacus assured, sensing her quandary. "The only payback is to yourself by using it wisely, and I'll tell you why. It's hush money to buy me off as a witness, paid by fathers of the twelve guys who abused you. It went down while you were still in the hospital and proves my point that they intended to do away with you."

Visibly moved, the significance of Dacus's caring concern for her welfare, the dissertation on surviving, and a plausible reason for the money dawned. "Why me?" she demanded, relenting. "It's your money."

"Compassion, my child. We share a world in common. I'm an orphan with no knowledge of my people, and you must never acknowledge yours. At your age, having family ties to discuss is essential. Our age difference makes me a prime subject to be father or uncle in building the history. The daughter life denied me from a failed marriage, or the girl from an unknown sibling offspring of mine, becomes your heritage and why there is a source of income," he bestowed.

A kindred bond unleashed, Marlene chided, "Where'd the extra thousand come from? A hundred sixty-one thousand can't be equally divided by twelve."

Caught, Dacus laughed. "It's something I wanted to do, Ms. Math. With that kind of mind, how about majoring for a career in accounting?" he challenged.

"Time's running out," Dacus asserted. "It'll take at least five banks, with an account opened in each to finesse money transactions. We'll start by depositing $2,500 equally into the five banks and renting a lockbox at each for balance of the money. Periodically remove a couple thousand in cash from the lockbox in one bank and move it to an account in another bank. Never take cash from a lockbox to deposit in an account of the same bank. Also, it'll be smart to disguise these cash deposits with incoming salary checks from a part-time job."

Reaching inside a breast pocket, Dacus pulled out a Social Security card, handing it to Marlene. "Here, you'll need this at the banks. Check out your new identity under the name of Marguerite Swann." Noting her puzzlement, he added, "Don't worry. It's a 'high-dollar' fake card, already recorded in the Social Security computer database, and one you can rely on."

"That's not it!" Marlene blurted. "How in the world did you pick a first name so close to mine? I'm going to have to call you my Wizard of Oz . . . You think of everything!"

Taken aback, Dacus deferred, "Why don't you call me your Uncle James Dacus? As for similarity of first names on the card, it was a fortuitous coincidence. But, hey! If we don't move on, our fortune's liable to leave us behind."

Afternoon hours evaporated in a flurry. They managed to open accounts and rent lockboxes in only four banks before closing time. Then it was a drive to the airport, rent a car, and secure storage space for the truck by five thirty in order for Dacus to put in a call to Ed at the motel.

Pushing noontime next day, Marguerite had opened her fifth account. Meanwhile, Ed made bank transfers from the Lafitte bank to two of her Little Rock accounts. Each deposit totalled nine thousand dollars and elevated her anxieties. Seated at a walk-in cafe, she exercised her right of authority. "What's the purpose of adding more money to that you've already given me?"

Pleased with her spunk, Dacus mischievously explained. "Well, let's say it comes with strings attached and a pay back when you go to get a set of wheels. Such items are too big to be purchased with cash and must be paid for by check. The payback is I keep exactly as much of your cash as was direct-deposited into your accounts today. By my math and standards, it's really just a dead even swap!" he joshed, reassuringly.

"The strings are easily detachable. Before buying and licensing a car, complete a driver's education course and have a driver's license that depicts you and your identity. Take your time learning as you go from leasing a place to live to buying a car. Always keep in mind that you are well fixed financially and that quick, rash decisions are not necessary. To answer your question, my motive is for you to be successful and above all to find happiness. For now, bear with me the rest of this day while a last detail is attended to."

On their short drive to a shop on Park Hill to select formal attire for a portrait shoot, Dacus divulged the layout for her to have a heritage base. "Marguerite, at the studio session a little later, we'll be dressed for poses of us together and individually. If anyone asks, hold to the story that we are a recently reunited niece and uncle, the only remaining members of our family, and want it preserved in pictures for years to come."

Touched and enthralled by their exuberance of the occasion, the older proprietor who had taken the late appointment tendered a proposal to befriend. "Could I interest the two of you to dine on my member status in a private club tonight? The Flaming Arrow Supper Club across the river in Little Rock, would suit your style and elegance with its superbly choice food and service, complemented by an artist on the piano."

The invitation accepted and the memorabilia package finished, Marguerite and Dacus embarked on a cherished evening. For her, his genuineness had finally been accepted. He had one last bit of advice to give her. "Marguerite, this is the beginning for you and not the end. Take this evening and what we've had and done together to help resist cheap entanglements out of sheer loneliness until you become established . . ."

CHAPTER 25

Rabbit, hard at work closing the opening to the cave, welcomed Dacus shortly after lunch. As Dacus scrambled up the mountainside, Rabbit's construction amazed him. An A-frame supporting structure ran parallel to the cave's mouth from bottom to top. Overlying it were three layers of mesh. He could see four-inch paving wire, then heavy chicken wire, and finally, a thick, quarter inch grid. The sixty-degree slope of wall support was barely adequate to hold the remaining concrete Rabbit slathered onto it with his trowel. As the last batch of mud was smoothed into place, Dacus praised, "Very innovative, indeed! Is there anything you can't do?"

"Once everything was done inside, it wasn't easy to disguise the opening and make it look like a part of the mountain," Rabbit elaborated. "Right now it stays as is to give the concrete a couple of hours to set up. Later, I'll mix up a mud combined with a little cement, rocks, and weeds in order for the two to bond while drying."

Entering the lodge, Rabbit retrieved a letter Maybelle had left for Dacus, who anxiously tore it open. In its contents, she wrote, "I don't foresee a chance of me coming back to the mountain. I beg of you to take charge of getting my things to the ship. You'll find all tapes in a large box in the closet. For my part, I'm skeptical of trying to burn evidence. My suggestion is to bring them secretly with you, and we'll bury 'em at sea. Hoping to see you real soon, Maybelle."

Eyeing Rabbit, Dacus inquired, "How many loads of equipment are at the ship now?"

"Two and a half," Rabbit counted. "You and Ed pulled a small trailer down. Following it, you and Theo carried a full load. The last one, Ed took with Sam, who brought Theo back. Now, Sam's prepared to go again with a fourth, and Art's scheduled to be an extra driver. There'll have to be another load hauled, when the equipment that's being used to generate our present supply of electricity is dismantled. Oh! . . . Maybelle took Harry on her trip to get the Jaguar reclaimed for you. On that matter, he's already made it back."

Dacus made an intuitive decision. "Round everybody up. Time is escaping us!"

Theo, thinking it was toasting time, went behind the bar to pour himself and others a drink. Dacus motioned him and everyone else to take a seat. "I hate to tell you, but what I've got to relate doesn't remotely call for a celebration! An untimely incident has happened. To make an otherwise long story short, while at the jobsite, a gruesome gang rape occurred, precipitating a kidnapping and an attempted murder. Results are, a man tried to kill me. Unfortunately, he instead crashed and died in a wreck, chasing me."

"How'd you do it?" assumed the cynic in Harry to vent.

"I didn't! He rear-ended a shell I had around my truck," coolly explained Dacus. "It's kinda like the story of a Miami dude, who showed up after being gone for a year."

"Oh yeah! How's that?" Theo pulled him on, half expecting graphic details.

"Supposedly," Dacus recited, "an acquaintance asked the dude, 'Where you been, man?' The dude replied, 'Been to Cuba, spendin' time.' After a pause, the inquirer posed, 'Whatcha doin' in Cuba?' And, without hesitation, the dude explained, 'Aw, I was just standin' on the corner of a certain street down there, cleanin' my nails with my pigsticker, when this cat comes runnin' aroun' th' corner and runs inta the blade of my knife—Thirteen times' . . ."

The story's irony caused an infectious chuckle, even from Harry. Its effect on Theo prompted a recurring question. "What's next, Dacus?"

"Even though I believe all the bases have been covered and everything's resolved," Dacus preferenced, "results of such events are beyond prediction. I want the mountain immediately vacated. We'll use Maybelle's vehicles for transportation and personal items. Eva, do you have a valid driver's license, and can you drive my old van?"

"I have, and I sure can," an enthusiastic Eva answered with utter confidence.

"Pay close attention to the rest of these details. If, and when, authorities come up here, it must appear that no one's been on the premises in years. Everything you own, except clothes on your back, must be loaded into the vehicle you're traveling in. Beds must be stripped and linens washed with bleach to skew DNA. Put on latex gloves to wax every stick of furniture, countertop, and cabinet front free of fingerprints after a thorough vacuuming. Wear them at all times until departure. When everyone leaves, Rabbit and I are going to make beds and spray each room with a thin layer of dust from two old Flit spray cans I happen to have. It must appear that years have passed since these apartments were used." His take on things had upped total awareness.

"Sam, I'll help pack your truck. If there's a chance in hell of getting the balance of electric gear in this one buggy, it must be done. Otherwise, the excess has to be stored in the Harrison office. Our immediate electrical needs here can be supplied from the portable unit in the one-ton I used at Garlington. Tom, you, Eva, Harry, Art, and Theo take the five vehicles down and fill their tanks at the nearest gas pump so loading can begin. Before taking off, two things . . . Exchange the license plate from my one-ton with the dealer's plate from off the Jaguar. Leave the proper license for my truck under the seat. Any questions?" he asked, expecting none.

Both the hustlers and cons were well experienced in getting out of town quick. Each scattered to begin his and her appointed tasks. Dacus commenced procedures for setting equipment on line in the one-ton to produce electricity. Once operative, he slowly shut down their main machinery in the old church house. Seeing him busy, the gals took over chores of stripping bed linens, utilizing the two sets of washers and dryers to speed the process.

Joining Dacus, Sam helped in dismantling priority equipment destined for the ship. Replaceable items, giving no clue as to their use, were separated into a pile apart from useable ones, resulting in a large stack of extraneous things. They followed the same format on required materials, assuring reality of hauling everything absolutely needed in one load. Dacus and Sam muscled the extras to be stashed onto the truck and headed for Harrison. Dacus drove his pickup in, staying around to speak with Ed at five o'clock. It allowed Sam to get back and finish loading for their final trip south.

At five, the phone rang in with Ed on line. Dacus asked if he had heard from Maybelle. Ed relayed she'd called and reported all money distributed in nine banks. The only domestic account left open was in Lafitte. "She's anxious to rejoin us," he included.

Dacus outlined their urgent departure schedule, advising Ed to confer with the Zallafino Don on where everyone could be housed in the next forty-eight hours. He recommended lending a hand to Tom and Viv on purchases of gold refining and testing equipment, since time was of a factor. "I'll be there in two days to help," he concluded. Before locking up the last time, he unhooked the two office computers and loaded them in his pickup.

Being updated on return from town, he found Rabbit had spent the balance of the afternoon on his cave project. The gals had cleaned out the kitchen, fixed sandwiches, and filled thermoses with coffee for prepackaged snacks later while traveling.

On schedule at 10:00 p.m., each in readiness for the journey, Dacus extended a cautionary set of remarks. "As I've told you in the past, we have won. Everything set out to accomplish, thus far, has been completed. The wrap down here and an uneventful trek to the coast puts us on line for the final goal. Be aware also that a group of this size traveling in tandem is conspicuous . . . So, be alert. Avoid attracting attention, especially of the police, and stay at least a quarter of mile apart on the road. If you make a stop for gas, food, or restrooms, choose sites offering multiple convenience service to disallow acquaintances. Use extreme discretion and save yourself for some good times."

In parting, Dacus reminded them that Ed would have the layout for their accommodations upon arrival and that he, Rabbit, and Lulu would be no later than a day behind them. As the last vehicle disappeared off the lip of the mesa, Dacus turned to Rabbit. "Damn! I forgot to mention that spending a little time in New Orleans before sailing wouldn't be a bad idea. What I can't lose track of is that I want to get up when you roll out in the morning. There's a full day's work facing you and me tomorrow before the three of us leave."

At first light of day, the two traveled thru the pasture on a four-wheeler to examine the disguised cave entrance from several points of view. Rabbit grew silent. Alerted, Dacus prodded. "If you're not satisfied with what you see, the logical solution is for me to climb on top and set off a stick of dynamite. Bringing down a part of the mountain might disrupt a beehive, however."

Without anteing any further information, Rabbit methodically moved around from point to point, scrutinizing the cave from every angle. Sheepishly, he allowed, "Personally, I think it'll get by. I hate to think what a dynamite charge might do to my work of art."

Dacus heaved a sigh of relief. "My sentiments exactly, but I figured you had the last say as the artist without a beret. Come on. Let's move away from here and down the line to where the four-wheeler can be tied to a tree, and we'll pull down a stretch of fence with the cable winch on front. It'll give animals a chance to forage off the mountain and is guaranteed to confound the curious as to how the fence came down."

An hour and a half later, they came in with ravenous appetites to find Lulu had made fresh coffee, toast, and fried bacon. She hastily filled a skillet with eggs to scramble and served her men. During regular course of the meal, Dacus instructed Rabbit on how to close down Lulu's house while he himself would eliminate Lulu's presence in the kitchen.

"If you have any clothes over there, bring 'em with you. Take food from here and arrange a half eaten meal on her table. Have Lulu choose the clothes to wear on our trip to the ship. All other items are to remain at her house as if she left, suffered an accident, or has disappeared. Your clothes cannot stay because you, like all the rest, are not supposed to have ever lived here. Since I own this place, the majority of my clothes can be hung up or laid about, except the clothes on my back. By the same reasoning, Maybelle's and everyone else's belongings had to go with them," he declared, adding. "When you get back, I'll have beds made that were slept in last night. You can help me spray a layer of dust in all other apartments, but mine has to give the appearance of having been occupied. It'll be time then to shut down electrical transmission from the old truck and crank up the forty-kW diesel powered generator. On our way out of town, we'll stop by the office long enough to take a call from Ed at five."

Motor running and the one-ton packed to leave, Rabbit stopped. Putting an arm around Lulu, he swept a gaze across every structure on the plateau before looking up at the sky. His sadness affected Lulu, and she cried with him, for him. Inside the truck, he wiped his eyes, confiding, "I miss it already. Meeting you is the kindest thing that ever happened to me, and this is the greatest place I've ever been." Traveling down the mountain, he never once looked back.

Tired, and waiting in the Harrison office, Ed's call ringing in brought them to reality. Dacus picked up, anxiously inquiring, "Is everyone safely there?"

"No problems," reassured Ed. "We're hoping you'll have as good a trip."

"Rabbit, Lulu, and I have iced the mountain," Dacus briefed, "and we're leaving promptly after this conversation. Barring car trouble, we should be along in about fourteen hours. For numerous reasons, I'm driving every mile of the way." Ed's reply had been gratifying when asked if there were any other problems he knew of.

Exiting Harrison down Highway 65 to Little Rock, Dacus mentally picked away at invasive, niggling feelings which had descended upon him. It came from an intuitive dread that something beyond control might happen, or already had occurred . . . All the way driving down, Dacus expected the worst. He watched every automobile and truck. He was especially apprehensive passing thru small towns. He mused to himself how unfortunate it was that no interstate superhighways were available until Baton Rouge. Even at access to enter the first estate gate he couldn't know the event he sensed and feared had already occurred . . .

In Harrison, during the wee morning hours, a fire had broken out, gutting small businesses in the strip mall. The fire department spent the better part of five hours containing and extinguishing the blaze. The mall's owner felt responsible for notifying tenants living outside of town. Rarely having seen Dacus, known as A. D. Mays, and no reference on a residency, he called the sheriff.

Sheriff Menton didn't relish the task posed to inform Mr. Mays. The disastrous fire became incidental, displaced to earlier years in his career. Decades ago as a deputy, he'd been called out on investigation of two other, still unsolved mysteries on that very mountain.

Assigning three deputies to accompany, he reluctantly took off with the mind-set it was a routine matter to be attended to. His apprehensions erupted, motoring up to the mesa, and accelerated as stragglers of cattle and horses on the slopes were encountered . . . Once again, it didn't seem normal. Considered safe, and with a vista, he directed his posse to park atop the plateau. It became apparent a torn section of the fence had allowed the livestock to roam. Puzzling, was the confrontation that so much fence had been laid to the ground by some enormous force. No clue presented itself as to an origin for the bizarre phenomenon. Sheriff Menton shook his head. Unlike former deputies had been guilty of, he told himself he wouldn't get hooked on his findings.

A forty-kW generator purred noisily along as they approached the lodge. Inside, they found no evidence of occupancy, except possibly by one person. Yet in the freezers, there was enough food to feed a small army and at the bar an equally impressive amount of whiskey. The previous report on file had not indicated a gambling hall as part of the first floor housing . . . Menton decided to disregard it by claiming ignorance.

Back in his office, he dated and dictated a memo to his secretary, who had it witnessed by the three deputies. In it he noted escape of animals, the massive stretch of fence laid flat, a lack of human habitation signs, except for one apartment in the lodge, and an old power unit running. He also described the enormous amount of food inside freezers and liquor at the bar. The only vehicle present, aside from a four-wheeler in an outbuilding, had been a white 1991 pickup. He concluded the purpose of his unsuccessful visit had been to notify Mr. A. D. Mays of the fire in a building he rented, giving closure to the memo. Switching off the system, he chuckled to himself, *I believe I covered my ass with this one . . . No matter what!* Little did he know then that federal investigators would later be crawling all over his territory for whereabouts of an A. D. Mays.

Minutes ticked past 8:00 a.m. as the one-ton rolled to a stop at the Zallafino mansion. All three, and Dacus in particular, were wiped out. Ed took charge, placing Rabbit and Lulu in a cottage on the grounds and telling Dacus his old room was ready. Ten hours after collapsing, Dacus showered, dressed, and came down to the library, ready to meet with Marc.

Seated and scanning one of the day old newspapers, Dacus didn't have time to rise for Marc's handshake and greeting. "Some trip, eh?" Marc began, not expecting an answer. "We were barely able to accommodate all your people on this estate, but the opportunity couldn't have been better for getting acquainted. I must say they're a classy, confident bunch. It's been refreshing to find no cliques and no individual game players among them."

"The cons have been together, off and on, for years," Dacus confided. "Like all artists, they have their own idiosyncrasies, but who doesn't? The hustler gals probably exercise more discipline than the rest of us to have maintained theirs within boundaries. Where else can you find seven good looking, professed prostitutes not hooked on even one perverted hazard of the trade? Their chief vices, sex, booze, and nicotine, are common among mainstream associates . . . My take is where's the damn for anyone condemning their indulgence?"

Marc changed the subject, purporting, "I want to meet Rabbit. I want to shake his hand and thank him for relieving me of that sorry, weasel, son of a bitch Lipscomb."

"I repeat," Dacus cited. "Lipscomb died by his own hand. Rabbit merely cut off his ears as a trophy." He had left no doubt about an earlier statement and proceeded in another direction. "Have you arranged for me to buy the high-tech communication equipment we discussed?"

Marc shook his head. "When I heard the price, estimated at five million, I pursued it no further. Figured it'd be too rich for your blood," he censured.

Dacus's face went stony. Finding his voice, and putting a damper on agitation, he submitted, "I told you money was no object." Assailed, he'd met his match in Marc. A professional liar has to have a super memory. From fatigue, Dacus's had just failed him.

Eyeballing him, Marc was unrelenting. "That's not what you said. You said everything has its price, and I agreed."

Dacus's shoulders slumped as truth of Marc's words hit. "My apologies. I remember, and you're right. Events of an unexpected seriousness are driving me to leave sooner than projected. If your plane's available and ready, Maybelle can be flown in with seven million cash. Just say the word. I'll notify her at five tomorrow afternoon, and she'll be here by the next evening."

"You constantly surprise and amaze me," saluted Marc. "In the morning, everything'll be set up, including purchase of the equipment . . . Now, help me in a delicate situation. We have certain customs down here. Would Rabbit be offended if he took meals in the kitchen?"

"It's already his preference," Dacus assured, "and Lulu's naturally, to be with him." Marc let out an overwhelming respire to being released of the matter.

The day dawned brightly for Marc's organized shopping excursion. Lulu, Rabbit, and Dacus accompanied Marc thru stores, replacing their apparel left behind. Vivian came along, solely to assist Lulu with purchases. While they shopped, Marc made arrangements on equipment Dacus had ordered and secured services of a communications expert to install it.

Also on the agenda, Ed chauffeured Tom in other areas to locate and acquire necessary tools and materials for processing gold. Their tour became arduous and slow. Tom insisted on haggling over prices of every item.

Precisely at 5:00 p.m., Maybelle rang the telephone in Ed's motel room. Dacus and Marc were both present to schedule the round-trip jet delivery of cash to a very private strip only fifteen miles out of Lafitte. In the course of their conversation, Maybelle asked Dacus if Jack could come with her and sail out as they did. "He's got women trouble, plural, and really needs to get away."

Dacus carefully selected his words. "We have another member of our group stationed in the Caribbean. He needs to make a business trip to the States. He's a fairly large man," he promoted to Marc, yielding. "It won't cause a weight or space problem, will it?"

Marc shook his head negatively, requesting the phone to give instructions on where and how to meet the incoming plane. "Maybelle," he greeted affectionately, "the northwest corner of the airport complex is site of the original airport years ago. You'll see two strips down there, a small fueling station, warehousing for light planes in bad weather, and tie-down markers. Every taxi driver in Georgetown knows its location. Our plane will be there in the morning between eleven o'clock and twelve noon, your time."

"Jack and I are all set, Marc. See you tomorrow night," Maybelle enticed.

Walking up marble steps to the mansion, and speaking briefly to Ed, Dacus learned of the headaches with Tom's obstinacy. Annoyed, he had Ed gather their cohorts for a session on board the ship. "The girls aren't invited," set an unmistakable tone for the meeting.

The entertainment area of the ship provided privacy and enough room for all. "Hear me well, folks," Dacus pounded. "Things have changed. Moreover, time's shortened for us to safely remain in this country. You know the goal was to pump less than three million bucks worth of electricity into power company lines. What you don't know is I tricked a meter reader, adding an extra digit to his computer. That single, punched-in number, brought total take to twenty-nine million, already deposited at nine banks in Georgetown." Instead of an exuberant scream or roar, the entire bunch audibly sucked in their breaths before he could finish. "Maybelle's bringing in seven million, or so, to pay for the ship. Just today, we've invested five million on high-tech equipment for monitoring government and other transmissions at sea."

Harry jabbed, "Are we going to war with the government?"

Dacus gave a measured reply. "Harry, I believe our goal is to con the precious metals market out of half a billion dollars. If you think it'll happen without a backlash cry to the federal government, then just keep your head in a poke. Our technology provides damn good protection. Having sophisticated listening devices gives us yet a greater edge in operations!"

"Sit down, Harry," stormed Tom. "Dacus is telling this to all of us, but he's directing it at me. Rightly so too! I can't get used to the sum of money we thought we had, much less the amount that's actually in the banks. My light bulb's turned on now, and who knows whether the power company's still in the dark? To quote an old sea captain, 'Damn the torpedoes—full speed ahead!' I'll have the gold processing equipment packaged in the next two days."

Looking over the group, Dacus mellowed. "Tom's a quick study, isn't he? My other priority is having necessary wire and other fittings for constructing a series of cathodes and anodes on a continuous electrical tail, measuring at least two hundred yards in length. It'll be used to drag ocean waters, capturing gold particles. In addition," he weighed in, "there's the new monitoring system to be mastered. I can't do my job and oversee everything else. I must depend on you to look for and volunteer to do the apparent. In the meantime, do not, and I repeat, do not talk around the amount of money we have, to either the girls or anyone else, especially Zallafino people."

Jack briefed Maybelle on the dangers of taking seven million in cash out of a bank without armed protection. Working together, they schemed a plan. Two identical light colored suitcases and a larger dark one were purchased. Back at Maybelle's digs, Jack cut the bottom out of the odd, larger suitcase, and removed its handle. Setting it over a smaller look-alike, the two became one via the inner handle. From there, he and Maybelle practiced a routine for deception until bedtime.

Separately, they entered the bank five minutes apart. Jack came in with a large suitcase, requesting access to his safe-deposit box. Once inside, he shuffled papers, pretending to be busy. Maybelle proceeded to withdraw seven million in thousand dollar bills, which she carefully packed in her suitcase at the teller's window. The luggage secured, she moved toward the door where Jack waited, and coughed. The signal triggered him to follow about fifteen steps behind her. She entered the elevator first, with him right behind her. As he sat his altered suitcase down, she became the lookout. Glancing around the upper lobby as doors closed, she mouthed, "Okay." Removing the outer suitcase shell Jack carried revealed a small suitcase beneath, identical to the one she held. In a matter of seconds, their suitcases were exchanged with the larger shell over her smaller one. Reaching through, he picked up her money case inside his fake and was waiting to step out as the elevator doors opened.

Jack purposely left the elevator first. Striding across the main lobby and exiting the bank, he entered a reserved, parked taxi. Palming the driver a fifty, he shot, "I'm waiting on someone else. There's more where that came from if it takes too long!"

Leisurely, Maybelle strolled out of the bank, waving a cab away, as if expecting to be joined. Sunglasses on, she peered back inside. Vice President Elbert DeBach watched from a third floor window of the bank. He hit redial on a cell phone, never losing sight of the activity below. Almost simultaneously, an automobile swerved toward the curb, three spaces down on Maybelle's right . . . Perfectly timed, a short man dashed unseen from her left around the corner, snatching her suitcase. Fleeing, he slung the suitcase in and dived in the car's rear door as it drove away. DeBach's head bobbed, rolling the executive chair to his desk and duties at hand.

Giving a Barrymore performance, Maybelle, half running after the car, arms flailing, cried, "I've been robbed!" Seeing the car peeling rubber as it turned the next corner, she ran toward Jack's waiting taxi, jumped into the backseat alongside him and the *for real* suitcase. Jack ordered the cabbie to U turn out into the street and head south. Traveling several miles with no sign of being followed, he directed the seasoned cabdriver to turn it around. Watching concourse signs as they were driven along the highway, Jack pointed out the exit to be taken for destination at the airport's north end, which accommodated private aircraft.

Marc's jet was on the ground being refueled when they taxied up. Maybelle proceeded to the plane, followed by Jack carrying the outer fake over the money packed suitcase inside.

"Hey! You're on the money," Marc's lieutenant saluted, unaware of the pat cliché. "Easier rendezvous than we'd expected" he commented and asked about other luggage.

Nonplussed, Maybelle flipped. "We're traveling light . . . Never know when you might have to run for your life. How quick can you get us off the ground?" she more or less demanded.

Three and a half hours later, the pilot set down on a private airstrip in the backcountry of Jean Lafitte. Two lieutenants, Maybelle, and Jack were off-boarded without killing engines. The plane lifted, arching toward a small nearby municipal strip, where the pilot knew he could pay off for having deliberately not filed a flight plan and receive a cover-up after the fact . . .

The chauffeured drive in to the Zallafino's mansion took a little less than an hour. The butler ushered Jack and Maybelle inside for introductions and a reunion . . . Coincidently, in a joint on the outskirts of Georgetown, DeBach and his cronies drank, pissed, and moaned, lamenting their con that got conned.

CHAPTER 26

Marcantonio Zallafino was a troubled Don. For weeks, his soldiers had picked up on rumors that lords of the drug trade were going to war with his family. *Now,"* he ruminated, *there's seventeen strangers in my home and on the compound. It's one day before Maybelle's due in with the money. To further complicate matters, my attorney, Gulliver W. Norton, has called in a message which turns everything upside down.*

Norton had received a letter from another lawyer under the nom de plume of Nathan. The letter stated his clients were aware of these rumors but that they were not true. It emphasized absolute familiarity with the boundaries of their turf, noting an early abandonment in drug trading by the Don could have been misinterpreted.

Quoting Nathan, Norton read, "Our status quo arrangement is enjoyed. We wish to inform you of same and do advise guarding your flank from whomever is slanting the rumors. If harm is to be dealt, we will not be guilty." Norton secured a stamp of authenticity by carefully examining the author's name, Nathan Bedford. Noting the last name contained exactly the same number of letters as digits in a telephone number, he transcribed them to corresponding numbers on a telephone dial, placing a call. An answering secretary announced offices of a classmate of his from law school days. "Mr Bedford, please," Norton requested. "Tell him G. W. is on the line." The two visited briefly, inquiring about each other's family, which assured the message had been received and understood.

Marc notified his troop leaders to be present on the grounds around 6:00 p.m. Slightly late, he and Dacus made it back from talking with Maybelle in Georgetown. Briefing the lieutenants regarding new developments, Marc directed a more intense monitoring of Nick Runshang's activities, including identities of any contacts. Dismissing them to inform the troops in their own way, Marc addressed Dacus. "You may not realize it, but this is serious business. I have no desire for you to be put in harm's way from my personal problems. Possibly you'd consider concealing date and time of the ship's departure, leaving some night after midnight, without benefit of lights."

Dacus grinned at Marc. "We've been down this road before. Forget what you think you know. It occurs to me these adversaries want to disable or kill at most, or at the very least, make an embarrassing statement. If you can finally trust me, leak word on time and day the boat is scheduled to tour a party of friends around the bay. Then, lay back for them to show their hand."

Qualifying, he subjected. "Of course, I'd prefer you and your brothers remain on shore with binoculars. The result of my action is guaranteed not to embarrass, and we won't be at risk. I'm smart enough not to commit delivering an enemy into your hands. My hunch is, it'll happen anyway. When it's played out, you'll grasp an understanding of why I'm not concerned."

"Well, I am apprehensive," vented Marc. "I know you're not a blowhard. Still, I'm not comfortable, particularly with so much hanging in the balance."

The next day, Marc busied himself with the troops, yet his mind kept drifting to the impending arrival of Maybelle and seven million. *This whole affair has become the warp and woof of an adult fantasy,* he decided.

Maybelle found all clothing, minus the tapes, in her assigned room. She luxuriated in the tub bath and would have missed the evening meal had they not waited for her. Dacus's cohorts failed to notice a spark in renewal of acquaintance between Maybelle and Marc. He lusted, seeing a beautiful and vibrant woman whom he had desired for many years. She saw a rather tall, handsome, and swarthy man of obvious power, who resembled a youngster she remembered from years past as too young and too green. Their eye contact and her body language invited—he'd be welcomed in her room later.

Marc eased back into his bedroom well before daylight. Both he and Maybelle, having exhausted each other, slept in and weren't seen until noon.

Dacus, up and out early, latched onto Rabbit and Theo to begin outfitting and organizing materials on board the ship. The three had a brainstorming session on most efficient ways to arrange equipment and commodities. Later, Rabbit and Harry were paired to make purchases and man the storage of foods and liquor.

During lunch hour, the butler announced the arrival of a box-type van and several individuals at the gate. Marc signaled Dacus. They left the table and proceeded hastily to keep an appointment. The entourage included one large storage van and two sleek, high-speed Jaguars.

A quick meeting in Marc's vehicle produced concurrence between Dacus, Marc, and a gentleman by the dubious name of Sardis Antonio, Marc's distant cousin. En route to the ship, agreement was reached for installation and demonstration of the equipment. Cash money was to be paid on completion. Marc granted one extra concession . . . An escort to provide security for the five million to an undisclosed destination would block any circuitous doubleplay.

By three thirty and the job completed, Dacus voiced satisfaction. Marc dumped the remaining five million from a dark handbag on the ship's wardroom table and counted it back into the attache. Following handshakes all around, Sardis declined a drink from the bar and left accompanied by an assorted contingency of personal bodyguards.

Toasting, Dacus celebrated another milestone. "I gather you're pleased?" Marc posed. "Certainly I am with the way it's worked out."

Dacus expounded, "I am, and I'm particularly grateful for these technical advances which have removed the need to break codes of any adversaries. When we deciphered the Japanese code in WWII, it was virtually over for Japan. Today, the technology of scramblers and decoders has removed necessity for poker, and/or, chess intellects, where one had to guess what an opponent's next move would be. You know, it's literally impossible to descramble a transmission without directly stealing its setup. The last unknown for us has been put aside. These present events allow me to set a date for sailing at early evening four days from now."

"What do you intend to do about Sloan Barnett? Are you going to use him or not?" confronted Marc, surprised by Dacus's last remark.

"Glad you brought the matter up," Dacus granted. "Getting a message to him is overdue. I'll send it by way of you and know it can't be misconstrued. Tell Barnett, *I am the captain*, and that I can function as both navigator and pilot. His sole value is in relieving me to perform other very important duties daily. If he attempts to communicate with anyone, including you, concerning the whereabouts or activities of our ship, I will place him in irons in the ship's hold for this odyssey's duration. And, his salary stops! If he jeopardizes the lives and safety of my company of friends, he'll be charged with mutiny and executed at sea. The only attractive part of the deal is ten thousand a month for eighteen months, guaranteed." Marc acknowledged by a slight thumbs up.

"Marc," Dacus implored. "Impress upon him that what's at stake amounts to him being able to truthfully answer one question for himself . . . 'Can you, for eighteen months, resist natural impulses to screw up the equivalent of a two car funeral?' You can tell him as well it's a no deal unless he's here tomorrow. Conditions are that he is to be packed and prepared to move onto the ship, continuously, until we sail."

The phone call made, and slightly amused, Marc relayed, "I'm surprised, but he says he'll report to you in the morning."

The next four days became a blur. Several fuel trucks were required to fill diesel tanks of the ship. Theo commandeered Sam to help dismantle, check, and reassemble the desalinization unit. The pair apprised Dacus on numbers of spare parts for replacement to offset the obviously corrosive effect of salt on metal. Tom redoubled efforts to secure all gold processing items, plus preformed, one ounce molds for making gold bars to serve as anodes. Maybelle and Viv busied themselves shopping feminine fragrances and toiletries of preference for the ten women aboard.

Rabbit finished a list to begin the purchasing and storing of food supplies while Harry and Art were occupied with stocking liquor and tobacco products. "It's a damn shame we left all that liquor on the mountain," Harry bemoaned.

"You gotta be mad or the humbug's lousy!" banished Art.

Toward the third day's end, a confluence of information being delivered caused tension to soar beyond its limit. Marc's surveillance team had located Runshang holed up in an ancient, three story house a couple of miles farther down on shores of the bay. Between that point, and the Zallafino's dock, rode a huge powerboat, partially hidden beneath high spreading oaks. Although he now considered the message from druggists as true, nonetheless, he couldn't conceal concerns. It had even cancelled nightly visits to Maybelle's room . . . Thoughts for her welfare invaded, leaving him cold and defrauded.

Ordinarily, Marc presented a smooth poker face, but his demeanor did not go unnoticed by the ladies. Efforts of Vivian and Maybelle were ineffective to calm them down. The girls simply lacked perception to follow urgings of their elders and were adding to the situation.

Of the men, only Harry and Sloan seemed to experience apprehension. They held it guarded and in check, neither wanting to show weakness. Dacus's attitude portrayed masked oblivion that anything perilous was afloat.

On the morning of the fourth and final day, Dacus suggested to Maybelle that the girls set up a recording session. "Tell them to tape favorite selections for a broadcast to be aired over the ship's speaker system during launch this evening."

The showdown came just as thin sun rays dropped below the horizon. The ship pulled away from dockside, its empty gunboat lashed firmly to the starboard side. Marc and his two brothers, positioned to see clear across the bay with their binoculars, watched intently and picked up on soft refrains of music. His lieutenants and soldiers occupied key positions relevant to the huge powerboat and to Nick Runshang's vantage viewpoint, primed to seize both instantly.

Dacus had stationed nearly everyone below in chairs, anchored, with seat belts buckled. In the superstructure, Rabbit manned the central computer located directly underdeck supporting the helm. His duty was to control the shell's hardness on demand from Dacus. Sam, youngest and strongest, had been lashed to the outside of the bulkhead containing the helm. In hamlike hands, he clutched a camcorder to document any action of an adversary. Sloan Barnett, at the helm, fell under a strict warning to unfailingly follow orders while in charge of the normal twin screws of the ship. Dacus controlled the auxiliary electric screws and had advised Barnett that these would be reversed, causing a sharp angle to the left if a turn to the portside became necessary.

Action unfolded on schedule. Leisurely, the ship motored out into the bay. Suddenly, the massive boat roared from its hidden cove, heading straight for the ship's portside. Barnett's eyes widened as it approached. Dacus called Rabbit to erect a transparent shell at 80 percent hardness and ordered Barnett to turn hard aport then straight ahead.

Reversing his engines twice, Dacus spun the ship into a direct heading for the powerboat. Gunners on board panicked. Opening fire, their ricocheting bullets off the clear, hard shell shattered portholes as they became their own target. At combined speed of double twin screws, the ship rapidly narrowed distance between the two vessels.

Collision with the transparent shell occurred at an angle, causing the powerboat to rear up in midair, split its hull, roll over leftward, and sink. Sam continued to film until it became apparent only one survivor was paddling around. Lying in wait, a smaller craft sped out to capture the struggling man and drag him aboard.

Simultaneously, Nick Runshang came madly dashing downstairs from his third story perch, to no avail. Running through the doorway, he was stopped, blinded by searchlights, and promptly doused with pepper spray. Both he and the survivor were separately whisked away to the estate.

The Zallafino brothers had witnessed the whole stunning scene. Marc, receiving notice that a survivor, plus Nick Runshang, had been captured, hurriedly left with his brothers for the mansion. "What did you just see?" he commanded subjectively.

"Seein' ain't believing what I saw!" argued Gitano thoroughly frustrated.

"Gitano is right! Can you explain it?" reacted Gilberto indignantly.

"We just saw how Lipscomb died! He and his men fired into an invisible wall, and ricocheted bullets killed them. They 'died by their own hand', as Dacus said. Sole inventors don't usually have a long life span or they're turned out into the streets as insane and irresponsible to survive. I cannot conceive of this man having obtained so much know-how. He's not a true scientist. He was not after knowledge for the sake of it, either . . . He sought power, and somehow, he's found it! Deducing what I have about their third scam, Dacus believes it'll be of such impact that the U.S. government becomes involved. My thoughts are, adding the new monitoring system to his repertoire for access to restricted government messages, makes him untouchable. I'd go so far as to say it might be another 'shot heard 'round the world'."

"I'd say, good riddance!" peevishly, Gilberto loathed.

"Ditto," echoed Gitano. "What if that shot ricochets? Are we in line for a hit?"

"I have a little secret to share," interjected Marc, ignoring Gitano. "I let him get away without paying me a hundred thou for the gunship, because I demanded cash. When they get on Grand Cayman, the cash will be presented to one or both of you at the airport in Georgetown."

"*Not me*," they chorused, appalled at the thought and refusing involvement.

"I'm disappointed," shrugged Marc. "I guess there'll never be another Don in this family."

"You bet there won't be if either or both of us are killed," predicted Gilberto grudgingly.

"How'd ya like it if I just pulled out and purposely disappeared?" threatened Marc.

"God forbid," the pair grunted, subdued and disconcerted.

Two drinks later, three lieutenants stood respectfully at the open door to the barroom. Setting his drink down, Marc walked over to them. Easing around to engulf him, they began to converse in low tones. "We took the survivor thrown out of the powerboat, and we also have Runshang. What are your orders, sir?"

"Keep them apart so each is not aware of the other. Give the survivor a pedicure until he confesses Runshang's his boss. When you're finished, put 'em on a launch and take'm fishing. Make no noise. Discharge no weapons.

Use plastic bags to suffocate them. Think wisely, make no mistakes, and be back prior to first light of day."

Before Marc could finish his drink, screams reverberated as a lieutenant slowly tore out toenails, using a pair of pliers. A five minute pause between the pulling and twisting of each nail made pain all the more excruciating. Twenty minutes later silence reigned.

Nauseated, the brothers kept their heads down in their drinks during the ordeal. "Why'd you have to do it, Marc?" raged Gitano.

Beset with his brothers' attitude, Marc spelled it out. "Foremost, we've had to contend with a circulated report that 'druggists' were out to get us. Thru Mr. Norton's contact, they disavowed any connection with the rumor. It made sense, since our soldiers had already linked the unidentified powerboat with Runshang's hideout. By chance, what if Runshang had learned of a move being taken against us? He'd have covertly taken us down, fingered the drug lords, and we'd still be looking for an unknown enemy out there. This way, the only survivor off the wrecked boat, under extreme duress, would finally give up his boss's name. Think about it! A confession from him seals Runshang's fate, as well as his own, and gives closure, ending problems with the fat bastard or another like him!"

Placated only by the reasoning, Gitano grated, "Now that it's over, I'm headed into town. I'm going to get this awful taste outta my mouth one way or another!"

"Wait for me," chimed Gilberto, reaching for his cap.

"I'd rather you didn't this night," counseled Marc, mounting the stairs to turn in.

The brothers learned the true meaning of "I'd rather you didn't". They were turned back by empowerment of guards at the gate.

Marc didn't sleep. Events of the evening were so bizarre he couldn't rid his mind of them. He also was provoked at himself, counting a third night not spent in Maybelle's bed, knowing he'd have been welcome. Perturbed, he phoned the gate, leaving word that he wanted to be promptly called when the lieutenants returned from their fishing trip.

His phone rang at 3:00 a.m. announcing the arrival of those from a fishing expedition. Meeting in the kitchen, over coffee, they reported no encounters with a living soul, neither in a boat, ship, or plane. The nude bodies, sacked in canvas, were weighted and dropped two miles apart in a deep part of the gulf. It was the closure needed, and finally Marc slept . . .

At about the time Marc dropped off to sleep, a meteorologist with the United States Weather Service, watching an intense storm at sea, immediately snapped alert. It had abruptly changed directions in the middle of an open, unimpeded ocean. The official couldn't believe his eyes. A storm of hurricane force is expected to change its course upon striking land—but not at sea! Sometimes, they followed the curved path of an arc, yet never is the course altered at the sharp angle seen. It appeared as if some gigantic being was out there playing bumper pool with this particular hurricane.

Dutifully, he reported these changes. New coordinates of the storm caused consternation to all ship and plane pilots dependent upon current weather reports in the area.

Unwittingly, Dacus and company partied or blissfully slept in calm seas under a shell ten miles in diameter and five miles high. Barnett, still at the helm and monitoring weather reports, was confused by reported change in the storm's direction. Especially so since coordinates given were comparable to those on readings and headings for their ship's log . . .

Docking on Grand Cayman, a day and a half after leaving the States, they were confronted by worldwide media coverage that seized upon extremely unnatural behavior of a storm at sea. It subsequently had been upgraded to hurricane status. Reports went on to say, "Some sources blamed the phenomenon on oddities peculiar to the Bermuda Triangle while others attributed it to the much publicized approaching millennium."

TV and radio evangelists were fairly evenly split on the subject. About half preached witnessing the last gasps of the devil before the turn of the century. The other half heralded the omen as signaling a Second Coming and a thousand years of peace.

Sitting dockside, under cafe umbrellas, newspapers became hand propelled fans. Dacus held forth for everyone, including Jack Rainwater and Sloan Barnett. "I promised playtime, but events caused a change, as you well know, which preempted New Orleans . . . Say hello to sunny Georgetown! We're taking off to play for a month! We'll rent cottages on the beach, buy local clothes, dine, drink, and party at local pubs and eateries. In doing so, the 'persona' of a pleasure ship and its wealthy passengers become broadcast," he said, noting key advantages.

"I plan for us to cruise from island to island, sampling cultures and creating lasting impressions of wealth. We'll visit Dominica and St. Kitts and Nevis, since both offer ten thousand dollar citizenships. Lastly, gambling in

Jamaica and elsewhere indelibly stamps us as high rollers. The benefits from sheer enjoyment of it all encompasses a miniature shakedown venture, and the means to locate an isolated island where gold can be processed. For now, take a break to hack this among yourselves. Later, I'd like to hear your ideas." Excusing himself, Dacus set off for the nearest news stand.

Ten minutes later, fresh coffee poured, Rabbit was first to resist. "Lulu and I want to stay on board the ship. We'll window-dress the persona you're talking about!"

"Why?" asked Dacus. "A cottage here is part of the lifestyle!"

"Nope! This is our private roots, now," balked Rabbit.

"It won't be so private," Dacus alluded. "I'm going to live on board, as is Mr. Barnett. The two of us intend to reconnoiter the ship in coastal waters to remove any kinks. Other than the four of us, I want everyone else living on shore, comingling with natives, and livin' it up. Don't forget to call it compensation for when you're working your asses off in the days to come!"

"What I want to know is why we have to reach an agreement to go party and have fun for a month?" Tom fretted. "To me it's redundant."

Sam snickered. "Let's have a vote and get it on."

Dacus didn't have time to open his mouth before every hand flew up. Maybelle detained them momentarily to have her say. "As long as it's understood we're building separate yet connected identities to carry off a scam, I have no problems within those of us assembled here. I do want my ladies to come to me if there's any confusion about how it's to be done."

Ed added an idea, suggesting, "Let's begin going ashore as a group. Afterward, we can split off, rent cottages, and do our thing."

Disbanding, Dacus signaled Ed, Maybelle, and Jack Rainwater for a rump session. "Jack, I'd like to pay you for some extra services. It'll include assisting Maybelle in transactions to acquire rental real estate for our people. I'd also like the two of you to take Ed around to each of our banks, presenting him as Big Daddy of operations. My intentions are for him to be seen doing business and for me to remain in the background."

Jack mulled Dacus's proposition. "Is that it, or did you have something else in mind?" he questioned, suspecting more.

"Yes, matter of fact, there is," surmised Dacus. "As our banker, would you also consider handling the extra services entailed to put our gold on the market in spot sales and in futures?"

"How much gold are we talking about?" puzzled Jack, mildly speculative.

Dacus bantered, "At current prices, an estimated half a billion dollars worth is projected to be sold in the next year and a few months."

"I want 2 percent," affirmed Jack, quoting on banker intuition.

"Done," stated Dacus and stuck out his hand. The deal valued at ten million dollars was consummated with a handshake.

In less than a week, after first night out on the town, waiters and bartenders acknowledged the gang's entry into the various establishments along the shore where they occupied beach cottages. During the frivolity, Vivian and Maybelle, along with her girls, became several shades darker against white-as-snow beaches, wearing a variety of new bathing suits and beach clothes, endearing themselves to local merchants and beach lackies.

The weather, customarily beautiful in the Caribbean, didn't reflect an unpredicted tornadic storm brewing in the greater Dallas, Texas, area.

Milton Q. Darcy sat in his tiny cubbyhole of an office at the home offices of Central Amalgamated Power in Dallas. A small wispy man, he had begged to not be laid off. On a whim of superiors, they'd retained him in an essentially boring job as a statistician.

Long ago divorced by a wife twice his size, the job comprised nearly a whole lifestyle. Aside from modest quarters in a shabby but genteel hotel, he habituated a cafeteria for meals. An only vice was vodka tonics, which he made, savored, and consumed within the confines of a three room apartment. It was rare that a neighbor visited or drank with him.

Mathematically inclined, he had instinctively gone far beyond simple requirements of assembling and categorizing related statistics. To himself, he maintained a constant pulse of affairs in the company. Consequently, a gong went off in his head when a twenty-nine million dollar glitch appeared in bookkeeping. Darcy knew instinctively, he must keep a low profile . . .

One thing most prized was possession of the company's secret access code to its mainframe computer. In a word, he tiptoed into the computer, leaving no trail to reveal his presence. He issued no commands, while merely seeking data, unobtrusively.

It took him two days of digging to finally isolate an irregularity in expenses of Arkansas Rivers Power Co. A thorough search revealed that the entire twenty-nine million had been spent for purchase of power . . . *Absolutely unheard of,* assaulted his mind, suspecting fraud.

Acutely aware of repercussions resulting from skipping steps in corporate ladders, he deliberated on what to do with the information. Choosing to make use of his only kinsperson, a cousin in Little Rock, he wrote requesting the stamped, sealed letter he'd enclosed be mailed out of Little Rock's nearest distribution center. It was addressed to Central Amalgamated Power, in Dallas, with attention specified for its president.

The correspondence, bearing a Little Rock postmark, duly arrived on Dawson's desk. Unsigned, the author claimed to be a retired employee of Arkansas Rivers Power, professing interest in its future for possible investment purposes.

Believing the letter to be the workings of a crank, nonetheless, Company President Roger Dawson made discreet inquiries, which verified purchase of twenty-nine million dollars worth of electric power from a company named Crown Alloys. Still believing there had to be a tempest in a teapot, he made further inquiries to find out how much electricity had been charged to Crown Alloys during this exchange. Shockingly, he discovered the figure to be less than five hundred dollars. He blew his stack! Demands for a full investigation reverberated.

Subsequent inquiry flashed through the internal structure of Arkansas Rivers Power Company. Tracy Cross, in conference, excused himself to call his buddy, Senator Eades. "Buster, we've got a problem." Eades waited, wondering.

"Shit's hit the fan. Words out from our holding company that Arkansas Rivers Power has bought and paid for twenty-nine million dollars worth of electricity from Crown Alloys at Garlington. Guess how much they paid Arkansas Rivers to generate it—a whopping half grand!"

Eades staggered back from the phone. "Twenty-nine million dollars? The hell you say! How?" he cursed, trying to shake the monkey he sensed climbing on his back.

Tracy twisted the knife he'd stuck in. "You were there, not me! I'm the guy you pressured to give 'em access. My job may not be the only one on line!"

"You shouldn't be in trouble," Eades soothed. "Y'all were legal to operate under a cogeneration contract between Crown Alloys and Central Amalgamated. Course, it mighta been forced upon Arkansas Rivers Power a little."

A long pause lengthened. "I'll give you credit for being a good country politician," Tracy fumed. "But you don't know squat about corporate politics. There always has to be a goat. In corporate affairs, just as in politics, that goat is not necessarily the guilty party. I can feel this goat's skin being tanned into fine, bogus leather as we speak."

Retaining his composure, Eades backslapped. "I appreciate the call. Let's keep in touch and stay informed. I'm sure I can help if the finger's put on you."

Once off the line, Eades's mind went haywire. Round and round he trod the same endless mental path. *How in hell could they steal twenty-nine million dollars by fabricating a supply of that much electricity? The key had to have been their insistence for a cogeneration contract . . . . Come to think of it, what a front to put up as a big company! Yet where were their employees? Oh Lordy! They may have my hide before it's over!*

Consequences of his dilemma were not long in coming. Rumors do not proceed directly from A to Z. Rather, they spread in a circular pattern, encompassing everyone in range, like tiny waves of a pebble dropped into water.

Within twenty-four hours, those rumors were carrying the message that Arkansas Rivers Power had been screwed out of a lot of money. The company, which initiated all the hype on building ten plants in Northeastern Arkansas, had taken them for millions. Eades stayed away from the public. He even contemplated taking a trip out of town until he heard the local prosecuting attorney intended making political hay by bringing charges against him as a co-conspirator with Crown Alloys. The prosecutor, Ralph Jenkins, having a latent ambition to run for governor, decided a case against the powerful Senator Eades would be a perfect springboard to launch a campaign for attaining needed statewide name recognition.

Eades dropped pretense and raged into Jenkins's office. "Stand up, you son of a bitch! I want you to hear this on your feet. When you propositioned me to help quash the rape case in violation of the law and your office, involving sons of prominent local people, I taped that conversation. If you think you're going to bury me in a crossroads and drive a stake thru my heart, think again. You'll lie there with me in infamy. Listen to your weasel voice . . . It's my turn to offer a proposition. I'm inviting you to the Ozark National Forest on a safari. Carrying rifles, I'll hunt you and you hunt me. We don't have to live on the same planet another day together, bastard!"

Jenkins blanched, pleading innocent. "That was the furthest thing from my mind," he lied. "Honestly, I'd never do a single thing to compromise your position!"

"You're not ready for the governor's office!" Eades slammed the desk and stormed out.

The theft of twenty-nine million, an internal matter of Central Amalgamated Power, had been leaked. These affairs took another turn under the fury of its President and CEO. His personal secretary engineered a conference call to all U.S. Senators from states within their domain. Explaining the loss and magnitude of damage, Dawson recommended the FBI be brought in to investigate. He encountered response of their pandemic attitude.

"Under what guise or law do you propose bringing FBI into such a case, Mr. Dawson?" a Senator questioned, before being one-upped.

"Under RICO, dammit," roared Dawson into the receiver. "You're the ones who passed that legislation at the insistence of Senator John L. McClellan from Arkansas. The Act's been hauled out and executed in situations never intended. We have been hit by experts. For once, initiate an investigation by the Feds under the Act passed to control racketeering! I want these conniving thieves identified and apprehended!"

It was at this instance that the FBI wound up going to the mountain outside of Harrison. Originating efforts from the site at Garlington, their best lead came through one of the crooked cops who'd been present at the rape scene. Easier than walking around to get a license number, he'd covertly jotted down the serial number off the doorjamb of Dacus's one-ton. Having secured an identity to pursue, they converged on Harrison, looking for an A. D. Mays.

The Boone County Sheriff led them up onto the mountain and into the complex. Going over everything with a fine-tooth comb, they were exasperated by the abundance of food and whiskey and only one set of fingerprints. It indeed did identify as belonging to A. D. Mays, verified through his military files. They spent a week searching the lodge and grounds but never once looked up at the slope of mountain Rabbit had disguised.

Poking in ashes of the burned out strip mall where A. D. had an office produced nothing. The local phone company unveiled its records, indicating the phones had been used to put two computers on line. Apparently, these had not been used for outgoing, long distance calls.

Finally, finding no evidence of substance and no further trail to link A. D. Mays to Crown Alloys, they folded up notebooks and listed the case in their Washington files as incomplete. Failure of the FBI to solve this Boone County mystery promptly took a chair in barbershops.

Stymied by lack of success in the FBI's investigation, Dawson handed down a directive. "Fly into Little Rock, taxi out to the Arkansas Public Commission and find who signed that cogeneration contract." News of the trip filtered through executive suites and was intercepted by Juicy Joyce's secretary, who recalled the connection. Digging through office files, she found a copy of the contract he'd signed and placed it on his desk.

He thanked her and asked for the door to be closed. For two hours he stared out the window, assessing his next move. Mind made up, he walked out of his office, took an elevator to the parking deck, and left the building. Forty minutes later, on Airline Highway at the edge of the city, very carefully and calculatingly he drove into the path of a speeding train . . .

CHAPTER 27

Partying at night, heightened by Jack's presence aboard, and concentrating on their tans in afternoons for nine days, they sailed in a self-imposed great circle from Georgetown to Kingston in Jamaica for a round of gambling. Once clear of port, work began. Dacus summoned the men to help construct a floating tail of electric wires to provide pulsed DC current to nearly sixteen hundred cathodes. Added were an equal number of gold anodes, suspended five feet under the water, to attract gold flecks out of the ocean.

Everyone pitched in vigorously. The ladies became Suzie homemakers in the galley. Harry worked as hard as anyone, only he wore a sour expression on his face most of the time. Emotion climaxed one evening as the meal ended. He stood, announcing profound disapproval of present activities as being nonproductive.

"I hadn't given much thought before we got down here on what it'd take to make this scam fly! Seeing up close what's being attempted drains every bit of my imagination. Looks ta me like we're workin' our nuts off, chasin' after a phantom cause and about to squander secured money. That people, leaves me damned discouraged."

Agitated, Harry tried to make his point. "Common sense says a piece of iron or steel falls to the bottom if thrown overboard. Gold, I happen to know, is at least two and one-half times as heavy as those metals. How in hell then can you expect an electrical attraction of the apparatus we're makin', floatin' less than ten feet under the surface, to find gold floating around in saltwater?"

271

In a two fingered salute, Dacus humored. "Excuse me a couple of minutes. I think I can explain what's got you jacked out of shape. First tho, give me a couple of minutes to get a prop."

He carried in a huge globe of the world, mounted on a pedestal, continuing. "I'm not blaming Harry for having doubts, because who hasn't been overly influenced by what I call junk science? It's the stuff promoted by members of the scientific community who're prone to shoot from the hip. They advance the theory that existence of this world is a happenstance, delicately and fatefully balanced, which can be upset by activities of man. To me, nothing could be further from the truth. From the tiniest atom to far reaches of the universe, all matter is in constant elliptical or circular motion and dynamically balanced by forces much greater than man's puny input," Dacus reasoned, highlighting the logic.

"You've been privileged to witness the awesome power tapped to produce a shell. Ceaseless interplay in this solar system is reflected in the same boundless energy displayed in our oceans. The earth's rotation around its own axis, plus heating or cooling of the two hemispheres, taking place on its annual journey around the sun, results in hundreds of currents. The more important ones have been named over time and are marked on globes. The physical energy of these currents causes them to dig the bottom of an ocean, bringing particulate matter up to the surface. Research confirms some of the matter is from unknown depths of the abyss, providing a food chain to support evolvement of more giant snow crabs and other large forms of sea life," he explained.

"Simply put, for our purposes gold is part of the stuff that's constantly being brought up by force of these currents. Subsequently, it is then returned to the bottom by gravity. Here, see for yourself. Read these names on the globe. There are countless thermodynamically driven currents shown. Their directions are influenced by nearby presences of landmass as depicted."

Tom bent forward to look, exclaiming, "I'll just be damned! I also have had misgivings but didn't know how to express them without seeming ignorant. I've got to hand it to you, Harry, for voicing your doubts. It sure makes things a lot easier to know the whyfors." Comprehension mirrored on other faces who were in the dark.

The intercom interrupted. Pilot Barnett's request for Dacus to the bridge came urgently.

"What's up?" Dacus asked, opening the cabin door.

"Here are coordinates of a storm we're presently heading into," indicated Barnett. "Would you like me to change course?"

"No. We'll ride it out at anchor. I'll have Rabbit set a shell ten miles in diameter and five miles high," came Dacus's response, anxious to rejoin the gang below.

Four hours later, Barnett buzzed Dacus in his quarters. Groggily, he reacted to Barnett's announcement, "Something is going on. The sea is relatively calm. However, according to our sonar, we are moving to shallower waters."

"I'll be right there!" yawned Dacus, quickly alerting to a problem.

On the bridge, his reactions shifted into overdrive. "Start the diesel engines, Barnett, and haul in the anchors. Signal me when anchors are aboard, and reverse the ship's direction. I'll add power from the two electric propellers," Dacus instructed.

Painfully and slowly, the ship inched toward deeper water. Twenty minutes later, the storm's vortex slid to the side. Just as suddenly and with a great lunge, the ship was free, rapidly increasing speed to sixty knots.

"What the hell happened?" erupted Barnett, maintaining a firm grip on the wheel.

"I can only surmise," speculated Dacus. "Suppose our maneuver put two curved surfaces against each other. By our use of power, the storm rolled off to the left. It had to, because it was whirling in a counterclockwise motion, with respect to axis of the earth. The shell provided a curved surface to the storm's action. Does that make sense?"

"Son of a bitch!" uttered Barnett. "You mean to tell me that when we go below the equator, a storm like this flip flops?"

"Exactly. Our position becomes reversed, and the earth appears to spin in an opposite direction," defined Dacus, proposing, "Let's get a weather update and a cup of coffee."

Moments later, the broadcast announced Kingston had been hit by the storm's fury. All ships were warned to stay out of the bay. Dacus mused to himself, *it'll be better to meet these storms 'head on', rather than at anchor. Otherwise, chances are to expect being pushed onto one of vast numbers of reefs in the Caribbean . . . Talk about disasterous!*

Breakfast found the rest of the gang totally unaware of the night's events. Even a lurch of breaking free from the storm went undetected in the deepest hour of sleep just before dawn. They were informed Kingston had been hit and their ship was off course.

"The Kingston basin is off-limits, and beaches probably closed," Dacus advised. "Art, at the helm, has orders to change heading so we go thru the channel between Dominican Republic and Puerto Rico. It'll take us past the

West Indies and into Sargasso Sea, where the North Equatorial Current offers better prospects to harvest gold, not to mention Bermuda, well known for its tropical pleasures and choice for a respite."

Having survived two storms at sea, everyone, even Harry, felt they'd become 'old salts'. Pitching in, they undertook completing the electric tail with greater resolve.

Two days later, the ship broke out of the Caribbean thru Mona Pass and into waters of the Sargasso Sea. After locating the North Equatorial Current, experimenting began on speed and variations of direction. They dragged the tail with the current and against it, at different speeds and numerous intensities of electricity. Dacus kept the statistics on operations, releasing bits and pieces of information to Tom and Vivian, who were sworn to secrecy.

"If you say it's a secret, my lips are sealed," Tom recast. "Don't worry about Vivian's. I have my own way of keeping hers occupied."

Dacus cut in. "How many stories have you read or heard where a band of men set out on a treasure hunt for gold, had a falling out, wound up in poverty, or killing one another? Point made is classified material cannot be kept secret between three people due to the greed of human nature. Counting both of you as a unit, once again, and myself as one, the data being collected can stay confidential and used to success in our operations. To leak the data invites speculation and controversy, which we don't need. What's necessary is your comprehension of how it was done, down to the penny, when processing begins. It'll guarantee everyone a fair shake."

Nodding her head up and down, Vivian reflected she'd grasped full significance of his remarks. "No more harassing you about our part," she promised. "There won't be time. It'll take both of us to fill the pair of shoes you've laid out. I haven't forgotten those ugly things you had me try for size our first night on the mountain either!"

"Well, now that you've gotten shoes on, help me wade through a little mud," Dacus said, drawing them on. "Do you have any insight on whether or not it's physically possible to process a ton of bars or more per week?"

"Yeah . . . Yes and no," Tom responded positively. "From our notes, I'd say yes if it weren't for oversized 'buts' in the way. The kind of time being allowed for collecting and transport of the gold to where it can be processed is a major factor. For us to actually do the work is another. But mastering a routine is about all that's involved. On the matter of getting it to where it can be cashed in is pretty much out of our hands . . . Your Baby, in other words!"

"You've touched on the basics, Tom, and they must be addressed," Dacus agreed. "I'm ahead of you, however, working on a 'game plan' which discreetly manipulates the end product into a certified depository," he contributed.

"Regarding supply and demand, it may be the smart thing to start off letting gold build up on an isolated island. From it, initially you could have us a fresh supply of anodes that would be picked up when we come in to drop off the gold once a week. Inasmuch, Theo's our man to keep electrical needs up and running, maintaining a shell for protection, with time to spare for assisting to muscle some of the weight around."

"Wait a minute!" stormed Tom, interrupting. "I'm not fixin' to be exiled and isolated on a godforsaken monastery island!"

Trying to defuse Tom's outburst, while not disclosing her own misgivings, Vivian teased, "See, you old fart, you just 'fessed up that I can't satisfy you by myself."

"Don't let her kid you, Dacus," Tom defended. "She craves variety as much as I do."

"Truce," Dacus declared. "Maybelle can assign Eva and Barbee for the three of you . . . That is, until they can't take any more!"

One day hence, a stop at Dominica proved fruitful. Ed and Maybelle were told by Dominican officials of an island eighty miles away bypassed by the usual trade routes. It was not under the jurisdiction of Dominica, although papers of ownership were filed in their records. Facilities had been built by an eccentric who died some thirty-nine years ago. Interest in the island had languished since no natural supply of water existed unless hauled in. Ed, a born trader, struck a two year lease for ten thousand dollars on the spot.

Their trip to the island revealed no deep water access. On over half of its shoreline, sandy beach faded to shallow sea. The remaining coast was dominated by mountainous terrain, ending in a sheer cliff and dropping into the ocean. However, beaching didn't pose a problem for the ex-gunship, a modified catamaran outfitted with a third hull.

They disembarked to find living accommodations abandoned years ago were surprisingly adequate under layers of dust and grime. The ladies turned to, cleaning to determine usability. Aside from antiquated refrigeration and no air-conditioning, everything else worked satisfactorily, proving favorable for habitation. The only things missing were electricity and freshwater. Those items were easily solvable with unlimited electricity and equipment to install a desalinization unit.

But then, Rabbit made a startling discovery. The structure had carefully crafted wooden guttering, connected in ever increasing capacities, that led to the back of the house. He escorted Dacus to his findings, pointing out a huge round wooden cover, maybe fifteen feet in diameter.

"What is it?" baffled, Dacus asked in ignorance.

"I guess you city boys never heard of a cistern, eh? They're to collect the rainwater comin' off the roof. This is the lid to its storage tank," chortled Rabbit.

Dacus was intrigued. "This would eliminate our water needs instantly. The existing water, decontaminated, plus annual rainfall, takes care of the rest."

"When I grew up, all we knew was to boil the water. Took lots of time and trouble," Rabbit recalled, relishing that part of his past.

"Techniques have come a long way, my man," prefaced Dacus. "It's easy enough to build an ozone generator to create a mild solution of hydrogen peroxide by bubbling ozone into the cistern's water. When all's said and done, bugs'll quickly be gone and water pure enough to drink."

Elated, Dacus conceded, "Maybelle and Ed made a stroke, to come up with this layout. Round up everybody, Rabbit, and let's head for the ship. We've got a date in Bermuda and plenty of daylight hours for getting on with an unfinished vacation."

On board the ship, following a brief conference with Jack Rainwater, Dacus called for a session in the lounge. "Our destination has just changed." Before anyone could react, Dacus pointed out, "Whereas Bermuda is still a dependency of Great Britain, I assumed it'd be the place Jack could establish contact with the London gold exchange. But he says the Bahamas, even though independent, offers us stronger ties through banking. Certainly, it's in a more convenient location for our needs and ample reason to change course. Nassau is under nine hundred miles and much closer than Bermuda. We should be there in no more than a couple of days."

The smiles of approval told Dacus that long stretches of living on shipboard would become more and more tedious. He logged it mentally, not losing sight that he wanted to check a potential for gold harvesting further north while en route. Locating a second island in the proximity for convenience of the processing crew had to be addressed in due time.

During the pause, Jack signaled, indicating he'd like to speak. Dacus acknowledged, appraising the gang, "Jack undoubtedly has something important to say. He's asked for, and I'm giving him the floor to be heard."

Standing tall in his traditional Indian dignity, Jack spoke softly, "I have been engaged to market your gold. There are significant things to be known regarding gold and banking. Gold is a most useless element to mankind.

Prized for scarcity and priced accordingly, it's too soft for use without help from another metal. Chieftains, kings, and queens reveled in its brilliance, rewarding craftsmen for ornaments created, always wanting more. Gold coins had their place in history. Presently, gold's just as impressive in thin layers adorning office door lettering, nail polish, books, as it was to repair teeth." For an example, he indicated a tooth's inlay.

"Focus with me, if you will," he encouraged, "on worth of this precious metal. Copper, readily available, is hawked at a thousand, five hundred forty dollars per ton, on today's market, to gold's incomparable price of well over ten million, for the same weight. Bear in mind also, it is a highly guarded price fix, effected by regimented supply."

Jack flipped a gold coin from his pocket into a radiant reflecting spin atop the table, fortifying, "The gold market is capable of great volatility, unless strictly controlled. Mark my word—this market is absolutely regulated! It's governed by a shadowy consortium in existence of very dangerous individuals with strong vested interests. These people, many who occupy high government positions in various countries, are astute in monitoring the market and not above use of unscrupulous tactics to enforce their will. After all, a sizeable loss from present value of three hundred sixty U.S. dollars, per troy ounce, will guarantee disastrous political consequences for them and the world."

Picking up the coin, Jack toyed it in his fingers, alluding, "A small army of well funded and equipped assassins exists in these matters. It is financed by the U.S., along with several industrial nations who rely heavily on their gold mining to buttress economics. Its purpose is to stealthily eliminate any threat to stability of the gold market, currently valued at about five hundred twenty-eight billion. Disrupt the market, which defines your actions, and it'll be tantamount to a siege on the 'fort'. After smoke screens vaporize, fangs of the wolf pack can be seen, if not felt!"

Diverting to more native antics, Jack advised, "My opinion is to be wise as an owl and cunning as the fox if you're going to dump half a billion of the stuff onto that market in one lump sum. It'll help to have the jump start of an antelope, the speed of a big cat in pursuit of prey, and a medicine man's magic to pull it off. You might consider war paint, if that doesn't work."

Out of the assemblage burst a loud, disruptive voice. "What's The Bottom Line, Chief?" All heads pivoted toward the sound.

Sam moved, squeezing in beside Harry. Gripping him by the biceps in one of his hamlike hands, Sam muttered, "One more word out of you and I'll break a bone!"

Dacus stood, placing an arm across Jack's shoulders. "The bottom line, folks, is that out of ignorance I've misled myself and consequently, everyone else. When I emphasized the legality of our scam, it never occurred to me there'd be a hidden, shadow entity, separate and apart from the UN which supports an actual police force to carry out its retribution for the accumulated leading nations in the world. Personally, Jack, I'm grateful to you for telling it like it is. I know I speak for us all in thanking you."

To the others, Dacus issued a directive. "Overtly, 'The Tale' must be altered, and a stronger resolve of silence is to be made regarding our operation. Jack's input at this stage in the game becomes more disconcerting than critical . . . Remember, members in Special Forces are just people doing a job. They are capable of being conned, if circumstances warrant. Whether its mob warfare or a special armed force retaliation, we have our own method to contrive an assault."

He cautioned, "You need to be aloof and unapproachable on such matters. Always portray yourselves as wealthy patrons of pleasure, not the least interested in concerns for welfare of others or affairs in politics or existing executive powers." Dismissing, Dacus posed, "The rest of the day needs to be spent mining for gold. I'm going to bend Jack's ear and reconsider priorities. See you right here after dinner tonight."

Bidding them a good day, Dacus ushered Jack into a cozy corner of the lounge and served more coffee. Before he could get seated, Jack raised a question, "What did you mean when you said the assassins could be conned into doing away with themselves?"

Dacus responded with a question of his own. "Is the deal still on for you to handle the financial affair of selling our gold?"

Jack gazed through a porthole. Squinting one eye, he finally took on Dacus. "You have powerful adversaries you didn't even know existed. I told you about 'em in detail. At eighty-two I'm an anachronism. Like any old man from the past, of necessity, I give thought to impending death. Searching for that perfect tree to sit under beats stepping in front of a speeding bus or jumping off a cliff. My problem is I'm not ready to sit down yet. Neither am I afraid to die. In short, the deal we made provides challenge over boredom rather than an execution. Now, tell me what you meant by proffering you could be in secret complicity with this matter."

It was Dacus's turn to stop and study. Gingerly he approached the subject. "It's surely obvious to you that we have access to virtually unlimited electrical power. Otherwise, we wouldn't be out here harvesting gold at a fantastic profit!" Then he delved into its cause and effect.

"The arrangement of our universe insures a reality of certain trade-offs. In this instance, results are either ham or beans for us. If intensity of electromagnetic vibrations, between earth and sun, were allowed to continue infinitely, our world would've exploded eons ago. Thankfully, the solar system itself, part of this rational creation, is dynamically balanced. Consider that the earth harbors something to provide a dampening effect without losing resonance with the sun. The enslaving of such energy for our purposes, produces an amount of electrical power far beyond any capacity to handle it . . ." Noting Jack attuned, he touched on the relevancy.

"The pioneer who discovered 'free electricity', Nikola Tesla, solved his problem by dissipating the excess through lightning bolts discharged between two globes, placed two hundred yards or so apart. The inspiration for my different kind of solution was triggered by Einstein's still unproven unified field theory. It includes his proven discovery that space is warped around an intense gravitational field, even to the point of curving electromagnetic waves, at the intensity of light, by the expense of its energy." Affinity prevailed and Dacus disclosed.

"With powerful PCs and Rabbit as my assistant, I learned how to erect a half spherical shell, of various dimensions and degrees of warp or hardness around an antenna of unusual design. Next, I succeeded in setting a second, smaller shell inside the first, with its own separate degrees of hardness. The mob, who came for vengeance after we'd knocked over their rigged casino, died by ricocheted bullets fired from their own guns while confined in a small clear, hard shell. They didn't have a chance! Neither did Marc's adversaries in a similar go down to destroy the ship after launch," Dacus solidified, reminding. "You missed that recent action when below deck."

"You mean to say you're warping space?" exclaimed Jack.

"Only in thin shells," expounded Dacus. "Space within these shells is not distorted. It's how we were able to deflect a storm at sea between New Orleans and Grand Cayman yet retain calm seas within our bubble."

"It sounds like science fiction," Jack grunted.

Dacus's reply was short and succinct. "Yesterday's science fiction is the science of today. Recall the reams of paper and buckets of ink exhausted explaining why mankind would never achieve flight through the air? Today, there's even manned spaceflights where no air's present. Now, Jack, let's skip the crap, as they say in Arkansas, and get down to the 'nut cuttin'."

Jack recoiled as a rattler ready to strike. "Rampant hillbilly bullshit! That's ranchers and cattlemen's lingo from cattle business in Oklahoma and all of the west. I've cut and made more steers than you can count!"

"Whatever," dryly consented Dacus. "Listen, I'm trying to furnish insight. This thing's shaping up to put you in as point man, exposed mind you, and without any protection. Possible consequences of such an arrangement leave me uneasy and damned uncomfortable."

"Don't waste your time. I've already told you I'm not afraid to die," reviled Jack.

"Nobody wants to die hard, much less in applied pain," contended Dacus. "How about you agreeing to wear an ankle bracelet for me?"

"As a memento?" Jack smirked, making light of his concerns.

"No! It'd keep you from being buried in sand up to your neck, with ants crawling all over, or forced to do a war dance until you spit up what you know. Your whereabouts would be known anywhere within twelve square feet on this hemisphere simply by bouncing signals off a satellite to your bracelet. The returns are processed back through my computers, not only on your location but a description of those surroundings." Dacus rose from his chair, waiting for a response.

In a steady gaze, Jack answered, "Neither anything you or I have said changes anything. I'm on board for the duration."

Dacus's shoulders slumped slightly. "It's a little off the subject, but you've said repeatedly you're not afraid of death. I've heard most of my life how Indians can die when they want to. Is it truth, purely myth, or nonsensical fantasy?"

"Not exactly." Jack smiled, interpreting. "The true legend tells of an old person or couple, too feeble to keep up with their tribe, who face an imminent death. Supposedly, they can go sit under a tree, facing the sun, while the tribe moves on. When the sun goes down, they meet their Maker . . . Death apparently must be about to occur, and an aura translates as such. Conversely, the white man's belief is that death can be held at bay by sheer willpower. They'll refuse recognizing death into their consciousness and avoid its discussion in conversation."

Unexpectedly, Jack scrutinized Dacus's body. "Let me see your fingers," he commanded. Dacus held out both hands. After running his fingers across Dacus's knuckles, Jack insisted on a further look at his elbows and knees. Rising from where he'd carefully examined the knees, Jack asked, "Am I correct that you don't have a clue as to who your biological parents were?"

"Yep. That's the way it is!" Dacus replied.

Jack articulated, "The anatomy of your joints proves to me there's as much Indian in you as I've got. By chance, have you ever been called a half breed?"

"Guess not. No doubt I'll handle it if I can *will* my own death," Dacus opted.

"Either you misunderstood or weren't paying attention. The real character of a person determines their unwavering belief. While our people were confined to reservations and no longer traveled, their traditions of the past made it possible for belief to preside. Maybe old Indians could die at sundown. Get this though, death had to be threatening. Besides, recognition and disclosure of ancestry enforces discipline for your own peace of mind, not to help you do tricks," Jack chided, extending his pipe.

Evening impending, the meal completed, Dacus tapped his wine glass to gain attention. "Earlier today, we had a 'set-to'," he commenced. "Revisions were outlined regarding 'The Tale'. Jack's the one who'll be spotlighted in his position of marketing. It's mandatory that the word *gold* be dropped completely from your vocabulary. Our devotion to pleasure, while in port, is eat, sleep, drink, play, and project. Forget *it* just once, and consequences will be so far reaching they consume everyone! Frequently, Jack'll have to be out from under our umbrella of safety as he's deployed in maneuvers within the gold market. He's wisely agreed to wear a sensor bracelet so we can keep tabs on his whereabouts. When we make port in Nassau, he'll try disappearing to check on its accuracy. If the sensor's in place, I have no doubt his welfare can be shielded . . ."

Having sized up events, Dacus enticed, "You've got the picture as clearly as this night is beautiful. What say we declare party time until eleven or so?"

Applause, a few hoots, and shouts of approval drowned out any 'afterthought remarks' someone may have considered.

CHAPTER 28

Sailing into Nassau, they were provided full docking accommodations, including freshwater, a sewage hookup, and electricity. Their lodging assured, Dacus, Sloan Barnett, Rabbit and Lulu, and most others spread out across the city like a shipload of sailors on leave. Jack, Maybelle, and Ed delayed making the scene until an in-depth search for established banking institutions could be located and earmarked.

On the third day, Maybelle flew over to Georgetown on Grand Cayman, planning to transfer assets into the five banks they'd settled on in Nassau. She rented a car and began making the rounds to set up new accounts favorable for their latest temporary headquarters. It flowed like clockwork until she walked in at the fourth bank. There, a swarthy man in dark glasses stepped up and handed her an open note card. The bold print read, "I need to see you." It was signed Marc.

Interesting! invaded her thoughts. "Where?" she asked the man, unaware of any interaction with Marc that had occurred, much less the unlikely disclosure of their activities.

"On the island," he relayed. "As soon as you're through here, I am instructed to take you to him. I'll be waiting outside."

At the teller's window, Maybelle described her business and went through the formalities of transferring funds into the new account. In addition, she arranged to withdraw a hundred thousand, in hundred-dollar increments, directing it be delivered to one of their private rooms. Once inside, she counted the bundles, burying them in an oversized purse, quite anxious to see Marc.

Less than half a block after leaving the bank's entry, a small wiry man cut the strap on Maybelle's purse, snatching it away. Going nowhere, her contact man in sunglasses caught the guy from behind, partially lifted him up by the neck, cutting off blood to his brain. Maybelle whirled at the interference, retrieving her purse from nerveless fingers. Unable to leave the Mafia's calling card of a broken leg in broad daylight on a public street, Marc's man pulverized bones in the dip's right hand. Without an audible outcry, the incident went unnoticed. He promptly placed a hand under Maybelle's elbow, steering her to his car.

"What about my car?" inquired Maybelle, a bit testy.

"It'll be okay," he assured. "When we get to the Mr. Zallafino's abode, I'm to get a partner and the instructions are to satisfy payment with the rental agency on delivery."

As they turned into the beach house driveway, Maybelle was startled to find that it was right next to the cottage she'd previously rented and had in reserve. *How utterly, utterly convenient,* flashed to mind. The door opened, and Marc caught her in a warm, lengthy embrace. Catching a breather, she couldn't resist chastising a little. "I'm impressed with the wide web of information you seem to have at your disposal."

"And I too am impressed with the way you and your friends orchestrated a storm at sea," he flirted while wanting to emphasize a point.

Rather intent on paying their debt to him, Maybelle let content of his remark elude her. Edging over to the couch, she dumped wares from her purse, allowing, "Don't get excited. I'm not about to buy choice favors yet! This is to retire our association's note on the gunship."

"You sure are blasé about it," Marc reacted, more enthralled with her than the money. Stutter stepping, he propositioned, "Can I entice you to my pad for the night?"

"Nope! Come onta my house," she invited temptingly. "I have rented a cabana, you know. Hope you don't get lost trying to find it."

Radiant, the next morning Marc followed his nose to where Maybelle was preparing a continental breakfast. He watched her bustling about the kitchenette, totally taken. "You're a helluva woman, Maybelle. I swore I'd never do it again, but would you marry me? We could do a wedding down here and have an island honeymoon," he proposed.

"Marc, you're a hunk to me. The trouble is I'm not interested in a binding relationship with anyone," she vowed. "You and I are like two trains, who are within touching distance as they pass, running on separate tracks in the night. It wouldn't work!"

"It's Dacus, isn't it?" hurt, Marc accused. "He loves you! Or is it the other way around?"

"He loves me all right, like the sister he never had. Dacus is obsessed with an idea he should never have been born. For starters, he couldn't uncover who his parents were. Later, the love of his life came along. She wanted children and discovered he couldn't produce, so she divorced him. It reeks of having been sexually emasculating and perhaps has caused a seething hatred of his own life. He hasn't personally killed although he's definitely beset with danger and he's perilous to be around." Impatiently, Maybelle reminded, "That part of him I know you've seen."

Still dissatisfied, Marc probed, "If that's the way it is, then why are you here?"

"Marc, stop it!" Maybelle sharply snapped. "I am a con woman. It's the name of our game. Not only has it been an opportunity for me to provide for my girls outside of Tulsa, it's become a challenge impossible to explain to you!"

Marc threw his hands up, ending it. "Okay, okay! Do me the favor of flying you to Nassau. While I'm in the act of begging favors, can I get you to ask Dacus to meet with me?"

Impishly Maybelle hugged him, committing. "Today, I have another transaction in one more bank. If it doesn't 'misput' your schedule, it'd be my pleasure to have your escort. And certainly, I'll be happy to ask Dacus if he'll see you, Marc."

The trip to Nassau would have been a short hop, except for time required to tack around Cuba's airspace. Marc's reservation was at the Sheraton British Colonial Hotel. He optioned being taken there before Maybelle's delivery to dockside, which was fine with her.

In the ship's lounge, Maybelle brought Dacus up to date on banking criterions completed in Georgetown. She fulfilled her promise to Marc, and Dacus contacted the Sheraton. A dinner engagement was arranged and a time set to meet.

Marc and Dacus polished off a sumptuous seafood meal in a private alcove, served by a waiter who only came when summoned by a buzzer. Furnished with brandy and cigars, they began a friendly verbal spar. "It was very considerate of you to fly Maybelle back from Georgetown," thanked Dacus, unaware of the go down between the two of them.

"I would've done it anyhow," Marc relented. "Fact is, I had in mind I'd like a visit with you. That show put on back in our bay could be seen by anyone present. To squelch any idle speculation, I put out a rumor that a rival gang trying to move on us had planned to blow up my ship. Instead, we mined their gunboat so it'd blow up when they pulled their cannon trigger."

"Neat and well executed," Dacus responded appreciatively.

"I put this propaganda out for my own protection as well as yours," confided Marc. "Matter of fact, now that we've gotten together, I have another subject to take up with you. Our business ventures have been fair, open, and aboveboard. In no way would I endeavor intruding into your affairs, first of all. My sole interest now is to afford you a means of reaching me, for whatever the reason, should it ever become necessary."

Dacus held up the palm of his right hand. "Come on, Marc. What's it all about? You know damn well it's easy, technologically, to locate me thru previous communications. I have a staunch responsibility to my people, just as you do."

Beset, Marc blurted, "Aw, Maybelle's turned me into a babbling high school idiot. I've lost my cool, and you've caught me in the act of resorting to terribly foolish tactics trying to keep the back door open to have contact with her. I can't think beyond she's turned me down, much less that she's not interested in having a lasting commitment with me. I've even accused her of turning me down because you're in love with her. She flatly denied it of course."

"She's right," Dacus confirmed, easing a finger across his moustache. "Our relationship is purely platonic. I won't disavow that I'm not enhanced in her company," Dacus quietly reflected. "She is a one-of-a-kind woman, possessing every kind of trait a man can lust for. The reality is, I'm just not in love with her."

To curtail the subject, he posed, "Marc, what say we get back to the case at hand? Oddly enough, you don't seem to understand there's potential danger in being associated with me. Your brothers sensed it tho! Perhaps fatuous passion involving Maybelle has obscured your vision. It's as if you've blocked eventualities since our first meeting." The irony had presented a recourse.

"Marc," he guided, "that initial scam brought in two hundred forty thousand, and you know the story of old man Lipscomb's attempted revenge. Currently, we've escaped retribution in our second one by well-covered tracks and leaving the country. That take secured just under thirty million. Most elaborate is the current working scam, and it's expected to net five hundred million. We've learned very recently that a covert armed task force lurks right along with it, which executes any infiltrating predators. You don't need the kind of trouble this one could provoke!"

Marc's eyes widened. Dacus's last two remarks had his full attention. "Half a billion!" he repeated. "I never heard of a scam worth that amount of money, unless politically originated. You can bet the powers protecting such an interest operate thru politics! Thanks, but no thanks. I might as well shelve what's brought me here, go back to the States, and get ready to meet a damned economic crash that's inevitable. I'm seriously considering putting most of my money in gold."

His remark galvanized Dacus. "No! Hell NO!" he reacted impulsively. "You can't! Not at least until after the gold market crashes, which it'll do."

"What are you up to, Dacus?" boxed Marc, sensing a misdirection.

Dacus punched the buzzer to buy a little time. The waiter arrived almost instantly. Dacus immediately deferred to Marc, who ordered a double scotch on the rocks. "Make it two," seconded Dacus, regaining composure to abate his outburst.

"You've heard me say that proceeds of present operations should produce a half billion. I'll agree with you that a worldwide depression potential does exist. To compensate for it, we intend placing our money in currencies issued by the seven leading world industrial nations. Use of gold as an international currency is passé, so follow me carefully. From 1952 to date, the price of day labor, thru inflation, has increased over ten times at a time when gold was already locked in at thirty-five dollars an ounce by the Bretton Woods Conference. Now, price of gold is around three hundred sixty, more than matching total inflation since '52. Even though gold was not freed to float with an international economy until the Nixon years, the current administration also touts it."

Intent on further masking the motive to Marc for his aggressive censuring of gold as an investment, Dacus did some touting of his own. "Insiders throughout the globe, you may be sure, will suck up wealth from the outsiders. The ensuing worldwide depression has to be controlled with absolute power, which necessitates destruction of freedom as known in our country," he predicted with woeful vengeance.

"I hate to even discuss it," Dacus confided, using the old bait-and switch tactic. "Especially, since it's a done, damnable deal. We in our Association are going to hang in there with the thieves. The insiders will see to it that these seven major currencies don't collapse. After all, money's only value is what people think it's worth. Gold's gonna crash, taking along the minor currencies. It'll rise again when the thieves buy it up cheap, consolidating more wealth within the few. Surely, you can relate to how this works, Marc. Neither you nor I have lived a life based on an honest day's pay for an honest day's work."

An uneasiness had begun to creep in on Marc. "Who and what the hell are you?" aloud he debated. "You've got more thought processes in your little fingernail than anyone else I am associated with or have ever dealt with in the past."

It rang a bell for Dacus to decide if the ploy was working that concealed their interest in gold. He measured his words, citing, "Historically, technology is ongoing whereby the obsolete lesser tech succumbs to advances of the higher. Venture capital seeks new horizons. A higher technology, that I have and control, became abandoned nearly a hundred years ago because it presented no apparent possibility for making money. Undoubtedly, as often happens, it was so far ahead of the times that the inventor died a pauper. I've reinstated and added a dimension to the old technology. Computer-driven, it can wrap space for designated areas into semispherical shells. What I haven't done is reveal it to the scientific community by applying for a patent."

Delving, Dacus exposed. "Wealth is the pure quality the lot of us search for. Power's not an itch of mine, or anyone else aboard I know about. There'll always be an adversary lurking, and what we've got is damn good protection. Only death or an unforeseeable mishap can prevent success. Don't forget, thieves orchestrate the world trade, and that we like being in the majority."

Marc's concentration disintegrated, spurred on by the nagging thought, *I know this is the last time I'll ever see you and I believe I know enough to keep you on my radar.* Forbearing the intrusion, he suggested, "Let's drop the subject and have a drink for the road."

Dacus agreed, putting the squeeze on Marc. "You and your brothers have quizzed me pretty good. Turnabout's fair play, they say. Tell me, are you to be the last of the Zallafino Dons? Neither brother seems capable of your succession. Nor, do you fit the popular concept of a godfather. Stance and dark, Sicilian looks pronounce you one until you speak. In that moment, Marc, you sound voluble and friendly, not taciturn."

"Touché," Marc saluted. "The 'shrinks' have a term for it, naming multiple personality disorder as the cause. Snap diagnosis! Who doesn't have a bunch of them that can't be applied to different occurrences and circumstances? I guess it becomes an abnormality when one can't muster the correct character to match a particular event. Evidently, personalities can take on a life of their own. I'd prefer to eliminate the term 'disorder' as describing one's exhibited identity, totally independent of an individual's control," he rationalized.

"Maybe I've outgrown the limited persona of a Don, or so it would seem to you. When time and tide demand, Dacus, I'm still competent to govern absolutely. As to who becomes the last 'Mohican', it's probably immaterial. I'm not at all sure our kind of organization can survive in 'the new world order' of boundary-busting international commerce." His lament showed.

Reaching the bottom of their glasses, and having exhausted all probing of each other, Marc rose. An essence of farewell descended over him. He grasped Dacus in a true Sicilian embrace, planting a kiss on either cheek before extending a cherished handshake. With one last look into each other's eyes, they parted without another word. Dacus was delivered to his ship. Marc was left to wrestle the unknown.

By seven, Jack waited expectantly for Dacus to show up at breakfast. Yesterday, he'd successfully completed researching all necessary facilities, with the possible exception of a suitable island for processing gold. When Dacus finally manifest himself, Jack had finished eating. "We need to have one of your so-called sessions, Dacus," Jack bestowed upon him.

"And it's got to be private," Dacus added. "Meet me in the wheelhouse in about fifteen minutes. No one'll be there to distract us since we're docked."

Jack beat Dacus to the pilothouse where he took the posture of intently staring out to sea. He began his briefing as Dacus entered. "I have mostly good news, but one thing frustrates me."

"Give me the good news first," Dacus quietly solicited, still slightly preoccupied.

Enthusiastic, Jack reported. "In a capsule, we're now established customers at the Carib London-Paris Bank, which gives us access to markets in both national capitals. The separation of banking stocks, bonds, commodities, and insurance markets in the States is about to end. It's never existed overseas, and we don't need it in our international banking."

"Do you mean to tell me it's possible to transact sale of gold in this same bank?" Dacus hesitated to ask, enthralled by the prospects.

"Not only that, friend," Jack professed, "but we can rent a ground floor vault. It'll be ten feet wide, eight feet long, and eight feet high, providing us a total of six hundred forty cubic feet for just a thousand a month. Payable on a monthly basis, of course!" Elation had preempted Jack's reserved stance, and he was in rare form.

Dacus's mind raced as he calculated space necessary to contain the total number of bars. Jumping up and all but hugging Jack, he spouted, "A half billion in gold occupies approximately eighty cubic feet. We could construct a six-sided table out of gold bars and still have room for chairs to pull up and hold a 'sit-down' poker game in that vault! Man, what a stroke of luck!"

Jack, no slouch at figures himself, assayed. "You're right. Eighty cubic feet is a cube measuring 4.31 feet to the side. If you're thinking of getting a smaller vault forget it, 'cause there's none available," he submitted, amused at Dacus's release.

"It hadn't entered my mind," Dacus shot back. "I just thought it'd be neat to be able to say that we'd once played two-bit poker on a table worth a half billion dollars. Now, before I unload my big surprise, tell me about the thing that's got you out of sorts."

"I don't claim to be a professional con man," Jack admitted, "but there's something amiss. I can't put my finger on it. It's wrong, and I sense it. Have an idea?"

Coming off his high, Dacus had to agree. "Something doesn't fit. Furthermore, you are wise to bring it to the table. The mere mention of something amiss puts me in tune with the cause. It's the same unbalanced sensation felt in the power company scam. The original plan was too drawn out, taking too long to complete, and open to a world of untold eventualities. Fortunately, time was shortened to a fraction of that in the initial plot. Risky business, but it worked!"

Dacus then outlined cause and effect for Jack. "Problem's the same, the scam is different! There are solutions, thankfully, on the front end here. The data I gave Tom and Vivian is flawed deliberately. I took the power off our electrical tail, except for twelve minutes out of each hour. When Tom and Viv analyzed weight of anodes after a day's run, declaring a ton of gold a week could be produced, my data projects five tons or more a week, as feasible. These figures have been verified on three different, daily excursions . . ."

Thoughtfully Dacus analyzed. "We're presented an opportunity," he assessed, "while encumbered by yet another headache. Instead of a year, the scam can be pulled off in a little over two months. The problem is one of time. Having boundless electricity to produce volumes of heat for processing deems it solvable. A ten week work schedule, start to finish, may tax the pants off all of us. Minor, though, compared to scoring a home run hit with bases loaded."

"That's it! It's the very thing that had me lassoed. By modifying the time element, the risk factor shrinks, givin the noose leave to slip off before it can hang ya," Jack abridged.

"Indeed. How we proceed shall be changed," rejoined Dacus, ready to explode. "While we're at it, Jack, I want all but a fraction of our accounts combined into the Carib bank."

Squaring two subjects, Jack reversed his tack. "I don't quite savvy this ankle bracelet. Daily, you've given me a printout map of my practical whereabouts over the past two sun-filled days. You got any, down-to-earth examples of what happens on a cloudy day?"

289

"Maybe," Dacus obliged. "A satellite contains an enormously powerful computer chip. In terms of its ability, it digests and processes vast amounts of data. Linkage between it and your bracelet is made possible through some of the equipment on board the ship that I paid five million for. Actually, the thing receives transmission of a signal, unrelated to light exposure, reporting the information back from space. In your instance, whereabouts are identified by coordinates on a large map. More precisely, detailed maps of increasingly smaller selected areas are honed in on a display for pinpointing a location within a square measuring twelve feet on each side."

Jack grunted, "I'll take your word on it. Proof of the puddin' is in the eatin', they say. Anyway, I'm a little long in the tooth to be concerned with mechanics of all this technology. Back to 'The Tale', Dacus, and any thoughts on where we go from here?" Jack regressed.

Assuring him of more involvement, Dacus prefaced, "My thinking, Jack, is that you'll become the focal person to spread inside word on antics of a wild bunch of rich 'oil money heirs' you're representing. Their reputation throughout Nassau is to perceive them as luxury-indulging, self-serving individuals with more wealth than sense, and absolutely no interests other than for living it up. While cruisin' about and acting out the role portrayed, the rest of us lend convincing credence to the most skeptical insider you've let in on the know."

Struck by sure questions expected to surface on Jack's connection to such clients, he cited explanations for consideration on answering them. "It occurs to me, Jack, that you'll be 'hit on' for a little 'how, why, when' rebuttal. My idea is to respond you're not exactly sure how and when they latched onto you as a financial adviser, but the ride hasn't been half bad for an old retiree. Referencing a few of them you'd known subsequent to Tulsa banking days is verifiable and suggests prime criterions why inclusion of the others. To redirect the inquiring, mention perks awarded as often exceeding your fee and hint at the 'goings-on' in their extravaganza bashes. Expanding on these subjects invites embezzlement tendencies and not research exploitations . . ."

Musing at responsibilities piled upon him, Jack subjected, "I'm going into Carib Bank this morning and move a sizeable amount of my money into its tender care. Three-quarter mil gets me a luncheon engagement with bigwigs of the bank, where I can start 'The Tale'. Any more green might raise their eyebrows to speculate why I was working. It's also the perfect time to inquire of an island for lease that can accommodate the idiosyncrasies of my clients."

CHAPTER 29

Except for a muffled thud of diesel engines, the catamaran glided silently on top of calm waters, separating hundreds of tiny islands and numbers of larger ones. Dacus was at the helm following instructions of a Carib Bank's employee while Barnett stood before a slanted drawing board, charting their course toward a particular island. At Jack's invitation, Tom, Vivian, Maybelle, Ed, and Theo were aboard, commissioned to join the voyage.

An hour and a half into the trip, a lush tropical island paradise rose on the horizon. A bone white, three story hotel summoned, nestled amidst tall elderly palms and a lawn sadly in need of care. Not a living soul appeared as the catamaran entered a huge deepwater harbor.

Tying off at the dock and power cut, Jack undertook to point out, "Before us are physical properties for ground-based headquarters. It's oblong, right at three miles in length to one and a half wide and encompasses three thousand acres, more or less. Along the backbone, there's a sizable lake whose bottom and shores of basalt have prevented water seepage for hundreds and possibly thousands of years. Its only loss comes either from evaporation or by overflow. Engineers in construction of the lake erected a concrete dam with a floodgate installed at the lowest point to give absolute control over water volume." The view superseded his remarks briefly.

"All facilities are workable, I'm told," he related. "The state of extended neglect is obvious. Investors promoted luxury of hotel life, the attractions of sunny days, mirrored seas, and sparkling white beaches, with a championship golf course, and spectacular sideshows of nature in action, hoping to assure an abundance of customers. Developers though, made a fundamentally poor misjudgment of nature . . . The island's a natural breeding and spawning ground for sea turtles."

A 'So what, Jack', interest stirred as he continued. "Suffice to say, word of mouth killed this venture. Homework had failed to be done on how invasive turtles can be. These creatures from the deep disrupt shallow sea edges, foraging for food, dig up beaches to lay and cover eggs, plus deposit tons of defecation in the sand. After an annual pilgrimage, up to four months of approaching and receding tides are required to restore beaches and borderline areas."

Engrossed in his role, Jack elaborated, "Through the course of my conversation with several natives, I've learned that the turtle migration ended around three months ago. Where this area still bears their effect, in another few weeks, and given the tropical rains, these beaches are destined to become pristine again, very shortly. That is, as acting trustee in a bankruptcy court for the property, they'd have us to believe for the sake of a signed lease. However, in consideration of a proposed lease, the bank has been admirable in dealings thus far. They have offered a minimum three-month lease for fifteen thousand and included an unlimited option for ensuing months at five thousand each. A perk they've extended is name of a local company in Nassau, who, for around twenty-five hundred, contracts in a service of cleaning rooms, washing linens, and grooming hotel grounds. Ten to one, the golf course could be renovated by inducement of a healthy tip . . . Then, again, who'd have time or want to use it?"

A cursory investigation of the resort and landscape by the group confirmed to Jack it was, indeed, a bargain quote. Exploring the interior of the hotel, dust flew anywhere a chair or couch was touched. Taking into account the number of rooms, the time and effort to reclaim it, the cost to refurbish seemed exceptionally low. Ed mentioned cause could be that subsidized upgrading of the premises may have been authorized by court order. If that were the case, bankers were holding true to form and would be dampening lucrativeness of the deal, at their expense!

Leaving shore, a fleeting observation of surrounding waters disclosed no close island neighbors. Once back in Nassau, Ed accompanied Jack to Carib Bank, negotiating the lease. It was to become effective with the signing date at Ed's insistence, plus have a written guarantee of all terms, conditions, and an adequate freshwater supply. He wrote a separate check to the company designated to perform services, hoping to squelch a kickback deal to the trustee.

The next five days were obliterated for the entire gang. Dacus called for an extended cruise, allowing four hours to restock supplies and prepare for departure. As soon as the ship left dock, he summoned everyone to the lounge, except Barnett.

Their customary interaction at being assembled ceased when Dacus formally opened the meeting. "Members of the Association, you possess the vested fiduciary interest in the whole of working affairs. The rest of you have strong viable interests through a sizeable authorized cut of the proceeds upon completion of our activities. What I've got to say embodies those interests, you as an individual, and time. It is precisely the purpose for each of you being here to grasp for yourself where I'm coming from. I don't want, and you don't need, to expend energies on hacking secondhand floaters!" he impressed.

"Recent events have changed prospects and set new timing precedents regarding this last scam. The turning point came when I shucked concerns the electrical tail might not be adequate to physically drag a ton of weight. While Tom and Vivian have been assaying gold collected, based on what they thought was a day's run, I'd been cautiously cutting current on the tail down to a fraction of minutes out of every hour. Their figures had satisfied a ton of gold could be harvested in a week. It couldn't rule out being in a rare, rich pocket in the sea, or the potential of increased collection on constantly acquiring mass attaching to the anodes. Repeated runs have since convinced me that gold particles are fairly abundant and evenly distributed in these waters." Vivian's not so subtle nudge and reactive glances at Tom didn't go unnoticed during his brief.

Choosing to ignore their interplay, Dacus formalized. "Later in the day, our first order of business is to determine capacity and durability of the electrical tail. Three or four, one-hour outings can spell out a multitude on where we stand in switching into high gear. If the gold holds up to be harvested, as I fully expect it to, and there is a dedicated effort by all, this operation can be wrapped up in a little more than ten weeks. To clue you in, success of the venture hinges entirely upon the time element to quickly produce, settle up, and vanish. It can only be done by a shoulder to shoulder work and no-play ethic. In fact, looking for your asses may be diversion of the day once we start. Jack, I'm with you on remarks about the golf course!"

The ending jest fell short. Dead silence was amplified and reverberated. Rebounding, and as usual, Harry threw his two cents worth in, coming up out of his chair, singing, "Grab your hat and get your coat. We'll be rich as . . . Rockefeller."

Sarcastically, Theo cut him off, "It's not a hundred percent done deal, Harry. A castaway donkey could kick a hole in the ship and sink it, or a Henny Penny disaster could occur."

The 'voice on opinion' dam broken, every Associational member began talking. Tom commandingly expressed doubts. In concise terms, he agitated, "I don't see how in hell fifty tons of gold can be processed in two and a half months, regardless of whether or not it can be harvested. We don't have anywhere near enough ovens to melt that much gold, much less twelve minutes worth. What'd you expect us to use for molds? Yours and everyone else's tennis shoes? I can't fathom, for the life of me, where you think you're coming from, Dacus. What I do know is this ship's fixed up pretty nice to haul the stuff in compared to our primitive setup."

Dacus didn't know whether to laugh, scorn, or assail Tom's inexplicable outcry. Prepared to combat his pessimism, Dacus altered course, slightly to 'one up him' in a way that retained focus of the others. "Tom, where were you down in Louisiana when the crunch was on to buy up every conceivable item that would be needed for you and Vivian to process gold? I hope you're not still spending time to haggle, 'cause time's running out for that. If you don't have something, we'll use the con's middle name, Improvise, and get it on!"

Shunning Tom for the moment, Dacus gestured to obtain the others' attention. "Your expertise is needed to help improvise a makeshift unit that'll handle melting down gold, quickest way possible, and poured into some type mold."

"For starters," Harry kindled, "what's wrong with the galley in the big hotel that you and the guys talked about leasing? Aren't the plans to stockpile the harvest there?"

Art's safecracking instincts whetted. "Did anyone check the cabinets? Surely, they're loaded with fine heavy-gauge steel utensils to put on stove top burners. You might even find a dishpan or two that'll fit in ovens."

Pissed with Tom's flack, Vivian hung her shingle out. "I tried to tell him we were retired from jewelry designing and that there was nothing to melting the stuff down. Our problem would come from size and weight of the pot used, tipping them to make a pour . . . And yes, I told you so!" she needled him. "We needed to buy those molds when we had the chance, Tom, and this 'go down' wouldn't be happening."

Julie bent over Sam's chair to put a bug in his ear. He passed it on. "How about using the small Grand Bahama outfit which carves objects in basalt to make us some molds?"

"That does it, Sam," Dacus approved. "Forfeiting laces to keep frayed tennis shoes isn't a bad swap. Neither is the intuitive input you've all contributed. We can turn the burners off on this one, except for means to guarantee purity of the product."

Sheepishly, Tom cooled the matter. "You don't have to sweat finding a spectrographic instrument, Dacus. It's the one item Ed insisted I purchase to have on board the ship. The wooden box is in Vivian and my quarters."

Ratifying, Dacus optioned, "I'd like to see extra support lines installed thru the electric tail before test runs begin. As late in the day as it's gotten, we'll try for three of the four runs to resolve doubts, even if it throws us after dark. Dinner, Rabbit," he singled out, while passing notice on to the others, "will be on hold until these exercises are over."

A tropical moon of near-daylight intensity had each one taking his or her turn staring wide eyed at emerging lumps of collected gold on the tail as it was reeled in on the ship's fantail. A random weighing of sixty lumps assured a 95 percent confidence level that indeed a ton of gold was on deck. Heightening amazement, Dacus causally dropped its value at ten and a half million.

By eleven o'clock, everyone headed for the lounge except Dacus, who relieved Barnett at the wheel, warning, "Don't be surprised or alarmed when you go to the bar and hear our mission can be completed in around ten or eleven weeks. Your contract's for eighteen months. It will be honored as such, whether your services are needed or not."

Inevitably, it got a little drunk out before the night was over in that particular spot of the Caribbean. In fact, the love wheel was cancelled because no one was in any condition or of a mood to indulge. Only Rabbit and Lulu held to their routine and retired early. Dacus dropped anchor at 1:00 a.m. and set a wind-breaking shell. Wearily, as much from mental fatigue, he sought the quiet only his quarters could provide.

Hung over and agitated, Tom and Vivian were the only ones present when he appeared for breakfast. He joined them, savoring a cup of coffee. Tom griped, "I don't know if it's crossed your mind, but I cannot pour molten gold on board the ship, especially in a choppy sea. At best, there'll be a certain amount of sway and pitching."

"That makes sense," Dacus humored. "We might come up with decks paved in gold. Talk about a sensation! But nah, Tom, it'll be done on solid turf. Our ship'll stand off in deep water if necessary, and the catamaran can taxi whatever's coming ashore to the dock. Short runs shouldn't affect power to heat your pots. Incidentally, I'd like to get far enough ahead on a supply of one-ounce anodes so we can 'blow and go' in harvesting."

Tom grumbled, "My boy, you got too much piss and vinegar for me to keep up. Viv and I are highly honored to be included, but I'm damn near too old to cut the mustard as it is." To take the edge off his sourness, he bantered, "Now lickin' the jar's another matter!"

Vivian intervened, "Tom, you're bein' rueful . . . Ease off. Apply the strategy of that old bull in competition with young ones chasing a heifer. That dude didn't get flustered with the odds. He stood back and waited for them to exhaust themselves before he walked down and laid it on her." Patting him, she purred, "Old honey pot, all you hafta do is think of all the enjoyment you're gonna have in about three months. It's attitude adjustment time."

"A good synopsis for all of us," Dacus assessed. "We can't afford to get bogged down on negatives. There'll be a labor force to help the two of you process the gold, even if now and then it puts the hurt on the ship's crew manning our electrical tail. One way or another, pots are going to bubble with success," he promised while pouring a cup of coffee to take topside.

A leisurely start up the steps turned to instantly bring alerted at seeing the peculiar looking sky. Current weather reports were far from reassuring. A backup tape of weather conditions since wee hours tracked a growing storm coming in on easterly winds that put it in line for the Bahamas. Deciding to make a run for the Berry Islands's lee side, Dacus had anchors hauled in while he cranked the diesel engines. Simultaneously, he dissolved the wind-breaking shell, cut in electric propellers, and headed due west.

Minus a wind shell, diesel props slowly maxed and soon achieved a speed of sixty knots. He observed, even though circular wind velocity was estimated at hurricane force of a hundred twenty-five miles per hour, lateral progress of the storm system was only moving from east to west by about fifty miles per hour. A gain of twenty miles an hour on the storm existed, as long as it didn't increase in intensity. That'd give them about an hour to tie off on a protected side of an island, put up a shielding shell, and divert the storm far enough out at sea to avoid problems.

Luck favored Dacus's reckonings. Minutes after dropping anchor, securing the ship off a most northern island, and setting a windproof shell, the hurricane hit twenty-five miles out. Once again, a storm had ricocheted off their shell's curved surface, sending it spiraling out to sea at a forty-five degree angle. The repeated curious phenomena, exactly twenty-eight days after an extravaganza of comments regarding another weather system, revived media speculation.

The inexplicable event defied scientific explanation yet had to be uniquely significant. The right wing tried linking the approaching millennium to Armageddon's final battle between good and evil. It succeeded in casting a pall over the sunny now stormy Caribbean, unaware these were but the first few sprinkles of a coming deluge.

In disregard of the ensuing media hype, Dacus and company eased out of the cay and away from their lee position in the Berrys, sailing steadily to

Grand Bahamas. On shore, a rush order was placed for size and number of basalt containers. Their downtime waiting took care of picking up essentials and incidentals, further cultivating the seed of filthy rich planters.

The Nassau service hired to renew conditions of the hotel and grounds had come and gone. Docking in tranquil waters of the deepwater port, the bunch debarked onto a whiter beach and was greeted by a freshly manicured lawn with activated fountains spurting. Flinging open massive doors to the hotel presented a polished elegance restored and their voiced appreciation. After scrutinizing the thirty rooms, the gang knitted to discuss the layout. In accord, their decision ruled out using the third floor, set resident rooms on the second, and reserved the lower level for basics and whims. Not one to quibble, Rabbit let it slide that he'd decided on a pad near the kitchen.

Sam, Theo, Art, Harry, and Dacus lugged equipment off the ship to the hotel's maintenance unit. The others began carting up and unpacking personal belongings, giving the guys time to rig reliable electrical power into the lines for personal needs and, ultimately, the task ahead. An air of confidence intensified. Everything seemed on track and life, for the moment, a bed of thornless roses. Utilities were on demand at the flip of a switch. Rabbit and Lulu performed their magic to serve up chilled appetizers and heated hors d'oeuvres to go with fare from the bar. For maybe the first time, even Harry appeared appeased with the circumstances and events. A solidarity reigned, and it would be sorely needed at a later date, if sustained . . .

Divided into two work squads during the next seven days, they settled into assumed routines. Tom and Vivian's group concentrated efforts on reducing two tons of gold from trial runs into one-ounce gold ingots for use as anodes. Ed's involvement ended with him manipulating the tonnage up a gradual slope from the water's edge to processing fixtures. Incited, he confronted Dacus after a five day run of harvesting, urging the purchase of a reconditioned Duck.

"Why, of all things, do you need an all-terrain vehicle on this small island? Particularly, why an amphibious vessel?" questioned Dacus, caught off guard.

"You forget that I'm an Arkansawyer," snapped Ed. "Hot Springs entrepreneurs put Ducks into use right after World War II. It's an established business, picking up tourists downtown daily and hauling them to Lake Hamilton on featured boat rides. Hot Springs doesn't have a franchise on Ducks! I saw a restored one advertised in Nassau for sixty thousand. It'd save on labor, getting gold from the ship up to Tom. More importantly, it'd also expand rumors of toys purchased for pleasure by the wealthy's eccentric behavior."

Dacus, exultant over picking up five tons of gold in as many days, obligingly consented, "Buy it! Cost is not an enemy with some fifty million in gold on board the ship, as we speak!"

Word swiftly paraded account of their new worth. No one felt ecstatic or stultified by the news . . . Rather, the more thoughts of it that invaded, the more unsettling it became. It became pronounced enough that comparisons of feelings surfaced. Harry buttonholed Ed to join an ongoing discourse in the lounge. "We need some answers, Ed. Instead of getting a high off of all this loot at our fingertips, it's causin' us strange mind miseries. You got any bright ideas on what we're experiencing, or any fast fixes to cool it?"

All eyes issued search warrants to Ed for the inquiry. "What we have here is not fatal," Ed judged, "but trauma imposed due to natural causes." His desire to divest intensity of their anxieties in order to connect worked. He set them up as jurors and vamped a case based on the whiff of information Harry had disclosed.

Resorting to mimicry of an expert witness, Ed was direct. "My uneducated opinion is that an abstruse matter has attached itself, and the problem may lie in how to come together with the reality of it. The fastest acting remedy would be to get the problem identified by name. Try calling it success, PGER, better known as the 'pot of gold at the end of the rainbow', a grand slam, or whatever, so long as it touches the root cause, literally . . ."

Short of outright suggesting it, he honed in on fact commentary. "The adage, 'some people cannot stand to have success' is a foregone conclusion. I sincerely hope there's not a soul among us suffering from such a recessive gene. Presently, I have no evidence to suspect it's remotely the case here. More than likely, the fear factor associated with waking up from a scary dream is as lethal a charge to levy as can be conceived."

In closing, Ed shed pretense of being a lawyer. "Sometimes it takes a 'ridiculous' to break a train of thought in getting a point across. By that, I mean your strange feelings are nothing more than one of disbelief. The 'seeing is believing' syndrome can be tough to cope with, and I should know! I went into temporary shock over the same thing. The difference is I've recovered, thinking time's wasting. I've gotta make plans on which country best suits my fancy to live in . . ."

"Well said, Dr. Bemis," Dacus applauded, catching the tail end of his dissertation. "In case it hadn't registered before, good people," he inspired, "may I remind you again we have won this one. A little over two months assures pursuit of your wildest passion on demand . . . Life on the Riviera, conquering the Alps, big game safaris, chasing rainbows, or whatever rings your bell!"

From his perch on a stool at the end of the bar, Jack Rainwater, unusually quiet, observed emotional aspects on display. An uneasiness crept in, suspecting a weak link in the tie that bound the group. He pushed it aside, telling himself the time was right to set in motion another matter.

Maybelle, obviously perplexed, sidled up before he could make a move. Compromised, Jack asked her to hold up a second while the bunch was receptive to hearing from him. Slipping off the barstool, he delineated, "Folks, there'll be no question about being able to sell the gold. The only problem anticipated is selling without 'jiggling' the market. For that, I've conceived a skilled sales pitch to fit the shrunken time frame we need. It's calculated to deceive and disguise true intentions." Perceptive of Harry's nature, he stipulated, "That's presently all I care to disclose."

Satiated from highs and lows of the past hour, the group retired to drinks, soft music, and putting their own spin on things. Maybelle confided her wavering to Jack of not being sure she wanted the affair to end, and small talk among the others escalated. It was a classic setting and time for the inevitable to happen.

Maybelle watched with passive interest as some gravitated into couples to discuss desires, their future, commenting on the what if's, and voicing few concerns. No forming bonds were obvious, but it was apparent everyone was listening closely to an opposite sex member. *Another damned reality check I can do without!* she swore to herself. *Lift the ban on festive pairing, kid. The universal questions, 'what are you like in bed?', 'what did I gather from the experience?', and 'how does it compare with what I want?' have been answered.* She made a mental note. *It's a shame there won't be a way to send donations in memory of this beloved Association and its Associates upon their passing . . .*

CHAPTER 30

Sunday morning found Dacus and Sloan Barnett on board the ship, readying for an evening departure. Their primary agenda was to have the crew in place to begin gold harvest the next morning. Focus of the run entailed trying for a maximum hoist in the shortest time possible. It set precedent on preparedness and required all kinks be worked out to the degree that little thought dawdled on the night before. Dacus had come away more satisfied with the group's attitude and conscious only of Maybelle being unusually distracted. He certainly had not attached any unusual significance to interaction between the gals and guys.

On the other hand, Sloan had sensed changes among the sexes but nothing to lose sleep over. He still interpreted it as foreplay, having been in the dark on Maybelle's rules governing her girls, and promptly dismissed it as such. For all he knew or cared, the girls were along for the ride with an eye out to hook a potential multimillionaire sugar daddy. It stood to reason a lowly pilot, expecting a hundred eighty-thousand draw, would be left out of the loop. No big deal. Their kind hooked at a hundred or two per trick, without the upkeep most anywhere he'd been.

Midmorning Ed showed up. He was on a crusade to bring the amphibious Duck in from Nassau and hit on Dacus to let Sloan pilot him over in the catamaran. They bargained. Ed abetted its expediency. A one-time shot from the ship to the melting pot, even for the first load in, rendered its value. Dacus expressed doubts. His load doubled without Sloan, and there was one less to get eight thousand ingots on board by dark. He relented, thus giving Ed the go ahead.

By afternoon, telltale clouds heightened Dacus's uncertainty on leaving dock at sundown. Threatening weather, verified in periodic bulletins on the ship's radio, steadily increased. He switched to government channels on the illicit system, where a new federal mandate required more detailed data be released. The gathering weather system, while not yet organized, was pinpointed on satellite at essentially seven hundred miles east, southeast from site of their current position.

It was being described as the mother of all storms. Ed and Barnett's departure vetoed using a protective shell over the island. Confronted by an ethical dilemma concerning mankind, Dacus projected a circle of six hundred miles radius around the ship's center point. The span he calculated would include islands of the Caribbean, plus Puerto Rico, and large portions of the southeastern United States. Satisfied he could fend off the storm without disrupting ships or aircraft, he set the immense soft shell, and eliminated any risky hardness.

Three hours in, and radio waves pulsating warnings, all flights were cancelled. Based on the announcement, he made a snap decision to reinforce the shell with strength to deflect physical objects, but not radio transmissions. Given time to contemplate what he'd done, second thoughts cropped up that there could be consequences from creating this largest shell ever . . .

Under the shell's massive security blanket, Caribbean islanders fared without damaging effects from the storm. The two excursionists, out to buy a Duck, made good time on their return trip. Barnett anchored the catamaran and climbed on board the Duck. With Ed as its first captain, the two rolled up to the hotel and to a welcoming entourage. "Land ho!" shouted Theo. "You're back in time to help cart those ingots to the ship," he indicated by pointing. "For a ride on your buggy, Ed, we'll even help you unload 'em."

Emotions somewhat quieted and formalities of an evening meal met, Dacus returned to the ship, unable to dismiss apprehensions. He dissolved the local shell after the storm abated to check back through numbers in the computer for specs on massiveness of the big one. Puzzled to learn its apex extended only one hundred fifty miles high, while the diameter of the shell had adhered to twelve hundred miles, he strolled out on the ship's bow to meditate. Determining there were no figures to predict such an oddity, the flatness of the shell must have been due to gravity. *Interestingly strange,* Dacus decided. *All the computations I know anything about involve two masses and the acceleration between them . . .*

Usurping morning tranquility, all hell broke loose across radio channels. Overnight, the largest storm of the season had disappeared! Rhetoric summarized comparison of fairly recent severe storms, which had bounced around at sea like giant billiard balls, to an enormously violent atmospheric disturbance over the past twelve hours that was predicted to wreak widespread havoc. How had it mysteriously evaporated became crunch question for speculation. Retained experts chattered on and on without having a clue. Their interest procreated, it aroused the gang to consult their own specialist.

Dacus, still a bit testy over his actions, spoofed reports slightly. "Yesterday afternoon, a healthy storm system developed. We had Ed and Sloan out of pocket in choppy seas and a lot to be done in the dry that a small protective shell wouldn't manage. I took it upon myself to alleviate the situation by setting a whopping six-hundred mile radius shell. And yes, according to my specs, it produced an unpredictable phenomenon, which had not been expected. The potential existed, I suppose, and it may have resulted in the mania you're picking up on . . ."

"Ante up, Dacus. There's more to this than you're telling us," Theo challenged. "Give us the straight of it and spare the technical stuff!"

Short with an answer, they'd have to make do with a theory, he concluded. "I'd suspected the storm to hit and bounce off the shell, as in previous encounters. Obviously, it didn't, and I later discovered probable cause. The apex in this sized shell only reached upward to one hundred fifty miles, producing a gentle slope up and over for the storm to follow. Between sixteen and fifty miles up, with no air to provide an interplay, the storm apparently spun itself off into oblivion by its own centrifugal force . . ."

Down playing the event as incidental, Dacus sought resource. "Regarding the subject, I'm not interested in releasing my take on a supposition to fame seeking paparazzi or media hounds. I am in favor of getting the lead out and putting an end to the procrastination, so the harvest and processing of gold can proceed. Let's see how much can be added by the weekend to the on hand supply projected for fashioning forty thousand more ingots by then."

Away for the next couple of weeks, Jack Rainwater stayed involved. Headquartered at the Sheraton, he lunched and hobnobbed with bankers, spreading the Tale about a wild bunch of spenders and gamblers he represented. During the same time, he was making numerous phone calls to the States, lining out purchase of the most updated science to verify the spectrum of tons and tons of gold. A singular specialty item ordered by Dacus, had to be requisitioned in the meantime. Details finalized, Jack flew to New Orleans, procuring a local interstate shipment of materials he'd ordered. Air transportation of the cargo to the Bahamas arranged, he played for two days and nights on Bourbon Street and climbed aboard his flight, satiated and pooped.

Landing in Nassau's international airport, Jack contacted the island by cell then taxied to the Sheraton to await transportation over. Ed, Tom, and Vivian arrived at dockside in the Duck a couple of hours later. Tom and Vivian were euphoric at the sophisticated spectrographic equipment, which made Tom's purchase look like a toy. "We're really moving on," Vivian crowed as Tom examined the contents of each package. Tired, Ed did a little pushing, shoving, and silent cussing, trying to move them off dead center, to load up and go. Maneuvering the Duck, he decided, was as good as a roll in the hay compared to their obstinacy.

Jack, tho pleasant enough, seemed guarded biding time 'til the ship came in. It heaved into port alongside the island dock just before dark thirty. The weary crew began to straggle up to the hotel for showers, food, and drink. After everyone had drifted into the bar, he engaged Dacus, bearing an extra cigar and brandy. "Where do we stand?" he asked.

Motioning out to the covered porch and leading the way, Dacus revealed, "It's no secret among us that there's a hundred fifty million worth of gold stashed aboard ship. Why I haven't stockpiled it up here is probably from being overscrupulous, but I can't be in two places at once. Lay it up to my gut feelings for using the ship in all aspects of the operation, except the melting down process. She's plenty capable of handling the fifty tons we're after, and I'm not the least concerned if weight displacement makes her ride a few inches lower in the water. She's mobile, and we'd play hell towing an island to gain security until the stuff's marketed!"

Jack, assured Dacus had finished his update, began unreeling a strategy for the marketing phase. "I've got a few intestinal thoughts of my own to take up with you, and I won't be making any bones about importance of concealing the glitter of gold, as you did. I don't have to tell you either, built-in, fail-safe stratagems are essential for second nature in response to doing business. You just gave me an example, not an excuse for actions taken." Dacus signified agreement.

"The futures market, I'm thinking, Dacus, might be the way to go in making the transfer of gold to money," Jack disclosed. "We'd play that sucker, based on what we'll call value of thirty-five tons of gold, knowing it should amount to more than three hundred fifty million at today's price." This strategy option brought Dacus to the edge of his seat. Jack however, was not about to be interrupted until he'd explained his offerings.

"Keep in mind, friend, the futures market involves the buying of contracts to sell for a tagged amount. Integral to that is after a contract's bought, and should a price hike occur, the seller's on line to make up the difference. Neither you nor I foresee this to be a problem. What is relevant in our case will be the dollar volume of purchased contracts being contemplated. It's destined to send up red flags to someone in the know. Instinctively, a professional is going to interpret it as an attempt to stampede the market, causing it to fall. A panic reaction does two things. It will raise prices, forcing us into answering margin calls, and makes the market extremely nervous." With a finger, he indicated there was one more point to make.

"In less than six weeks, projections are you'll have enough tonnage of processed gold to begin playing it in the futures market. That, Dacus," Jack advised, "is the time when the climate's perfect to buy up contracts on short-term paper. The contracts need to be for the same amount as current value of gold, and it puts one in the catbird seat to cover margin calls by selling some of the gold held at a higher daily price. The market could weaken, or 'have a stroke', at the sight of actual gold for sale. Be mindful of the fact that you are holding purchased contracts and they are the key."

Jack's concept was sound. Dacus thrived on complexity and appreciated its portrayal in others. "Maybelle sure had you pegged right, Jack," he complimented. "You have contributed far more than you'll be paid. That's troubling to me, and it's become a real concern of mine for you to be in the line of fire if it brings termites swarming out of the woodwork. I may want to rethink the 'banker protection program' from security in the ship's hold, if there's any gold left to sell, to outfitting Sam in a tailored suit over double-shouldered gun holsters to be your bodyguard."

"Let's meet that problem when it becomes a problem," Jack drawled. "Nothing's wrong with your fox hole idea, except you left the *y* off fox and failed to insert lady's after it!"

Dacus and fraternity heaved ho while Tom and cohorts melted and poured. Jack's mind wouldn't be stilled. There were trifling matters lying just on the edge that bothered. He looked for an outlet by walking around and exchanging stories with the guys and took sport in suggestive flirtation tactics of the ladies. Not until his path crossed Art's did a lever trip to pinpoint the mental hold he'd had since outlining a marketing strategy to Dacus. On impulse, Jack canvassed, "Art, I'm told you're an expert in cracking safes, and I'm confronted with a need to get educated . . . Reckon you could help me out?"

"Sure. It'll hafta' wait though, until we quit work. I'll meet you in the bar, if that's okay," the man of few words relinquished.

Jack clued Art in on their lease of the vault at the bank and his interest in its susceptibility. Art consented he'd check it out, and Jack made plans to go over the next day. Art left in worker's blue duds, wearing a cap printed with Ace Lock & Safe Co. and carrying his tool case. It was quite a contrast to Jack's suited finery.

At the bank, Jack was greeted from every cubbyhole, guiding Art through the lobby to depository vaults. At ease in his element, Art spun a few dials, listening to the tumblers. He sat back on his heels to rise from a crouched position, quelling one concern. "You've got as crack proof a safe here as there is made . . ." It set Jack back on his ear when Art asked, "Do you have any idea who else has the combination?"

"Hell no! I hadn't given it a thought, much less asked the question," Jack reacted, irate with himself for such crass ignorance.

"Well," Art deduced, "someone's give you the combination which says to me someone in the bank has it too . . . Don't know's I'd wanna put much of value in here, 'specially any thing ya wanted kept secret." He diddled with his tools, before putting it to Jack. "What say we open this doll up and change the combination?"

"Have at it!" Jack spat out, too flabbergasted to think.

The backplate quickly removed, and in examining the mechanism, Art totally blew his character, expressing exuberance, short of shouting. "The majority of safes you mess with are only complex enough to give seven hundred and twenty combinations . . . This'uns got two extra options and no less than forty thousand, three hundred and twenty possibilities. I can't believe it!"

Regaining his wits, Jack rebounded. "I can believe it if you do! You amaze me with your ability, and your insight is solid," he bragged, favoring him with his first question. "How did you pick up on options and possibilities built into a safe's combination?"

"Simple, I guess you'd say. My handle on it came through a perfunctory understanding of the mathematical law of permutations." Art dismissed it as nothing and picked up his tools.

They relaxed for the ride back on the catamaran, with Jack highly influenced by Art's aptitude to deliver on things that were plaguing him. "If you didn't have the combination to that particular safe, Art, would there be any way to break into it?" he wondered aloud.

"Yeah! Blow it, and the bank up," Art obliged and for a second time expounded. "You couldn't torch it today. You gotta get in and out in a hurry if you plan to crack a safe. Alloys developed in the space program they use today are too tough to cut through."

"I owe you, Art . . . You've just about cracked a nut I've been trying to get the kernel out of for days. There's a tiny piece of shell left," Jack explained.

"I need your 'take' on whether or not you'd be willing to put your cut of the gold bars in that safe."

"It depends on the turn key," Art rectified. "Put my gold in there and nobody knows what it is going in, then I got pretty good odds nobody'd think it worth jil flirtin'."

Jack Rainwater didn't proceed from a half-breed Indian boy in Oklahoma with limited education to respected president of a renowned bank in Tulsa, by being slow witted or dumb. All he had to overcome was ignorance, and he met it by self-education. His mind had never let him rest. Back on the island and true to form, the matter of discreetly moving tons of gold into the bank's safe had him on another bizarre conquest.

He checked in at the Sheraton again. Daily, he shopped Nassau trying to find some type of self-propelled, wagon-like vehicular contraption small enough that a person could appear to be pulling it. Exhausted from looking, Jack drew up a diagram, went to a machine shop, and ordered the cart fabricated. It had to be restructured a few times until closely matching his mental image. On the Duck's routine run, he hauled it to the island and waited for Dacus's return.

A productive week's run under their belts, the crew and Dacus came ashore in good humor. During the intermixing, sharing, and catching up, Jack took part. Later, motioning to be followed, he brought Dacus up to date. "While I'm at it, I might as well tell you we changed the combination on the bank's walk-in safe."

"Art didn't have anything to do with it by chance?" Dacus intervened. "The 'we' was a dead giveaway, and that's part of his bag. Along with being a helluva confidence man, he's a master at cracking combinations to open safes."

"I'll attest to his skill any day," Jack praised. "He's fixed it so the only way into the safe now is to know his combination or bring the building down. Finessing tonnage being hauled into the bank and avoiding attention as to what it is was his brainchild. I've been busy this past week trying to design a disguise and had a beginning model made, which I brought over. You'll see it's a takeoff on those totes on wheels used in airports. You know, and I know that one man can't budge, let alone pull five tons of anything on such small wheels. The end solution has to be something that is covertly self-propelled and appears effortless to maneuver."

Dacus grunted, looking at the model. The dim vision of a con within a con began to materialize. "Yes!" he finally reacted. "Don't sweat it, Jack, I'll take it from here. At sea it'll be easier for me to modify and come with the needed end results. You shop the canvas wrap to complete the look, and next week we'll give it a trial run."

"Whatever you say," nodded Jack, elevated by recognition it had merit.

"Unless you've got a hot date lined up," Dacus proposed, "let's put your 'play pretty' on the Duck and take it out to the ship, where there's privacy. Our Tale is taking on an interesting new twist. You and Art have substantiated one or more key persons are likely to be on the take."

The model stowed, Dacus and Jack ambled toward the lounge, where cool comfort under a fan could be had. Dacus, anxious to pick up on where they'd left off the week before, bridged, "You've been damned adept at how important it is to apply measures that cover the bases, and it was sweeping ingenious of you to suggest we deal in the futures market. At some point, you used weight of thirty-five tons in the discussion to compare value in dollars. I'm coming around to think it's more realistic than the fifty tons I'd set. A lot hinges on pulling this one off in the time allotted. It shouldn't have to allow for stress-driven mistakes that the stretch to glean fifty tons could incite. Particularly, when there won't be a team of shadowy assassins breathing down our neck initially. It changes the perspective to focusing on our mark! Scratch a six sided gold poker table and we'll shoot for seven loads to get the thirty five tons deposited in the vault." Primed, Dacus unfolded more expected byplays.

"As it stands, the bank will be operating between us and the gold market. Instinctively, the con in me manifests itself. They, or it, should be tagged as our mark. I've tabled a foregone conclusion that within this large a financial web, there's a kingpin and possibly an accomplice or two on the take. It behooves us to gain identity of the culprits early on by observing reactions. Mentioning gold in conjunction with futures is a sure bet to finger a mark. Dropping a few hints your outlandish clients think they've commandeered a gold find, Jack, puts the wheels in motion and ups a mark's telltale suspicions to check out the claim's validity. With access to the safe's combination, it'll be a natural to venture a peek inside after our very first trip to the vault. Human nature doesn't mask being one-upped well, and to come up short on a try at the combination should do it. They are at bay to broach such an incriminating subject to anyone. Speculation becomes their only recourse and it's strong . . . Gold and vaulted secrets!"

"No problem there," Jack lauded. "Planned curiosity is virtually ready-made and can be vigorous enough to tap a gas gusher. It'll start with the safe's combination they can't open and dare not question why. Once or twice weekly, some Joe pulls a plaid covered tote across the lobby to vault number

105, spins dials, and disappears inside for an hour. The blasted cart's too easily maneuvered and too small for much weight . . . Or is it? Gold of any volume gets bumped as too heavy to pissant in on the rig. What's being concealed becomes suspect . . . Bags of currency? A Styrofoam block with a few gold nuggets stuffed inside? Or, even less—a bluff, maybe?"

"You capsuled that well, Jack! Nothing like covering the bases, eh? By the time we're ready to buy futures contracts to sell the gold in a few weeks, they'll have convinced themselves it's a setup. Without access to the vault, all they've got to go on is your casual remark referencing gold and outlandish clients. It seems logical then for them to append gold as the commodity and us as buying up cheap gold for a profit to cover the contracts in a plot to drive the market down." Dacus rubbed hands together with the prospects . . .

"What I'm after is the bottom line in clarifying the bank's position for being the mark. Correct me if you have a different take on it being the bank who'll be tempted to pluck our feathers by booking the contracts when we purchase futures. Wouldn't they be the ones who'd fake a run-up in price to skin us out of the margin money we've already put up, from second guessing there won't be enough actual gold to fill the contract? Does it not stand to reason that the swindlers would time a run-up to coincide with maturity of our futures contract? Considering this as a likely script and if you are in accord, Jack, my opinion is to counter by selling gold on the spot market to pay up and have the bank's ass in a sling the next day."

"The questions you've brought up aren't worthy of the breath it'd take to answer them," Jack preferenced. "Banking rules of those in the States don't apply down here. It's open hunting for predators to bag game anytime. I don't have to remind you it took plotting and props to get Maybelle out of that Georgetown bank with her roll of cash. Neither can we forget the bird on a windowsill at another bank that made a setup in a matter of minutes to rip Maybelle off of Marc's indebted money. To expect anything less from ethics of Carib Bank officials, Dacus, would be authorized robbery."

"If there's a secret to the perfect con, it has to lie in the ability to cover all possibilities. It'd be deserving of your attention, Jack, to come up with the government agency who audits banking activities in the area. Get a feel for how they dress and operate. Do they adhere to business suits or prefer regimented uniforms? Who's in authority, and how much clout do they wield? What's the dominant accent of inspectors and any slang terms they apply? I'm of an opinion it might not be a bad idea to have a battery of our own auditors on standby. Having auditors' intimidating presence on the mob's agent, who was dealing from under the table at a Mississippi casino, certainly paid off."

"A word of advice, Dacus," Jack extended. "Two factions exist to be dealt with through the Carib Bank. In its capacity as agent for the world gold market, I'd consider the conjecture to scam as likely to be moot. On the flip side of that, officials in the bank's routine operations would be the individuals suspected to screw someone around. If it comes down as an independent bank scheme, their game will be trying not to pay off on the same day of transaction. You can't afford a twenty-four wait, Dacus, and I can imagine how an impromptu visit by auditors would rattle cages in the accounting department . . . They'd want to avoid a controversy!"

"Before we put this one to bed, Jack, come by my office," Dacus persuaded. Inside, a computer was up and running with nearly a ream of paper stacked beside it. "Ever since we left the States, I've religiously collected daily data from DTN, specifically concerning the gold market. It's programed to spit a printout of activities on days the market is open. Why don't you scan the current as it comes in? It'll give us a chance to compare notes?"

Ferrying Jack back to the island, Dacus discussed the see and be seen tactic be increased to supplement complexity where the clients were concerned in Nassau. He prevailed on Jack, with little effort, to do lunch with Maybelle and one of the girls during the week and to squire them by an elite fashion shop for some binge buying.

Unable to settle in for the night, Dacus revisited every detail the two had outlined and underscored. *Why,* he asked himself, *didn't I mention to Jack the Percival family's attempt to corner the silver market? It's a benchmark case for instant recall on someone suspected of trying to shill the market. Our 'mark' is going to pick up on every seed we've planted. Their reaction is going to be, "I knew it," "They're bluffing," and "This is some kind of scam waiting to be capitalized on." Hopefully, whoever it is will be so intent on a rip-off that they overlook a mathematical obvious. The amount involved, roughly 175 percent of the weekly restricted international gold production, can't be handled like cashing in a healthy bank certificate of deposit. Consequences of nixing stability of the world gold market has a long-time history of being deadly, but that would be their misfortune, not ours!*

CHAPTER 31

Englishman, Henry Aston and Frenchman, Norbert des Lauriers are the closest of friends, having met several years back as co-officers of Carib London-Paris Bank. Young married, their families interacted, partying together and children rotating daily between neighboring homes. Bonds for an alliance forged early on from these and mutual dilemmas.

Being individually multilingual, it had fallen their lot to be assigned to the Nassau Carib branch. Over time and in spite of loyal friendship, both longed to return to their native country from the relatively small island, where chances for advancement had become stuck in time. It urged on the need to explore each other's propensity to profit from certain salacious opportunities for feathering a nest egg, by whatever means, retire, and find solace in the motherland.

A union of minds solidified, and as vice presidents in the bank, they prowled throughout every banking day, looking for that promising break. Having taken Jack Rainwater to lunch a few times, an interest began flowering in the man's friends. High-rolling gamblers and money to burn struck a nerve. The reality that it had taken a wad to restore the island to a first class facility, prepaid extended rent on a huge vault, and profiling an eight-digit cash-deposited balance registered as potentially the break they needed.

Henry ran a confidential check on Jack's resume. It came in revealing Mr. Rainwater was everything he appeared to be. As a highly regarded and successful ex-bank owner from Tulsa, his reputation, Bert and Henry determined, lent credence attractive to the wealthy clients he called friends and associates. "If they're as loaded as things suggest, what's to keep one of our gambling entities from offering them a high-stakes game where the winner takes all? Our cut to arrange the introduction on something this big affords reason to expect a passport ticket home," Bert allotted.

"I won't call you a stool pigeon, Bert, if you don't call me a dupe," Henry chided, quite encouraged at prospects of his proposal.

Considerable progress had been made by the bankers toward aligning the gamblers when Sam and Rabbit showed up at the bank with their first wagonload of gold. Sam backed a fancy low-slung, dual wheeled, superduty truck, flush with curbing at the bank's service entry. He lowered a counterweight from beneath onto to the pavement before stepping from its extended cab. Rabbit pulled light fold-out screens stacked on the backseat and struggled into the bank with an armload. Sam swung the custom-hinged tailgate to the side, eased the load to the sidewalk, and followed, appearing to effortlessly pull the self-propelled cart. Mesmerized, Bert and Henry never batted an eyelash taking in the whole scenario.

Giving ample time for the pair to secure the safe and leave the bank, Bert and Henry quelled any personal interest in the goings-on, by waiting to confer. "What do you suppose went into our number 105 vault for safekeeping under guise of all that fanfare?" Henry couldn't resist the downplay to get his cohort's immediate reaction.

"I got the notion it was made up with more bulk than weight for what it's worth! Quelque chose, but we'll know as soon as the bank closes," Bert declassified.

Banking hours over, they lagged behind until everyone left the building. Anticipating discovery of what had been cloaked in secrecy, the two hurried to the bank's lower level. Fifteen minutes led to frustration and flat out certainty the combination had purposely been changed. "Something tells me our playboys aren't quite so innocent," Bert grimaced. "Our old banker friend may not know what he's up against either! For me, the gambling bit becomes questionable. I can't believe we'd be the duped decoys for these misfits! What do you make of it, Henry?"

"You know and I know, Bert, we cannot afford to make any mistakes," Henry digested for both of them. "I agree, there are too many outsiders involved to press for a rigged game of chance. We may need to come at this from a different angle, playing it close to the belt. Let's wait for a show of hands before we get too far out on a limb."

"Suits me fine," Bert relegated, influenced by a growing distrust of events.

A week and a half later, Sam and Rabbit hauled a seventh load of gold to the safe. The time had arrived to purchase futures. Awaiting Friday, Ed and Jack sauntered into the bank, engaged a clerk, and stated their interests. Assuming a routine transaction, the clerk turned gray upon hearing they wanted 10,206 contracts in gold sales of one hundred troy ounce lots, at the day's market price. He pressed a button for management, assuring Ed and Jack assistance would be with them shortly. Answering the distress call were Vice Presidents Henry Aston and Bert des Lauriers, whom Jack had met previously. He greeted them smoothly in a genteel manner.

It was all they could do to keep their composure when apprised of the sales' amount. For appearance, Henry ran calculations on it and then Bert. The figures tallied to the dollar for an overwhelming $367,416,000 in guaranteed future sales two weeks and three days hence. Politely astute, they commissioned the clerk to fill in 10,206 contracts at $1,300 each and advised Jack and Ed the total for same would be $13,267,800. Without blinking an eye, Ed drew a check for payment in full from their account in Carib Bank, where $18,500,000 had been deposited. He scribbled in the number of contracts on the check and on the stub.

Exchanging niceties while the clerk finished, Bert offered the bank's security services, tempting, "We'll be happy to put your contracts in a lockbox for safekeeping."

"Thanks," Ed declined. "They'll be quite secure where we put them."

Alone in their office, Henry and Bert could hardly contain themselves. "Viva la bagatelle! This is it!" exulted Bert. "N'importe, they've finally shown their hand. I never dreamed they'd be so naive and stupidly cocksure. We've watched every trip to that vault, and there's no way they could've hauled in enough gold to cover that many contracts. Seven trips on that two-bit cart won't cut it! Who do they think they are fooling?"

"Nah," Henry synchronized. "The thirteen and a quarter million is ours. Shunting these contracts aside from the market for the next two and a half weeks will be easily enough done. There's nothing to keep us from faking a rise in price and demand a margin call before the maturity date. Everything ceases to move when they fail to have the product on a forced call. Think you can design a fake margin call, Bert, that will virtually clean out the other four million left in their current money market account?"

"Henry," Bert accused, "you're losing your British polish by associating with damned Americans. You are even beginning to sound very much like them. Here, stick copies of the contracts in a lockbox and get our hats. The rest of today, we toast our good fortune."

While the pair celebrated daily, the gang consolidated its plans. Under Jack's tutelage, Theo, Tom, and Harry rehearsed roles and duties, mimicking auditors. One thing kept troubling Tom. He knew that if a demand for purity assay of gold were made, he couldn't counter without causing a delay. That potential glitch could not be addressed until Dacus sailed in over the weekend. Reluctantly, he put his mental disturbance on hold.

Distance narrowed between ship and the dock, and a zealous bunch congregated at the shore. As it tied off, they rushed aboard to relate Jack and Ed's entire episode at the bank. Amid the talking, a beatific smile spread across Dacus's face. The gang caught it and quieted. Looking back out at sea, Dacus reflected, "We've come all the way and are possibly five days short of reaching the fifty-ton goal. I am not returning for more! You've put the 'coup de grace' on this one!" Cheering excitement drowned out Dacus. He took a Roman's approach and joined them.

When the stimulus subsided, Dacus pulled Tom and Vivian aside. "Tom, before you hit on me again, I have the answer to your expressed concerns." He pulled out the item he'd ordered through Jack and handed it to him.

"A balance scale?" Tom questioned, puzzled. "How's it supposed to speed things up, much less satisfy a demand of purity?"

"Ah, come on, Tom. Get your head out of the poke. How do you think purity of gold got established in the last century's California gold rush? Electricity hadn't been harnessed then as a useful tool for mankind. Analysis by a spectrograph instrument wasn't available, yet you know the gold rush was a roaring success." Dacus had his attention and made the most of it.

"The scale succeeded because of the peculiarity in weight of gold. Gold's purity can only be adulterated by addition of another metal, and you are quite familiar with what they are and their associated weights. Gold cast in a bar at precisely forty-four avoirdupois pounds is standard measure and identifiable by weight alone for its purity. The scale you hold in your hand is American made, certified accurate under rules promulgated by laws of Congress and will thwart controversy. Our whole thirty-five tons can be quickly certified in thirty-five separate increments."

"Hold it, hold it, hold it!" pressed, Tom erupted. "Where do you plan to hide out a crane contraption in that bank, Dacus, that's big enough to pick up one ton of our gold to weigh? I'm sure as hell in the dark on how you expect me to use this small a scale to weigh that much poundage!"

"Your gotcha, Tom." Dacus laughed. Less intent, he more or less relieved Tom of having to take an active role in certifying accuracy of the gold's purity. "This bit of someone being in a position to steal from either us or the bank becomes more of a likely factor. Ed and Jack's short brief a while ago, recounting buying up futures contracts, left a lot unsaid. Gold traffic within the market is generally confined to small lots of it, retrieved from sunken treasures off pirate ships. Banking officials are experts and are notoriously nosy at getting someone to disclose even their dirty underwear. So, get this, Tom. Preposterous, and as unheard of as it was, two guys walked into the bank and on the spot requisitioned futures contracts for thirty-five tons of gold without the first question asked. That's some kind of 'gotcha' in itself! We'll be prepared, but I'll be surprised if one bar of gold gets weighed under these circumstances."

Tom reined in the high horse he was on to corral thoughts. "Let this dust settle, Dacus. I wanna see the whites of your eyes when you try tellin' me this is no-man's land where cutthroat bankers can skin us out of our gold and money. What the hell kinda scam they got goin'?"

"Conditions down here in this tax haven for western hemisphere entrepreneurs, Tom, are little different from what went down in our own Oklahoma territory. Right now, we're not a hundred percent sure of the 'mark' but certain enough that a game plan to counter is in the mill. You are aware contracts to sell have been secured. If it goes as I predict, a fake run will be presented to us that price of gold has gone up. Such a move is destined to take the balance in our account to square with the margin call. A pure con in anyone's book, except . . . The exception will be having proof to the contrary that no price hike occurred. It'll be ours via Delta Transmission Network. Day after tomorrow, Monday's results of gold market trading, both in spot and futures, will be downloaded in print off the Web. Make no mistake about it, that single piece of paper is as lethal as it gets to squash a coup!"

The weekend, and well into the following week, a push was on to load refined gold and get equipment stored aboard the ship. Dacus manned the task, doing with help from Sam, Art, and Ed. Tom, Theo, and Harry had to groom themselves in tropical-weight suits and complete courses to graduate from Professor Rainwater's investment academy as certified auditors.

On Friday, Jack called on Carib Bank. He was promptly informed the price of gold had risen, necessitating a margin call for his clients the next banking day, which would be Monday. Wearing his best poker face, Jack thanked Mr. Aston and later left for the island in high spirits.

"I've scooped 'the mark'," reported Jack. "According to DTN, price of gold is steady. Our greedy bastards issued a margin call of $4.60 per ounce, coming to within $37,500 of cleaning out your bank account. The only reason they couldn't get it all is because gold prices move in ten-cent increments. It fingers those two vice presidents in the bank as having stolen from both the gold market and the bank and making their move to steal some more from us. Incidentally, Maybelle must be in Georgetown early Monday to receive a bank transfer from Carib Bank."

As bank doors were opened on Monday morning, three auditors strolled in, led by a short, round older man wearing a hearing aid. He had probing brown eyes peering over pince-nez glasses perched on the arch of his curved nose. There was no question as to who was in charge. Certain books and records were requested delivered to a conference room in the bank. News of the auditors circulated quickly. Henry and Bert put in an appearance, pledging cooperation. They were met with cold indifference and retired to their office.

Picking up on a signal in his hearing aid, Tom hurriedly left his coauditors for Henry and Bert's office. He huffed in, minutes prior to Ed and Jack's arrival, demanding to see all of the bank's capital accounts. Henry scurried to assemble them. Accompanied by Jack, Ed stormed into the office, confronting Bert. "What's the meaning calling for margin when DTN reports the market is unchanged since purchase of those contracts?"

Bert blanched, stammering, "T-t-t-here must be a mistake!"

Ed sat both hands on the desk and in Bert' face asked, "Whose mistake? Last Friday, when your buddy here visited, didn't you tell him the market was up, and it'd be necessary to settle a margin call today? I guess you'd have me to believe he lied to us and is in here now, trying to cover his ass." Slapping contracts on the desk, Ed issued a warrant. "These are the paid-in-full contracts! Where'd you put your copies?"

Walking in, Henry heard Ed's last question as Tom interrupted him, "Sir, are those futures contracts? Let me see them, please." Portraying the experienced, Tom scanned the pages then ordered, "One of you get me the bank's copies."

Sensing the squeeze, Henry tried to misdirect by implication. "The bank wouldn't have copies of forged contracts."

Rainwater came up out of the seat he had taken, seething with indignation. "You can't get by with claiming those contracts are phonies! Where's the clerk who filled them in? I'm an eye witness to the transaction! I watched this man write you a check for the unheard-of amount of better than thirteen million to have the privilege of gambling on futures. I'm the one who advised using this bank to clients where gold trafficking interests were favored. You're not about to taint my reputation with such unprincipled accusations! Where's your CEO?"

Trembling, Bert managed, "Henry, we've got a problem." Searching, he pleaded to the auditor, "How can we begin to undo this?" Still defiant, and eyes blazing, Henry stood at Bert's side, lending deteriorating support.

Staring them down, Tom chastised, "You got greedy on this one, boys, and didn't take time to read the tea leaves. Neither of you seem aware your bank will cease to exist ninety days from now due to the enormity of your gamble. So I tell you what." He reversed his mood to one of compassion, bargaining, "These innocent people won't be hurt if contracts are honored today, and my official business did not entail uncovering the likes of this to be reported on!"

Relieved no immediate inquiry was on docket but aghast at prospects of the bank's closing at their instance, the two asked, "Why?"

Speaking with authority, Tom improvised. "It's the Euro dollar and an error of the British in refusing to join its currency when it first came into existence." Waylaid by Ed's rehearsed question, Tom failed to get said that it was his opinion.

"What makes you think Carib Bank will have to close its doors?" Ed implored, implying they had every intention of keeping the account open.

"Financial institutions, such as Carib and others, have operated through a comparison of British pounds and French francs in their relationships with U.S. dollars." Tom glared. "You do realize, don't you, that all currencies can be expressed in relation to the U.S. dollar? Simply put, it's a matter of limited time before the franc vanishes and is replaced by the Euro dollar. Obstinately, Britain prefers to remain aloof with the pound. It'll thrust associated banks into a period of instability, and buy-or-sell situations become inevitable. Risk to assets is that they can be swallowed up by one or the other side or by outside investors." Tom had masterfully composed, devising on spur of the moment when needed.

Adhering to the rehearsed script, he placated, "Purpose of the audit in progress is for governmental study relevant to what's being discussed. A bank's current balance sheet of assets and liabilities is based to construct analysis of existing strengths and weaknesses and easily can determine a bank's solvency. I may get a reprimand for not reporting the kind of discrepancy found today, but I'm of a mind to lift a rug and sweep it under and not have to deal with it. If I'm willing to take some heat, and all else is in order, are you fellows ready to complete this transaction?"

Addled by shock, Bert and Henry nodded agreement. Tom confronted Ed, "Do you have gold to back up these contracts, or were you in here on a devious attempt to stampede the market?"

"Sir, we have the gold in one of this bank's vaults. And no, to your second question. We had no intentions of market tampering when . . ."

"It is a bloody bluff!" Henry charged belligerently, cutting Ed short.

"Okay, boys, let's finish the sequence of events before we get ahead of ourselves," Tom cautioned. "Assuming gold is present, the bank's the buyer on the spot market for these contracts, the money's direct-deposited into the gentleman's account, contracts are invalidated and destroyed, completes the transaction . . . Correct?" Tom sent a heedful glance to each. "You, sir," he told Ed, "are to withdraw cash in the amount of profit this transaction would have given you and hand it to these two idiots. I want the affair finalized by three o'clock."

Ed tried to negotiate. "It seems unfair that I get no return on the thirteen million put up with this kind of deal and these guys get reimbursed for trying to scalp me!"

"I can tell you're a novice," Tom interceded. "I've made it possible for you to recoup your investment and these two 'no-brainers' to resign and retire outside these islands. My concern is for this bank and a paramilitary organization subsidized by many governments with vested interests in gold sales. I'm not up to date enough to know whether this much gold could cause repercussions but smart enough not to try discounting it or the consequences." Tom left unsaid to register with the two vice presidents that there were assassins who policed the gold market and who used terroristic methods to quell its crashing.

Resigned, Ed committed, peevishly, "Okay, mister. It's your tea party."

Taking offense, Tom put it to Ed. "You got anything other than your word on how much gold there actually is in that vault?"

Ed managed a tight smile. "Well, when slapped with a margin call that didn't tally with today's quote, and suspicious of a stall, yes, I came prepared. In the vehicle outside is a certified scale from the States, which accurately weighs up to a ton. You don't have to take my word. Count the bars, multiplied by weight of each, gives undisputed verification!"

Composure lost, Bert reached for rationale. "It's not physically possible to weigh that much gold by three o'clock," he lamely cited.

Tom agreed and consigned it shouldn't be necessary to weigh the entire lot. Picking up a calculator, he punched in numbers to confirm his decision, relating, "You say the bars are of a standardized weight and you know total numbers. In such cases, a 95 percent confidence level by random sample of weight on sixty bars is acceptable math for a certainty. The curve goes fairly flat when the number is doubled and would not be worth the effort. In consideration of these facts, what are we waiting on? Complete the bank transfer on this piece of business and resolve any need for me to file theft charges in banking activities . . ."

At two thirty in the afternoon, Maybelle was notified in Georgetown that three hundred eighty million, four hundred sixteen thousand dollars had been transferred to an account identified with her PIN. She promptly transferred equal amounts into three other Georgetown banks. Before leaving the bank, using Jack Rainwater's PIN, she made sure that three-quarters of a million had been entered to his balance.

Wrapping down a delicate business day, Jack and his client, Ed, left the bank sometime before the fallacious auditors, Tom, Harry, and Theo, clocked out at four. Bert and Henry shunned being drawn into discussions by other bank employees on their bout with auditors. They occupied themselves in frenzied moves from the vault, carrying briefcases to their office, as if to finish a complicated transaction by quitting time. It threw them a little late in leaving, assuring the new safe combination worked, and in retrieving briefcases and shopping bags stuffed with the cash gratis. Caught in rush hour traffic and consequential reflections, Henry reasoned, "Bert, maybe that gold should be sold methodically. We cannot be guilty of starting a panic in the market by large sell-offs. Do you think we could persuade the auditors into our way of thinking tomorrow?"

"It's wa-wa-worth the try," Bert stammered, absorbed more in freezer space at home to hide his cash than a debriefing of the day's occurrences.

Alarm oozed in on Bert and Henry the closer ten o'clock came the next morning, and no auditors had shown. Henry picked up the phone and called the government controller's office, hesitantly inquiring if auditors scheduled for today had been changed for a return visit to Carib London-Paris Bank. Emphatically, the clerk dispatched. "Sir, all auditors had previous engagements on Monday, and none are shown booked for today at that bank." Henry dropped the receiver and made a mad dash toward the men's room. Bert reflexed to hang the phone up and hurried into the toilet. Henry, bent over with a hand on the towel rack, was retching his guts out.

Drained, Henry washed up and motioned Bert back to the office. He took a half-pint out of a desk drawer, gulped about half of it, and passed the remainder to Bert. Bert declined, and Henry unloaded. "You'll need it when you hear what I got hit with over the phone," he told Bert.

"There weren't any auditors at Carib Bank yesterday, and none are expected here today. The bank's in arrears by thirteen million dollars, a vault full of gold that dares not be sold, and we're in one helluva compromised position. One thing's for certain . . . We're victims of some very slick confidence players, as I think about it, and few, if any, viable options to operate with."

"What about this paramilitary group those so-called auditors spoke of? Do you think we need to put substance in what they said?" Bert opted to evaluate, his stuttering blocked by the insinuated crises predicted.

"I've never heard one story on an extreme group of their kind since I've been down here. True, there have been a few unsolved notorious murders reported in the newspapers, but nothing ever suggested mob involvement by the press. Under the circumstances, I'd have to consider the source and promptly discount it as more con. Our best option," Henry forecast, "stands to dump the gold, get things squared at this bank, and bow out with the money while we can."

Pacing, Bert allowed, "I have an idea those high rollers shipped out yesterday. Let's charter a plane and fly over the turtle island. It'll help to know how fast we must move."

The pilot brought the plane in high over the island. Unable to locate the moored ship with the naked eye, they buzzed the hotel. Nothing stirred. The place had obviously been vacated with unused rented time left on the books.

Frantically, the two foreigners dumped gold on the spot market, under Carib Bank's agency contract. The market immediately went into a power dive. From London and Paris, to all major cities, angry messages and questions jammed bank fax machines. Phone lines were red hot, and Websites were clogged with incoming e-mails.

On board ship, the DTN reported gold had been dumped and the market was in free fall. The ten tons of gold stored in the ship's hull was worth a great deal less than when they left. Dacus decided to keep the market news to himself. The gang, already in a state of nervous disarray over the sudden departure, didn't need any further distractions. They muttered to themselves. "What're we running from?" surfaced to question when told the Florida Straits would be skirted en route to a rendezvous off Cozumel. It hadn't helped, to learn Maybelle couldn't complete Georgetown banking affairs in time to make their departure schedule and would have to meet them later.

Two days after the market crashed, the badly mutilated bodies of Henry Aston and Norbert des Lauriers were reportedly found on an isolated beach by Nassau patrol. Descriptions at the scene left little to doubt. The tormentors had what they had come after, in detail, and would waste no time in organizing a hunt for wealthy oil heirs on a luxury cruiser.

CHAPTER 32

News of two banking associates' murder and torture deeply affected Dacus. Instinctively, he knew their ship would be spotted through technology available to assassin agents from a governmental cabal. He felt Maybelle would be safest in Cozumel, yet the obvious could not be ignored. Retaliation efforts of the worst kind, no doubt, were imminent.

Weighing every conceivable possibility, he decided their best advantage lay in forcing the enemy to come to them. Proceeding slowly thru Florida Straits into the Gulf of Mexico, a soft shell, set at five miles radius around the ship, gave shelter from the unexpected. Certainty rising, Dacus began monitoring all channels accessible on the illicit transmitting equipment.

On day two, about four hours after dawn, he logged on to a transmission. Interplay between a pleasure craft, gunship, and reconnaissance plane came in explicitly clear. Tracking a satellite report on three contiguous sectors of the Gulf, coordinates were being passed to the survey plane on a purported ship's position. The epitome was to fly in close and verify the mark's registration number with those on file in Nassau. If it was a 'match', the pilot was to go into a holding pattern and wait for counterparts.

Dacus summoned Ed, Jack, and Rabbit to the wheelhouse for a briefing. "Repercussions from our business dealings with Carib Bank, predictably, have fallen to the akin of an aroused eight armed cuttlefish. The gold cartel's octopus tentacles have already reached out and extracted a description of who and where we are from the now-deceased, bank VPs."

Jack's vim snapped. "When did this happen?"

Dacus equalled the energy. "It doesn't matter, Jack. The SOBs ignored every piece of advice given, swamped the market, and inflicted the assassins worst wrath. That fallout apparently is upon us. Shortly, I suspect we will be under attack from it!"

Urgency mounting, Dacus indicated Rabbit would be closest to hear an update. "If you have occasion to check in on audio being taped in the office, key codes to listen for are scout, hash, and decoy. Currently, it's been disclosed that a plane, referred to as, scout, is flying in to ID our ship's registration number. Two sea vessels, a gunship coded, hash, and the other, a pleasure craft tagged, decoy, are en route to make the first contact on a mission destined to destroy us. Our only recourse boils down to one of kill or be killed."

"Where's the difference now, Dacus, from all the times you related you couldn't deliberately kill?" Ed posed, perplexed at the gravity of the situation.

"Considerable, friend!" Annoyed with the timing of his trivial question, he cut Ed off. "I had a choice when Lipscomb invaded the mountain for revenge with his mob. Except for Rabbit here, you and the rest of our bunch were evacuated to secured ground . . . I can't submarine you and our crew to safety nor can I hide you out on open seas with assassins breathing down our neck. The term used to defend the helpless, whether innocent or not so, is admirable I believe. Besides, this encounter will amount to self-defense," Dacus scoffed.

"I brought you guys up here to help organize a counterattack, not find myself before a firing squad of questions. The ship's being hunted with maybe an hour's lead time. It's readily apparent the subjects expect to find it at sea, not hidden out in some dock, which is the best of alternatives for us." Wearing a headset with one earpiece, Dacus suddenly bolted for the office . . .

Picking up on beginning banter between the plane and the two ships, Dacus made certain their system was recording and increased volume. Exact location and a fair description of their vessel were detailed. Disclosure followed that primary thrust would be to target, capture, and restrain everyone left alive on board. How various methods of interrogation were to be exercised became flagrant. The diabolical plan basically evolved use of obliterative torture on the men to occlude interference for perverted raping of females. Nauseous, spastic giggling began interlacing, heightened by lurid expectations. Dacus killed the sound and squeezed past Sloan, Jack, and Ed for the topside. His avenging rage had to be floodgated.

Volatile rebuke shrouded Dacus's departure. Barnett seized the opportunity to confide a lingering impression. Rabbit eased in to catch his story. "Guys, you might not have seen it yet, but our man, Dacus, has a very dark, violent side to him. Unrestrained, he's capable of going beyond physical conceptions to do damage. It was the think process he had during an episode in Louisiana backcountry that has stuck with me the most. Outnumbered by some big bruisers, I saw him take on redneck punks who'd tried to pick a fight so they could get off their jollies. I don't mind telling you, I was lookin' for the door, when Dacus didn't back down, and plain stupefied at watching him wipe out the whole bar of 'em. Teeth were flyin', bones crackin', and blood spurtin', all by usin' his bare hands. He was on the verge of being out of control and stopped short of a killer punch once! Driving him away, a sort of reaction tremor set in. Take my word, it took a while for him to get a handle on himself period." The incident met with interest to his listeners.

Sloan whipped around to the pilothouse. Rabbit turned the sound up slightly to be alerted on any updates coming in, and Jack eyed Ed. Obliging, Ed aired his opinions. "For some reason, Sloan's recount didn't spike my curiosity, Jack. Could be it's been my forgone conclusion that Dacus is a powder keg. It hasn't affected the utter trust I've had in him toward doing the right thing in all the years I've known him, though. I also got the idea Sloan personally likes and has complete confidence in Dacus. You know, Jack?—What would get my interest is hearing the other side of that story, and the part Sloan might have instigated . . ."

Dacus had to first accommodate barbarism intended on his people. To hear the cruelty described by supposed humans for those in his immediate charge came as a blast on his composure. Once digested and stowed, he pooled mental resources to find satisfaction. No sooner had he stepped inside the cabin than Jack set upon him. "Clue Ed and me in on our roles, effective now. I'm aged, but we're both choice prime meat for these vultures circling out there. Our bit at the bank stands to get us singled out for special treatment."

"It won't happen, Jack! You're the one who forearmed us with knowledge that a shadow army existed. Right now, hindsight is our heavy grievance. We shirked the duty of planning an early retirement for those two VPs. They deserved better than what was dealt. A small isolated island miles apart from others would have given them plenty of leisure to use accounting skills counting their money."

Clasping Ed and Jack by the shoulder, Dacus assigned, "You'll draw the duty to inform everyone below of what's happening. Use your own judgment on how to handle things from what came across the wire to strategy you've heard that is to be employed. Our technology stands us in good stead to counter the last hurdle it'll take to come away clean with the three hundred eighty million . . . Providing we can execute this one to prevent a single message of distress from being transmitted by our misanthropic attackers. The coalition forces won't nor would they waste much time trying to pick up on a cold trail if it appears a sunken blowout occurred at sea. Also, caution no one's to be visible from inside a porthole, and absolutely not one foot is to be put topside! Rabbit, you're in to man the computer, Sloan's in as pilot, and I'll be master of ceremonies." Dacus wished them good luck and turned his attention to finalizing microstratagems.

Roughly an hour later, the recon plane appeared on the horizon, aimed at making a midhigh pass over the ship. Signaling Rabbit as the pilot banked a turn to come back at deck level, Dacus ordered a hard, two-mile radius shell set. Only two words, 'identity confirmed' were broadcast by the pilot before crashing twelve seconds later . . .

Viewing from a distance, Dacus, Rabbit, and Sloan watched the barely visible wreckage sink below wave actions. At such a low altitude, with no chance for bailing out, a human could not survive an impact at six hundred miles per hour. Activating the ship's intercom, Dacus announced, "One down and two to go. Plane and pilot changed course and are in route to the bottom of the gulf as I speak."

Dacus directed Rabbit to soften the two-mile shell and prepare to welcome in two ships. Passing diapers to Rabbit and Sloan, the three dropped their pants and suited up for combat, anticipating possible use of the ultrasound machine. He parlayed, "Everyone below deck is shielded, as you will be, when these plugs go in your ears."

Rabbit flinched resentfully. "Why must we go back to using this damn gimmick?" In the dark on the matter, Sloan gave Rabbit, then Dacus, a strained look.

"They intend to flaunt the pleasure craft as decoy to get in close and use radio coordinates with the gunboat for it to make the hit," Dacus outlined. "The last thing we want is for this decoy to send out a Mayday. Belly cramps and spontaneous erupting shits can squelch any thoughts of reaching for a panic button until it's too late."

In that moment, the pleasure craft crested the horizon, traveling at a relatively high rate of speed and approaching them at a right angle. Cutting speed, it made a sweeping ninety degree turn and heaved to the portside of their larger vessel. Matching speed, it cruised along parallel. Dacus alerted Rabbit, "I'm going topside . . . Back me up."

Dacus stepped on deck with a remote palmed. A huge fat man wearing a captain's hat jovially hailed, "Are you the captain of this fine luxury ship?"

"Yes. I'm owner and captain of her," Dacus confirmed.

"Well, I say, old chap," the red faced captain bellowed, "would you happen to have a bit of Grey Poupon on board?"

"Sorry, sir," Dacus responded with a forced grin. "For a discriminating taste treat, could I interest you in some chitlins?"

The fat man's smile faded into a sneer. Sunlight reflected off metal of a rifle barrel from within his cabin. Gesturing a salute, Dacus aimed the remote and activated ultrasound waves. He felt its familiar effects despite the earplugs, but neither the gunslinger nor his captain seemed acutely affected. Unable to react, Dacus saw the rifleman draw a bead on him and fire. The bullet entered the fat captain's shoulder, rendering his left arm useless. He pulled his pistol to take out Dacus. The rifleman's face exploded . . . "Doing your thing again, eh?" Dacus dropped as Rabbit came on deck. "Where's your automatic?" he asked.

"Didn't need it," Rabbit drawled. "Seein' things goin' on you wasn't, I got a little worried and used your trick with a small shell. From the way it looks, 't weren't a bad idea neither."

"Yeah right, and I owe you," Dacus thanked. "Let's get a quick playback on final moments recorded between the two vessels to see where we stand." The last words, "element of surprise is gone, blow 'em out of the water, and sink the ship", were stark. Adjusting to meet the criterion, Dacus ordered Rabbit to harden the five-mile shell to immediately block electronic activity to the outside. Still scanning, he heard the gunship's delayed response follow. "Ten-four. Hang on 'til we get there, fellows."

"Standby!" Dacus commissioned Rabbit and Sloan, having been told all he needed to know. "Rabbit, dissolve the shell around the fat bastard's boat, and Sloan," he shouted, "give us a hard left rudder when Rabbit signals you." As the ship swung around, he conveyed full power ahead with an extended forearm. Distancing their ship a quarter mile from the spoil craft, Dacus directed a clear, hard shell of five hundred feet from the ship's center be set and relaxed momentarily as soon as Rabbit notified compliance.

"This one's in the bag, friends, waitin' for the finale," Dacus adduced. "Both vessels are now contained in an area outside our hard shell and inside one of five miles radius, without contact through the walls. The renegade captain's hit to the shoulder must have been low enough to penetrate a heart valve since he's had nothing more to say. No response from him will bring the gunboat in at maximum throttle, and we'll use a squeeze play on it by shrinking the outer shell. When it's within distance, the simplest thing is to trap the two vessels in a narrowed, circular slot around our shell until they break apart and sink. It'd sure be nice if we had their call code to report mission completed. Speculation would be delayed a good while, that is, until someone woke up to ask why no one was being heard from."

Sloan was incredulous. "Do you mean these shells can crush steel ships?"

"The forces of nature are far more powerful than any man made structure," Dacus delineated. "An awesome part of the fabric of this solar system has been tapped, and I can assure you nothing is capable of standing up to it."

Interrupting, Rabbit sang out a computer-generated estimate of two miles distance, and closing, on the rapidly approaching gunboat. Dacus called for reducing the five-mile shell to a smaller one of two and an eighth miles in radius, and to retain same specs.

The crew staff aboard the gunboat was smart enough to maintain radio silence. Lack of bullshit declamation, after contact from their fat cohort, suggested trouble. Coming within range, its captain ordered a self-guidance missile be readied for launch. The closer the gunboat drew in on its target, the more Rabbit shrunk the outer shell, correlating it and the other craft in an alleyway between two shells. Programed to activate on contact, the gunboat's captain signaled launching of the missile. Dacus watched as it propelled the conformed path, circling their cruiser to hit the pleasure craft, blowing it to smithereens. In panic, the captain ordered another missile fired. It completed full circle, destroying the gunboat . . .

Dacus, Rabbit, and Sloan watched last remnants of this wreckage sink into the deep. For thirty minutes they waited, observing the area. No survivors emerged. When none surfaced, Dacus switched on the lounge intercom, declaring, "Our would be assailants have given up the ghost. They fired misguided missiles that got them instead of us," adding, "I guess." Rabbit dissolved the shells before erecting a soft one of two mile radius. He and Dacus went below.

It was an agitated, disgruntled bunch that met the pair. Acting as spokesman, Ed minced no words in telling of fears, emotions, and reactions unleashed in confinement. "None of us bargained for a pot of gold turned so blackened. Your description of what a legal scam on the gold market would be, Dacus, and what's occurring bears no resemblance. It's time to disband the organization and to go our separate ways."

Deploring the timing to meet the inevitable, Dacus was in accord. "I totally agree," he allowed and advised. "After today, and except for anywhere in the States, you should be free to pursue a lifestyle of your own choosing. As for sine die of the Association, only one function is left to be addressed. It's our duty to settle commitments to the contributing associates and divide the remaining money among members."

Harry interrupted, "I want a strict accounting of all cash. I've got serious doubts about goin' along with you dippin' into my part for so-called expenses." The outburst from Harry sent ominous, disconnected vibes thru Rabbit. He left the lounge, put a pistol in his pocket, and eased back in to find nothing going on. Everyone seemed subdued and lost in thought. A couple who'd decided to go away together would cast a glance over to the other once in a while.

Dacus finally broke the silence. "We're headed toward Cozumel as quickly as possible. The ship'll be moored just outside its ten mile limit, and from there, Maybelle'll be contacted by cell phone. Pilot Barnett and one other are to embark in the catamaran to pick her up. Only then, when everyone is present, can the business of money be expended."

Outraged by the circumstances, Jack broke in, "I joined this operation through my long term acquaintanceship with Maybelle. I considered there to be a solidarity here . . . Mainly because she's a solid, responsible individual. My services, at a price, were retained to perform two functions. Having fulfilled the obligations of supervising bank transfers and assisting in sale of gold on a commission, I hereby resign from all associational activity. It's too flaky at its core for me to stomach. You are relieved of any bindings to me, except for the 2 percent commission on gold sales. The instant I'm paid $7,348,320, I'll be outta here on the first raft going ashore."

"What? You mean you're not going to escort us to Switzerland and supervise bank transfers for a fee there?" ridiculed Harry.

"Not no, but hell no!" Jack fired back. "I want to be as far away from the likes of you as I can get. You've substituted greed for guts and responsibility and destined to fall on your dead asses." Visibly upset, he stalked out.

Hard on his heels, Dacus tried to rectify, "I respect your decision Jack, but Harry doesn't have the last say here. It was a business agreement, and you are entitled to be reimbursed."

"I don't want it," grunted Jack. "I've never quit in the middle of anything in my whole life. This thing stinks like a lighted fuse to a keg of gunpowder. I hope you can diffuse it!"

"If you won't stay the course, would you go over with Barnett to meet Maybelle? You can do your bidding while there and inform her of developing affairs here," Dacus supplicated.

"Yes!" conceded Jack. "I'll do that for you."

Pleasure showed at seeing Maybelle again as Dacus helped her aboard ship. Proclaiming her arrival to the gang, Harry obnoxiously shouted, "Showdown time, missy."

Dacus, ignoring Harry's uncouth behavior, called the meeting to order. Without ado, he opened by declaring the cash kitty account to be $380,416,000. "According to my bookkeeping, we are obliged to pay expenses, deducted from this figure. And, Jack's assessment of his commission on contracting gold sales at 2 percent, indeed comes to $7,348,320. He has flatly refused compensation due for these services rendered."

Exhaustion crept in from excercising ingenuity of power and wit and from too many intense hours of self-restraint for a vested cause. It was at saturation now having to contend with disenchanted associates turned avaricious. He threw a fisted forearm into the wall beside him and charged ahead to assess rights of the money. "Rabbit, although not a member as such, has been a vital arm throughout our entire operation. Each and every one of us has benefited 24/7 from his contributions. Just a few hours ago, he saved my life for a second time. In so doing, your safety and mine was assured once again. I propose five million for him and Lulu to live on in comfort the balance of their life."

Making eye contact with each one present, Dacus cited, "The ladies adopted us midway of our venture and understood rewards were contingent on its success. They can't be accused of not holding up their end of the deal. For prosperity, at least two million apiece is recommended."

Seeking to make a point, he phrased to invite comment. "Now, unless Tom and Vivian are not satisfied to be considered as a unit, the original eight members' share is $44,258,460 each and takes into account all deductions proposed, including the pilot's salary."

Vivian and Tom molded to confer briefly. Facing peers, Tom sternly relayed, "We're one item and not about to change the arrangement over money this late in life!"

Chiming in, Vivian agreed, "Sure, we can scrape by on forty-four million during our golden years. Beats Social Security, but Tom, you'll have to be careful about your spending!"

Dacus continued, "Our ship's pilot contracted the job with us for a hundred eighty thousand. I'm adding a million out of my proceeds to his guaranteed salary. I'd much prefer he part company overcompensated, with better things to occupy him, than to be vindictively tempted to rat on us."

"Rots of ruck," chided Art without malice, bothered by Tom's put-down.

"You bet," echoed Theo. "Your money, your risk, chum."

Heads jerked around as Harry jumped almost in Dacus's face, confronting, "Who the hell do you think you are? God? What gives you the idea you were to decide what to pay Rabbit or anyone else when part of it comes out of my pocket?" A unanimous frown of disapproval crossed the faces of eight women, spreading a disquieting reality of things.

Harry was far from through. Turning on Dacus, he accused, "What about a ship worth seven million dollars and over fifty million in gold stored in the hull you didn't bother to mention? Thought you'd get away with it, didn't you?"

Provoked, Dacus shoved him aside. "Everyone's entitled to have my comments and be reminded of debts owed! Granted, I've assumed you'd all know, instinctively, the ship couldn't be sold any more than the gold can be fenced now. It'd be insane to put the finger right back on us. Where were your senses just hours ago when last traces leading to us were wiped out and sunk at sea? Consumed by concern for Rabbit and me out there risking our necks to save your asses is doubtful! You wanta stay and liquidate proceeds to be split? Fine! We'll tough it out together, along with every bloody ramification it'll present. But, if you think I'm going to pick up the tab on marked merchandise while you're living it up on some Riviera, then you're woefully mistaken!"

Infuriated, Maybelle came in beside him, pointing to Harry. "Take a good look at Mr. Self Righteous. Doubting Thomas has both hands out of his pockets and is reaching. His negatives damn sure didn't put forty-four million in the bank for anyone! This same sorry attitude has caused nothing but dissension, including incriminatory accusations over this boat and balance of the gold." Her anger ascended to a higher pitch.

"I got a lot more to get off my chest, while you, Sam, Theo, and Art slouch a little lower in those chairs. It was Dacus who fought to get me into this organization. As a member, it fell my lot to do something not a damned one of you would've done. That act could have left me dead or still behind bars instead of being the key to seed money which has brought you squabbling over proceeds . . . Pitiful!" she scorned.

"I had two million, coming in. None of you had a pot to piss in, much less a window to throw it out of. My money would've earned more interest in a bank than it has working for the likes of you. I'd have walked away if I'd dreamed you people were the scum you've proven to be. No thanks. No gratitude for an opportunity to make it big on someone else's wits and money. Frankly, you're not worth forty-four million, and I've got news for you. You've all put yourself at a real disadvantage letting this two-bit son of a bitch take over your minds! If you've got a head on those shoulders, hear me and hear me well . . . The more than three hundred eighty million kitty account is under my PIN. You're gonna get your money, but it'll be on my terms. When it's done, I don't ever want to see you again. Not one has shown an ounce of appreciation to Dacus for dumping these millions into your laps. I despise an ingrate!"

Without warning, Harry lunged, grabbing Maybelle by the throat with deadly intent. Reacting, Dacus reached for him as a shot rang out. A bullet to the back of the head had felled Harry instantly. Standing there with a small, twenty-five gauge pistol in her hand was—Julie! Stepping forward, she released the gun to Dacus. "I can't go anywhere," she mustered. "Do whatever's necessary to me later."

A state of shock gripped the gang. Dacus asked that Rabbit fetch a blanket while he and Sam removed the body to Harry's stateroom. Rabbit spread plastic across the bed, covered by a bedsheet, to lay out the body on.

Dacus hurried back to the lounge, dreading what he'd find. Still too stunned to show emotion, they were huddled in around the bar. Taking a position from behind it, he consoled, looking into each agonized face. "We've lost something precious here, today. I, for one, can't give it up. I'm not mad at anybody, not even Harry. Fact is, all of us must carry our excess baggage, and that hurts. Harry's burden had to have been a paranoia. Something we had as much problem coping with as he did. I believe he's at peace now, and I am truly sorry he is gone. I feel it's my solemn responsibility to be available to each of you. You'll be welcomed in my quarters at any time." He lingered only a moment before going out in search of Julie.

He found her leaning against the railing, looking down at passing water. Putting an arm around her shoulders, he uttered not a word. As if talking to herself, she began a monotone. "It's an old story. Two couples become friends and go out together. One half of each marriage decides to cheat on the other half. Generally, it leads to divorce and remarriage of the cheaters. The other couple often'll marry out of devastated feelings, clinging to each other in bottom of the barrel depression and lose their self-confidence. I guess Harry and I subconsciously identified and suffered from wounded pride. Everyone else had chosen partners to pursue a life of luxury leaving us, not second but sixth or seventh best. Naturally, we'd gravitated to each other," she cried, bemoaning the tragedy at her spurring of wrongdoing.

"Something in me couldn't let Harry destroy the only stability I ever had by hurting Maybelle. I'm sick. I'm ill with myself and wanta die.

Where'd you put my gun?" she demanded. "Use it, or let me have it to end my misery."

In one motion, Dacus gathered her into his arms, held her tightly, and stroked her hair. "You're not guilty of anything, except of being human, Julie. You didn't shoot out of hate or jealousy. You reacted in defense of a friend. In his crazed frenzy, Harry could have crushed her windpipe and Maybelle would be gone. She has plans to stick around, along with Rabbit and Lulu. Why don't you give thought to staying around?"

Sobbing, Julie managed, "Thank you. I really don't have another place I'd rather be."

"It'd be a mistake to wander after the others," Dacus advised. "You've always been set apart with a specialty difference. It might have the same effect as puttin' a Rhode Island red chicken among a pen full of white leghorns. Chickens can be cruel. Their pecking order is to eventually peck a victim to death, and you wouldn't deserve that."

Wanting to quell her anguish, Dacus took up a tangent discussion. "Did you know our legal system in the U.S. is based on the English common law? It might interest you to know legal accusations were influenced by the code of Moses transcribed in the Old Testament. In the States today, our legal profession has abandoned that code of Moses, whereby one person could not be convicted by testimony of another person without corroboration of a second party. It's a shameless legal ax! One person can now convict a half dozen others by being offered a plea bargain of amnesty for testimony of his or her part in a conspiracy or other crime. In essence, the law is reduced to wallowing in muck with a convicted felon and justice is mocked."

He patted her hand. "That, my dear Miss Rich, is why the States is not an option for any of us. No matter how much money you have, footin' it alone's no fun. Make plans to move in on Grand Cayman beach, as we did before. The rest of the bunch has sights set on Europe and are flying out in a few days. Right now, Julie, I need to go below and give a hand on building the casket. You need to do yourself a favor by putting cold compresses on those eyes. Be ready when we lay him to rest just before sundown."

The funeral proceeded speedily and perfunctorily by protocol of the ship's captain at sea. After reading from The Book of Psalms, Psalm 23, Dacus concluded, "Harry was not a morally bad man. He became very sick, afflicted by a progressive form of insanity we weren't recognizing. May God rest his soul and offer solace to us."

The weighted casket, lowered gently into the water, slowly disappeared into calm seas . . .

CHAPTER 33

Docking on Grand Cayman held little resemblance to their first godown with its sun-soaked, pleasure-drenched atmosphere. The tension of an impending hurricane could more describe the demeanor of Association members and others accompanying Maybelle ashore to finalize their banking. Jack Rainwater, knowing when to consolidate, had directed a concise schematic of banking accounts to expedite the end settlement.

Acting on Jack's advice and with fluid expertise, Maybelle moved their remaining three Georgetown accounts into a Canadian-chartered offshore bank having close ties to a Swiss bank. In short order, personal accounts for each associational member, one for each of the ladies, Rabbit, and Sloan, were set up. She transferred funds from her newly established PIN account to open each of theirs with designated shares of the money. Jack had indicated he would be transferring his account to take advantage of Swiss banking privileges later at his instance.

Issuance of individual PINs for the group required a thumbprint, slowing the process somewhat. When documents were notarized, the Canadian bank faxed reproductions of the information to their Swiss associate bank. As courier for hand delivery to the overseas bank, Maybelle took charge of the originals and would add Jack's if he chose to go the privacy route.

Paperwork completed, Maybelle summoned everyone to a borrowed boardroom for briefing. "My sole purpose of being here is the strong responsibility I feel for my gals and to Rabbit," she stipulated. "Those others of you present may benefit from what is said as you prepare to go abroad. Bear in mind, all and any communication made hereafter, for the obvious, will be through fax at this bank." She passed bank business cards around with its printed number.

"Girls, you now have a secured base with the opened bank accounts. It is my opinion you should withdraw ten thousand in cash, or equivalent paper, today. You'll go through half of it in a hurry, buying luggage, plane tickets, and incidentals for the trip. Before I leave for the airport to fly out, set up a flight itinerary, purchase your tickets, and claim the reservations for departure. I'd consider it urgent to move on and expedient to establish credentials over there with a residency and credit cards. Jack is adamant and, of course, holding true to his word not to have any part in this transition. In other words, you'll be on your own, kiddos!"

As Maybelle's plane lifted into the air for Europe, the gang, including Jack, sought temporary beachfront quarters. Perversely, Dacus, Julie, Rabbit, Lulu, and Sloan stayed on board the ship. Julie opted, and got Lulu's help for the next couple of days, to air the place out and put the shine on all staterooms. Dacus involved himself, Rabbit, and Sloan with a maintenance check of equipment. The five were lacking in R and R. Light chores during the next couple of days and tranquil evenings did a number to catch-up on time lost.

Only twenty-four hours after moving on shore, Ed had a 'head-on' with withdrawal pains. He broached the subject to other association members. They too were being struck by a mixed bag of uncertainties. And yes, if he could arrange it, one last time together might remedy the harshness felt from severing all ties. Ed managed to wedge into the packed schedule for departing, a session in the ship's salon with Dacus's blessings.

"From the beginning of our reunited association in Little Rock," he addressed the group, "I've been privileged when advice was sought, or you trusted me to be your spokesperson on our whirlwind excursion. I'm already missing the interaction and having a problem adjusting to the void it'll leave. Whatever else comes out of my mouth, you'll probably consider it as trite. Without a doubt, this parting brings deep, sweet sorrow to me."

Ed wavered as impact of the significance sunk in. "Good-byes really are taken for granted," he exposed, "and that's what makes ours so difficult to accommodate. There won't be any letters, phone calls, e-mail, or planned reunions to keep it touch. Our mental video is all we take for remembrance, and that's hard-core for real stuff to abide by. In absence of contact with one another, we can only hope time eases the empty space with a promising new direction in life, money, and a partner who has shared some of the same experiences."

Determining that emotions were running too high for any of the others to voice a remark, Ed engaged Dacus. "Although second chances at our stage in life aren't easy to come by, you made it happen! I, Dacus, and I think I speak for the whole of us, am grateful to you for the salvaging. I know for sure I'd become wormy. We're all indebted to the driving forces which motivate you and for rewards we have gained from being participants. They'll go with us the rest of our lives and should be a source of peace and contentment to you. You are an honorable man. It's been a pleasure having known you." Barely handling emotions, Ed sat down beside Randi.

"Thanks, Ed, for your remarks and for the many mutual years of friendship we have all had, off and on," Dacus managed, clearing his throat. "As a man with a dream of sorts, constricted by a recondite technology, and the burdens it bears, I'm pretty grateful myself. Without your bonding and the capabilities each of you possess, none of what we have today would have been possible. Certainly, not the tapestry of memories we take away. Let them be our support to bridge the parting. Best of luck to each of you."

Dacus moved around to shake hands with everyone. Comments were briefly exchanged, and moods had lightened in acceptance of the separation. Catching Ed and Dacus, Theo came up to shake Dacus's hand and drolled, "Our man Ed put together a fair wake for the bunch, don't you think? Too bad he didn't bring along Irish whiskey. As a memento, we coulda passed it through the body before sprinkling it off the lower deck."

It set off a ripple of amusement as they, and others who heard, moved on to give farewells to Rabbit and Barnett and affectionate hugs to Julie and Lulu. Wisely, no one suggested opening up the bar nor indulged in a solitary moment of reminiscing. Neither did anyone make mention of Maybelle, question Jack's whereabouts, inquire of Sloan's and Rabbit's plans, or ask about Dacus's intentions for the future.

Maybelle's fax arrived at the Canadian bank two days later from Switzerland. With little fanfare, last items were packed, cottages vacated, and a tourist-clad, luggage-loaded group boarded a one-way flight to Geneva.

Jack had been quite busy and had his nose to the ground in some unlikely places, picking up on tidbits being dropped by 'banker groupies'. By an uncanny intuition, he knew the Europe bound group had departed. It was an occasion to go by a package store for champagne, get cigars for the guys, find flowers for the girls, and enough time to retouch base on the ship. He instigated a little benign merriment in passing out the favors and popping the cork on a bottle of bubbles, waiting for the right time to talk with Dacus alone.

After Julie and Lulu left to put the flowers in water and when Sloan and Rabbit excused themselves, Jack approached Dacus on news he had to incite his curiosity. Wasting no time for Dacus to speculate, he abruptly and solicitously introduced. "What're your thoughts if just maybe an unusual opportunity presented itself and we were able to sell the balance of gold stored in the hull? It goes without saying there would be no ties remotely connected to cartel intervention."

Dacus reacted favorably and drew him on to hear more. Encouraged, Jack obliged. "Even though Cuba is ostracized and relatively isolated, their government is circulating that time is nearing for U.S. sanctions to be lifted. If there's any merit to it, it'll mean their trade access to the world community becomes enhanced . . . You get the gist," Jack stated, rather than asked.

"At the moment," he summarized, "Cuba is awash with cash from increased worldwide tourist trade and from drug money. Castro has leaked wanting to buy gold with some of these dollars while the price is down, believing it will come back up in a year or two. To feed our particular interests, the word is out that he wants to own it secretly!"

Dacus smiled, reflecting on the Indian's tracking instincts and on a new challenge well worth the consideration to pursue. As if it'd make any difference, he stamped his approval offering a proposition, "How much do you want, Jack?"

Knowing Dacus, Jack laughed outright, quoting, "Ten percent!" The amount came as decisive, yet he'd emitted it with a twinkle in his eyes.

Reinforced, Jack retired to his quarters on shore. Zealously, he continued courting his 'Cuban Connection' while waiting for Maybelle to fly in from Switzerland. It occupied energies and his mind, formulating the deciding terms.

Concurrently, Dacus consulted with Rabbit and Sloan for their approval then withdrew into his personal shell, holing up in the office. The DTN had already convinced him the gold market was, with great effort and expenditure, stabilized around a benchmark of two hundred ninety dollars per troy ounce. Quickly figuring the probable troy ounces in ten avoirdupois tons, he determined the current value of unsold gold to be close to eighty-five million. It certainly proved a large enough sum to induce temptation. In anticipation of launching another venture, he consulted Caribbean area maps. Drawing up contingency routing plans, he included an alternate course, just in case of some type of unpredictable trouble.

Unexpectedly, Jack reappeared the next day. He briefed Dacus on negotiations in progress with the Cuban contact as being ardent. Dacus readily countered, instructing Jack to relay ten avoirdupois tons of gold was available.

It's worth of eighty-four and a half million U.S. dollars to be based strictly on the current troy ounce price. The cargo, if a deal were struck, would arrive by ship. Her captain preferred to dock and make delivery at Manzanillo.

Timing became geared around Maybelle's schedule. Three days prior to her coming in from Switzerland, Dacus gave a crash course on the subject of 'Gold Mission II'. He rehearsed and drilled Rabbit and Sloan on procedures to follow in all eventualities. Encountering a double cross by the Cuban government could not be ruled out by any means, and he intended to be prepared! Maybelle's arrival signaled Jack it was time to move back aboard the ship.

A task of loading the ship to capacity began with replenishing supplies of engine oil and diesel. Rabbit took advantage of the women's fare to select fresh vegetables, dairy products, and staple goods in preparation for possibly an extended journey. Julie joined the cause, suggesting a stock check on office essentials, batteries, and tape.

Within a week, Jack met for a last interview, finalizing understandings with his Cuban representative. The ex post facto seven completed readiness to leave port for Manzanillo . . . Before casting off, Dacus hurriedly took time to get everyone together, relating, "The proceedings from the venture at hand should bring in eighty-four and a half million. Jack has put this entire transaction together, asking only 10 percent for his part. The differences to consider is that he is present, as surely as we are, and fair is fair. Counting Rabbit and Lulu as a unit on this one adds up to six of us and a potential take of roughly fourteen million apiece. Let's settle on the front end and before leaving, to make an equal split in all proceeds." The proposition unanimously agreed upon, the ship eased out to sea from Grand Cayman.

Squared away after an hour or so at sea, Dacus called for an assembly in the pilothouse. "I'm inundated with a common, fairly routine occurrence to use as strategy for wreaking chaos, if it becomes necessary on this jaunt," he divulged. "The wherewithal to execute it on a large scale is at our fingertips. Just how operative it'd be in a full-fledged initiative, needs proof. I think it can be determined with your help enacting out the scenario."

Aware of the ship's current position being at its farthest point from shipping lanes or airline routes, Dacus, unobserved, had covertly set a bubble five miles high and ten miles in diameter. It would be the field of action to check on response time and reaction to absolute darkness. He gave few hints of what was about to take place, offhandedly commenting, "It's two o'clock this bright afternoon and perfect conditions to put my strategy through a trial run. We'll want to observe aspects of the experiment for pros and cons to be used in a crunch situation. If you're ready, let's see how your reaction is to an unexpected, reoccurring incident contended with numerous times. You'll have a prior inkling. Whether or not it'll register in time to make an adequate response, I'm not sure. Countdown is in three minutes . . ."

Instincts of a feline being whetted by prey or danger visibly surfaced. Eyes flitted, taking in every inch for any thing that could accost them. Rapidly dimming lights distracted, rather than activated a preparedness to meet the situation. An unexpected blackout is an experience in total disorientation . . . It caught them off guard and on the verge of panic, except for Julie. She calmly took a lighter out of her jacket, flipping it once. It illuminated barely far enough to see the oil lantern setting on a ledge across the cabin. In the panicked moment, both Rabbit and Sloan scurried to get it lighted so flashlights could be retrieved. Without matches handy, their response time was cut, again, having to call on Julie.

A flashlight finally in hand, Sloan frantically fanned its beam across the ship's instrument panel. It hadn't registered until then . . . No electrical power, no lighted computer display! Compounded by lack of compass direction, Sloan was on the brink of losing it when Dacus intervened. "The shell is being dissolved so we can think rationally. Neither an individual nor a mass of people experiencing what has happened here reacts on an even keel. It renders helpless floundering, unless advance preparation is programed in."

Sloan didn't wait for daylight to return. "That was some wake-up call, Dacus," he beefed, trying to shake the adrenaline rush. "Where do you have a magnetic compass stashed? It is the dregs for someone like me to rely on computer-generated directions and never question it. Look for a cold day in hell before you find me on a ship without a flashlight, spare batteries, a waterproof container of matches, and a trusty compass. With those items, I'd be prepared to find anyone's ass, set it on fire, and see which direction it took off in."

High fives around confirmed appreciation for the rigged precept, keyed to enhance readiness responses. It had worked, and Dacus was rewarded by Sloan's stimuli and amused with his reactions. "You're very familiar with my hang-up on having three identical pieces of equipment for every function," he reminded and justified the idiosyncrasy to disclose. "Having them eliminates downtime to make a repair, naturally. However, when faced with circumstances as we're now gearing for, spare parts and equipment can prove their usefulness in an emergency power play. I'll fill you in on where I'm coming from in a minute."

Dacus had watched Sloan not lose focus of the compass value during the trial exercise. After he'd made such an issue of it, Dacus decided to reveal his activities on two days the three of them were on maintenance duty. "Both this ship and the catamaran have an automatic pilot by which the helmsman is relieved from manually steering if it's set on a single, continuous course. Each of these crafts were equipped, as you know, with a standby unit until I took one of the gyroscopic devices to mount in a free-standing position on ball bearings and secured it in a frame bolted to the deck. It came about as a latent decision, attached to the blackout ploy, and satisfying a preparedness fixation of mine. As pilot, Sloan, or any one of us, there is now a reference point, even in the absence of a standardized compass. Start the gyro, point it due south, and it'll stay constant in that direction as long as it's running. Inky black conditions plus lost sense of direction equals confused disorientation and a faltering reconnaissance I hope we benefit from."

"Let me get it straight," Sloan tendered. "I take it your game plan is to go in with this device up and running, holding true to the preparedness bit. If worst comes to worst, and defense calls for using your blackout theory, I won't have a problem if I swing the ship around parallel to the heading we're on and know it is either north or south?"

"Exactly," Dacus concurred. "I'll go you one further my man. By placing a red dot on the north indicator and a black dot for the south heading, we'd be relatively comfortable even then if Maybelle had to spell us at the wheel."

Maybelle, followed by Jack, ambled out on the sun-filled deck. "Fascinating, for lack of a better term in my ignorance," she confided, enthusiastically. "Imagine having the ability to create total darkness, with sunlight this brilliant, and have the foresight to use it to one's advantage. You got any earthy thoughts on the matter, Jack?"

Feeling good in his role and about the whole of operations, Jack was projecting ahead. "This one is staking up with a wealth of potential. I believe Castro better play 'er straight or hide his balls in pubic hair transplanted from that 'trademark' wavy beard."

"Oh sure!" Maybelle burst out laughing, swatting him across the rear. "And I guess your next career move is to become the giant icon of lascivious-talking radio hosts!"

CHAPTER 34

The millennium is not far away, and there is a whisper of unrest. In a time when astrology charts are still printed in daily newspapers, it's not unusual for predictions of Nostradamus, Edgar Cayce, and other reputed prophets to be bandied about. An added emotion from a prevailing doctrine of fundamentalism, stating, "A thousand years of peace will be preceded by Armageddon," causes the World Wide Web to jump with apprehension.

It is little wonder then, on report that radio contact had been lost between the U.S. Naval Base at Guantanamo Bay and the Pentagon, a frenzied scrambling of personnel occurred. Two U.S. reconnaissance planes were immediately dispatched to its base in Cuba. All hell broke loose in the Pentagon when both planes radioed back Cuba had disappeared off the face of the earth. "That's impossible!" shouted the Colonel, who had been patched in. "How in creation can you lose anything the size of Cuba?"

"Beats me, sir," the pilot in charge answered curtly. "We've flown this exact pattern from Jacksonville to Guantanamo for years. It's the first time our compasses have suddenly gone haywire. The whole island's nowhere to be seen, sir."

In a reaction to crisis, the Colonel interrogated, "Do you have heat sensory cameras aboard?" Knowing full well the planes were totally equipped, it was an asinine question.

The pilot responded, "Yes, sir. We've already used them, and they're of no benefit."

"Return to base and prepare for debriefing. A team from the Pentagon will meet with you in three hours." His over and out, killed the connection.

Long before time for debriefing, an older Pentagon staff member suddenly recalled an undersea telephone cable. It had been installed from the States to Guantanamo during the Batista regime. Some thirty minutes into a continuous series of dials, letting it ring, and redialing, an enlisted man picked up, hailing, "First Class Yeoman Stennard speaking."

"Yeoman Stennard, this is Colonel Yarnell in Washington at the Pentagon. We have been unable to make base contact by radio. Reconnaissance planes can't seem to find the island. We'd like an update on conditions there."

"Colonel, all I know is that around 1700 hours, it got dark for no apparent reason. And I mean really black dark. You can't see a hand in front of your face outside without a flashlight. Everyone's scared! The Cubans have already converged on the base. They thought we had sabotaged them someway. It hasn't helped much seeing firsthand we've got the same problem."

"Yeoman, whose charge is it to man this phone?" demanded Yarnell, upset at seemingly lack of organizational 'hump-to'.

"Sir, I can't say that I know. I happened to be passing by this old office and heard the phone ringing. The place was empty, so I answered it. Come to think of it, sir, I thought the line was dead. It's the first time I've heard it ring in the three years I've been stationed on the base."

"Admittedly, it hasn't been ringing into the Pentagon, either!" ranted the Colonel. "But this is an order. Get someone on duty to have the phone continuously manned until further notice. Take down these numbers. I want your officer in charge to call me as soon as possible."

His command received an 'aye aye, sir'. Forty five minutes later, U.S. Navy Captain Roland Adams deferred duties to respond. When Colonel Yarnell answered, Adams reported, "This is Captain Adams at Base Position G, acknowledging as requested."

"Captain, Colonel Yarnell here in the Pentagon. Can you brief us on current conditions? Incoming classified on the situation down there is highly irregular. What's your MO?"

"It's suspect, Colonel! Our overall status is absolute, total chaos from an unidentified blackout and reactive dysfunction among personnel. Four to five hours ago, daylight prematurely ended. Oddly enough, nothing's been visible from the skies since. Moveover, the problem seems to be universal. At this hour, the cause remains a mystery. Utter mayhem exists, hampering efforts to solve it, and complicated by a delegation of fear-ridden Cubans, who descended on the base about two hours ago. It's taken a while to turn them toward the logical basis of 'fact' thinking. The terror of a supernatural occurrence had to be ruled out to their satisfaction. Following that, a mounting grievance festered to avenge a crisis we'd surely created and it had to be stifled. Now, in more of a rational discourse, the group has come out with scuttlebutt we're presently looking into." Adams summarized their mode of operations, relating breaking details . . .

"It's becoming evident these extreme conditions result from an undetermined outside force. The Cubans' leak of a megadeal gone bad suggests retaliation of such magnitude as consequences. The 'who and how' of this is stumping intelligence. Initial information received from sources out of Havana is that there's a conflict between the government and a ship in its port. It has something to do with gold, purportedly gleaned from salvage operations off the bottom of the sea, worth millions. As leads filter in, the likelihood of such takes on merit, Colonel."

Reinforcing, Adams revealed, "The latest, unofficially, is Castro's government made a hushed deal to buy an undisclosed amount of gold. A coup to swindle the supplier went sour. The regime declared the gold confiscated merchandise as soon as the ship entered Manzanillo harbor by assuming a position that gold harvesting at sea was illegal under Cuban law. An attempt to arrest the ship's crew failed. Almost simultaneously, the blackout occurred, and the Cuban forces met astonishing defeat in some strange manner. The ship has withdrawn out of the harbor, and a search by air has proved unsuccessful in locating it. Incoming reports indicate, Colonel, the captain of this unknown vessel may be responsible for overriding all broadcasting facilities. Stranger yet, it's being said Cuba's seeking guidance from the United States."

"What the hell for, Captain?" erupted Yarnell, disconcerted by the prospects.

"It seems they've got a problem, sir. The phantom ship's captain issued a threat . . . 'Pay for the gold in U.S. dollars, or the blockade continues until the Cuban sugar cane crop is destroyed from lack of sunlight'. Their expressed apprehensions include fear of a revolution in this extended midnight. The bearded man cannot afford that," he confided.

"Shortly, Captain Adams, there's to be a debriefing of the reconnaissance pilots who couldn't find the island of Cuba. I'd appreciate it if you'd stand by for a conference following the session, at which time we'll attempt to develop a coordinated plan of action."

Hanging up the phone, Colonel Yarnell spun his chair to address a listening aide. "I never took any stock in the Bermuda Triangle crap, but damned if it doesn't seem like we're dealing with something equally as bizarre. Find out if an area satellite shot at this odd hour is of any value."

Twenty minutes later, pinpointed computerized imagery appeared on screen in Yarnell's office. Cuba was not completely gone. A small tip of the island, running southwest of Havana was indeed visible. Nothing else of it remained. Other abnormalities were observed. Part of Andros Island in the Bahamas was gone as well as a portion of the southern peninsula of Haiti, plus all of Jamaica and the Cayman Islands. "What in god's name does it mean?" the Colonel muttered to himself and no one else in particular.

His reverie was disrupted by the aide. "Colonel, check on the blanked-out area we know should exist. Don't it look like it'd fit in a circle?"

"You're absolutely right, son. Irrevocably correct! Get the precise coordinates of its center. We may have stumbled on to something!"

Addressing his staff, he theorized. "If this is what it appears, a perfect circle, then whatever the phenomenon is, we'll take the stance it's man-made. Refocus your inquiry, adduced along these lines, and we should be able to eliminate or, at least, gain insight into the problem. Begin by running a check to see if radio contact is possible with Jamaica or the Cayman Islands."

It was quickly determined neither Jamaica nor the Cayman Islands were in communication with the rest of the world. As a report summarizing events was being prepared for higher command, an urgent phone call for Yarnell came in from Guantanamo. "Colonel, we've just received word the Cuban government is in the process of submitting to demands the gold be paid for. It will alter the criteria. As an equal ranking officer, I'd appreciate your input," Adams aired.

"If the Cuban government decides to act unilaterally, without consulting our government, then, for the present we'll do the same, Captain. Also, there's certain satellite imagery now available. How effective it'll be to intercept the unidentified ship when the confrontation is over remains to be seen. Moreover, until further notice, this and any future information from the Pentagon is declared classified. The receiver you're holding is probably black, so label it red until other communication modes can be restored," Yarnell directed, emphasizing the primacy of Pentagon authority. For a harassed Adams, he hadn't needed brass pettiness.

With priority urgency, the report was compiled and sent up the chain of command. First of the U.S. Congressional Joint Chiefs of Staff to be reached, General 'Pink' Sherman, a giant redhead, happened to be holding forth at a private dinner party. He contacted his personal staff with instructions to meet him and departed for the Pentagon in a chauffeured limousine.

In the meeting, agreement of the Joint Chiefs of Staff was sought on proposed action, addressing two points. They wanted the applied use of an unknown technology identified and how an invasion of U.S. sovereignty at Guantanamo Naval Base should be categorized. It was resolved no recourse should be initiated without notifying the White House. General Sherman deferred, "It's a damn shame we have to approach the President through his 'whiz kid' advisor."

His remark created a rumble. A resolution to involve the White House immediately passed and was promptly recorded in the minutes.

The Presidential conference briefing went as expected. Present were a number of staff aides to the Joint Chiefs of Staff, as well as the astute, brainy advisor of the President seated on elevating cushions at his boss's side. The report met with lax indifference from the Chief Executive. Undaunted by the contents, he questioned, "What are the chances of ignoring this one? Better yet, would be to not let it surface . . ."

Anticipated by the Chiefs, their answer was direct and pointed. "Surely you're not suggesting such a damaging dilemma be suppressed. Think of the human rights element, if nothing else. The entire world knows what loss of sunlight can do to the environment and effects it'll have on Cuba's staple crop, not to mention impoverished Haiti and the recreational trade deficit to the Cayman Islands, Bahamas, and Jamaica, who are also unnaturally affected. When Castro's officials comply with payment demanded by the ship's captain and communication is restored, you'd better believe, Sir, it'll be followed by a media backlash, the likes of which has never been encountered at a White House press powwow."

The cold, stark facts of realism overrode his disregard of the situation. With a pained expression, leaning forward to place his chin in the palm of his hand, the President listened to his whiz kid's whisperings. He was reminded the polls were decidedly down and the administration was being labeled as wimpish and indecisive in crisis . . .

Regaining composure as Commander in Chief, he cleared his throat and backtracked. "Gentlemen, regardless of cost, I want that ship seized and its captain brought in for questioning." In dismissing them, he added, "Incidentally, finalize minutes taken of the meeting as soon as possible. Dispatch a copy to me in this office. I'll be here for a while longer."

Under Pentagon orders, the U.S. Navy launched a small flotilla from its Guantanamo base to sail toward coordinates calculated to be center of the blackout. In absolute darkness, with unreliable compasses and vision limited to searchlight beams, they succeeded only in suffering from several collisions, incurring minor injuries. The trashed mission had to be called off and the

Pentagon notified by the single red-colored phone. Being bearer of bad tidings, Captain Adams compounded it to relay other unconfirmed rumors. "Cuba has lost two fighter planes. It's supposed to have occurred when they tried to strafe the unidentified ship as it sailed out of the bay and after mysteriously defeating a cadre of Cuban police in the Manzanillo port."

Continuing, Adams informed, "The Cuban government has refused to confirm these rumors officially. Personally, I'm of the opinion they'd like to see us fall flat on our ass. They have to be in a state over their cover being blown to buy up gold and our having inside knowledge of it."

Armed with Presidential blessings, the Pentagon craved action, launching two more planes to fly from Jacksonville toward Guantanamo. The pair of pilots, briefed of circumstances in advance, radioed back more accurate descriptions of their observations. They reported experiencing a mammoth force, altering the intended flight pattern. It pressed them increasingly westward in spite of locked-in controls on both planes. Finally, swinging around in a northeasterly setting, it became possible to maneuver after passing over a part of Haiti.

The inky blackness, a lack of charted direction, and impaired communications presented a state of affairs without precedent. It had thrown the Pentagon staff into a dither, and the Latin-based intelligence became exasperating. Actually, at the very time the U.S. Government was trying to become involved, Dacus had already carried out most of his contingency plan in response to Cuban duplicity. Two Cuban fighter planes, commissioned to apprehend him, had crashed into the side of a clear, hard shell as he exited Manzanillo Bay. Once in open sea, he headed almost due south to a spot just north of Jamaica's Montego Bay. Employing both diesel-powered propellers and the electric ones, he reached a preassigned position in slightly less than two hours.

The catamaran, cut loose from the ship, was firmly anchored fore and aft in the shallow sea. Under Dacus's guidance, Rabbit and Sloan began generating electricity with equipment aboard the trihulled vessel. When voltage potentials were high enough, they erected a bubble of 666 miles in radius and quickly extinguished all lights.

Utilizing precise split timing, Dacus, by generating his own electrical supply to supplement diesel power, had only hesitated before roaring back toward Cuba at top speed. Left in charge with Rabbit, Sloan pondered, "How can he do that from inside a shell?"

"I don't exactly know," Rabbit speculated. "It has something to do with the fact that electricity, at somewhere around a hundred fifty thousand cycles, is easy to transmit through the earth's skin . . . I'm no whatshisname, so you figure it out."

En route to Manzanillo, Dacus overrode Cuba's facilities to broadcast. Taking advantage of Maybelle's bilingual capability, he threatened the Cuban government in Spanish. They'd had enough and their response was swift. In a shade less than four hours, he'd returned and pulled along the catamaran with money in hand.

Dacus invited everyone to come aboard and hear the rest of the scheme revealed. Satisfied every planned detail was explicit, he eased the ship away from the catamaran, bringing along Maybelle, Julie, Lulu, and Jack. Very slowly, it sailed around the island of Jamaica to Kingston, where they docked, aided by searchlights. Amid staged hoopla coming ashore, they all had multiple questions to be asked on what was happening. Dacus said with emotion, "Our compasses are out of commission, and we've been lost for hours. Worse than that, we have two mates out on a catamaran exploring low, shallow islands, and they've disappeared! I need help to get a search party organized tomorrow, with planes or whatever, to locate them."

When asked if accommodations ashore were required, he declined. "Thanks, anyway. We'd prefer sleeping on board if we can buy a little electricity from you, good people."

Early, shortly before sunrise, Dacus started the process to restore normalcy, as prearranged. Blackness eased up to a dark blue gray, metered into lighter and lighter tints. The huge shell dissolved completely at daylight. Relieved of its responsibility, Rabbit and Sloan leisurely brought the catamaran into port at Kingston. Its reunion with the ship became noisy and boisterous, as witnessed by the native residents, awake and awakened. The con was complete . . . Almost!

There are elements in the affairs of men, which preclude positive predictions to base a future on. Interested in picking up where he had left off with satellite reception restored, Dacus asked Rabbit to turn on the monitoring system. He also requested the intercom be activated loud enough that it could be heard from anywhere on board. Rabbit, in his weariness and giddy elation, instead flipped on the system's *send* switch . . .

Routine, monitored CIA taping of Dacus's little party was recorded, and someone made the connection it had to do with the shady Cuban affair. Feeling skunked by the whole of the incident, Guantanamo's reflex action kicked into gear. Using the previously pinpointed 'center of darkness' for reference, a small civilian plane was dispatched to circle Jamaica, looking for the 'devil ship'. When the pilot reported in there were no ships at sea around Jamaica, he received orders to land at Kingston Airport and take pictures of all ships in the harbor. Posing as a tourist, he randomly snapped photographs, including a fair description of the nine ships in dock and their registration numbers. He flew back to Guantanamo, bearing damaging goods.

The Pentagon, in processing information, concluded it advisable all ships be categorically identified before making any firm resolutions. Hamstrung by unpredictable notions of the sitting President, they decided the suspect ship must be seized in international waters. It was further resolved that apprehending it in a port of another country's jurisdiction would only serve to complicate matters. Surveillance teams were considered, then scrapped . . . The possibility of the observed ship's crew observing their team was too risky. For a successful capture, they had to avoid alerting the ship that it no longer was securely anonymous!

The registration numbers, fed into DC's computerized network, came up with an interesting and disturbing printout. The owner of one ship in dock at Kingston was none other than the Zallafino family of New Orleans. Scanty details, evolving from conflict over money and gold, profiled known styles of a Mafia's Don . . .

CHAPTER 35

Awaiting birth of dawn's first light, the Pentagon, according to Cuban authorities, had overstepped its jurisdiction by sending an aerial armada of planes in search of the so-called devil ship. Concurrently, Guantanamo launched all its vessels into flotillas to interrogate ships sighted by the planes. While the series of maneuvers were proving to be an exercise in futility, Dacus's party resided safely docked at Kingston with an airtight alibi . . . They thought!

As the day progressed, international news coverage began growing on its own momentum. Ever hungry, the stampeding media interviewed individual members of Congress and solicited opinions. Party hacks on both sides of the aisle were selected to stimulate controversy. The ruling party in Congress, not occupying the White House, naturally censured the mismanagement and timidity. The seated administration defended the armed forces' action, blaming Cuba for double-dealing, corrupt tactics.

Reacting to being scooped, the Pentagon attempted to demonstrate they were on top of things. A press release stated the circle of darkness to be geometric. The radius measured exactly 666 miles, establishing the area's existence as man-made and thus reversible.

The announcement was the straw that broke the camel's back, igniting fire and brimstone from Reverend Hamlich Gordon. The wealthy televangelist and fundamentalist prophet proclaimed in televised ministry that 666 indicated the Devil's number. He ascertained the circle had been created by Satan. The latter days were at hand, and he referred the listener to Revelations.

Immediately, fundamentalist preachers took up the cry in their pulpits. Response of the secular movement became as vocal and as certain on radio as in telecasts. Through close ties with the environmental movement, new 'scientific' data was introduced supporting man's involvement. "Most assuredly, it might, possibly could upset the delicate balance of nature in our accidental, 'godless' universe," they testified repeatedly.

In unity, these messages from both sides reverberated essentially the same. "Send money. It's tax deductible for a very good cause."

The President was furious. Already branded as gutless and ineffectual, the train of events began reinforcing that image rather than dispelling it. Adding insult to injury, a member of his loyal opposition openly and artlessly compared the efficacy of his Pentagon to the one which sent ill equipped helicopters in for desert warfare to rescue several captives held hostage. A perplexing crisis descended on the administration.

Dacus, unaware of having been compromised, assembled his gang, outlining everyone needed to move ashore for a while. He noted each had plenty of ready cash on board, separate from proceeds of the latest gold transaction with Cuba. Interaction with it and the local merchants would be good therapy for all concerned. "Just in case some of the recently acquired money is counterfeit or marked in some way, don't take a chance spreading one cent of it around here," he advised.

Rabbit begged off. Beach living didn't appeal to him. "Let me guard the ship and man the equipment," he opted. "You've been interested in keeping a thumb on orders sent to U.S. troops. I'll get anything of importance to you in a hurry."

Knowing Rabbit quite capable of taping Pentagon intercom via satellite, and sensitive to Rabbit's disenchantment with the beach, Dacus nodded agreement. He needed the break . . .

Settled and unwinding in new 'digs', Dacus invited Jack in when he came calling. After a few casual remarks, Jack got to the point. "I find myself in the position of a fox who's had sex with a lady skunk. I've enjoyed about all of this I can stand. Not to say you remind me of a skunk, but the pace of ongoing operations is faster than my old frame can, or wants to maintain."

"Well, I can't say I haven't expected it," replied Dacus. "I know you're interested in getting back to the States, and I'm for it. There shouldn't be any problems, considering vital facts. Both you and Maybelle, untarnished by law violations, have valid passports that would allow the freedom to move on.

Even Maybelle's free of fear from conspiracy charges now that the man she conned, 'Juicy Joyce', is dead. That has to be a cold trail," he reflected.

"Let me pass a proposal by you, Jack. Our relationship is a 'one in a lifetime', and I'd like being able to keep in touch. Use of satellite phones would stultify our positions. Too many cell phone hacks out there listening in! Online computers are far less invading. Intercepting messages from the volumes being sent, for the most part, are confined to tracing on sites where subversive activities are suspected. Our folksy exchange would be hard put to raise eyebrows, much less an NSA tap inquiry. I know you're not a computer buff, Jack, but it won't bankrupt you to get online with a PC. For that matter, Maybelle's clean and, like you, is planning on staying around. A link with her would be damn convenient. The three of us could get our heads together before you leave to decide on unpretentious addresses."

Jack thought a minute. "I think I like the idea. It'd probably be benign enough and certain to occupy my curious mind. Keeping abreast and being informed on future intrigue you come up with does hold an interest for me."

Ambling by a small open-air market on the way to his beachfront cottage, Jack savored the salty breeze and basked in tropical sun warming his skin. Approaching his abode, he was surprised to find Maybelle waiting outside on the glider. She walked in with him, soliciting grapes, a plum or two, and the chaise lounge. "What's the occasion? You horny?" he teased.

"Don't start that, Jack. I need a favor," she pouted.

"I just offered you one, my dear," Jack feigned insult.

"You ole sweet fart!" Maybelle rebuffed wickedly.

"Okay, what's up besides me, and how am I to befriend my friend?" he asked, becoming seriously curious about her motives.

Maybelle's body language spoke that something was afloat without her windjammin' question. "I suppose you realize I'm staying with the ship, don't you?"

"Sure, I'd gathered as much." came Jack's nonplussed reply. "And I've detected there's more to it, too. You've decided to make a move on Dacus, haven't you?"

"I wouldn't call it that," she argued. "You men just don't seem to grasp the deep, instilled motivation of womankind is to nurture the human race."

"Call it what you like," Jack soothed. "I can't help you unless I know what your angle is."

Maybelle took longer than usual to confide. "The con game's over. Dacus conceived the ultimate, achieved it, and won. Subsequently, he's back to square one now. What's left for him? Another capital performance? Hardly! The man's due a downer," she predicted. "You and I are both aware of the worth in having someone to off-load emotions onto. Generally, it's the opposite sex that fills the void after a letdown. In his instance, who better than a woman!"

"Whoa", Jack reined her in. "I don't need to be proselytized, and it's not like you to be fronting a cock-and-bull rationale for outright desire."

Tipped, Maybelle candidly chided, "Damned if you didn't have me pegged before I knew my own score, Jack!"

Lending a hand to Maybelle rising from the chaise, Jack squeezed hers. "Sweet, sweet woman, and I do mean 'all woman'! Your zealousness for a conquest is unequaled by male counterparts. I wholeheartedly approve, but let's not be sidetracked from this scenario. Get me closer in to where you're coming from."

"There's not a lot more to be said really," she contemplated. "I do think Dacus suffers from an obsession he's impotent. It won't contribute in adjusting, and probably he's going to need some outside help. Sure there's more. As a woman, that's where I'd like to come in. The problem is how to go about finding the necessary concoction to proceed. I was hoping to rely on your expertise in purchase of choice specialty items . . . Got any suggestions?"

"Money buys anything you want down here," Jack laughed, attaching, "And a few things you haven't bargained for. If you need a laundry list, jot down a vacuum pump, a cock ring, syringes and the medicine to inject, vibrator, and latest on the market, Viagra."

Still chuckling, he added, "That pill has to be the 'cock's meow' according to televised testimony from a retired reliable, who had a retired one. Why not try the Viagra first? Slip a potion of it into his food, or a drink, and the magnificent erection that results will be attributed only to your womanly appeal . . ."

"Oh, Jack! Off!" Maybelle reacted, a little frustrated. "Up until now, the only trouble I've had with men has been the other way around. The things you're talking about aren't fanciful. They're cold, jock hardware. Oil of essence is the only support item I can recall using, and you haven't even mentioned it."

Without touching, his eyes undressed her, assuring, "And well you shouldn't have." Patting her thigh, Jack craftily propositioned, "I'll go gather up the paraphernalia and be back shortly to demonstrate 'em."

"And you, sir, are a naughty, devious devil!" she just as wily flipped in return.

A routine check on ship ID numbers docked at Kingston showed registry of one listed in Panama. It was the break the Feds had been looking for. The owner was registered as none other than Marc Zallafino, a Mafia Don in

Louisiana. They bypassed local law enforcement with an inquiry. His known attorney, Gulliver Norton, received a call regarding their interest on status of the ship. Sensing the inevitability of a meeting, Norton mentally assessed and countered, soliciting name and number of a contact person. He promised an early reply.

Marc, stunned at Norton's disclosure, recovered quickly. "Set up an appointment in our usual chateau suite two hours from now. I want you present."

Holding to the schedule, he and Norton were met by a couple of agents who flashed badges briefly, without offering any names. The spokesman addressed Marc pointedly, implying entanglement. "Your ship has been involved in an incident in the Caribbean."

Marc stared at him. "Would you be referring to all this crap about the millennium, darkness, and the sugar cane crop in Cuba?"

"Why do you want to know?" the agent questioned, short of insulting, to intimidate.

"You've just announced to me an alleged ship's embroiled somehow in the Caribbean when I don't own one. In case you don't read papers, or listen to the tube, the news is consumed by what I've asked you. You're invading my time by asking questions that are of no consequence to me. I'm entitled to be informed on the wherefores of your prying into my personal affairs. Are you ready to charge me? If so, I want to know of what?" He shot a glance at G. W.

The agent backed off. "The incidents and the ship seem related. It is of a potentially troubling concern to our government. Would you voluntarily answer a few questions?"

Marc glared at him before committing. "First of all, it's not my ship. I sold it several months ago. What happened in the process of it being re-registered, I'd have to check on."

"Who did you sell it to?" asked the agent courteously.

"I don't know," Marc convincingly alluded.

"How is it you don't know who you sold your ship to?" pursued the other agent.

"If it'd been paid for by check, I would've known. But it wasn't! It was a cash transaction," Marc snapped, well aware of the statements' vulnerability.

"How much money changed hands?" Marc's assailant pressured, unrelenting.

"I don't see what that has to do with anything," Marc tendered. "However, and to move on, the party paid two million," he disclosed, setting up his interrogator.

The agent took the bait, accusing, "Well, you're going to owe a lot of taxes!"

Marc's face became stony. "I am going to make a statement," he carefully intoned. "You might want to take it down, word for word, because I believe it's going to be over your head. For the record, I purchased the ship through one of my companies. The ship was capitalized, as were all of the alterations. Because it was acquired for personal endowment, not one cent has been depreciated from the total cost of two and one half million dollars. When this year's books are submitted for audit, I will be legitimately declaring a half million dollar loss. That sirs, is out of your bailiwick and in the capable hands of IRS . . ."

Standing, Marc dismissed his interrogators. "This interview is over. In a living will, why don't you donate your bodies to medical research? Perfecting painless hemorrhoid surgery is high on the list to be investigated!"

Royally insulted, fury raged in the agents' eyes. Marc strode to open the door, allowing two of his soldiers to enter. It was a 'cut and dried' statement that an available escort service had been waiting, as the agents exited into the hallway.

"G. W.," Marc imposed as the door closed, "I've got to go to the Caribbean!"

"Why, for Pete's sake?" Norton questioned its sanity.

"Why?" Marc refuted. "I've been hit with a bag of incriminating shit, and I want answers. Right now, I'm the goat! Associating me with the ship thru registration is damning. Cash sale, no invoice, and no re-registration tightens the noose! Something's amiss . . . It's not like Dacus to put me in this position. There's a reason why the FBI is out beating the bushes for the CIA, trying to locate the ship. I suspect the Pentagon has an ax to grind, and this visit says to me that the hunt's on. Dacus has got to be informed!" Marc paused, pondering, "G. W., if they're asinine enough to try setting a trap for him, all hell's gonna break loose. That display he put on off our coast here in Louisiana won't be a drop in the bucket compared to what possibly went down in Cuba or the bloodshed potential of these ramifications."

Marc dodged a confrontation involving his brothers. Taking one soldier, his pilot flew them to Georgetown on Grand Cayman. Without leaving the plane, Marc sent the pilot in to file another flight plan on to Kingston. Proximity in news releases of a so-called center of darkness to Jamaica, told Marc he was on course in locating the ship. The why Dacus would return there eluded him. It seemed all the more reason to move on, though.

On touchdown in Kingston Airport, Marc assigned the soldier to rent a car while the plane was being secured. Confident their movements weren't under scrutiny, the three drove down to the docks. Sure enough, there sat Dacus's ship in gentle, perpetual motion of the sea. The soldier went aboard, astounded to be confronted by Rabbit. Receiving the fractured message, Rabbit hurriedly went ashore to the waiting car.

Marc grasped Rabbit's hand, urgently emphasizing his need to see Dacus. "Let me go back on board to leave word where I'm going then I'll take you to him," promised Rabbit, sensing an uneasiness with the visit.

Driving up in front of Dacus's place, Marc gave the two aids instructions, "Take Mr. Washington back to his ship." Noting their questionable glances, he didn't waiver in respect addressing Rabbit. "I'll always be grateful to you, man, and equally glad to know you. Thanks also for getting me over here on such short notice." After shaking Rabbit's hand, Marc signaled a farewell as they drove away.

Sitting down across from each other at a small table in Dacus's villa, Marc's anxieties were running high. He made no pretense for being there, relating, "Less than twenty four hours ago the Feds came in on me, investigating your ship's involvement in the Cuban incident. It seems registration of ownership was never changed, and they tried implicating me." The look on Dacus's face stopped Marc cold. Realities were instantaneous. Dacus obviously hadn't suspected his cover was blown, nor had he any inkling the Feds were closing in on his whereabouts.

Impact of the revelation was crushing. Marc attempted to buffer the brunt of it, allaying, "I told G. W. something was way out of context, and I had to come down here. I flew in to warn you in case you didn't know what you were up against. As it's turned out, I'm damned glad I did now, for the both of us. Maybe it'll buy you a little time having me focused squarely in their spotlight, speculating the raucous Castro money deal . . ."

Shock overrode reactions. Dacus peered out the small window. Aimlessly, he turned to Marc. "I appreciate your efforts to inform me. Where you are concerned, I'll do anything and everything possible to minimize a showdown with the Pentagon. The last thing I want is for this information to be given to my bunch at the present time. Hopefully your men are discreet."

"Absolutely," assured Marc. "As you've probably guessed, discretion is paramount in my business. It's preferential that we have no ex-members in the organization. Firing someone who breaks a confidence is not an option!"

Dacus nodded, needing an outlet. "Let me bring you up to date on our party. The only ones left with me are Sloan Barnett and Julie, Rabbit and Lulu, Maybelle, and Jack. Once the gold hit had been accomplished, the others took their cut and split for Europe. The bulk of our money from that caper is safe in Caribbean banks. Proceeds from the Cuban venture, which brought you down here, are on board the ship. From what you're telling me now, it could be in jeopardy. Jack's weary of the fast-paced kind of life and interested in going home. Neither he nor Maybelle must be confined to exile, as are Rabbit and myself. Why subject them if it's avoidable?"

The question dislodged itself. "Marc, I'd consider it a great favor if you'd smuggle these two back into the States, along with their latest cash. It'd make life simpler. Jack could address our concerns on whether or not any of the cash is counterfeit or marked, solving another problem. We'd all be helped by this information and any other updates he gathers."

A mere hint that Maybelle might return to the estate surged blood through Marc's veins. He contained himself to ask, "Do you think she'll go for it?"

"She'll go for it if she hasn't a clue about these latest developments and the government having knowledge of our whereabouts," surmised Dacus, regaining his wits.

"It won't be easy pulling wool over that gal's eyes," mulled Marc. "At the pace we've got to set, let's hope she's preoccupied and doesn't try to second guess us. First off, you'll have to lie about my presence here. It should be believable I came down several days ago to gamble. The recent disruptions in this part of the world upset the game and dropped odds of me winning. Restless and bored, I decided to check out of the unfavorable climate tomorrow. With time on my hands, I toured the docks and, lo, found your ship sitting in port! Make a point of telling her I went aboard, made contact with Rabbit, and he put me in touch with you. It'll also make sense to her if you relate I thought I'd detected your handiwork in the blackened events that ruined my game."

Satisfied with the impromptu plot to deceive Maybelle and Dacus's acceptance of it, Marc bid, "I'm outta here. Give me a cell number."

Jack showed up at Maybelle's villa midafternoon. Walking inside carrying two brown paper totes, he dumped all of the sexual stimuli on her couch. One by one, he explained their use and function, pointing out, "Aside from the Viagra, the rest are items of last resort. Hell, just the thought of a needle shot into a pecker shrivels mine. Your best bet, honey, is the Viagra . . ."

Maybelle, diverted from her intent to select one with most promising prospects per Jack's dissertation, became enthralled at how much Jack's chant mimicked a doctor's. "It's a nitrite, specially compounded to expand blood vessels in the central body region, increasing blood supply required for an erection. It comes in a pill form, and perfect for you grind into a powder. It'll be a made-to-order prescription to put in a portion of highly seasoned food! Sic 'em, hon," he encouraged. Reacting to how he'd sounded, he pretended to unbutton and shuck a white lab jacket.

Laughing affectionately, Maybelle ravished, "You're a rare gem, Jack." She stood on her tiptoes, kissing him on the cheek as he wished her luck.

Gathering up and disposing of the undesirables, Maybelle took only a minute or two before making her move. When Dacus answered the call, she invited, "I'm cooking my specialty dish tonight. Care to join me for the evening?"

"What time do you want me there?" affirmed an unabated readiness she hadn't really expected. It was spur of the moment appealing, and Dacus had surprised himself.

"Sixish be okay?" Maybelle improvised. Gathering her wits, she proposed, "Would you mind going by the ship and bringing a bottle of dry red wine with you?"

"Sounds like a winner!" he agreed, enthused by expectations of escaping the mundane.

Totally out of character, Dacus stepped into her bungalow, carrying a bouquet in one hand and a bottle of wine in the other. Assailed by rich, savory odors of Italian cooking, he followed his nose. "Hey, it's smelling great!" he said, lifting a lid. "How did you keep this attribute hidden?" he complimented. "Rabbit's a good cook, but I can already tell it won't compare, any more than that from Marc's professional chef!"

Pleased, Maybelle humored, pecking him on the cheek and directed, "Ice is in the bucket, scotch's in the cabinet and your favorite brand of cigar. Pour yourself one, light up, and enjoy them outside in last rays of sunlight. Space in this kitchenette is restricted to one body and never intended for cooking a meal. I'll call you when it's ready to serve."

Promise of a rising tropical moon showed on the horizon, and ripples of a tide change were evident as she engaged him to come in for dinner. Dacus poured wine and pulled a chair out for Maybelle before sitting down at the candlelighted table. A pineapple salad nestled in a bed of lettuce with hot herb buttered, Italian bread preceded serving spaghetti with meat sauce. Toasting her again after first samplings of the main entree, he raved over how delicious the food was and that it surpassed anything he'd ever tasted.

Dacus devoured the serving as if it were an appetizer. Maybelle picked up his plate for a refill and did the same for herself. Getting settled, she saw a puzzled look cross Dacus's face with the first bite. "Still good," he praised. "Somehow though, I'm detecting a little difference in taste of this and the other plateful."

Prudently, she nonchalantly laid it on thick. "Oh, I should have told you. Except for the years with Brian, my food prep has strictly been limited to one person . . . Me! Tonight, I'll confess, has been no exception. To make sure we'd have enough, I cooked two batches of sauce. If you must know, on the second one, I touched the hot edge of its pan, adding more wine than I'd intended. Come to think, it may have a tad less thyme."

"Well, both batches, as you call them, were a hit," Dacus applauded, leaving only a few bites of the spaghetti. "Let me help you with the dishes."

"No, thanks," Maybelle differed. "I'm not about to spoil valued time over a sink of dishes. In the short span since we've met, it seems a lifetime of experiences have been shared, with precious few, togetherness moments. Grab the bottle of wine. I'll get the glasses, and we'll sit outside under that yummy full moon. I want you to put your arm around me and hold my hand. Nothing's wrong with indulging the old basic physical attraction that's always been lurking."

Sitting down beside her, he poured their wine by moonlight. Stardust drifting in, he leaned across Maybelle to refill her glass as strange, old familiar urgings rose in his body. Putting the bottle aside, he pulled her to him in a long embrace, kissing her neck, while slipping off straps of the sundress to expose and caress her breasts. His passion left him groping elsewhere like a young sixteen year old . . .

Maybelle never lost her cool. She accepted the uncouth responses and subtly urged him on in her own inimitable way. He pressed himself against her, and she felt his firm reply. Responding, she unzipped the fly, increasing urgency and desire to enter her, transcending their awkward position. Accepting his hand to get up, Maybelle led him inside and to her bedroom, where she momentarily retired to remove her scant apparel.

Emerging from the darkened bathroom, she feasted him with her nakedness in moonlight. In the inviting comfort of her bed, without boldness or lasciviousness, they consummated satisfying desires of each other, the depth of which neither knew existed. The mental dam broken, their passions erupted well into the night until they fell asleep in each other's arms.

Coffee brewing and heading for a shower late the next morning, Dacus stopped in front of the mirror. He faced the person he hadn't seen in years. Stark reality also intruded. Maybelle must be informed of Marc's presence on the island. He had to present her with the possibility of her and Jack taking advantage of an opportunity to be smuggled into the States aboard Marc's plane. Their total take lying in temporary limbo, from the Cuban connection, might turn the trick . . .

She resisted, instantly in denial to consider going anywhere. Urging it was in the best interest of everyone, and touting an agenda of lesser, unexpected priorities needing attention, Dacus got her to agree. She had finally relented and became especially convinced when he encouraged her to oversee Jack's setup with a computer. The value of providing the ship access to information from within the United States regarding their latest money proceeds spurred her incentives.

Another stimulus that sealed it for Maybelle was Dacus's list of humorous code names to be used in a computer link. The more preposterous the 'handle', the better for concealing identity. Ridiculous as it seemed, he succeeded in blanketing a mockery of confusion, which defied association. Synonymous with the last name, Rainwater, and sometimes his temperament, Jack would become Stormy. Influenced by suggestion of Indian heritage, Dacus claimed Tonto for himself and squeezed Maybelle in to reflect the era as Buffalo Gal. Lover Boy, a nomic title, suited Rabbit with his uncompromising love and affection for Lulu, who would fare well with her own name. Sloan Barnett, already a pilot, kept his common place title. For Julie, he decided it wasn't necessary to change an identity that had no history of association.

Establishing a computer link reassured Buffalo Gal she wouldn't lose contact with Tonto. Another powwow couldn't be ruled out either . . . Not if she had anything to do with it!

CHAPTER 36

Vested interests of the Precious Metals Cartel had been slammed. The act resonated with revenge. Their shadow army had been dealt a destructive blow. The culprits were elusive. The longer it took to apprehend them, the more the cartel stood to lose in respect from an underground world, serving as source for recruits. They wanted satisfaction!

Unlike dime a dozen special interests in and around Washington, this type of entity paid for insurance and collected premium returns. After the Joint Chiefs of Staff were hastily called into emergency session, a cultured rug-rat aide confided the cartel's first solid lead in weeks. Strings attached to coddled puppet officials were yanked, and yanked hard, at suspicions hinting that a sizable gold deal had gone down in Cuba.

A dead-end alley opened into an expressway with verified news the Zallafino family had been linked to their problem. No time was wasted in Washington's arena directing key aides on how their Chiefs of Staff were to be manipulated for end results. The vendetta would be covertly honored, without overt risks of any identifiable association made.

From every direction, pressures were mounting. Cries for action escalated to bring closure to the incident. The President faced a vigorous force to respond. His poll was headed for ground zero and still in free fall. Certain disaster awaited any unplotted or irrational strategy. Subject matter this controversial could and would be misconstrued in serving fixed interests, unless disguised in such a way that no leaks occurred.

Impeded by a 'damned if you do' and 'damned if you don't' situation, the President gathered top advisors and select aides in for a put session. Their analyses of circumstances were in total agreement. This and another consensus prevailed at the meeting. Foremost, they dared not target the ship while moored in a foreign country. Sending in intelligence for surveillance would be of first priority. Their condensed mission was conceived to unerringly keep track of the subject vessel without being detected until it left Jamaican waters. Included was recognition that it should be continuously monitored by use of satellite imaging until other orders superseded.

His personal advisor pointed out a missing element. "We need to initiate a critical turn in commentary. Don't you think it'd be expedient to instigate media feedback? Why not leak an imminent confrontation is in the making, pressing necessity to take action? Backed up by word the U.S. Navy and Naval Air Force have received orders to impound the suspect ship, should do it. Qualified by suggesting resistance cannot be ruled out would bring a turnabout of opinion . . ."

Enlarging on strategy, he proposed, "Let the media be the ones to tout a war crisis. Bottom line to the press is that our national security has been threatened. Define how an engagement to capture the ship and its crew is mandatory for the ultimate, more desirable outcome to such an emergency. Once it's established, political funds become available to provide housing and other accouterments for accommodating on-site sympathetic media presence."

He further subjected, "A least attractive alternative, which could be voiced, is use of any premeditated speculation that necessitates destroying the ship and crew. The position of certain fundamentalists hammering the end of the world's at hand, or secular doctrine teaching man's upsetting a 'godless, delicately balanced universe', must be neutralized. Otherwise, eventualities may be seriously misinterpreted. Worse yet, Sir, is if it's deliberately misrepresented by your opponents for their own political gain."

Resounding words of the Whiz Kid, Roscoe Ramsey, were acutely sharp, "Nothing, but nothing, must be allowed to connect this Administration with either of those two activist groups!"

Jack was enthused. The prospects of going home and managing to have his and Maybelle's twenty-eight million in cash smuggled into the United States put him on a high. As the two flew in on Marc's plane to the coast of Louisiana, Dacus had a coincidental conference with his remaining bunch. They were entitled to know the gravity of despair facing them.

"In spite of our efforts, we've been located, and the ship is identified. Apparently, the Feds don't know who we are, but they damn sure know where we are. Just in case you're wondering how I know, it was the purpose of Marc's staged visit. He and I finessed Maybelle into leaving. The profile being presented didn't fit her natural disposition, and I felt it might have gotten in the way of what has to be done. Jack, sitting on ready, didn't need a boost. It is under these circumstances, you are also being encouraged to leave. Actually, I'm imploring you to gather things up and get out while there's still time," Dacus pleaded, imploring further.

"The odds stink. As you well know, except for Sloan, the rest of us are traveling on phony passports. Rabbit, you and Lulu can be unobtrusive, traveling the world over. However, you'd play hell and be apprehended trying to get back into the States. Sloan, if you do decide to move on, you'll have the same advantages as Maybelle and Jack. Marry Julie down here, and as your wife, she'd have amnesty. Don't forget for a moment though, at any port of entry, U.S. Customs stands between you and the amount of money you'll be carrying."

Dacus, having made a last-ditch effort to inspire and inform them of other recourses, added, "The slate's clean. I've laid out your options and covered the waterfront. You have no obligations to me and are free to go your own way."

Reacting quickly, Rabbit spoke assertively and in no uncertain terms. "I ruined my first life. The time with you has given me a second chance nearly every convict longs for, but can't ordinarily come by. This is my life. I'm not about to give it up! Neither is Lulu."

Thoughts and emotion gripped Sloan, wrestling with words to express himself. "Life's been a bitch for the most part. It had left me pretty bitter when I met you, Dacus. I won't give you all the credit, because it ain't my nature. Truth is, I never dreamed of being so happy, of having money, and falling in love with a sweet girl like Julie. We've tossed it about to get married down here. Sure, there'd be only limited hassle to travel, but neither of us can imagine abandoning you, or the ship. We're here—for a showdown, if that's in the cards, or until you run us off!"

Expecting the four of them to pack it up, Dacus mulled the dilemma of how to pull off a vanishing act from their dockside location. A weather bulletin, detailing a massive tropical depression, might hold the answer. It gave him an idea.

"Rabbit, it helps that you and Lulu are residents of the ship. But you, Sloan and Julie, must find a way to covertly get your possessions from the villa back on board ship. I've gotta do the same. Our submarine batteries are fully charged. Under cover of this hopefully dark, forbidding night and an impending storm, we'll ease her out of port on battery driven-propellers. Once clear of the bay, and later in weather related turbulence, it'll be easier to cut in diesel-powered props and run like hell out to sea," he assorted, detailing means for a stealth departure.

"Now, for our vested audience, who don't know we know, peering thru binoculars, or from across the street, we'll design a script for playacting. As we go ashore, Julie and Sloan set off on a shopping spree for small items wrapped in big birthday packaged, boxes. Buy large decorated totes, containing more tissue than gift, and three helium filled occasion balloons. Before going to your bungalow, drop by its office with the stuff to pay another week in advance. I'll time my visit in there to do the same, and we can have a little 'hacky sack' over a party. When we separate, take your goods inside and repack them with any and everything that's going on board. I'll hit the shops for my own oversized, boxed package, and buy staple foods to fill a couple of sacks before seeing you back at the bungalows. If the boxes and bags aren't adequate, we'll ad-lib a beer bust and lug a big cooler down. Given an interval, let's troupe out to the ship, bearing gifts, have a little party in plain sight, and wrap it up by sundown for all to see. We'll gear up, depending on location and intensity of the storm brewing and plan to leave the beach houses shortly before midnight. The remaining bare essentials we'll carry hidden under dark rain ponchos."

Sloan nodded comprehension, plotting input far beyond the night. "I have the coordinates on an uninhabited island of poor beaches, uncovered yesteryear while on duty in the Bahamas. At one time, there must have been a hell of a lot more rainfall that supported an ancient river, which I assume barely flows now. Essentially, it's brackish. The riverbed is very narrow, hardly able to accommodate the width of this ship with its companion alongside. A tropical forest has formed an arch over the waterway, absolutely obstructing anything beneath. We stayed there twenty days one time and never saw a soul. It's the perfect place to hide. The 'if' is in being able to reach the island's sanctuary before an all-points bulletin is issued."

A stream of weather reports throughout the day caused much activity in battening down hatches and securing tie-downs before sunset. Subsequently, it stepped up timing of their charade. Spiking rain riddled the water's surface. A brisk wind from the south, forerunner of the coming storm, blew directly toward the dock. Slightly after midnight, Dacus slipped the moorings, silently easing the ship away and into the bay.

He set a heading straight into the wind until out of the bay. Clearance gained, he directed Rabbit to erect a wind-deflecting, clear shell of five miles radius, before changing course from south to southeast in an effort to skew any monitory devices. Sloan in the engine room was instructed to crank up and cut in diesel-powered propellers.

Geodetic survey placed the ship's course at some risk. Dacus debated. He decided to compute tracking of the storm's center on radar with their current setting for interception of the two. Results were less than conclusive. It'd take between three and four hours later to be in a part of the sea fairly free of shoals and worth the chance. Once the storm could be deflected and hazards minimized, he would route a previously traversed heading of east-northeast for Mona Passage. He briefed Rabbit and Sloan of his decisions.

Receiving a disturbing report of the ship's undisclosed flight out of Kingston port, the Pentagon duly forwarded notice to the White House. An immediate session of White House staff was abruptly scheduled. While an account of the missing ship fell under discussion, Ramsey withdrew down the corridor to a room whose walls were an imagery of global maps and weather conditions. Two hours lapsed. Around three thirty in the morning, he observed a sudden change of direction in the storm pattern. His suspicious speculation was confirmed. He hadn't been tagged the Whiz Kid without reason. Twenty minutes later, using vectors, he'd mapped the ship's position. It took only a few more minutes to ascertain its current heading.

Sitting back in on the meeting, Ramsey emphatically presented probable tracking of the ship. "Surveillance shows it'll be traveling through a strait between the Dominican Republic and the Commonwealth of Puerto Rico. Topographical features of this Mona Passage actually suggest conditions conducive for an encounter with the vessel due to its relatively massive displacement. Also, Puerto Rico's Dorado Beach, with its condominiums, golf, entertainment, and cuisine, is an ideal location to reserve luxury quarters for the media."

In that soft, penetrating, controlled voice, Ramsey cajoled, "We must work thru what's left of the night, and all of tomorrow, to prepare for an engagement. My prediction is, the ship can't possibly arrive until near nightfall. It gives her captain two options. Either he'll try to go through the pass at night, or wait for dawn on the next day."

Gesturing, in a half spread of arms, palms up, Ramsey tossed it to them. "In any event, there's adequate time to be in full readiness with our armed forces and a reciprocal press."

The President expressed doubt. He wanted to be convinced. He knew foolproof strategy would be needed to issue a news release. Using the National

Weather Service's series of bulletins to locate and project timing of a ship entering the Mona Passage simply lacked clout to create a media rush, and he said as much. Aghast, his staff sat, too stupefied to comment.

Undaunted, the Whiz Kid fortified his think process. "For several months, the National Weather Service has been marked with the stigma of relaying unheard-of abrupt wind changes by hurricanes at sea. These are documented occurrences. It's as if these weather disturbances rebound off unseen objects and only in the Caribbean." No one cared to dispute him.

"We're confounded by and contending with some type of esoteric technology. Assign your public relations department to get to the bottom of it. Turn them loose on its strange and demonstrable ability to destroy communications over megamile areas while you're at it. They'll surely come up with an explanation for the sealing off of electromagnetic radiation from the sky, which disables compasses within. Given plausible cause, the PR staff can splash how these phenomena are directly related to each other. This will cause an avalanche of investigative press teams scurrying to use ink. In a matter of hours, they'll promote you into a wizard of awe, Sir!"

The President turned a quizzical look toward the other aides. Rather than saying it, he made eye contact and assumed his characteristic 'there ought to be' expression.

Solving the awkward silence, a staff member spoke out. "What else is there to draw from, Mr. President? Seems to me our stash of options are pretty damn slim at the moment. Has anyone thought to consider classifying this misfeasance as potentially a subversive action?"

"Finally, you've put it into context, Trey. Notify the Pentagon of my decision," he ordered. "Alert our chosen friends in the media, Ramsey. Brief them on preliminary protocol and tell them to exercise utmost integrity."

Adhering to Ramsey's advice, the Chief Executive's orders were expedited to General Sherman's office. Upset at being disturbed 'with a piece of shit', Pink raged, fumed, and ranted to his aide. "The sons of bitches have staged a media event with no battle plan. This Administration knows nothing about fighting. They're made up of 'love children'. All they know how to do is talk, sniff, and do the hanky-panky. We're destined to lose personnel, planes, and equipment. More than likely, some of the press people could be killed!"

Alarmed, his aide blurted, "Sir, if you openly go about opposing an executive command, they'll ruin your career. And what about me?"

"No shit! Protect your flank at all costs, son!" he warned. "It doesn't make me like the prospectus, or my position, one damned bit! The fact I'm not a MacArthur, helps! In five years, I'm history except for the name on a monthly check."

Just before daylight, Dacus unwittingly threw a monkey wrench into a master minded hypothesis. He shut down diesel motors and disconnected the electric ones driving extra propellers. Ordering all anchors down, fore and aft, he told the slim crew it was bedtime. Essentially, everyone needed to get a full night's sleep. It would be night because he was about to turn out the lights, also thwarting any aerial surveillance or other probing devices. He set the hardest possible shell twenty thousand feet in diameter and ten thousand feet high at its apex before retiring to his cabin. Drifting into sleep, he marveled at and reflected on the awareness of how easy it is to hide in an ocean by using this type of shell . . . *Satellites are totally disabled. Their ability to 'see' is compromised by bending of electromagnetic rays in the spectrum of visible light. As these rays strike the shell of warped space, they are bent around its edge, giving the effect of a continuous, seamless expanse of water. The only exception is the chance of someone in a vessel accidentally stumbling onto the shell and being forced to sail around it. But, these odds are in the millions. As far as aircraft are concerned, the shell is far below the normal altitude of twenty-five to thirty thousand feet for commercial craft. Thankfully, the odds are equally as scarce.*

At the Pentagon, observations being reported from space declared no ships present in an area outlined by the White House. Ramsey was adamant. "Do not abandon this mission!" he screamed in denial. "That ship is there! It's obviously shielded from your scopes! Find out why!"

The President had no opinions. Based upon findings presented, he offered no input and blindly backed Ramsey's assessment. Leaving one person in charge, the other staff members were ordered to bedrooms in the White House for remainder of the night.

Awakening ten hours later, Dacus roused his bunch out of the sack. Sleep and rest had improved attitudes, except for an adjustment to be made for time of day. The sun was setting. Descending to the galley, the five began cooking up a hearty meal. When prepared and while sitting around eating, Dacus diagrammed a scheme for playing a game of leapfrog.

"You know what they say the *if* is about a frog, don't you?" Barnett joshed.

"Yeah!" Dacus answered. "And that *if* is the concern to me. In wee hours this morning, before hardening the shell, I set the ship's gyroscope for a direction needed to travel. At the time, my thoughts were of trying to shove the shell by momentum of the ship. After sleeping on it, you don't have to remind me, Sloan, of how difficult it was to push a soft wind-diverting shell in the hurricane that took us into the shallows, nor have I forgotten Theo and Franco's fiasco. The plan here is for a leapfrog effect of shells over the ship and catamaran to allow undetected movement. We'll try for a synchronized set on the shells and use direct radio contact to create a new center near the perimeter of the old one each time. The go'll be slow and an awkward way to proceed, but at least we can't be observed."

Two hours into sundown, their vessels had traveled only twenty miles. Dacus rationalized, "Whatever the risk, we must have an update on weather reports." Dousing all running lights and killing engines, he softened the shell enough to receive radio and television signals. Hearing reports that a general rain was in progress, he dissolved the shell entirely, telling himself, *Nothing ventured, nothing gained.* The decision came easy to make a run for it under cover of the night's widespread rainy umbrella.

Holding steady at sixty knots, with both power sources wide open, they roared through the deluge toward Puerto Rico and Mona Passage. Eight hours later, the tiny isle of Mona came into sight. Dacus maneuvered to hide the ship on the island's lee side in thirty fathoms of water.

For the past hour and a half, illicit communication equipment purchased in New Orleans had once again reimbursed its cost while monitoring classified transmissions . . . Information being released by the Pentagon was general. Moreover, it didn't take some clever rocket scientist to conclude armed forces had invaded Mona Pass and were fully occupying its space. To advantage, other masked items of interest surfaced. Out of palaver and chatter, Dacus was able to glean a little government conspiracy cropping up. Deducing that they plotted to stage an event for a captive media whetted his senses to learn more. By scanning, he tuned in on a frequency where government forces were communicating with friendly allies in the media.

Leaning back in the chair to listen, Dacus swiftly surmised, *They're creating a scenario for capturing a scapegoat. The pretense has to be based on trumped-up charges that sovereignty of the U.S. had been invaded at Guantanamo Bay, and that sucks! With the extent of denoted force being proposed against one ship and a five-man crew, they surely haven't factored in the far-reaching repercussions it would have on the present Administration in the event of a failure . . .*

A direct connection to network television in the States was uncovered in the government's electronic link with the media. Instinctively, Dacus spotted a golden opportunity. By flip of a switch, he could broadcast to an entire national audience. Exhilarated, he assessed plans of how to partake. The media always groped for material, desperate to fill time until action occurred. Undoubtedly, they'd seize upon audio of a quarry's interruption if an attempt were made to communicate directly with the armed forces. An inevitable retort would then be pressured from the Administration. Dacus rubbed hands together at the jarring repulse it was capable of exciting.

Overriding the media's frequency with superior broadcasting power, Dacus opened the mike, addressing the naval brigade sent in to occupy Mona Passage. "We are not hostile people. We pray for a peaceful journey through Mona Passage and beyond. I repeat. We are not hostile, and pray for a peaceful voyage through Mona Passage, and beyond . . ."

The interposing message electrified all in its listening audience. Tape of the episode was being cut and spliced for rebroadcasting, even as Dacus repeated the message for the third time. The media simultaneously sought reactive response from administrative chiefs.

Upon a briefing of the incoming message, military brass on location made a snap decision. They sent an official warning to the ship, broadcasting, "You are hereby ordered to cease activity and surrender. Maintain your present position. Await further orders." The command was duly cataloged by the media and relayed, unedited, to stateside networks.

Unyielding, Dacus set a clear, missile-proof shell, moving into entrance of the channel. The press could stand it no longer. Stimulated, broadcasting of the total backdrop of operations began. They were primed to pick up on future conversations between the captain and certain armed forces, including any play-by-play description of the ship's defiant movement. One thing not available to be reported on was the existence of a nondetected, protective shell surrounding the vessel two miles in diameter and a mile high.

It was herein that the Administration found itself exposed by media coverage and labeled as 'not in control' in a questionable national crisis. A lone ship identified as the adversary was challenging, yet claimed to be benign, and the command's plausible cause shrunk. White House media pundits pounced, demanding a news conference with the Oval Office. Furious, the President raged in his quarters, while Whiz Kid Ramsey, feigned off the press using the limp excuse, "No comment until the military engagement is terminated."

Churning at twenty-two knots thru several miles of the passage, Dacus gradually reduced the shell's diameter to one mile. The military command had independently reached a consensus to destroy the ship. A small fleet of five fighter jets lifted off to strafe a final warning before bombers were to finish the mission. At combat speed, four of the five exploded on impact at the shell's wall. The fifth barely turned aside in time. Resulting actions were captured by media photographers poised half a mile away from the disaster in a military helicopter.

An armada, sent from Guantanamo, had rounded the tip of Dominican Republic. Aimed at the target ship, the lighter and speedier vessels roared through the passage to get within range, temporarily postponing a bombing run. Without prior warning, the armed crafts reared up, broke into pieces, and rolled aside, sinking beneath waves of their impact and those being pushed by the shell. Striking the shell head had been deadly. The sea claimed all combat evidence. Its surface revealed nothing even though helicopters were in the air and available for sight and rescue . . .

In a last, desperate attempt to salvage the operation, a bomber came in too low. It skimmed the shell's apex, blowing up from the explosion of its own bomb. Aggrieved onlookers were mentally tattooed with the horrible image. Senseless destruction of service personnel had occurred without any visible weaponed retaliation from the unscathed ship.

The unbroken series of disasters precipitated the on-site command to halt operations and confer with the Pentagon. General 'Pink' Sherman took the call, facetiously ordering, "Withdraw and claim victory." He had already seen the calamitous events on television, along with the rest of the United States, and perceived damaging consequences.

Shortly thereafter, the General received a summons to appear immediately before the Senate Subcommittee on Military Preparedness. All networks scrambled for leverage to report on the expected debacle, and the whole world looked in.

The first directive to General Sherman, asked, "Are you prepared to accurately detail our losses in terms of equipment and personnel, sir?"

"Yes," he gravely replied. "Four fighter planes and one bomber went down. Ten warships sank. Assuming each plane and ship was correctly manned with a full complement, total loss stands at two hundred and five personnel."

The inevitable question followed. "To your knowledge, how much firepower did the adversary possess, and to what extent was it exhibited on our forces?"

A perturbed look crossed Sherman's face. "None!" he refuted. "Apparently, all planes and vessels inexplicably self-destructed, without any display of weaponry. This Committee observed, as I did, the precise account captured on television. No evidence of self-defense tactics are recorded, and nothing has been suppressed regarding the matter."

Stilled by his expression, and trying to absorb impact of the General's statement, the stunned Committee sat transfixed. Sherman used it to pause before planting, "Pertinent to an official understanding of the overall encounter is a message delivered through the media to advise our government, stating. "We are not hostile people. We pray for a peaceful journey through Mona Passage and beyond." I might add, it was repeated numerous times, even as fighter craft were dispatched. In case of an override, that purport was not issued idly!"

As these proceedings were taking place and being viewed worldwide, another act was unfolding. Methodically, Roscoe Ramsey laid his resignation atop the Presidential Oval Office desk and purposefully took leave of his position.

Televangelists began having a field day. They were split down the middle as usual. Those placing great emphasis on key phrases of the message, 'not hostile', 'pray for peaceful journey', 'beyond', believed these words to be from a harbinger of God's arrival. Others advanced thetheory Satan was involved, reviving the adage, of 'a wolf in sheep's clothing'. "After all," they interpreted, "Jesus calmed the wind whereas this devil's advocate manipulates storms!" Just as concurrently, the secular movement became oddly silent. It became suspect they were awaiting more particulars before professing a position.

Confusion reigned at the White House. Turmoil reverberated in all walls of the Pentagon. The press, blackballed, were reduced to reporting on health breakthroughs.

Dacus proceeded into the western Sargasso Sea. There he erected a blackout shell under which position and direction change occurred several times before dropping anchor. In eight hours, darkness would give cover to hide them.

Roscoe Ramsey's resignation leaked out around the White House soon after midday. Press mavericks stampeded, promoting an audience with the Chief Executive. Remaining advisors to the President urged him on the rectifying value of requesting a joint session of Congress in a prime time telecast. With reserved acquiescence, he agreed. They went to work on a speech for him and scheduling of the event. At two in the afternoon, the President reneged. A call cancelled the Congressional session. On its heels, an announcement circulated he would address the nation. It was promoted to air at nine o'clock from the Oval Office.

Time hung heavy. Dacus and his tiny band noiselessly glided along, hugging inner edges of the Sargasso Sea. Spent, yet anticipating the President's speech, they became ghost voyagers using only their electric power to wait him out.

Standing beside his desk, clutching a sheaf of papers, which he then carefully laid aside, the President addressed, "Fellow Americans, we have come together this night to memorialize and pay honor to the two hundred and five brave servicemen and women who have lost their lives to a horrific recondite force. The battle scenes that flashed across our screens are as equally gruesome as any ever recorded in history of this nation . . .

"I give you my solemn promise. We will sacrifice no more of our precious people in the face of an unidentified technology, which wantonly destroys. The perpetrators of such an outrageously wicked act ought to be brought to justice. At this time, we dare not disclose a future course of action. The powers that be are working and will prevail in the end to bring peace and safety for our citizens. You have my word!"

Proponents of the loyal opposition party had not bid for equal airtime. They took the diabolical attitude, ascribing, "Let the bastard hoist himself on his own petard."

Disgruntled, the Commander in Chief retired, escaping into quarters and shunning any interchange of opinions. He preferred his own council and attacked party politics as sick. The two factions had become too rich and powerful. It convinced him they had warped the separation of powers. Slipping out of custom-designed footwear and stretching out on the leather sofa, he talked himself out of running for a second term. Before one of his flash naps claimed him, he sentenced aloud, "To hell with soft, easy money and avaricious power."

CHAPTER 37

"Absolutely no regards!" scorned Dacus following the President's speech. "Live telecast? You couldn't prove it by me. It mimicked an old forty-five record with the needle hung in a groove—same tune, over and over. Why won't he get writers with some originality? Projecting a modicum of genuine concern to go along with meaningless rhetoric would at least be a change. God knows there wasn't an ounce of compassion shown over loss of those lives. He had to treat it like someone else's terrorist attack, or a foreign conflict, or a school shooting, where absolutely no responsibility has to be assumed. No rationale and no explanation off the 'Hill' for the asinine motivation, which initiated such costly action. It's a good thing the cold war's passé, or he'd have tried to implicate its big bad bear. God help us . . . Where is the sense?"

Kicking at a chair, he left to vent emotions away from the others. Still on a tirade, Dacus swore, "I'd damn sure like to meet that rakish General who got hauled before the Senate committee today. It's apparent he didn't approve and let 'em know they'd crapped in their britches. He didn't mind spelling it out for the wimps in no uncertain terms either."

Under cover of darkness and fixed on Sloan's heading, the ship sailed stealthily toward the hideaway island. A light, salty mist, picked up by the movement and slight winds, felt soothing as Dacus stood against the railing. His thoughts seemed be on an endless merry-go-round, mixed with snatches of reality. According to computations, it'd take a total of three more nights to reach their destination. Using diesel to expedite the time had been ruled out. The ship could no longer appear in any port, and their remaining supply of fuel had to be held in reserve. Fleetingly, it crossed his mind to send an e-mail to Jack and Maybelle, but it left him much like a feather swept up in soft breezes. 'Catch 22' invaded his consciousness only to exit without pursuit. The hours stretched into another long night . . .

By the time they reached the secluded island, Dacus had fallen into a depressive blue funk. Sleeping by day and traveling in relative darkness, no one had noticed Dacus's distress. However, fortune was a lady. She provided a full setting moon of near daylight brilliance and a couple of hours left before arrival at dawn to get oriented. Things couldn't have been more ideal for circling the island to gain a feel for its layout and to find the mouth of a river Sloan described as hidden by tree bowers. Entering, each nook and cranny was explored heading upriver to locate the thickest arbor for concealing both the ship and its companion vessel. Too exhausted to show exuberance, everyone crawled into their beds and slept until sundown.

Last rays of light from the setting sun had disappeared when Rabbit and the moon began to rise. He put coffee on to brew, picked up, and cleared the table of last evening's leftovers. The rest straggled into the galley, still trying to wake up. "I don't know whether to start cooking breakfast or supper," he joked, feeling less pressured.

"Why not call it what it is," Dacus jawed, pouring coffee. Holding his cup up, he tried to make light of things. "After this, let's do breakfast hors d'oeuvres. Bring on the ham and egg quiche, crab fingers, and plenty of olives to go in Bloody Marys. We'll proceed to have our 'catch of the night' caught and ready to be broiled for dinner. And, oh! Happy hour starts right now over at the bar with a salute to whatever is caught. Who knows we might get days and nights evenly straightened out in one 'go down'. If everybody crashes early tonight and sleeps late tomorrow, we ought to be back on our lost schedule."

Stress had taken its toll. Not surprisingly, the after-midnight party turned nostalgic. Longings for the full gang and 'good ole days' crept into conversations. Moody, thought-filled interludes occurred, and the jukebox didn't sound the same. No one was turned on to dance or cuddle. A bottle of club soda held the only fizz to be found on board.

By one o'clock, nearly everyone had a snootful. The night ended the way it had begun. In reverse, they began straggling back to bed. Julie poured a second nightcap, so Dacus spiked more scotch into his glass and stayed. They exchanged no small talk, just drank. Each in their own obscure world of thought, words would have been superfluous. Tipping glasses in a good-night gesture, Julie staggered off to bed in wee morning hours, leaving Dacus to close the bar. He lingered, nursing the drink in hand, knowing sleep would not come easily if he retired.

For better than an hour, a haggard, half-sober motley crew came and went through the galley, guzzling coffee and opening cans of juice. Sloan made three attempts at rolling Julie out of bed. As a last resort, he picked her up, depositing her in the shower. Being extremely silly, Lulu tried to help Rabbit put together a brunch to serve around noontime. More than once, he took issue with her behavior. Except for refills of coffee, Dacus made himself scarce, walking the deck.

The crew, assembled about a table of scarcely touched food, watched as Dacus finally came in to join them. He seemed somewhat disconnected yet stated matter of factly, "The showdown is over. We've made the cut. Now, it's time to talk. Every underground nobody and most others around the world have seen this ship and the battle it was in plastered across TV screens. Its registration number is on government files, accessible off the Internet, and logged into computers of sea pirates and shadow militias. The ship could not be more finished than if it had been blown to smithereens in Mona Passage. She's no longer of use to any one of us as an option for survival. Sink her in the deep, separate now, and move on is our only recourse and chance to survive." Wavering, he stopped.

"What about it, Sloan?" Dacus regrouped to ask, "Got any thoughts?"

Sloan didn't hesitate. Winking at Julie to alleviate a sobering situation, he lightened, "What do you think we did on those long nights while trying to stay awake journeying to this place? Seriously though," he added, "we did make some plans. She and I decided to buy a ketch, put a good kicker motor on it, and sail back to my ole swimming hole territory. There, I intend to initiate contact with my former employer's dock. I don't have the know-how to launder money smartly, but I do know where it can be found. A real possibility is to exploit bayou living for a while. Julie needs an introduction to authentic Cajun vittles."

"There's something you need to realize." Regressively, Dacus cautioned and launched into repeat of an earlier update. "Marc wasn't coincidentally in Kingston on a gambling trip, just prior to our hasty departure. The Feds had paid him a visit after our little jaunt to see Castro because I had never posted change of ownership on the ship. They thought they had him dead to rights by association . . . Gold and a Mafia's registration on a ship involved provided plenty to make a strong case. Always prepared, Marc kept his cool, put 'em down, and played it smart. He let 'em know they'd have to look elsewhere for the ship's owner."

Relating Marc's influence prompted recall of other involvement he felt compelled to voice, again. "Interested, Marc kept abreast of any and all releases put out on the Cuban incident. What gave him an edge over the Feds to pinpoint us was a reported byte he'd retained. A center of darkness, in and around Jamaica, keyed our profile to him only too well. Cuba, gold, and a blackout left the ship as missing link to the Feds' inquiry and reason to trace its ID number. Guessing we'd dock back in Kingston if we were unaware of a search and seizure warrant, Marc made his spur-of-the-moment flight to alert us . . ."

Dacus wanted nothing taken for granted, affixing, "I don't know if you picked up on its significance at the time, but Marc is owed a debt of thanks for another 'go down'. He and I cooked up the gambling story for more than one purpose. We didn't need a panic situation, motivating someone trying to find a logical solution to our dilemma. Jack was already disgruntled, ready to go home, and Maybelle had no place on a fleeing ship. Marc agreed to fly them back to Louisiana on pretense of taking care of their money. When they were airborne, the four of you were also encouraged to depart. I don't mind remindng you that little good it did!"

Reflecting, he cautioned. "In any chain of events, one thing calls for another. I guess what I'm striving to say, Sloan, is to be careful not to compromise Marc if you go back into the States' intracoastal waterways. He's probably still under the Fed's surveillance, which could cause scrutiny of you with a domino effect."

Sloan took his elbows off the table and tipped the chair back, acknowledging he'd taken in every word imparted. "I've never been one to find an iota of bliss in ignorance, Dacus, so this is important for me to know. However, it won't change my plans for returning to the Lafitte bayou area south of New Orleans. Being familiar with these circumstances, I'll be much more discreet in how things are done and use safer methods in accomplishing what I want. Once back in the country, there's an intricate, but reasonably foolproof system available to me for contacting the Mafia. I'll wait for the right time and opportunity to make it work."

Finishing touches to details were applied by Rabbit and Sloan to fashion the next calculated move for an appearance in public. The catamaran was rigged to the hilt for deep-sea fishing excursions. Rabbit took on the role of a native tour guide. Julie and Sloan, honeymooning, were to do less rod and reeling and more lovey-doveyin' when they closed in on the nearest island, where they planned to hop a ferry for Nassau.

It went as smoothly as the sea had been that day. Even Rabbit got caught up in the excitement. He bid farewell to the couple, wishing them luck and good fortune in finding just the right ketch to purchase and ideal sailing conditions on the final leg of their journey.

The same couldn't have been said when the catamaran pulled away from the canopied ship, moored upriver. Goodbyes were short and uncomfortable. Moods were tangled and seemed bogged down under a weighted burden. Unobserved in the emotional hassle of departure, fears, lingering from an early-in-life abandonment, showed on Lulu. Symptoms of withdrawal surfaced. Retarded traits became more pronounced . . . Then, she simply disappeared!

Oblivious to her whereabouts, Dacus busied himself on the computer setup to make an overdue link with Jack's personal computer for communicating by e-mail. In the beginning, it became toilsome for him. Completing final hookups to receive messages, he found one waiting and was startled to see Maybelle's transmission coming in. The date was a week old . . .

>>>Hi Tonto,
>>>Buffalo Gal ridin' herd.
>>>Stormy in hospital with 'heart incident'.
>>> (vet chose to call it).
>>>His offspring here. Too many for corral,
>>>so we swapped.
>>>Smoke signals circulate better here.
>>>Incidentally, Big Bird that landed,
>>>dropped two eggs not far away. Good site.
>>>Ass sets for real. Not encumbered.
>>>No mortal danger on Stormy.
>>>Anxious for Pony Express run.

Dacus read the e-mail again, thinking. *It's just like Maybelle to mess around with a guy's mind and at the same time put the hurt on someone who might try interfering in her business. Let me see,* he mulled. *What is she saying?* In a flash the mess translated itself. *She's had to take charge due to Jack having a heart problem. Bad enough, the children were called in, yet hopefully, not life threatening now. His condo was to have housed the computer for their e-mail correspondence, but it must have been too small to accommodate his kids. Apparently, she moved in to his to let them have the larger one. Big Bird has to be Marc. The plane probably made an unauthorized landing on the estate. Jack and Maybelle obviously were the two eggs deposited, and they decided to network financial institutions down there after learning assets were valid and wouldn't be subject to impediment as counterfeit.*

Aware the message he was about to send required no mask put on its content to obscure identity, Dacus began typing . . .

>>>Hello Dear,
>>>>It's hard to discuss the transformation
>>>>you've worked in me. I must also believe
>>>>you saw some potential in me that I couldn't
>>>>see in myself. I'm free at last of a crush-
>>>>ing, self denigration, because of my murky
>>>>beginning and loss of Claire. For these, I
>>>>do love and thank you. But, that's not all!
>>>>I don't want to misuse the word 'love'.
>>>>Therefore, I declare I'm 'sweet on you' be-
>>>>cause of the thrill from your body and person.
>>>>I still tingle over the thought of 'flesh of
>>>>one flesh', if I've described it correctly.
>>>>I know Bryan was the love of your life,
>>>>but I want you to know that, if it is a
>>>>part of existence, I will carry my memory
>>>>of you into eternity.
>>>>
>>>I am faced with somber decisions. This
>>>>world is not ready for the technology I
>>>>possess. The ship is hidden and will
>>>>never sail again. Soon I will dismantle
>>>>the electrical equipment on board and
>>>>destroy some key links in the apparatus.
>>>>
>>>I'm not concerned about convincing Lover
>>>>Boy to disable the catamaran, when he gets
>>>>to where he's going. He won't care for
>>>>the danger of a direct link to the tech-
>>>>nology, and has enough money to buy all
>>>>the electrical power he'll ever need.

>>>>
>>>The reality is that national sovereignty
>>>>is fast becoming passé. The contribution
>>>>of both Democratic and Republican parties
>>>>to the demise of the most powerful nation
>>>>on earth, is starkly apparent to me. An
>>>>accumulation of vast amounts of financial
>>>>resources has tempted them both into
>>>>loosening the restraints which separated
>>>>the three branches of government for two
>>>>hundred years.
>>>>
>>>All three branches, themselves, have co-
>>>>operated in abandoning antitrust legisla-
>>>>tion, opening the way for the present crea-
>>>>tion of corporate monstrosities, surpassing
>>>>the powers and control of any nation. I
>>>>dare not remain available for imprisonment
>>>>or torment to force me to reveal the tech-
>>>>nology I have.
>>>>Aside from these considerations, I am con-
>>>>sumed by a crushing sense of guilt. When
>>>>old man Lipscomb and his gang came to avenge
>>>>no innocents died. When one man came after
>>>>me on the road from Joy to Floyd, he was al-
>>>>ready a murderer, and not innocent. When
>>>>Runshang and his gang sought revenge in the
>>>>bay, they were out to murder, and were not
>>>>innocent. And, when the assassins protect-
>>>>ing the gold market, wanted to take life,
>>>>they surely were not innocent.
>>>>
>>>But, I fell prey to the common affliction
>>>>of mankind. The Biblical statement, 'The
>>>>love of money is the root of all evil', is
>>>>true, true, true. Oh! How I wish I had
>>>>dumped those ten tons of gold back into the
>>>>ocean. We were home free. No one knew who
>>>>or where we were. Each of us had forty

>>>>four million safely in a bank account. I
>>>>apparently had to have a little more. So,
>>>>today, the blood of two hundred and seven
>>>>innocent people is on my hands, two from
>>>>Cuba, and the rest from the United States.
>>>>
>>>Please indulge and believe me when I say that
>>>>I'm not afraid to die. As an engineer, I've
>>>>had to rely on numbers . . . Absolute numbers . . .
>>>>The existence of this Universe as a happy
>>>>accident, delicately poised and balanced,
>>>>goes beyond mathematical impossibility to
>>>>mathematical absurdity, in the time frame
>>>>allotted to it by science, itself. The
>>>>Universe I perceive is both a deliberately
>>>>Kind and gentle creation . . .
>>>>
>>>I'm leaving a note for Lover Boy, when he re-
>>>>turns. I depart from you with my love. Tell
>>>>Stormy that a half breed can actually die at
>>>>sundown by watching the sun go down.
>>>>
>>>Love, Tonto

Elation at finally hearing from Dacus was short lived as Maybelle read on. *My god, has he lost it? How could he be so depressed? When's Rabbit due back?* were a few of the questions flooding her mind. Getting a grip on emotions, she fired back an e-mail, hoping he hadn't left the computer to begin dismantling equipment.

An hour, then two hours, passed without a response. A sickening devastation replaced anxieties. He'd left no doubt as to his intent. Nonetheless, neither was it her nature to accept without trying to intervene, having known the man. Helplessness won out in a wrestling match on how to proceed, replaced by an emptiness of dry-eyed grief. Feeling sorry for herself, she thoughtfully quizzed, *What now, old girl? Does everything you've ever loved or cherished have to die? God, I wish I had his faith and compassion for life.*

Passing through rooms of the town house, seeking some kind of comfort, she stopped in the kitchenette to pour a bourbon on the rocks. The first sip out of the glass didn't taste right. On a second sip, there was no mistaking the drink was too distasteful to fill a gap. She poured it down in the sink and stared out the window into space of her tidy but artificial backyard.

Unable to focus on anything else, a kaleidoscope of their association spun, reflecting many and varied facets of an unusual, bonded relationship. *Maybe, just maybe, there was purpose for our chance meeting,* she comforted herself.

Five days later, in the evening's quietness, Maybelle heard sounds from the computer that an e-mail was being transmitted. It was from Rabbit, crudely written, in an obvious state of shock . . .

>>>>Much trouble. Many problem when I come
>>>>back. Mind of Lulu back to when we met.
>>>>Dacus dead. Had been shot. Lulu hold on
>>>>gun in lap, rockin. no talk. Note in
>>>>pocket. He in unmarked grave like he say.
>>>>
>>>>I taken Lulu away to get fresh start and get
>>>>her better. Will stay down here. Live on
>>>>catamaran til Lulu improve. Say hello to
>>>>Stormy.
>>>>
>>>>ps: I throw his fourteen million in ocean
>>>>like he say.
>>>>
>>>>Lover Boy

Maybelle pushed back from the computer desk to stand, a twinkle returning to her eyes. For the first time in days, a grin eased away stress lines on her face. Joyously, she exclaimed, "You lovin' devil!" Going over and opening the window, she blew a kiss into the star-studded sky, devotedly proclaiming, "Once a con, always a con, Dacus, my Dear!"

Impulsively, she sat down at the computer, sending a torched message . . .

>>>>Tonto, I will find you!

FINIS